THE GIRL IN BETWEEN

A Next Door Series Novel

By Miranda Silver

D0877337

COPYRIGHT

Cover design: Concierge Literary Designs (front), Betty Lankovits (back)

ISBN: 9780463728352

Manufactured in the United States of America

Paperback edition October 2020

For L, my partner in crime

Also by Miranda Silver

The Girl in Between (Next Door #2)

Priceless: A Dark College Romance

Crave: An Erotic Story Collection

CONTENTS

Prologue

Sunlight teased Diana's eyes open. Blinking, she closed them again, snuggling under the warm covers. Then a curl of panic tightened her stomach, and she bolted upright.

She'd overslept. She'd missed a test. She'd blown every chance of getting into Yale.

She was...outside.

Blue sky spread overhead, edged by maple leaves. She sat halfway in, halfway out of a sleeping bag. Instead of her lacy nightgown, an oversized T-shirt draped her curves, and when she touched her hair — usually a straight dark bob — her fingers met a matted tangle. Her glasses were dropped on a book by her pillow. Her panties lay on the lawn, and her crotch throbbed unmistakably.

Summer was here.

She'd graduated high school two weeks ago. Yale waited at the end of August. In between — freedom.

Her sleeping bag still held the shape of Ian's body. She'd drifted off against his bare chest last night, listening to the lazy music of her record player cross the beat of his heart. He must have gotten her into his T-shirt and taken the needle off the record before he went home.

But, just like Ian, he hadn't bothered to help her back into her panties.

It all felt like the best dream of her life, but she was wide awake.

Only one person knew Ian jumped the fence between their houses each night, Huskies blanket tucked under his arm, to wrestle her onto the grass and share kisses and whispers and moans.

Only one person knew she'd been seeing Ian for close to a week now.

Only one person knew that their love rose from the ashes of a threesome so hot, it had almost burned her up.

And she trusted that person not to breathe a word.

She was just beginning to see who Brendan really was, but one thing she knew about her boyfriend's twin: he was very, very good at keeping secrets.

Chapter One

Summer evening sun slanted through broad windows into the diner booth. Music pulsed from the jukebox, boosting the laughter of Diana's friends, and ceiling fans stirred the humid air.

Diana was laughing too, but she'd already forgotten who'd told the joke. Was it Marissa or Janelle? Batting David's hand away from her fries, she pulled her foot back when she kicked Shaun's guitar case under the table.

She was hanging out. Having fun with no plan or purpose. All through high school, this would have been unthinkable. And if guys had been part of the group? She would have kept her legs crossed, her eyes on her iced coffee, and her mind just out of the gutter. All while managing the occasional comment that sounded smart in her head, but plain bitchy out loud.

Now, she was chattering away, like sitting at a table with boys was no big deal. Stuffing her face with fries, leaning across Marissa to smack Shaun's shoulder. Her sailor dress clung to her curves with sweat, and she wasn't even self-conscious about it.

But her head was only half there. And her mind was still in the gutter.

It was Friday. The end of her first week interning at a biology lab. She'd applied for the internship months before the boys next door had seduced her in their treehouse. And she'd assured the head of the lab that she'd give it her all, even though she wasn't in college yet.

I'm very focused, she'd promised. *I keep my eye on my goals. It's pretty much impossible to distract me.*

Now, six days into being a couple with Ian O'Brian, she was walking around in a fog. Half the time, she wanted to squeal out loud. The other half of the time, she wanted to race to her room, peel off her clothes, and squeeze a pillow between her legs. And those were the times she wasn't with Ian.

Times like now.

Red satin track shorts hid in the tote bag between her feet, shorts she'd never worn outside the house.

"I can't believe people are still hanging out on the lawn at school," Shaun yawned. "Smoking and playing Frisbee. Time to cut the cord. It's summer now."

"They're the same people who never came to school during the year." Janelle tugged on the basket of fries. Diana pushed it absently toward her.

"Like that's not what you do with your ass every day, Shaun." Marissa blew a straw paper at Shaun's guitar case. "You sit outside strumming while the rest of us go to work."

"I'm writing music for my band," Shaun protested. "Full time. You're all coming to our next show, right? Bring everyone you know."

"Yeah, Diana." Janelle poked her arm. "Bring everyone you know."

"What?" Diana said distractedly. Somehow, her fries had ended up on the other side of the table. She reached for the basket. "We know the same people."

Marissa leaned close, speaking slowly in case the message wasn't clear. "You know your neighbors."

Diana took off her glasses and toyed with them. "Oh, you mean the DiStefanos? They're old. They wouldn't like Shaun's decibel level."

"My God, your *neighbors*, Diana," Janelle broke in. "*The* neighbors. The O'Brian twins." She fluttered her fingers in front of her face. "When they showed up at graduation, all tall and muscular and hot and standing two feet away from me — and fucking identical — I

10

honestly couldn't breathe."

"We noticed," Marissa said drily. Shaun was grumbling and unzipping his guitar case. "Shaun, don't play right now. We're in a restaurant."

"And when they both had their arms around Diana and were posing for pictures... You've been holding out on us, babe." Janelle pointed her fork at Diana. "How did you even stay upright?"

Good question. Her friends would never know how close she'd been to melting under her graduation gown.

"I told you," Diana said airily, though her heart was pounding, and her dress felt much too hot now. "I don't see them that way."

From the corner of the booth, a chord strummed — pissily, if that was possible. David's eyes darted between Marissa and Janelle like the conversation was moving too fast for him to follow.

"Marissa, we need to see those pictures you took." Janelle reached for Marissa's purse on the table.

Marissa shook her head sadly. "They're all on their phone."

"Brendan's phone," Diana put in. "They don't share a phone. They're two people."

"Oh my God, you touched his phone. And those green eyes—"

"Hazel," Diana sighed.

"Are you sure?"

"Yes." *Very sure.* "They're just eyes," she added.

Eyes with their own unnameable color in the moonlight when Ian crouched over her, his muscles tensed. Eyes that went wide and hot as she tugged on his sweats and trailed her fingers down his skin, eyes that narrowed with lust as he peeled off her nightgown. Eyes that explored every curve until her nipples puckered in the cool air, her breath sped up, and her legs opened in an obvious plea...

"Who are these people and why do you care about them?" David looked perplexed.

"Oh, right." Marissa patted his arm sympathetically. "Transfer

11

student. You never witnessed the glory of the O'Brian twins. They graduated two years before us. Total jocks and cocky as hell, or at least the bad one was, but no one can deny the legend. Diana's been hanging out with them. She never did in high school."

"We have a history, that's all." Diana pushed up her glasses and smoothed her dress. Sweat gathered between her breasts. "Sometimes it just feels really good to hang out with people you've known forever, who know the real you. It's not a big thing. They're busy, I'm busy. I do see Brendan every morning." *And Ian every night.* "He has some financial internship downtown and he leaves when I go to the lab. We have a nice good morning hug ritual," she couldn't resist adding, because it felt safer to talk about Brendan right now. "Brendan gives really good hugs."

"What's involved in a really good hug?" David squinted at her, while Janelle motioned to Diana and mouthed, *Least huggy person ever.* "Can you give us a step-by-step?"

Oh, could she. First, Brendan rested a solid arm on her shoulders and smiled down at her like he'd been waiting for this moment since he'd rolled out of bed. *Morning, cutie.* Next came his other arm, wrapping easily around her back and pulling her close. Close enough to breathe in a hint of cologne, close enough to feel hard muscle against her soft curves, close enough to hear his deep voice murmur the compliment of the day. *I like your dress. You smell amazing. You look so happy, Di.* Close enough for her body to throb as she hugged him back and teased him about wearing a tie.

His hand, tousling her hair, told her she was strictly a little sister now. When it dropped to her waist for a brief squeeze, it told her he hadn't forgotten when she wasn't.

No one but Brendan could pack that much into a two-second hug, and she doubted anyone but Brendan could pull it off. She wasn't complaining.

"You know." She pushed ice down in her coffee with her straw. "A friendly cuddle. Not too soft, not too hard. No expectations, so you can relax, because you know nothing's ever going to happen."

Janelle was hanging on to every word. David had his phone out like he was taking notes.

"I give good hugs," Shaun announced between strums.

"You give great hugs, Shaun." Taking pity on him, Marissa began playing with his hair. A month ago, Diana would have looked awkwardly in the other direction, the way she always had when her friends got up close and personal. Now, she just smiled.

"Why don't you want something to happen with Brendan?" Janelle demanded. "Oh, right. They're like your brothers. Better for the rest of us."

"Not like anything would," Marissa chimed in. "No offense, Di. You're hot. But I don't think your neighbor twins' tastes run to scary-smart."

"We don't have to talk about them," Diana said quickly. "We were talking about Shaun and his band."

"No, we weren't." Marissa turned to David. "Janelle used to drag me to their games to drool over them."

"Me? You were all over that."

"You went to their games?" Diana asked, startled.

"Yeah, remember? We tried to take you once. You closed us down like that." Marissa snapped her fingers. "We couldn't even convince you to bring homework, and let me tell you, they were playing Woodside and there was such a display of man-flesh on that basketball court..."

"Sounds like overkill," Shaun grumbled.

"It was perfection. And everyone heard about how hard they partied afterward. Ian got totally thrashed and streaked through the neighborhood. Rumor said he was the only guy who was naked, but he got some girls to take their clothes off too," Janelle giggled.

"Oh, I believe it. Brendan's the responsible one," Marissa

explained to David. He nodded and reached for a handful of Diana's fries. "And Ian's the troublemaker. He is such a party animal and a manwhore…"

"Who's shaking the table?" Janelle grabbed her milkshake to keep it from spilling. "Diana? Jesus, sit still."

Diana took a quick sip of her iced coffee. Half an hour from now, she'd be walking into Ian's territory in her red satin shorts. Had she really thought caffeine was a good idea? Her heart raced, and butterflies were invading her stomach.

"They're different once you get to know them," she said out loud. "And I just have a lot of energy. I was sitting on a bench all day."

"Yeah, how's that going, Miss Lab Rat?" Marissa dragged a fry through ketchup. "Forget the O'Brians. Do you have to wear a white coat?"

Diana slurped more iced coffee, buying time to calm down.

On her first day at the lab, eager to make a good impression as the youngest person there, she'd volunteered to wash a huge tray of glassware. Two minutes in, she'd knocked it over. Everyone heard the smash, everyone watched as she swept up the pieces, and everyone saw the head of the lab tell her that she'd be paying for that glassware.

That night, still hot with embarrassment, she'd asked Ian to make it better. Seconds later, she'd found herself naked in her dark backyard, grass pressing into her hands and knees, obeying his order to hold still.

In a low voice, Ian told her she was all alone in the lab. So busy, so hard at work, she never heard him sneaking up behind her. And wasn't she surprised when he started feeling her up under her white coat?

But so was he, because she didn't have anything on underneath. All he felt was soft skin, an incredible ass, and tits that begged to be squeezed. How dirty. He knew she was a bad girl, but naked at work? She really was a slut, wasn't she?

When she'd tried to turn around, already dizzy with arousal, he told her not to pay attention to him, to keep doing whatever she was doing with beakers and shit, while he growled the filthiest words imaginable and played with her nipples until she whimpered with need.

I'm not here. Just keep working, baby. Don't let anything explode.

God, when he'd finally plunged into her with a deep thrust that made her gasp, she'd been dripping wet, beyond ready for him even though he hadn't touched her pussy yet, and —

"Not too bad," she chirped. "Everyone else in the lab is more experienced than I am, which means I do all the bitch work, and I spend most of my time pouring things in test tubes and watching them, and I smashed about a thousand flasks the first day because I was nervous. But overall — not too bad." She took another freezing gulp from her straw. "And yes to the white coat."

"You were nervous?" Shaun's head jerked up from his guitar. "Seriously?"

Diana spluttered through a mouthful of iced coffee. Everyone was staring now.

"What?" She grabbed Marissa's napkin to wipe her face. "I just snorted coffee up my nose. No big deal. It happens."

"Not to you." Janelle waved one of Diana's french fries. "You don't do the klutzy stuff the rest of us do. You're always so together and… careful. Really, you were nervous?"

Diana nodded, too shocked to answer right away. *Buttoned-up ice princess,* Ian had called her that first night in the pool. *Stone-cold fox.* She'd been shocked then, too.

"Nervous like you wouldn't believe," she said firmly.

"Well, I guess it happens to the best of us. Even you." Marissa gave her a teasing elbow to the ribs. The motion knocked Diana's purse off the side of her chair.

Shit, she hadn't zipped it. Keys jangled to the ground while lipstick skittered down the tiles. Her phone landed with a gut-wrenching crack. And in plain view, lying next to her red leather journal— Fuck. Oh, fuck.

The lube.

Not just any lube. The lube Brendan had brought to her bedroom on graduation night, right before she'd taken him and Ian inside her. Together. The first part of the twins' gift, and just to make things obvious, the tube was clearly marked *Anal lubricant: for intimate pleasure.*

Marissa had seen it too. No question. She goggled at the floor, then Diana.

"What?" Shaun leaned over the table, craning his neck at the mess.

No one else had seen. With two sweeps of her arms, Marissa scooped up Diana's things and dumped them back in her purse.

"Sorry. So sorry. What was Janelle saying about being klutzy? I need to go be a girl now." She picked up her own purse. "Come with, Di?"

She looped her arm through Diana's in a way that made it clear she wasn't asking. Her face on fire, Diana grabbed her purse, along with the tote bag under her chair.

"Sure. Absolutely," she babbled. "Let me just see if my phone will start. Good, it's okay. I need to head out soon anyway."

"Where?" Janelle asked, but Marissa was already rushing her across the diner. Past the kitchen, up to the door — Marissa opened it and pulled her inside. The restroom was mercifully empty.

"Did I just see *lube* in your purse?" Marissa was clutching her arm, her face working in delighted shock. "Did I see *anal lube?* Am I having some kind of hallucination? Did Shaun dope my drink? Because I thought the only drug in my system was caffeine."

"Calm down." Giggles burst from Diana's mouth. "Just calm down, okay?"

"Right. 'Cause you've been so calm this whole time. You're like… lightning, looking for a rod."

"Hey, that's poetic. Are you claiming that line? Because otherwise, I'm writing it down." Diana reached for her journal. Her face was scarlet, she knew.

"What's going on?" Marissa blocked her hand. "And where the hell are you going after this? I brought a tank top, like you asked. Since you apparently don't own any." Fishing in her purse, she pulled out a plain white tank top. "But after the lube, this seems so...boring."

"No, no, it's perfect. Thanks." Diana took the tank top and disappeared into one of the stalls. Her cheeks still flamed. "I'll go ahead and change."

"You can't change in front of me, but you're carrying around anal lube?"

"God, stop. It sounds so *dirrrty*." She couldn't keep the giggles back.

"It is dirty! It's incredibly dirty! Have you even had your first kiss yet? Are you trying to be prepared, like the world's worst boy scout?"

"Oh, I just have it on me to get a reaction." Diana tried to sound nonchalant as she unbuttoned her collar, wriggled out of her sailor dress, and tugged Marissa's tank top over her head.

Dear Lord. She let out a breath. Though, to be honest, she barely had room to breathe. Describing the shirt as skin-tight would be an understatement. The white ribbed cotton was painted on her exaggerated curves, stretching over her breasts and clinging to her slim waist.

On went the thrifted shorts, oozing seventies charm with St. Xavier High School pride marching up the side. The red satin hugged her rounded hips and ass.

Yes. She really was going to wear this outfit in public, all because she'd dared herself to do it. Before she lost her nerve, she kicked off her flats, pulled on white pom-pom socks, and laced up a pair of white Keds — the only option from her closet that got anywhere near athletic shoes.

"I'm like Jen Pagliucci, freshman year," she announced through the stall door. "Remember how she'd always stick a beer can in her backpack and 'accidentally' knock it out during class? And be all 'Oops! How'd that get there?'"

"Please don't mention yourself and Jen Pagliucci in the same sentence ever again."

"What's she doing now, anyway? Did she graduate?"

"You're changing the subject."

Diana came out of the stall, her dress and shoes in her bag, feeling next to naked in the tank top and shorts. "Then can we please be mature about this?"

"Damn, woman." Marissa's eyes caught just below Diana's neckline. "You're about to break my shirt."

"It's my secret." Humming, Diana pulled her dark hair into a ponytail. Loose strands slipped from the hair tie and tickled the back of her neck. She smoothed down her bangs, and they brushed the top of her black-rimmed glasses.

Marissa took her arm, leaning close. "Is it Alex?" she whispered.

"Alex?" Diana blinked. Oh God. Alex Noriega, and the date last week in the movie theatre. She hadn't said a word to her friends. After she'd jumped in the O'Brians' pool the next day, whispering *I love you* to Ian had knocked that night out of her thoughts. "No. Uh-uh. There is no Alex."

"I heard you guys went out." Marissa squeezed her arm. "And he's been talking about how you're not the girl he thought you were. He seemed kind of shell-shocked. Have you stopped telling us things completely?"

"How can I stop when there was nothing to tell before?" Blushing again, Diana felt in her purse for lipstick, doing her best to avoid bumping the lube. She'd sweat off all the lipstick where she was going, but who cared? Leaning toward the mirror, she touched up her rosebud lips with red. "Anyway, I'm just heading to the gym."

"You? You refused to even walk past the gym at school, and you never said why. And who wears *lipstick* to work out? Diana, can you please tell me what the hell is going on?"

Diana dropped the lipstick in her purse and zipped it closed. "Not yet." She turned to face Marissa, whose expression hovered between curious and concerned. "It's— It's really new. I don't even know what to think yet. It's crazy and amazing and it's a lot—" She broke off. "I just know I'm really happy and it feels right."

"So it's good."

"Really good." She let out a breath. "Which is why I'm not ready to talk about it. I just want to protect this and see what happens, okay? Without telling anyone."

"Even me?" Marissa looked hurt. "You tell me things."

Diana blinked. So far as she told people things, yes. Marissa knew more than most. Diana had shared bits and pieces about her epic crushes — boys she hadn't had the nerve to talk to during high school, boys who seemed very young now. And she'd gotten an earful from Marissa over the years.

But she'd kept so much under wraps. The lonely year away, the secrets in her underwear drawer, the dirty fantasies at all hours. Everything she'd wanted to do, and everything she'd done.

Some of those secrets, both the twins knew. Some of them, only Ian knew. And when she opened up and started to really share, she wanted him to be the first.

"I will, I promise," she said out loud. "When the time is right."

Marissa glanced at the door. "Just one thing. Does it hurt?" she asked in a hushed voice.

The question caught Diana off-guard. Never had she ever thought she'd explain anything about sex to Marissa. Marissa, who'd been on-again-off-again with Shaun for months, and seemed to be both off and on with him right now.

"If you're really turned on," she whispered back, "and you're relaxed, and you want him in there, then no. It doesn't hurt. He has to go slow, and it feels strange, and you need a lot of lube, but it can be amazingly hot."

And if his twin brother's easing into your cunt while you kneel over him and he soothes you with kisses, and your boyfriend-who-isn't-yet strokes your clit to sharp excitement as he sinks into your ass, and they keep moving and moving and moving until you pitch over the edge — "amazingly hot" doesn't even come close.

Diana's fingers closed on the edge of the sink. Graduation night had been a one-time thing. Her threesome with the O'Brian twins had been crazy, overwhelming, explosive — and it was over.

She'd chosen Ian. She was absolutely certain that she'd made the right choice.

"It's about trust," she finished. "That's all I'm going to say."

"Sounds romantic. That—" Marissa pointed toward Diana's purse, raising her eyebrows, "—doesn't."

"I know. But believe me, it is. It's romantic. It sounds weird, but it is."

"Okay, Di." Marissa was giving her a very strange look. "I believe you. And I don't think that lube is in your purse because you're faking anything. But at some point, I want details. I've always given them to you."

"All I ever wanted and more," Diana murmured. Shouldering her tote bag and purse, she opened the bathroom door. Marissa followed.

When she walked out of the ladies' room in her gym clothes, a chorus of catcalls filled the diner. Thank God they only came from one corner table. Her friends were making all the noise. Shaun and David eyed her with open interest.

"What's with the outfit?" David wanted to know. "Do you have a cape and boots to go with it?"

"I'm just going to work out," she exclaimed.

"Voluntarily?" Janelle jumped out of the booth. "Great. I've been needing to work out forever. I'll go with you."

"Not tonight," Diana said quickly, grateful that Marissa was shaking her head at Janelle. "I'm just checking out the gym near my house. It'll be boring and I'll probably last five minutes. You don't need to see me make a fool out of myself."

"I do," Shaun piped up. His face had brightened when Marissa came back. "I'd pay good money to see Diana Cooper make a fool out of herself. I don't think it's physically possible."

Diana cut the conversation short with a round of goodbye hugs. Janelle was right — until recently, she hadn't been a hugger. Now it felt natural.

Hurrying through the swinging front door, she hopped on her bike. This time, she checked to make sure her purse was zipped shut.

Mature. Romantic. It had all sounded convincing in the bathroom. She pedaled around the corner, feeling the breeze rush past more bare skin than she'd ever shown while riding a bike.

Then she coasted downhill to the neighborhood gym to play a prank on Ian O'Brian.

Chapter Two

Bells jangled as Diana pushed the gym door open. The smell of sweat, metal, and rubber rolled over her. Pounding music greeted her ears, and a blur of pumping bodies filled the room.

Diana had counted on the gym being quiet this late in the evening. Prayed for it, in fact. Did every fit person in town need to be working out right now? She hesitated just inside the door, getting her bearings.

She was in a long, bright room. Mirrors ran along both walls, multiplying the bodies in motion. Behind the receptionist's desk stood rows of workout machines, all of them occupied. People were lined up behind the machines, waiting their turn like a treadmill was worth waiting for. Past the machines, racks of weights sat alongside rippling muscles.

How had she gotten here? The gym was all fluorescent lights and hard surfaces, a place so far beyond her territory that she expected a flashing imposter sign to go off.

She tugged her tank top up to cover her cleavage, her shorts down to hide her thighs. Her glasses were sliding along her nose. She pushed them back up and tightened her ponytail.

She felt so exposed, and there weren't any twins here to protect her or friends to distract her. Right now, she was on her own. Heads were starting to turn as she lingered by the door. Her skin prickled from the attention.

Memories crept in, old memories of gym class. She remembered all the stares when she was a kid in sixth grade — and God, she had been a kid, too young to go through that. The hissed whispers, the boys surrounding her when they were jogging the fucking mile out on the field, teasing her about the body that made her look five years older, while she looked straight ahead and tried her hardest to tune them out.

She hefted her tote bag. Was she really still stuck on the year her family had moved away? Sixth grade was a long-ass time ago, and she was done caring what other people said and did.

If you really didn't give a damn, a little voice said, *you wouldn't be hiding your relationship with Ian. You'd be shouting about your steamy threesome with the O'Brian twins from the rooftops. And there was that little orgy after graduation, when you were high as fuck and ready for anything...*

Jesus. She flushed. Maybe it was impossible not to care about people's opinions.

Quickly, she retreated to the safety of the nearby water cooler, where she drained half her water bottle just to refill it and stall for time. Ian had to be in the gym somewhere. Maybe Brendan was too, since he came here to work out. But in the busy room, she didn't spot either familiar body — tall, bronzed, broad shoulders traveling in a vee to narrow hips.

A group of sweat-stained guys walked by, towels around their necks, close enough for her to smell their perspiration. She focused her gaze ahead as their eyes cut toward her — toward the white tank top straining across her full breasts, the red shorts hugging her flared hips, and all the leg she was showing.

Her first instinct was to shrink. Instead, she stood up straight and managed a smile in their direction.

"Do you need some help?" one of the guys asked. The question was friendly enough. He'd been obvious about checking her out, but he was looking at her face now.

No one here was out to get her. And dammit, she wasn't a kid anymore. She'd done more than she'd ever imagined these past few weeks, learned more than she'd ever dreamed. She'd closed her books for the summer, but she remembered Ian's teasing voice: *This is where your education begins.* She'd walked into this gym for a reason.

"No, thanks," she said, her voice firmer. "I'm fine. I have an appointment."

The guy nodded, she nodded back, and her own legs propelled her to the front desk.

The receptionist looked up with a smile.

"You're right on time. I've got you down for his seven o'clock, Samantha."

"Fantastic," Diana heard herself say. "Thanks, Molly. Should I wait here?"

"Nah. Go look around, check out the gym. Make him wonder where Samantha is." She gave Diana a wink.

"If you say so." Diana grinned back. A few weeks ago, she wouldn't have believed she'd be standing here chatting with the kind of girl who'd intimidated her almost as much as boys: outgoing, breezy, sporty.

"Trust me, he has it coming." Molly gave her keyboard a few frustrated pecks. "When you showed up a couple days ago, saying you wanted to prank him, you came at the right time. You know he stole my office supplies that afternoon? I was running around freaking out, and he says, all innocent, 'Take it easy. Everything's in your car where you left it.' How he got my keys I don't know, but there was all my shit, right in my car. I almost killed him, but we were all actually kind of relieved. He was really quiet last week. And his yummy twin brother hasn't come in for a few days." She sighed. "Brandon. He's such a *gentleman*. Brandon would never do anything to drive a girl crazy."

"Brendan," Diana corrected automatically. Of all the words she'd use to describe her boyfriend's twin, "gentleman" wasn't one of them.

"Right, Brendan. You know if Ian was okay?"

Diana let out a breath. Her heart fluttered in her chest. "He is now."

"Good. Hey, he's coming. Go, go. Hide!"

Diana swerved in the other direction, away from the male figure sauntering up to the desk. His black tank top and athletic shorts showed acres of lickable tanned skin. At the last minute, she veered towards him. Hiding wasn't part of her plan. She'd spent too many years hiding already.

Ian's head was turned as he called to someone over his shoulder. He didn't see her, which gave her the chance to drink him in.

Gorgeous. It wasn't just his long-lashed hazel eyes, his mischievous white grin, the deep dimples in his cheeks or his defined jaw. The sleek, muscled body helped, but it wasn't the whole story. The way Ian moved...did things to her. He was so unconsciously graceful, so comfortable in his own skin.

Ian. Ian O'Brian was her boyfriend. The boy she'd grown up with who'd done everything in his power to irritate her, the guy who was hot enough to make her gulp her water, now climbed her fence every night to kiss and fuck and talk. It felt so right and so unbelievable at the same time.

Everything since her first kiss — with her boyfriend's twin — felt that way. She was in a fever, and she hoped it would never end.

A loud clang made her jump. Someone had dropped a giant weight on the floor. No one else seemed to notice. Everyone was busy with machines and mats, running and jumping and grunting and sweating. And, in some cases, staring. At her. Her blush seeped down her neck, but she kept her head high and her eyes on Ian.

He saw her. His mouth actually fell open, and he blinked. Then he closed the distance between them, a grin splitting his face. As he gripped her arms, he dropped a quick kiss on her neck.

"Ian!" she hissed. "We're in public."

"Trust me, baby, no one you know is here."

"What are you saying about my friends' athletic skills?"

"Nothing. Jesus, what are you doing here?" His eyes traveled over her scant clothing, stopping on her hips. "Nice shorts. The seventies want them back, but they can't have them. Not 'til later tonight."

"I'm pranking you." She itched to smooth Ian's damp hair. She wanted to lick up the drop of sweat trickling down his neck.

"Excuse me?"

"I'm Samantha." She held out her hand. "It's nice to meet you. We have an appointment."

Ian took her hand and didn't let go. Warmth spread up her arm. "And?"

"What do you mean, 'and?' Look at me. I showed up. I surprised you. I'm wearing…this." She gestured at the tank top and shorts that were plastered to her curves.

"Diana." Ian shook his head. "A prank is more than a surprise. I mean, this is pretty good, but the best pranks take planning. Groundwork. Details. I need to, like, turn around and see my shoes on the roof across the street, or find you sitting on my car wearing a bow that I have to untie to get to you and the car, or— What?"

She snickered. Standing on tiptoe, she let her lips graze Ian's earlobe. "You're a nerd. You're a total nerd when it comes to pranks, aren't you? I've found your nerdy side."

Ian looked alarmed. "Fine. Okay. Don't tell anyone. We've got work to do."

"You're going to train me?" She tried a seductive whisper, but heat flooded her cheeks.

"Hell, yes. Or did you just show up to set my gym on fire with those shorts? Are you scared?" Ian's face was a challenge now.

"I'm not scared." She held his gaze. "Do your worst."

Red crept over his ears. He led her across the crowded gym, their fingers still linked.

"Okay, Diana. Samantha. Whoever you are. Leave your bags by the wall. If you think I'll go easy on you, think again. Stand up straight. Shoulders back. I know you bust ass to get an A. You're gonna do all that for me and more."

Shit. She really was going to have to work out. She leaned her tote bag against the wall and set her purse and water bottle on top of it. Then she straightened her spine, threw her shoulders back, and looked up at Ian. A smile tugged his lips, and an answering grin broke across her face.

The gym felt twenty degrees hotter, but dammit, she was doing this. Brendan's encouraging whispers cut under the pounding beats of the music in the gym, taking her straight to the treehouse where everything began as she sprawled between the twins.

Trust us. I promise, Di, you can do it.

"Just like that." Ian's voice was close to her ear. He wasn't touching her, but he stood near enough to feel the heat coming off his body. Sweat molded his black tank top to his chest. "I'm going to look at you."

An answering drop of perspiration trickled down her cleavage. She rolled her shoulders back again, blocking out the nerves of standing half-dressed in the middle of the gym, seeing Ian's tongue catch between his teeth as the movement thrust her breasts out.

"I thought you were going to train me."

"We'll get there. Breathe normally." Ian circled her, looking up and down her clingy tank top and shorts. His eyes pricked her skin wherever they moved.

"So you're getting paid to check me out?" She tweaked his tank top. "I know this is a free session, but I expect the real deal."

"I'm assessing your posture," he said briskly. His tone was businesslike enough that she let go of his shirt. "Relax those shoulders, Diana. I said *relax.*"

She huffed out a breath and let her shoulders fall back.

"Good. That's it. Now bend over and touch your toes."

"You're really getting off on ordering me around, aren't you?"

Ian smirked at her. "Baby, if you thought Brendan was bossy, you have no idea. No fucking idea."

The gym was warm, even sticky, but Diana shivered. In the world of the twins, she knew the truth: Brendan had been running the show for a long, long time. That had changed in the past week. If Ian enjoyed telling her what to do right now, she wasn't going to argue. Her body had no arguments either.

She reached to touch her toes, flushed and damp. God, people were all around, she was bending over in a pair of tight shorts, and obviously, the prank had backfired.

But doing this on Ian's orders, exposed for him, sent pulses of excitement over her skin.

She held the pose, feeling the stretch in the backs of her thighs. He wouldn't touch her when she was bent over like this, would he? Not in the gym. But she almost felt his hands closing over her rounded ass, fingers sliding into her crotch, maybe landing a smack on one cheek. The uncertainty got her hot. Hot and nervous.

She straightened up, pushing her glasses into place, and smiled at him. Ian's eyes looked a little glazed. But his pat on the back encouraged her. He waved her over to the wall.

"I'm gonna touch you now," he said, like he'd read her mind. "Is that okay?"

"Of course," she breathed. Ian probably asked people that question every day. But knowing he'd touch her in front of everyone — runners bouncing on treadmills, guys lifting huge weights — made her heart beat faster.

"Good. Hips and shoulders against the wall. Like that, Diana." Ian held her hips, angling her in place as his eyes flicked down her body again. His skin burned hers through the thin shorts. Diana swallowed. "Now walk for me."

"Walk," she repeated.

"Here to there." Ian pointed to the far side of the gym. His dimples showed in a broad grin. "Pick your feet up, put them down."

Oh boy. She could handle this. It was just a walk. She hadn't even started working out yet, but sweat pooled between her breasts.

Heads swiveled as she started across the springy gym floor. Ian stood nearby, watching her movements intently, but she felt every inch of the distance between them, widening as she walked. Eyes raked over her, more and more eyes, and now it was too hard to stare back, to know if the gazes meant lust or laughter or something else.

Self-consciousness flickered again, getting stronger.

She wasn't in Ian's arms, or, oh God — sandwiched between him and Brendan. She wasn't surrounded by her friends. She was alone and exposed under the fluorescent lights, and the other side of the room was a mile away.

She should have eaten something in the diner. She should have drunk more water before "Samantha" sprang her prank. One solo walk across a rubber mat in a ridiculous workout outfit shouldn't matter. But here in the gym, halfway across the length of the room, all the old memories rushed in. Jeers filled her ears.

Come on, Diana, we wanna see you run. Show us what happens when you run.

Her eyes closed. It was hard to breathe. The floor tilted under her feet.

"Diana? Diana." A voice — Ian's voice. His hand closed on her shoulder. Fingers pressed into her skin, bringing her back. She blinked, focusing on his face.

"Hey," she said weakly. "I'm okay."

"This way."

One arm supporting her, he walked her towards the front of the gym. They turned a corner into a more private area near a small empty office. The wall at her back was solid and reassuring.

"Drink." He thrust her water bottle in her face. "I want to see this gone."

She gulped water. Thank God the gym was noisy. Machines whirred, music blared. If anyone had witnessed her little breakdown in the middle of the room, they didn't think it was noteworthy.

"I'm okay, really."

"The hell you are." Ian was holding both her arms now. "What happened?"

"Ugh, nothing." She pressed her forehead against his chest. "I just thought I was through feeling this way."

"What way?"

"Shy," she muttered. "Embarrassed. Scared. I've done a lot, and you've seen most of it. You were there. This should be nothing."

Ian rubbed the back of her neck. "You mean, because you've fucked a few times, gotten drunk and high, and jumped in my pool twice when I didn't invite you, you're never going to feel scared again?"

Diana sagged against him. Then she laughed. "Pretty much. You forgot the graduation speech and the declaration of love."

"I haven't forgotten. I never will."

He kissed the top of her head. When she wrapped her arm around him, she felt the restraint in his bunched muscles. No one seemed to be able to see them in the alcove by the office.

"Is this like that night at the club?" Ian's voice was soft now, barely a whisper. "Are you flipping out because there are too many people here? Believe me, you don't want to hook up with any of them." He nodded toward the water bottle in her hand. "But they'll look better if you drink some more."

"It's not that." She shook her head, slurping more water. "It's the past. I shouldn't care, it was such a long time ago, it's not even a big deal…"

"Spit it out."

Diana pushed her bangs off her forehead. "Gyms scare me." Her voice dropped. She waited for Ian to say something, but he just watched her, standing very close, squeezing her arms. "They scare me shitless. I know they're probably the greatest places in the world for you, but being here makes me remember the year away. You know, when my family moved." Voices filled her head again, making her flinch. Ian's hands tightened on her arms. "Gym was the worst. That and the bus. Being teased all day, and it never let up—"

Strong fingers gripped her shoulder. Ian was whispering in her ear. Breath, turning into words.

"It's over, Diana. It's not gonna happen here. Look around." She stepped forward to see the bustling room around the corner. "See? Everyone just cares about themselves. Everyone's trying to beat their personal best and check out their own ass in the mirror. No one's laughing at you. I'm not laughing at you."

"Okay." She heaved a breath.

"Okay?" Ian's gaze, unsmiling now, held hers.

"Okay."

"Do you want to tell me what happened? Because what you said about it not mattering anymore is bullshit."

"I thought it didn't matter." She looked right back at him.

"And it came and bit you in the ass."

Her gaze moved across the busy gym. Ian was right. Everyone was huffing, sweating, checking the view in the mirror.

She took one last drink of water. "I'll tell you. Tonight. I'm ready to go out there."

"Good. Let's do this." He led her swiftly out of the office area.

The clang of another dropped weight made her jump. Ian watched her with a hint of a smile.

"If I didn't know you already," he leaned down to murmur, stopping at a mat, "I'd wonder if you really swing your hips that much when you walk."

Diana's face flamed, and she let out a surprised laugh. "Only when you're around."

31

"Uh-huh. Watch me." Ian went into a squat.

Jesus, that was one instruction she had no problem following. Every move Ian made was pure muscled grace.

"Now you." Ian kept a hand flat on her back, resting his other hand on her stomach to adjust her stance. Diana lowered herself, wincing at the pull on her muscles.

As Ian guided her through sets of squats and lunges, pushups, crunches, and five minutes of biking faster than she'd ever tried to do before, she kept waiting for him to give her a hard time. None of this was easy for her, and Ian had seized every opportunity to tease her mercilessly when they were kids. She'd learned to fight back, fight harder. But Ian wasn't laughing at her now.

"You're doing great, Diana." Approval lit his face as she eased herself off the bike. He gave her waist a squeeze. "You'll do even better when you lose those." He jerked his head toward her white Keds. "Cute. But get some real athletic shoes for next time. I'll help you."

Next time? She groaned out loud. Her body argued with every move. "Absolutely. Next time. I'll get them myself."

"Diana, let me help you with that one, okay?"

She pushed out a breath, then gulped her water. Her whole body was flushed and sweaty now. Ian led her to the back of the gym, chose a weight, and wrapped her fingers around it. Diana looked at the hunk of metal in her hands.

"You gave me the smallest weight."

"And I'll take it away if your form is bad. Now swing like I do. Twelve reps."

Diana gritted her teeth. She'd signed up for this. She swung the weight, imitating Ian's easy movements.

"Okay. You can help me pick out the right shoes."

"See? That wasn't so hard." The words pulled her attention to Ian's flexing muscles. Her own body tightened, and he gave her a knowing grin. "You can let nice people help you with things. And no charge for our sessions."

"What?" she protested. "Of course I'll pay you. This is your job. I'm working too. I can afford it."

"Baby, believe me." Ian leaned against a column. Dimples marked both his cheeks. "I'll get a lot out of this."

She frowned up at him, giving the weight a harder swing. "You think I'll have a better body? You've never had a problem with, uh, my physique."

"It's not how you'll look." Ian's grin widened. "It's what you'll be able to do with it."

"Meaning...?" She let her arms follow the weight in rhythm.

"In the *bedroom*." He kept his voice low, exaggerated, and near her ear. "Not making your boyfriend do all the work."

"Oh— Ohhhhh," Diana breathed as understanding broke through. A dozen hot fantasies surged through her mind. She set the weight down and shook out her arms, trying to stay focused. "Don't complain. I work too."

Ian laughed and motioned her to the pull-up bars. "Dip your hands in this." Diana eyed the bucket of chalk, then shrugged and dipped her hands in the white powder. "Stand on this." He kicked a wooden box under a bar. Sighing, she climbed onto it. "One pull-up."

Diana gripped the bar overhead. As she stepped off the wooden box and hung, her arms trembled. Her palms were slippery on the metal, even with the chalk. Every muscle in her body shrieked a protest. Without a doubt, she was going to fall.

"You got this, Diana." Ian's voice was patient. "You can do more than you think."

Her fingers strained to circle the bar, her arms were on fire, her body swung in the air, and pulling herself up even once seemed impossible. But so many things had seemed impossible a few weeks ago.

Inch by inch, clutching the bar, she lifted her body. At the top, she managed to murmur, arms straining, "You too."

Hazel eyes flickered. "That's enough for now. Let go. Easy does it." Diana dropped to the box and stumbled onto the mat. Ian rubbed her aching arms briskly as she groaned. Then he leaned close.

"You look really hot," he said in a low voice. "I like seeing you sweat."

Heat flooded her cheeks. Ian was already showing her another stretch, back in professional mode. But she had to admit — she liked sweating. A lot. It felt good to push herself.

"I like seeing you work," she whispered. "Love you, Ian."

A slow smile spread over his face, dimples deepening in both cheeks. She felt warmer, lightheaded and dizzy again.

"Bend over like this." Ian demonstrated, then guided her into the same pose. His hands on her in public, their movements obvious under the fluorescent lights, made her even warmer. He bent close. "I love you too," he whispered.

"Do I look like an idiot?" she whispered back.

Ian laughed softly. "You look amazing. Come on, Diana, you're so fucking good at everything else you do. Seeing you a total beginner like this..." He shook his head.

Diana bristled, about to snap back, when she realized the expression on Ian's face was more lovestruck than teasing.

"I'm trying," she said softly.

"Oh yeah, you are. You're trying really hard." Now his grin was mischievous. "Bet you can try harder."

When Ian helped her deepen the stretch, she groaned. But the reach of muscles she'd never known she had, Ian's warm hands wrapped around hers and the lights gleaming on his rippling body — it was all really, really hot.

"Ooh," she gasped. "Ian..."

"I'm not going to take you anywhere you can't go," he whispered. "You're safe."

She squeezed her thighs together. Here in the gym, yards away from where she'd panicked earlier, she was starting to get wet. She needed Ian to hustle her back to that empty office, slide a hand into her red satin shorts, and find out how excited she was…

"And if I wasn't here," Ian went on, his voice all tease now as he pointed for her to sit on a mat facing him, "you would have injured yourself in three seconds, lifting the heaviest weight, trying to impress the guys who've been eye-stripping you."

"I'm not that crazy," she sniffed. "Give me some credit. Ooohhh…"

Ian stretched her arms, his fingers laced through hers. "Pull back."

She pulled. His words came to her, from the first time with the twins in the treehouse. *Push back.*

"Does it hurt so bad, Diana?" Ian's voice was soft enough that she barely heard it underneath the blaring music, the whir of the exercise machines, and the clang of the weights. His low tone went straight between her legs. "Or does it hurt so good?"

"It's good," she breathed.

"Then harder." He grinned at her. "Show me what you have."

Gripping his hands, she leaned back. "You don't know yet?"

"I bet there's more."

She flushed, but she managed to retort, "A lot more."

Chapter Three

"You did it." Ian slapped her on the back. "Congrats."

Diana bent over the rowing machine, panting. "We're done?"

"For tonight." He let her catch her breath, then held out a hand. Diana took it. She climbed off the machine, muscles aching. "Ever worked up a sweat like this before? I bet you haven't."

Ian was right. She thought she'd known what it meant to sweat — with nerves, with excitement. But not like this. Wincing, she stood on wobbly legs and stretched her arms.

"Dare you to come twice a week." Ian looked much too pleased with himself. "You'll see the best results if you're here a lot."

"I had no idea what I was doing."

"The more you come, the faster you'll learn." He cocked an eyebrow at her.

She nodded, too wrung out to laugh at his suggestive tone, and pulled at her damp tank top. "I borrowed this." Her voice was hoarse. "It's going straight to the laundry."

"Can it wait?" One finger stroked her shoulder, and her breath caught.

"Why? Are you taking me to a place that's not my backyard?"

"That's what I'm thinking." He gave her a half-smile. "Somewhere nice and private that I've always wanted to show you. We can talk."

Warmth ran over her cheeks. "I bet you've used that line a lot."

"I mean it." He rubbed her arm. "You were about to collapse back there. Time to get that shit out."

"Okay," she said slowly. She was tempted to skip the talking. It would be so much more fun to bury the bad memories and focus on Ian, here and now. Go someplace alone, get him out of his workout clothes as soon as possible. But the conversation didn't have to be long. She'd rip the band-aid off, toss the hurt away, and get on with her life. "No shower?"

He tugged her ponytail. "You're hot like this. You okay with a little sweat? Some dirt and mess? I know the ice princess wouldn't approve, but—"

She smacked his arm. "Don't start. You know that's not the real me. This is fine."

As they left, Ian insisted on refilling her water bottle by the door. Molly fluttered her hand in a little wave from the front desk, calling out that she hoped "Samantha" had a good session.

Outside, orange stained the sky — the beginning of sunset. The twins' Jeep waited by the opposite curb. As her fingers linked with Ian's and they crossed the street, she looked both ways. Not for cars, but for people she knew.

"Where's your worse half? Doesn't he take the Jeep to work every day?"

"Worse half." Ian chuckled. "Nice. I'm telling Brendan."

"Go ahead. We all know it's true."

A breeze cooled the sticky air. They stopped on the sidewalk by the Jeep. Ian backed her against the passenger door and brushed damp bangs off her forehead.

"Yeah, he takes the Jeep. Used to be, he'd drive over, work out near the end of my shift, and we'd leave together."

"And now?"

"He's been dropping off the car. It's close enough to jog home."

"Why'd he stop coming? Molly's pining for him."

Ian grinned. "Yeah, she'd love to get in Brendan's pants."

"She thinks he's such a gentleman," Diana giggled. The passenger door was warm against her back. Ian leaned over her, one hand resting on the car, smiling down at her.

"Her and the rest of the world."

He ran a finger along the low neckline of her tank top. No one on the sidewalk seemed to notice, but Diana shivered. The move was public and very obvious. When he tweaked her shoulder strap, she laughed and pushed his hand away.

"Why'd Brendan stop coming to the gym?" she repeated.

Ian shrugged, his smile gone. "We've been doing more things apart, babe. It needed to happen. Once I got with you — okay, once everything went to shit after that crazy night out — it wasn't a matter of if, but when."

There was a lot she wanted to say, so many questions waiting to be asked. The one that popped out was, "But where's Brendan going to work out?"

"You're worried about him losing his manly muscles?"

She sputtered with laughter. "I'm more worried about finding mine right now. Am I going to be this sore every time?"

Ian's lips brushed her ear. "Are you as sore as you were the first time we fucked?"

Her body tightened. Her hands went to his hard waist. "No."

"Same thing with the gym. It'll get easier, I promise." His dimples were back, marking both cheeks. "You'll learn to love it. You'll wake up craving it. You'll think about it all the damn time. *When do I get to work out? Ian, pleeaaase make me do push-ups. Oh God, I need more.*"

Diana blushed. "You talk a good game."

"I'm more than talk, baby." Ian kissed the corner of her mouth.

Yes, they were in public. But leaning against the Jeep with Ian standing over her, his body inches away, felt private. A world just for the two of them.

Diana took his face in her hands and pulled him down for a real kiss. Ian's mouth opened in surprise, but he quickly recovered, one hand going to the back of her head, sucking her lower lip into his mouth, turning her insides to mush. All her senses went into that kiss.

When they parted, Ian looked down at her with a dazed smile.

"What?" she murmured.

"I still can't believe it."

"Me neither. I can't believe we're together." She ran her palm over his damp hair. "But it's so right."

"So fucking right." Ian kissed her again, lightly. He unlocked the Jeep and opened the door for her, jogging to his side when she climbed in.

As she settled into the seat, still dizzy from the kiss, she decided not to point out that Ian hadn't given her an real answer about Brendan. What happened between the twins was their business. Even if a small, insistent part of her still wanted a share.

Ian pulled into the lazy evening traffic.

"You're almost driving carefully," she spoke up.

"I know, right? Me and the speed limit are getting acquainted." Ian turned on the radio, but he kept the volume low.

They rumbled down one street after another, music pulsing through the car. As Ian rounded a corner, Diana's heart leapt into her throat. Not because of his driving — this had to be the slowest Ian had ever taken a corner — but because the pleasant neighborhood streets now looked a little too familiar.

Up ahead was her house, all lit up with both cars out front. In the side yard, her dad crouched over the flowerbeds. Next door stood the O'Brians' house, the garage door open. All her nerves went on alert.

"This is the someplace private?" she asked in disbelief. "You're taking me *home*?" She gripped Ian's leg, and his muscles tensed under her touch. But he just laughed, braked sharply and veered into the O'Brians' wide driveway.

"Wait here. Don't get in trouble." Putting the Jeep in park, he jumped out. His long legs streaked toward the porch.

"Hey!" she called. Ian waved and pulled the front door closed.

Diana leaned back against the passenger seat, her heart thumping. People were mowing their lawns, sitting on their porches, strolling down the sidewalk. Her throat was dry. She reached for her water bottle.

Of course she wouldn't hide. If anyone noticed her in the O'Brian brothers' Jeep, she was ready to deal with raised eyebrows about good girl Diana Cooper and the sweat-soaked tank top plastered to her curves. Not to mention her flushed cheeks and messy hair...

When the DiStefanos' door opened across the street, her stomach lurched.

"Damn you, Ian," she muttered. She slid down in one long stretch until she was crouched on the floor.

As her breathing returned to normal, she rested her head against the seat. The black leather was smooth, and the car smelled like both the twins: salt, cologne, and aftershave. There was an undertone of beer that might have decorated the back seat at some point. Slowly, she began to relax.

The twins loved this car. Countless times, she'd ogled them from her window as they worked on the Jeep, stripped to the waist in hot weather. Sharing a car had never seemed to bother them.

They'd never guessed she was spying on them, either. Except for one morning in high school...

It was the fall of her freshman year. The twins were juniors, and she hadn't had the nerve to talk to either of them since the epic fail of her ride with them on the first day of school. Ian's license was still suspended and would be until February, as she learned from eavesdropping on Mrs. O'Brian's mournful conversations with her mom. Whenever the twins drove by, or climbed into the Jeep at the end of a school day, Brendan's easygoing frame filled the driver's seat, while Ian slouched in the passenger seat.

But this morning, as Diana headed outside, buttoning her jean jacket and adjusting her bulging backpack, she spotted Ian in his driveway. He stood in front of the Jeep, tinkering under the hood.

His breath made white puffs in the October air. He wore an expression of total focus, one she'd never seen on Ian. Brendan was nowhere in sight. The only clues to Ian's identity were his messy hair and lithe movements. She wasn't close enough to check for the freckle under his left eye, but oh shit, she wanted to be. So badly.

The morning was chilly, and she tucked her scarf more firmly around her neck. But Ian looked completely at home in a ragged T-shirt and fraying jeans. His feet were bare. She couldn't believe he wasn't shivering.

As she lingered in her own driveway, holding her bike by the handlebars, the clock ticking toward her first class of the day, she stared openly. The lines of Ian's shoulders were perfect. The lettering on his T-shirt was almost gone, impossible to read. His back, bent over the car, was so smooth. What would it be like to touch that back? Fascinated, she watched as he stroked the hood of the Jeep like a favorite pet.

Of course she'd been noticing both twins for awhile now. Having...thoughts about them. But always from the safety of her bedroom. She wasn't prepared for Ian to glance up.

From a few feet away, he took in the bob she'd just chopped, her colorful chunky scarf, her backpack heavy with books, and the oversized glasses perched on her nose. His eyes flicked from her to the Jeep, sending a mocking message: *Want a ride?*

Like she'd ever get in a car with him. With or without a license. She valued her life, thank you very much. Not that Ian meant it, anyway. She managed a sniff in his direction before she tore her gaze away.

Then she unsteadily climbed on her bike, praying he wasn't watching her, praying that he was, and sped through the neighborhood toward the brick high school, thinking righteously about how late Ian was going to be, if he even showed up at all.

Now, she shifted position and propped the back of her head against the seat. A long scratch scored the ceiling of the Jeep. There had to be a story behind that. There was a story behind everything with the twins.

"I wish I'd talked to you, Ian," she said to the ceiling. "Just one hello. I wish I hadn't been so scared."

In the distance, a door opened and closed. Footsteps came toward the Jeep. She climbed out of her crouch and straightened up.

"Where were you?" she began indignantly. "...Oh."

A twin leaned against the open driver's window, wearing a striped button-down with the sleeves rolled up. The collar was open, showing tanned skin.

"Hey, cutie." He smiled down at her. The setting sun deepened the cleft in his chin.

This was Brendan. The signs were obvious. If nothing else, the "cutie" was a dead giveaway. He'd given her that nickname about twenty-four hours after she got together with Ian. Coming from him, the word put her squarely in little-sister territory.

"Hey yourself." God, Brendan was the last person who should make her blush, but her cheeks felt hot.

"How come you're hiding?" He looked like he was trying not to laugh.

She waved Brendan to lean in the window. Instead, he opened the door and slid into the driver's seat, closing the door behind him.

"My parents still don't know," Diana whispered in his ear.

"About you and Ian?" His smile broadened. "Figured."

"I'd like to keep it that way for now."

Brendan stretched out his legs, leaning back comfortably. "You're going to have to tell them." His voice was reassuring, but Diana stiffened.

"I will. Soon. It's not like I'm ashamed." She spun the radio dial, bouncing from station to station.

"Easy there." Brendan's hand closed on her wrist. "Pick a song and stick with it."

"Control freak," she teased. The contact made her skin prickle. Brendan laughed and let go.

"Have at it."

She played with the dial to have something to do, because honestly, she didn't know what to do with Brendan. Every morning when they hugged hello, she repeated the same words to herself: *Brendan equals brother.*

"It's just so much easier with no one knowing about us," she said quickly. "Me and Ian, I mean." Brendan nodded understandingly. "I tell my parents I'm going to be out with my friends. They say, *have a great time, we're glad you're enjoying yourself after all your hard work in high school. We're glad we have a daughter we don't need to worry about.* Then I go out with my friends. I come home after my parents are asleep, Ian meets me in my backyard — you know about that part — and we...well. Yeah." She let go of the dial and straightened her tank top.

Brendan looked at her innocently. "What do you do, Di?"

"Listen to records." She gave his innocent expression right back to him. "Talk. Look at the stars."

"Ian's not a big talker." Brendan's dimples were on display. "At least, not out of bed."

She wrinkled her nose. "He is with me."

Hazel eyes flickered. Then Brendan cocked his head. "The sneaking around isn't bad for an amateur." He rested a hand on her shoulder. "But you need to go big or go home. Push it more, or tell your parents."

"What?" She stared at him. "Uh-uh. This is perfect. If they find out, I'll lose all my freedom. And if I push it more—" she broke off. "I'm not risking that."

Brendan turned the radio dial until it landed on a mellow station. He hummed along for a minute, then winked at Diana.

"Secret's safe with me."

"Better be." Diana shot a glance at the closed front door. "What's Ian up to?"

"Dad's talking to him. It won't take long."

"Is everything okay?"

"Everything's fine, cutie."

The soothing tone was pure Brendan, and so was the squeeze on her shoulder. But Ian would tell her the truth, pretty or not. She'd hoped Brendan was heading in that direction too.

Crossing her bare legs, she smoothed down her shorts. The red satin had ridden all the way up, wedging into the vee between her thighs.

"Where are you going tonight?" she asked quickly.

"Out." Brendan flashed his dimples. "My ride's on its way. I figured you guys would want the Jeep."

"Thanks," she murmured. She shouldn't feel guilty. The twins were used to sharing, had shared for years.

"Don't sweat it. Ian hasn't used the car all week. He needs to take you out already."

"It's not his fault. I haven't let him out of my backyard." As confident as she meant to sound, her face was warm.

Brendan chuckled. "I bet you haven't." Reaching over, he pulled her hair. The tug on her ponytail was all big brother, but her body felt the pressure in one long wave.

"Well, have fun, wherever you're going tonight." She flicked his collar, trying to breathe normally. *Brendan equals brother.* "I feel underdressed. I wanted to surprise Ian at the gym, so I showed up like this." Brendan's startled expression sent a little curl of pride through her. "He trained me really well."

"I bet he did. You're in good hands, Di." Hazel eyes moved to her legs. God, she really was tugging the hem of her shorts down now, inviting his gaze. "Cute outfit." His smile was friendly, without the tease she'd begun to see from Brendan, but she felt close to nude again.

"It's what everyone wears to work out. Didn't you know?" One sneeze and Marissa's white tank top would unravel completely.

"Mm-hm." As Brendan studied the patches of sweat under her arms, his dimples deepened. "Looks like Ian worked you over."

"Not even close," she retorted.

When he raised his eyebrows, her cheeks went hotter, and she stretched up both arms to hide her blush.

"Oooh...ow," she groaned. Her body felt like it had been run through a wringer. "Somehow I have to be able to walk by Monday. I promised Ian I'd work out with him twice a week."

Brendan chuckled. A large hand closed on the back of her neck, massaging where the ache began.

"Is that the right place?"

"One of them. There are about a million."

"We'll start here, okay?" He smiled at her.

As Brendan rubbed her neck in slow circles, Diana's eyes slid closed.

"That feels so good," she confessed.

"Nothing wrong with that, Di." The smile in Brendan's voice was clear.

"I didn't say there was— oh," she sighed.

He'd found a tender spot where her neck met her shoulder. Brendan's touch was so relaxing, she didn't feel any need to open her eyes.

It was just a friendly massage. Affectionate, nothing more. Fingers slipped under her tank top, kneading her bare back.

"I probably pushed myself too hard," she mumbled. "I wanted to show him I could do everything."

"We already know you can, cutie."

God, the "cutie" may have been all little sister, but there was a world of history behind that "we."

"You're too nice."

"Di, remember when I said that when you graduate, you can do anything you want?"

"Mm-hmmm." All her limbs were loosening. She leaned back into Brendan's palm. "That was a long time ago. We were all in high school."

He kneaded her neck. "When are you going to believe me?"

"Right now."

"Good. Bend over."

The command was so casual, she obeyed before she knew it. Brendan's hands moved over her back, pushing up her thin tank top to find all her knots, melting every tight place that he touched.

And where was Ian, anyway? What could he possibly be up to in the house?

She blew out air and sat up abruptly, trapping Brendan's hand between her back and the seat.

"You guys said this wasn't weird for you." She looked into bright hazel eyes. "But it's weird for me."

Brendan's movements stopped. He stared up at the ceiling of the Jeep for a long minute, then back at her. Outside, across the street, a lawn mower started up.

"It'll be okay, Di." Easing his hand out of her tank top, he patted her shoulder. "You guys are in love. It's so fucking obvious, you won't be able to hide it for long."

"But I want to," she said quietly. She couldn't read Brendan's gaze.

"Maybe you can, but Ian won't. He's wanted you forever."

"Yeah." Butterflies began to flutter in her stomach again, and her heartbeat accelerated. "That. I'm still wrapping my head around that."

Brendan gave her shoulder a squeeze and let go. "It's always been you, Di. It's not like we talked about it, but whenever you came up, he acted different."

"Really?"

"Come on." Now his pleased smile was back. "Remember the time you slept over when we were kids? Ian put fake spiders in your bed, and you put a caterpillar in his Cheerios? He kept the caterpillar. He put it in a jar with some leaves. He poked holes in the lid and everything."

"That was ten years ago. You're making that up."

"Ask him. I came into our room the next day and caught him talking mushy to it."

"You didn't." Diana started to laugh.

"You know how Ian's ears turn red." He winked at her.

"I've seen it once or twice."

"He got embarrassed." Brendan's innocent look said he couldn't imagine why. "Let it go in the backyard right after that."

"Why didn't he just tell you the truth?"

"That's the part I don't get." Brendan shrugged. "It's the part I never did get."

Diana let out a long exhalation. "I kind of get it. I haven't wanted to tell anyone about us because it's too private. Maybe Ian felt that way too."

"I'm not 'anyone,' Di." Brendan's tone was mild, but he was looking right at her, all the charm gone. His intense expression could have come straight off his brother's face.

Impulsively, she grabbed his hand. "I'm really glad you're my big brother," she blurted. "I don't know what else to say."

Her front door opened.

"Diana!" her mother called. Diana started. Both her parents were coming down the front path, passing their own car to head for the Jeep.

"And Brendan!" Mrs. Cooper added as she came closer, sounding profoundly relieved.

When Diana turned to Brendan, she saw why: he'd cranked the charm back up, giving her parents a dimpled smile like seeing the two of them made his whole evening.

Both her parents glanced from her to Brendan. They looked surprised, but pleased, as she and Brendan dropped hands.

"Hi, Mom," Diana said quickly. "Hi, Dad."

"Please." Her mother beamed. "Don't let us interrupt."

"We were just finishing up," Brendan said smoothly.

"Didn't you say you were out with your friends tonight, Diana?" Her father looked confused as they reached the Jeep, while her mother was saying "It's *so* nice to see the two of you together."

"I'm about to meet up with them," she lied. Her heart was pounding. "Brendan's going out too. We were just talking."

"Well, don't let us interrupt you," her mother repeated. "Brendan, how's your job going? I heard from your mom that you're volunteering at the mayor's office on top of your internship? How do you find time for everything? And here we thought Diana was busy. Did you know she's doing groundbreaking research?"

Diana buried her face in her hands as her mother grilled Brendan about every conceivable aspect of his summer. So much for not interrupting. She'd tried telling her mom that her job in the lab involved more dishwashing and data entry than groundbreaking research, but it didn't seem to matter.

A creak caught her attention. The O'Brians' front door cracked open a sliver.

At least Brendan was being less chatty than usual — pleasant, but brief.

"I better finish up with Di," he said finally, giving Mrs. Cooper an apologetic smile. "She wanted some advice about college, and my ride's almost here." He leaned out the window to shake Mr. Cooper's hand. "Always great to talk with you both."

"We should be going too, Julie," her father said, steering her mother by the arm.

"Of course. Diana, what are you wearing?" Her mother stopped and peered at her skimpy tank top.

"I was just at the gym," she said nonchalantly. "I decided to try something new this summer. I can't spend all my time indoors."

"Well, I can't argue with that. Is that your influence, Brendan? Very well-rounded."

"Very," Brendan agreed. "Very well-rounded." Diana clamped her lips together to keep back a snort of laughter. "Take care, Mrs. Cooper. Mr. Cooper. Have a great night."

Diana let out a sigh of relief when her parents made it safely to their own car and drove off in the other direction.

Brendan leaned over. "It's okay, Di. I understand about secrets."

She found herself squeezing his hand again. "I hate lying," she muttered. "I just want to protect this."

"I know. I get it, cutie." The charm was turned on again. Lips pecked her cheek, just as the sound of feet pounding the driveway made her look up.

A tall figure jogged toward the Jeep. His hair was wet, his broad shoulders outlined in a black T-shirt. The bundle tucked under his arm looked suspiciously like a rolled-up blanket with a thermos on top. A scrap of paper peeked from his jeans pocket.

Brendan climbed out of the Jeep. "Keeping your seat warm."

"I see that." Ian crushed his brother's shoulder under his palm.

"Your girlfriend needed company. She was all alone in the car."

"Did you shower without me?" Diana demanded. "You did, didn't you. And you left me sitting here. How evil is that?"

Crossing to the passenger side, Ian buried his face in her neck with an exaggerated sniff. "Nah, you smell good. Bet you'll taste good, too." He grinned at her, deep dimples marking his cheeks. "There's no way to get you clean anyway, dirty girl. Inside or out."

Heat trickled down her neck. "You haven't tried yet."

49

Brendan just laughed. "That's what took so long? You missed Di's parents, bro."

"Yeah?" Ian tossed the blanket into the backseat through the open window and dropped the thermos on top. "I'm crying. See these?" He leaned an arm on Diana's doorframe and pointed to his cheek. "Wipe my tears, okay?"

She smacked his face lightly. Once her hand was there, it had to slide into Ian's brown hair, wet and curling over his forehead. The clean shampoo scent was familiar and sexy at the same time, and she just wanted to bury her face in him...

"I don't think I can date someone who takes longer to shower than I do," she announced. In her mind, a little voice whispered it was crazy she was dating at all. "What else were you up to?"

"Stuff." Ian's dimples flashed again. He nuzzled her neck. Then he sprinted around the Jeep and jumped into the driver's seat.

Brendan glanced from Diana to his brother, shaking his head. "It's okay. Di was hiding out from her parents too."

"Like you're so straight-up. *How do you find time for it all, Brendan?*" Ian's voice went high in an uncanny imitation of Mrs. Cooper. *"How do you do everything and everyone?"*

Diana was about to give him a good hard pinch, but she caught the look the twins shared through the window. A private look, with the same half-smile flickering across two pairs of lips.

"Did you have a nice chat with Dad?" Brendan asked in a low voice. Almost like he didn't want Diana to hear.

"Always."

"I find time for everything because I'm organized. You should try it."

"I don't do your kind of shit." Ian's tone was amiable, but Diana shifted in her seat.

"If you guys need a moment, go right ahead." She picked up her tote bag and purse. "I'll just run into my nice, empty house and take a shower. Even though Ian doesn't think I need one, ever."

"Sorry." Brendan's shoulders relaxed. "You two go have fun."

Ian reached through the window frame to clasp his brother's arm. *"You* go have fun. Don't do anything I wouldn't do."

"I'm going to do a lot of things you wouldn't do." Brendan smiled broadly. When Diana's mouth fell open, his smile just got bigger. She busied herself fixing her messy ponytail, but strands of hair kept sliding out. "Have I told you you're cute, Di?"

"A couple times," she murmured. Her imagination was spinning out of control, picturing Brendan doing what Ian wouldn't. Jesus, what would that even involve?

Brendan chuckled. "The cutest."

"Okay, that's enough." Ian twisted the keys in the ignition. Brendan strolled to the end of the driveway, giving them a friendly wave as they backed out.

"Do I want to know?" Diana asked.

"My brother's all talk." Ian drove down the quiet street. His wicked smile didn't make her breathe any easier. He looked way too amused. "Don't let him scare you, baby."

"I'm not scared," she retorted. "I just don't want him to get too crazy."

"Why?" Ian's hazel eyes were genuinely curious. "Are you worried? Brendan's the last person you need to worry about. He can handle himself."

"What about everybody else?" she murmured.

For a minute, Ian was silent. He'd turned on the radio, but the volume was low. Mellow chords spilled from the speakers, loud enough for only the two of them to hear.

"He can handle them too."

Chapter Four

Ian was driving more carefully than she'd ever known him to, but Diana squeezed his knee hard when he suddenly swerved off the main road.

He chuckled softly. "Meant to do that, baby." His hand left the wheel to flick her ponytail. "I haven't had a traffic citation in a month."

"Ian..."

"You're a good influence."

"So are you."

Ian's eyebrows lifted. "No, I'm not."

"Yes, you are." Diana squeezed his knee again. "I won't tell anyone. But you are." Ian's mouth opened. She rushed on before he took over with a joke. "I wrote my graduation speech because of you. And that's just one example. The gym tonight? I never would have gone in there if it wasn't for you. And if I had, I would have raced back out and kept on running."

Ian didn't say anything, but he put his hand over hers. Seeing him drive one-handed made Diana's nerves fizz. She wasn't about to let go of him, though.

Rustling trees surrounded them. The road curved and climbed into a wooded area. Ian clearly knew where he was going. The Jeep came to a stop under a thick cluster of trees — a lookout point, where the ground crested in a hill. Below, lights spread out under the deepening dusk.

Ian turned off the ignition and dropped the keys in the cupholder.

"Looks like we've got this all to ourselves." When she turned to him, he unhooked her glasses and set them on the dashboard. "And I've got you all to myself."

"And the other times you've been up here, it's been full of people?"

A finger traced her lips. She flicked out her tongue to taste the salt and sweat on Ian's skin. He smirked at her.

"Yep. I'd come up here in high school and sit all by myself in the Jeep, thinking about you, while everyone else was doing it."

"Right. You were never alone." She folded her arms. "You were with Brendan, or girls. Or Brendan and a girl. Don't pretend otherwise."

He tugged her ponytail. "You mean, don't pretend that I didn't think about touching you? And kissing you? And being inside you?" Her breath quickened. "And wondering which guy would melt your ice princess act, because you wouldn't even look at me?"

"It wasn't an act," she murmured. "You know that now. I was scared."

The car was quiet. Ian's hazel eyes held hers. With her glasses off, the rustling trees behind him fuzzed to a shimmer. But the burst of green on brown in Ian's eyes was so clear.

"Of what?"

"Everything."

"How'd that happen?"

Ian's gaze, moving over her face in the near-darkness, made her feel more naked than she ever had. But she wanted to be naked with Ian. Strip herself down, show herself to him.

When she touched his face, she caught sight of a white scrap peeking from his pocket.

"What's that?"

Ian pulled the paper from his pocket and handed it to her. Smoothing out the creases on her lap, she recognized the spiky scrawl she'd seen in her backyard last week. Late at night, scarcely believing her eyes: *Can we talk?*

"You saved this?"

Ian nodded, his eyes on hers.

"Okay." Rolling up the note, she let it fall on her tote bag, resting by her feet. "Let's talk."

"Come on in back." His voice was low.

She crawled between the front seats. Ian followed, reaching into the trunk, pulling out a towel and draping it over the back seat.

"Look at you, all prepared," she murmured.

"Always."

He sat down comfortably, his long body taking up most of the available space, and patted his leg. Diana climbed into his lap, feeling the stretch of every muscle she'd worked at the gym. Strong arms pulled her close.

"How much do you want to hear?" she asked his shoulder.

"As much as you want to tell me."

The bulk of Ian's body felt safe, but she pulled back to look at him.

"When my family moved away," she began softly, "I was so nervous on the first day of school. I didn't eat. I was practically shaking. Sixth grade is awkward anyway, and when you're at a new school — I was just looking for anyone who'd smile at me. I was such a kid."

"You were supposed to be a kid." Ian brushed her bangs off her forehead. "So were we."

Him and Brendan. Now that she thought about it, Ian used "we" a lot less than his brother did.

"Weren't you kids?"

"Not as much as you. Maybe we shouldn't have been in such a big hurry to grow up."

She stared out the open window. There was a bench under the largest tree. Carved initials and arrow-pierced hearts speckled the weathered wood. The light breeze blew an empty Coke can across the gravel.

"My homeroom teacher asked one of the eighth grade boys to walk me to the office." Her voice wavered, and she forced it steady. "He said he'd show me around the school. He was cute, and he reminded me of you and Brendan, just a little."

Ian's body tensed against hers. "Fuck," he muttered.

"You know where this is going."

"I can guess."

"He took me outside to the field. I trusted him. I even held his hand. It was dumb, but I wanted a friend, and I missed you guys already. You have no idea." She traced the peeling letters on Ian's t-shirt. "I worshiped the ground you and Brendan walked on. I wanted to be just like you. Everything you said and did—"

"Wait, you worshiped me?" Ian broke into a huge grin.

Diana started to laugh. "Don't let it go to your head."

"Too late, baby." He rubbed the back of her neck. "The damage's already done."

She snorted, but her stomach knotted up at what was coming next. "Go on."

"The boy…he tried to stick his hand down my shirt." Ian grunted, his arms tightening around her. "He wasn't even looking at me, just at my chest. He didn't care about me at all. I was so shocked. All I remembered was the times you'd teased me and I'd done you one better. So I kicked him in the balls and rushed back inside."

"Good." Surprise and approval crossed Ian's face. "I hope you did permanent damage."

She laughed again, but it died away. "Not enough to keep him from telling everybody I'd wanted it. By the end of the day, the whispers were everywhere. In the halls, in class, on the bus. I couldn't escape, I couldn't believe it was happening. I started bringing books to read at recess and lunch. I got my homework done at school. I hid in the library. Anything to block it out. I thought people would forget, but it went on all year."

"Those little shits," Ian muttered.

"They really were." She sighed shakily. Telling Ian about that year felt like uncorking a bottle. Everything was pouring out, too fast to control. "Gym — oh my God, gym was torture. I hated my body because of the way people looked at me."

"That was them." Ian gripped her shoulders. "Not you."

"When I came back…" she turned her face to his chest. "I didn't know who to trust anymore. Boys were scary. Girls were scary. I didn't know how to talk to my old friends here, and you and Brendan — God, I missed you both so much, but I was too nervous to even say hi. I felt like something was wrong with me."

Ian stiffened. "There wasn't." His insistence startled her. "Jesus, there wasn't, Diana. None of this was your fault."

"I knew that. I did know that, deep down, but it didn't make any difference. And in high school — I was thinking about boys all the time. I wanted so much, but I was so scared it would be like that boy out on the field, grabbing me, instead of — this." She gestured to Ian's arms around her. He pulled her closer, holding her tight. "I thought if I even looked at a guy, he'd get the wrong idea. Or he'd just laugh at me and not want me. I tried so hard to hold it together, and I know you thought I was a priss and a goody-two-shoes, but really it just took, uh —"

"Me and Brendan."

"Yeah." She nestled her cheek against his warm shoulder. "It couldn't have been anyone else."

"I know that now." He gave her a half-smile. "Probably knew it even then."

A lump filled her throat. She swallowed, but it didn't go away. It didn't dissolve into tears, either. It stayed, heavy and insistent and making it hard to breathe.

"I was so scared," she whispered. "Do you know what that's like? I couldn't control what happened to me. I couldn't control what people said. All I could do was study and tell myself it was a fuck-you, every time I got a hundred per cent. It stuck, because it was the one thing I *could* control. I hated hiding. I missed you and Brendan so much. I missed my old friends, I missed the way things used to be."

Ian's silent grip was all she wanted right now.

"Tighter," she whispered.

Then she gasped when powerful arms crushed her in a bear hug. She squeezed back, hard. Ian's T-shirt bunched in her fists. His neck was warm, his scent calming, his breath matching hers.

"Okay." She rubbed her face against his shoulder. "I'm okay."

Ian's arms relaxed. "Diana, remember the time you lost your shit?"

She sputtered with laughter. "Which time? There were so many."

"The orgy."

"Oh Jeez." She buried her face in his neck, laughing harder.

"Hey, if you regret that, tell me now."

She shook her head against his shoulder. "Uh-uh," she hiccuped. "I regret that I didn't talk to you guys for a week. But I don't regret that night."

Ian let out an audible breath. "See? You were out of fucking control, screaming, coming like crazy, and it was okay. I was looking out for you. Brendan was looking out for you, even though I got mad and told him he wasn't afterward. I'm not saying let's go do that again, but I am saying that you don't have to control every single thing. You're safe."

"With you." She kissed his neck. "I'm safe with you."

A light breeze blew through the open windows of the Jeep, stirring her hair. The only light came from the moon outside, the only sounds from the whispering trees.

"Always." Ian's voice was gruff. "Can I show you?"

Her breath quickened. "Yes."

The next thing she knew, she was being guided off of Ian's lap and gently pushed back onto the seat.

Warm hands slipped the straps of her tank top down her shoulders. She grasped the hem, sitting up halfway to pull it over her head. He helped her tug it free.

She reached for Ian's black T-shirt. He stripped it off quickly, dropping it on the floor of the Jeep in a dark puddle next to her white tank top. He planted one knee between her spread legs, the other foot on the floor. Steady pressure eased her down.

At the first contact of his hands with her breasts, she gasped. His fingers sparked currents through her body, and he wasn't even touching her bare skin yet, just fondling her through the lacy cups of her bra. She reached up to play with his chest, her fingers finding two tiny flat nipples. When she flicked one, Ian made a low male noise.

"Remember when I told you that you have the most gorgeous fucking tits I've ever seen?"

She arched her back, wanting more touch, as he ran a teasing finger inside white lace over the tops of her breasts.

"Nope," she giggled. "I forgot. You better tell me again."

His hands worked into the cups of her bra, then withdrew, waking up every inch of her skin.

"Shit, Diana. Your tits are incredible."

"When you said that for the first time —" she broke off, unable to speak for a second. "That was when I stopped hating them."

Ian's fingers tightened on her breasts, his body tensing above hers. Anger flashed across his face. She'd never actually seen Ian mad. Intense, yes. But between the serious moments, Ian made a joke of most things.

Then his expression and touch softened.

"I'm gonna keep telling you, then."

"Are you all talk?" she murmured. "Or are you going to take my bra off?"

Ian palmed the full curves. "What do you say, baby?"

She wasn't in the mood for games right now. She didn't feel like playing or pushing back. She just wanted to be as close to Ian as possible.

"Please," she said simply. "I need you."

His eyes slitted. A hand slid under her back to unhook her bra. The lacy cups peeled away, exposing her heavy breasts to Ian's view. He rubbed his thumb over one puffy nipple.

"Beautiful," he whispered. "You've always been so beautiful. Everything about you."

Her breath caught. Her nipple was exquisitely sensitive under Ian's slow caresses.

"Even that time that I made a mud pie and snuck up behind you and got it all over both of us, and you were wearing your brand-new jersey?"

"Definitely that time. Lift your ass for me."

The sweetest words possible. Eagerly, she raised her ass off the seat. Thumbs hooked into her shorts and panties and pulled them down her legs. They dropped on the floor, a bright heap on the growing pile of clothes. All she had on were white socks and tennis shoes. A breath hissed from Ian as he stared down at her.

"Such a nice ass." He cupped her cheek in one hand, squeezing the generous curve. "Your body's perfect, Diana. It's always been perfect, even when you didn't think so."

Pleasure heated her face. "Nobody's perfect," she protested. "Definitely not me. I don't expect you to be."

"Don't argue, baby." When he gave her a good hard pinch, she gasped. "I'm telling you the truth." A light smack followed.

Oh. God. She wanted more of that sweet sting, but she moaned when his fingers found the sticky warmth between her legs.

"Mmmmm, and here's the sweetest little pussy. Just right for my fingers and cock."

"I trust you so much," she said abruptly. Ian looked up from her pussy, startled.

"Where'd that come from?" A finger brushed her clit, as if by accident.

She knew. *Say you trust us,* Brendan had whispered that first night in the treehouse. "I just do. I trust you completely, Ian. I'd do anything with you."

Ian's eyes widened. He stroked her opening, then worked inside her, fingering her slowly, making her quiver. "Good. Because sometime, Diana…"

"Yes?" she whispered.

"I really want to see you fucking lose it. No booze or drugs. Just you, letting go."

Diana's stomach lurched. "I will if you will."

"Nah." Ian massaged her clit until she relaxed and melted against him. "You don't want to see me lose it."

"Trust me. I do." When his strokes lengthened, the "do" turned into a breathy moan. "I know who you are," she murmured into his skin. "You're Ian who's so good. Ian who deserves kisses everywhere." He inhaled sharply as she explored his chest, nuzzling the patch of hair. "Ian who makes me want to learn everything and do everything."

His fingers flexed inside her tight warmth. "You already are."

"Take your pants off," she whispered.

He flashed a sudden wicked grin that gleamed in the moonlight. "You do it."

She unzipped his jeans, too excited to go slow, and pulled down his boxers. His cock sprang free, dark in the dim light. She wrapped her fingers around the warm shaft, letting Ian deal with pulling his pants off as she stroked the velvety skin. Clear dew spilled from the tip. When she massaged it in, Ian let out a grunt. His heavy length twitched against her palm.

He was naked now, half-kneeling over her on the back seat.

Parting her folds, rubbing his fat head over all her secret places. She lifted her hips, excited and eager. He found her entrance and pushed.

"Ooh..." She wriggled on the seat, slippery but tight, taking him in. "You feel so big like this."

"Mm-hm." He crushed her nipple between his fingers, making her dizzy, holding himself inside her. "You want that?"

"Yes!" She welcomed the stretch and the twinge of discomfort. "More," she urged.

He gave her more. And more. And she wanted to push back, but there was barely room to maneuver in the back of the Jeep.

"I can't get the hang of this," she gasped. "I'm trying to move, I promise."

"I know, baby. I got you." He pushed her knee against her chest and held her in place on the seat. Flexing his hips, he sank deeper. "It's an awkward position. That's why you need to keep coming to the gym." His voice was soothing, hypnotic, and so much like his brother's that she spasmed on his thickness in surprise. Wrapping her other leg around his waist, she let out a cry when he hit a sensitive spot. "Soon, you'll be able to take me inside you in every way."

"Fuck," she groaned. Her pussy clutched Ian's cock. "I need you every way." Fingers tightened around her ponytail, pulling. "*Yes*. Harder."

Ian's eyes, smoky with lust, widened. He gripped her hair, yanking it, just as he drove into her with a ferocious thrust.

"*Oh* God."

"Like that? Is that what you need right now?"

"Yes..."

"You need it a little rough?" He growled and plunged into her, his body heavy and slick. "You need me to fuck you into pieces?"

She gasped and tightened around him, because it was so right. "Yes. And put me back together."

Ian was fucking her so deep that it almost hurt. But she wanted the intensity. She needed the hugeness of him pushing inside her with all his male weight.

"I'm — I'm going to cry," she panted.

"Do it."

"It won't be cute."

"Let it out."

The ceiling blurred above her. Tears spilled down her cheeks, hot and fast, and pooled in her neck.

"Ian," she sobbed.

"Let it all out." She could barely see Ian's face through the tears clouding her eyes. But his deep growl, his heavy strokes, his hard pull on her hair, made her shudder. "Let it out while we fuck."

The mix of feelings threatened to overwhelm her. She clutched Ian's hard waist, fingers digging into his bulk, tears still falling, pushing back. As fiery pressure built, her hand worked between them to seek relief.

"Oh yeah," Ian muttered. "Touch yourself, you bad girl. You've done it so many times, haven't you? All alone in your room, playing with your hot little pussy, wishing and waiting so long to be fucked. Waiting for the guy who wants the real you. Show me how you come on my cock."

Breathless, she circled her clit, soaked and spread open to Ian. The pain dissolved, and every juicy plunge felt good now. Her cunt quivered on his thick shaft.

When a finger probed her ass, pushing into her rosebud, she cried out. She surrendered to the pleasure of Ian's cock, her own touch on her clit, the intimacy of his finger buried in her slick cleft. She couldn't get enough of his hot breath and hungry lips on her tearstained cheeks. He was a sleek weight on top of her. She bucked into him as a spasm shook her body, then came in a long, rippling orgasm.

"That's it, baby," Ian whispered, husky. "Just let it all go on me. Do another one. You know you want to."

Oh. Oh God. Her fingers slipped over the swollen bud of her clit again and again as his words spurred her on. Tightening again, releasing again.

"Mmm. Christ," he grunted. "You're having such a huge fucking orgasm. You have so many dirty needs, don't you, Diana?"

"Yes." The words dropped from her lips.

"Do you want my cum?" His thrusts sped up as he held her firmly on the seat. "Because you're going to get it. You're going to get it all."

"Wait." She gripped his shoulders. "Not yet."

Ian halted, his face dark with desire. He breathed in and out hard. "You better have a good reason, girl."

"In my ass. Please, Ian..." The begging just got her hotter.

His cock jerked in her tight embrace. "Fuck, yes. But I don't have lube."

"I do," she breathed. One hand scrabbled on the floor as she tried to keep her perch on the seat. Unzipping her purse, she rustled around inside until her fingers closed on a tube.

She put it in Ian's hand. Through the haze of lust on his face, she saw an unmistakable smirk.

"Damn. You really are a horny girl, Diana." A swat on her ass made her jump. "Turn over, baby."

The Jeep floated around her. Dazed, she felt Ian's cock slip out. Hands helped her onto her stomach. Fuzz tickled her breasts and belly, sending shivers over her skin — the towel.

Sure fingers spread her cheeks and rubbed lube into her rosebud. The glide of the slick liquid made her shiver. A knowing finger slid inside, massaging her in the most private, intimate way. More fingers surrounded her clit. Ian caressed the sensitive opening of her cunt, stroking her everywhere. Her ass squeezed down on his finger, then relaxed.

"That's it, beautiful." Ian's deep voice was heavy with desire. "Just let me in."

More pressure opened her rosebud, but not enough to be Ian's cock. Diana sucked in a breath as her ass fluttered around sudden thickness. The touch felt strange. Willing herself to trust Ian, she slowly yielded to the firmness sinking inside her.

Then she realized — two fingers. Twisting and stroking, massaging in and out. She let out a low cry. Her cunt was absolutely dripping.

Suddenly, Ian withdrew, leaving her empty. Warm flesh pressed against her cleft. Diana focused on opening to Ian completely, focused on his cock, huge and hard, the friction of his velvety skin.

No words. No moans. Only the sound of their breathing. When her ass clenched sharply on Ian's cock, his lips found her neck, soothing her until she relaxed around him. His shaft was so hot and slippery and silky smooth, easing in and out. In the sweet silence, every nerve in her body felt Ian's impossible thickness moving in her ass.

"Ian, oh God... talk to me, Ian," she pleaded. The sudden twitch of of his heavy cock made her cry out. Fingers closed over her clit again. A comforting hand surrounded her breast, rolling the tight bud of her nipple.

"You're amazing," he rasped. "You're so sexy. Your ass is so soft and hot and right." She whimpered, spasming on his cock and fingers in a surge of pleasure. "This is what we need to be doing right now, Diana. This is where we need to be. My cock, your ass. Fucking over and over and over and over."

"I love you so much." Saying the words made her ass flutter around Ian's cock.

A low groan was all she heard. That, and ragged breathing. "I love you too," came a murmur near her ear. "Go ahead, baby. Make some noise."

She moaned louder as Ian rubbed the tiny bud. Her face pressed into the backseat of the Jeep, the towel imprinting her cheek. Her ass rippled around his cock. Ian eased deeper inside her, slick and pulsing, murmuring soft words that blended together. Soft, unspeakably dirty words. Loving words.

She caught *sexy ass* and *your first fuck* and *belong to me*. *Beautiful* was in there too. And *slut*, and *bad girl*, and *I love you*.

It was all so right, and her moans shook the car now. Her clit was so swollen and sensitive under Ian's fingers. Her ass opened to accept his sinking cock again and again. She couldn't take it, it was too much sensation, too much sharpness and sweetness, she was teetering on the edge, until she gasped and her body clenched and she exploded in an orgasm. Warmth flooded her body as she convulsed with pleasure.

"I'm yours," she panted.

"Fuck yes, you are."

His cock throbbed inside her tight channel. And then, oh God, hot spurts of cum soaked her from the inside. She would never get over how that felt. More than anything else, feeling Ian come, buried in her most secret place, made her completely his.

Her ass tightened around Ian in little aftershocks. She shivered when he pressed down on her clit, guiding her through more ripples of pleasure.

"And you're mine," she whispered as their breathing slowed.

He laughed softly. "That too."

Exhausted, Diana collapsed on the backseat. She was dimly aware of the rumpled towel beneath her, against her cheek and naked skin. The emptiness as Ian eased his cock from her cleft, the brush of his skin on her back as he climbed over her.

Moonlight outlined his arm as he reached down, and fleece settled over her body. She breathed in a familiar clean scent — the blanket. Sleepily, she reached for Ian.

Somehow, they fit together in the backseat, curled up in the confines of the car. The dark freckle under Ian's left eye stood out against his skin.

"Fuck, Diana," he breathed into her hair.

"You're beautiful," she whispered. "I can't take it sometimes."

The moonlight showed just enough of his grin. "Blame my brother."

"Oh, so you got his face?"

"It's a joke." He closed his eyes, his heavy body relaxed against hers. "And you're dirty. Sweet and dirty, like I always knew you were."

"Always?" She pinched one tiny hard nipple, and Ian's eyes flew open. "We were kids together. I know you were a gross boy, but *always*?"

He laughed softly. "Long enough."

"Now you say that." Diana sighed when he tugged her hair. Then she saw the tube of lube on the floor, and the sigh turned into a groan.

"What?"

"One of my friends saw the lube tonight." Her face flushed hot. "She knocked down my purse in the middle of a diner and it fell out. I thought I was going to sink through the floor..."

Shaking. Ian was shaking. With laughter. Grabbing his shoulders, she pushed herself up to glare at him, then dissolved into laughter too.

"I made her promise not to tell anyone," she wheezed, collapsing onto Ian's chest. "I didn't tell her about you. I said I needed to keep things private."

"Oh yeah? You didn't tell her your boyfriend's brother gave you some lube and a butt plug for a little graduation present?" He smacked her ass.

"Jesus, Ian. That present wasn't so little."

"That's what I like to hear."

"Shut up," she giggled. "You feel huge. Enormous. Immense. Happy?"

Instead of answering, he kissed her. "It'll be okay, Diana. We don't have to tell anybody right now. Brendan knows and that's cool. I like it this way too." Ian's voice was low. Soothing. A warm palm covered her stomach. "You probably made your friend's day. Which one?"

"You don't know my friends." She tickled his abs, following the trail of hair downward.

"I saw you with them at graduation. Right? Those kids with a million cords around their necks, who were almost as good at school as you? I bet they never left their rooms either."

Diana pinched his waist. "They left their rooms more than I did. It was Marissa. Brendan gave her his phone to take pictures of, uh, the three of us."

"Oh, her. The girl whose hair is three different colors? You'll be fine. The one who forgot how to talk 'cause she was drooling over Brendan — you'd be in trouble there. She'd tell everybody."

"Janelle? Yep. She would." Diana looked at Ian curiously. "She was drooling over you, too. She went to your basketball games to lust after you guys—" She broke off. She'd asked Marissa to keep her secrets. She didn't have any business spilling other people's private comments.

"Whatever." Ian shrugged. "What else are you hiding in that purse? Your butt plug? Or do you keep it in all day at the lab?"

"You wish." She snorted with laughter. "Lifesavers, lipstick, phone, and random napkins with poems. Totally innocent."

"Got anything to clean up with in there?"

Blushing, she felt around until she found a little bottle of hand sanitizer and dropped it on Ian's stomach.

"Strawberry. Cute." He poured it out. The fruity scent mingled with the sweat and sex perfuming the Jeep.

"You didn't come prepared," she teased.

"Sure I did. See?" He leaned down and handed her another towel. The soft drag spattered goosebumps across her skin. She started to pull it between her thighs, then stopped. "Oh, you need help, baby?"

Holding one leg up, he wiped her clean with quick strokes.

"Okay...okay...that's good," she said breathlessly. Ian bundled up the towel and dropped it on the floor. "I just didn't know if you wanted me all over your towel."

He squinted at her like she was crazy. "I want you all over my everything."

"Same."

All through high school, her friends had talked about being careful with guys.

Don't put all your feelings on the table right away. Make them sweat. Keep them guessing.

Forget that. There was no being careful with Ian.

He picked up the thermos from the floor. As he unscrewed the lid and held it out to her, the scent of hot cocoa met her nose. Little marshmallows bobbed on top.

"You did it again," she murmured. "The blanket, the thermos, the note from last week." They'd sat in a neat pile in her backyard while she blinked awake late at night — lovesick, confused, convinced she and Ian would never work.

"Yeah, I remember this used to be your favorite. Seemed pretty sad that you didn't drink any last time."

"Is it spiked?"

"Nope. Do you wish it was?"

"That's okay." Diana sipped. The night was sticky. Her heart still raced and sweat was cooling on her body, but the cocoa took her back to cozy scarves and snow angels with the twins. "This is just right."

As she licked melted marshmallow off her lips, Ian sprawled in the backseat with a stupid grin on his face.

"Damn, baby."

Diana passed the cocoa to him. "You better drink up," she said sympathetically. "You look worn out. I guess that's what happens when you're old."

"Watch it." Ian gave her ponytail a yank. Half her hair had come loose, hanging in a total mess around her shoulders.

"You watch it." She flicked his bare chest. "I've got a lot of making up to do for all that 'little baby Diana' crap you gave me when we were kids."

"You mean you've got a lot of showering to do. I'm sneaking you into my house when we get back."

"Ian—" Apprehension pricked her skin.

"No one will know." He squeezed her knee.

Of course. Ian knew all the best ways to sneak into his own house. He'd probably been escaping and coming back from the time he could walk.

"I guess I need your help to get clean," she giggled. "It's so hard on my own. Don't you think?"

Ian tipped his head back, then looked straight at her. "I think it doesn't get any better than this."

"Oh, I think it does." She stroked his wrist. "This is just the beginning. I'll let you train me twice a week, but the next time we go out—" She let out a breath. "I'm going to take you somewhere you've never been before."

Outside the Jeep, crickets chirped. Ian's voice was so quiet she barely heard it.

"You already do."

Chapter Five

The bookstore was busy for a Tuesday night. Diana lingered by a display of greeting cards, eyeing the entrance over the top of a random book.

She hadn't told Ian where they were meeting. She'd just texted him an address, with instructions: *Meet me inside the front door. Come after you're done at the gym. Don't dress up.*

Ian's shift ended at eight. The bookstore closed at nine. It was eight-thirty now, and it shouldn't have taken him more than fifteen minutes to get here.

Maybe she'd made a mistake. Asking Ian to a date at a bookstore — and springing it on him as a surprise — might genuinely be his idea of torture. At least she'd known what she was getting herself into at the gym; she'd planned her visit, thrift store shorts and all. She'd been back once since 'Samantha' showed up and both the twins were right: the second time was easier. But Ian had no idea what he was in for.

She'd been joking when she promised to take him someplace he'd never been, but it might be true.

Her tote bag hung from her shoulder. Inside was her red leather journal, bulging with all the poems she'd ripped out, turned into paper airplanes, and stuffed back inside. Ian still didn't know she'd almost flown those poems to his backyard.

She carried her journal everywhere now. It didn't live hidden in her underwear drawer any longer.

Snapping her book shut, she pushed it back on the shelf and toyed with the greeting card display.

"Okay, Diana." A deep voice spoke up, so close that she jumped. Ian stood in front of her. "Nice one. This is the real prank, am I right?"

"No prank," she said cheerily. Glancing both ways, she stood on tiptoe to kiss his cheek. "Just a surprise."

The look of sheer confusion on Ian's face was priceless. He eyed the walls of books, hands in his pockets.

"So we're here because you want me to buy you a book?"

"You don't have to. We can just browse."

"What does that mean?"

"We wander around and look through books to see if there's anything we like. It's fun."

'Fun' was not written anywhere on Ian's pained face or hunched shoulders. "This place is stressing me out."

Diana touched his hand. Ian's palm was warm, the way it always was. Large, giving her flutters. But alarm radiated from his body.

"The gym stressed me out," she said softly. "And it's where you go to relax. This is where I go to relax."

Ian nodded a few times, like he was trying to convince himself. "I get that this is basically your heaven, but I don't like books."

"What did they ever do to you?"

They were blocking the doorway. Someone coughed behind them. Ian circled her shoulders with his arm and pulled her to the side. At least they were still in the store, instead of out on the sidewalk.

"I was kidding about taking you someplace you've never been," she added.

"No, you weren't." Ian's lips twitched.

"You've never been in a bookstore?"

"Not really."

"I can't believe that. What about when you have to buy books for your classes in college?"

Ian shrugged, but a faint flush crept up his neck. "Brendan takes

71

care of it."

"Oh."

"Yeah, oh."

"What's going on here, Ian?" She was being just this side of obnoxious, she knew. But Ian had pushed her so many times...and she'd pushed herself for him...and she sensed the best way to get to Ian was to push back.

Ian sighed loudly. "Okay. I'll spell it out for you. Books mean school. I don't like school. I don't like teachers. I don't like sitting in class, I don't like being told what to do, I don't like grades and kissing ass and playing stupid games. It's boring and fake and has fuck-all to do with what I want to do."

"That's not books' fault. You've never liked school for a single minute?"

He leaned against the wall and raked a hand through his hair. "Listen. The only reasons I graduated high school — the only reasons I got into college — were my brother and Mike Harris."

"Who?"

"Um, Coach Harris? The basketball coach?"

"I'm sorry, I never knew his name. I really paid zero attention to sports."

"Yeah, okay." Ian closed his eyes. "You never came to any of our games either. I know you didn't care."

Dammit, her date was rapidly going into a tailspin. Ian had been so supportive when she came to the gym, so encouraging. She'd blubbered all over him when they'd had sex in his Jeep, and he'd just urged her to let it all out.

"Of course I cared." She squeezed his arm. "I cared so much that I stayed away. I don't know if that makes sense. But I'll take the bus for two hours in the winter to see you play, I'll learn how the game works, I'll cheer you on. I promise. I'll be your biggest fan. I know it's the most important thing for you. I brought you here because this place matters to me. I want to share that with you."

Ian exhaled. "I get it. But Diana, I came that close — *that close* —" he held his thumb and forefinger a millimeter apart — "to being expelled from high school. You know why I wasn't? Because I cared enough about playing basketball to skate that line and be good after I pulled some shit, and because Coach Harris massively helped me out, over and over."

"I wish I'd known," she said softly. "I would have been there for you too."

"It's better that you didn't."

"Where was Brendan while you kept getting in trouble?"

"We had a lot of agreements in place." Ian didn't blink, but his leg was jiggling. "I benefitted too. I'd be lying if I said I didn't. He helped me graduate."

And probably, more than one outraged parent had found Ian fooling around with their daughter, only to get a dose of puppy-dog eyes from "Brendan." She knew. She'd been there.

She leaned against the wall next to him. "Look, you like me. I like school."

"Really?" Ian folded his arms across his chest. "Do you really, Diana? 'Cause I've always wondered."

"It's how I win." She flushed and looked around to see if any random book-browsers had overheard. "I know I'm not supposed to say that. But I like being on top."

"Bloodthirsty bitch." His face broke into a grin. "You're not much of a team player, are you?"

She began to laugh. "I like learning too. I've had some really inspiring teachers. I'm excited to go to Yale and broaden my horizons…"

Ian swiped her glasses and held them high in the air. "Forget the college essay, baby."

"Hey!" She smacked his chest.

"Listen to yourself. I know you like broadening your horizons, bad girl. How about we broaden them a little more tonight?"

"You're such a dick." She made a snatch for her glasses. Ian held them out of the way and messed up her hair. As she dove to yank on his wrist, she bumped into the greeting card display.

"Oh shit," she wheezed, grabbing the rack to steady it.

A woman passing by gave them a shocked look.

"Sorry." Ian flashed her a charming smile and patted Diana on the shoulder. "I can't take her anywhere."

As soon as the woman walked off into the nonfiction section, shaking her head, Diana dissolved into laughter.

"I'm going to kill you," she gasped, tipping her head into Ian's chest.

"In the bookstore, or outside? You're already killing me slowly in here."

She made a split-second decision. "Ten minutes." She leaned close to whisper in his ear. Softly, urgently. "Ten minutes here, and if you want to leave after that, we leave. Okay? We go home or go to the gym or go do it in your Jeep or whatever you want."

He gave her a reluctant grin. "You memorized that little speech from the club, huh?"

"It was very persuasive."

"You're really fucking stubborn."

"Takes one to know one."

He exhaled. His breath stirred her hair. "Where do you hang out when you come here?"

"Usually here." She pointed to the fiction section. "Or over there." She gestured toward poetry. Taking Ian's hand, she pulled him down the aisle towards the back of the bookstore. Then she shot him a smile over her shoulder. "Ten minutes to do whatever I say."

Ian's mouth opened and closed. Oh, she'd remember that look on his face for a long time.

"Okay," he said, as they approached the poetry section. "Yeah. You write poems that you never show anybody. And you said you're gonna show them to me."

"I will."

"When?" They halted in front of the bookshelves. Ian's hand was warm around hers, his big palm giving her goosebumps.

She opened her mouth to say *soon*. What came out was "Now."

Ian's eyes widened.

"You're going to sit down right here and read them," she added, before she lost her nerve. Three shelves formed three sides of a square, a quiet alcove in the back of the bookstore.

"Here?"

"You heard me. Sit."

He laughed. "Yes, mistress."

Easing his long body to the floor, he spread his legs in a vee, his knees bent, and looked up at her expectantly. His feet touched the opposite bookshelf. She settled down opposite him, between his legs, her back against the books.

Holding her journal over Ian's lap, she opened the red covers and shook out a snowfall of ripped paper. Poems went everywhere. On his legs, between his legs, on the floor to either side.

"What's all this?" Ian ran his hands through the poems and let them fall. He looked the way she'd felt for the past month: confused, nervous, excited. Dazzled. His broad shoulders were hunched, his mouth hanging open a little. Hazel eyes wide, the dark pupils almost swallowing the clear green-brown of his irises. She wanted to kiss him, but she held herself back. "Why do they say *Ian* on them? Did these used to be paper airplanes?"

He picked one up and folded it back along its creases. She expected him to pitch it at her. Instead, he turned it over in his hand.

"They're my poems." She touched his knee. "I've been writing in this book since the beginning of high school. After that night at the club with you and Brendan, when we weren't talking, I tore them all out and was going to fly them into your backyard. That's why they say *Ian*. They're not all about you, but there are a couple…"

"We weren't talking," he repeated. His fingers linked through hers, holding her hand loosely. "You mean, you weren't talking to me."

"I didn't think it would ever work," she said softly. "I didn't know what to do with how I felt about you."

"That makes two of us." A grin split his face. "Now I'm hanging out with you in a bookstore. Does that change your mind?"

She kissed the back of his hand, because *yes* didn't seem like enough. "Read something. Pick anything. Before I lose my nerve."

"You're not going to read to me? I forgot to tell you." Ian leaned forward to whisper. "I don't know how to read."

"Ian," she groaned.

"Kidding." He picked up the poem he'd refolded into a plane and flattened it out, reading silently. Then another. Diana watched every half-smile and flutter of his eyelids.

After he'd read through a handful, he stacked the papers in a neat pile and squeezed her knee.

"You were lonely," he said quietly.

"Yeah." Ian had cut to the heart of it so fast, it took her breath away.

He held up a poem in each hand. "I know you said that when you told me everything in the Jeep, and all the shit you went through, but this makes it a lot more real. And — damn." His voice dropped. "Horny as hell on top of it."

"You knew that."

"Yeah, but I didn't know the extent." He folded and unfolded one of the poems. "No wonder you were so ready when I — when we wanted to fuck you."

Ian's crude words, in the quiet of the poetry section, sent hot pinpricks over her body.

She glanced down. She was leaning forward, her dress gaping open a bit to reveal her cleavage. Her light tan made a vee that reached the tops of her breasts. Below that, a ribbon of paler skin showed above her polka-dotted dress.

Ian looked down too. He licked his lips.

"What do you think of the poems?" Diana whispered. "Besides me being all lonely and horny. I did have a life, I promise."

He held her gaze. "I don't know anything about poetry, but what you write is making me feel things."

She felt warm, sticky, her pulse throbbing. "That's the best I can hope for." She'd clutched her poems close for so long, but sharing them felt...powerful. She was powerful, making Ian feel things.

He picked up another poem from the pile he'd read. "Is this about me and Brendan?"

She glanced at the looping handwriting and the scattering of dirty words.

"Yes." Her cheeks were red now.

His slow smile made her stomach lurch. "You're a very bad girl, Diana. I saw the date. This is from before we took you to the treehouse."

"You thought about it too." Heat trickled down her body.

"All the time." He grinned. "While you were walking around being all prissy with your nose in the air, you have no idea how many times I thought about melting you from the inside out."

She shivered. "Did you ever think about the three of us?" she whispered.

Ian leaned back, hands clasped behind his head. "Sometimes. After the first time me and Brendan were with, you know, Lauren, my old girlfriend, yeah, I thought about it." The tips of his ears were red. Hard to believe this made him blush, but it was adorable. "That day we ran into you by the gym vending machine when you were just an innocent little sophomore—"

"I remember that," she put in.

"Yeah, innocent little sophomore, except for this." He waved the poem he'd just held up. "And these too." He rattled a pile of paper.

"Are you sorting out my dirty poems for future reference?"

"Hell, yes." He flashed white teeth at her. "Anyway, after we saw you at the vending machine and you would only talk to Brendan, not to me, and then Lauren showed up and we went outside to the bleachers—"

"Did you...?" she asked in an undertone, trailing off. She glanced out of the poetry section. The back of the bookstore was quiet, empty for now.

Ian raised his eyebrows at her.

"I'm curious!" she exclaimed, throwing up her hands. "I'm very curious. I want to know."

"Yeah, you're a curious cat. And yes, we did."

"Was it good?"

"Not as good as it was with you, bad girl." Ian hesitated, like he didn't want to go on. "She had more experience than you, but Brendan and I had a lot less at..." He waved both hands in mirror movements to illustrate working together. "And you know the three of us have a history since you were born, and I've been in love with you for longer than I'm going to say, and there was that part under the bleachers when I closed my eyes and pretended she was you."

"Wow." Ian's hand rested on her bare knee, squeezing lightly. She picked it up and played with his fingers. "I don't know whether to be happy or freaked out."

"It was a long time ago. She never knew. I was behind her, and Brendan—" he broke off.

"Was in front of her," Diana finished. "I get it. I've been there, I know what it's like. And thank you for not dragging me under the bleachers."

But no, she realized. In her crazy whirlwind with the boys next door, they'd never tried that. She'd never had Ian take her from behind, heard his pants and growls of desire, while she opened her mouth to Brendan. She'd never come around Ian's thickness, rippling helplessly with each rub of his finger on her clit, while Brendan fell apart the way he only did when his cock was being sucked.

The other way, yes. More than once. But this arrangement was something she'd never done — something she'd never do, now.

"Diana?" Ian's voice was teasing. "Where'd you go?"

"Sorry. Just, uh—"

"You really want to hear this?"

"Part of me wants to hear everything you've ever done and everything you and Brendan have done together with girls. And another part of me knows that once I hear something from you, I can't unhear it."

"Yeah." Ian rubbed her palm with his thumb. "If it's all the same to you, I'd rather not go into details. Besides what we're talking about now."

"That's fine," she said, surprised. "I can't believe it, I was so envious of Lauren when I saw you guys, but now I feel bad for her."

"It's okay. Lauren was happy, Brendan was happy, I was happy enough. Especially when I thought about you. Afterwards, though, it hit me like a truck, the way it always did: I'd never have you." He squeezed her hand, shaking his head. "And Lauren was like, 'what came over you? You turned into a beast back there. I know you like it a little rough, but damn.'" Ian stopped and looked at Diana. His ears were completely red now. "This is way too much information, isn't it. I know you're curious, but I'll stop now."

"That's fine. I do have a poem about you — just you," she added quickly.

"Oh yeah?"

"I started it yesterday."

"Gimme." Ian sifted rapidly through the creased and torn pages.

"It's still in my journal." Dammit, she was supposed to be in charge here. "It's on the last page, and it's not ready yet." She grabbed his hands. "It's totally rough."

His face lit up. "That's what I like to hear."

"I mean, it's a rough draft," she said hastily. Ian looked at her with a knowing smile. "I haven't revised it yet. It's still in the terrible stage. It's really bad."

"Then I want to hear it. I want to know everything bad about you, Diana."

"Okay." She scrabbled for control again. "Not here. In a bed."

Ian's eyebrows shot up. Since they'd gotten together, everything had happened in her backyard or his Jeep. "Whose bed?"

She thought fast. "Yours. You said you're the best at sneaking into your own house."

"You got it." He was already snatching up the poems and stacking them in a pile. She joined in.

Soon, her journal bulged again, her tote bag hung over her shoulder, and she and Ian were hurrying to the front of the bookstore, holding hands.

"Pick something out," Ian said in her ear.

Her heart was pounding now. "What about you?"

"Nah, just read me your terrible, rough, awful poem. That'll be enough for me."

"Thanks." Diana rubbed her forehead against his shoulder. Did Ian realize how much it meant, showing her poems to him? She scanned the displays near the door and reached for a journal. "This. I'm on the last page of my old one."

Ian frowned at the red leather binding. "That's exactly the same as the one you have now."

"That's the point. Things are changing. And that's good, it's great, but I want something that's the same."

"Nothing stays the same." His voice was low in her ear. "And no two things are ever exactly the same."

Heat poured over her body. "I know that." She locked eyes with Ian. "But I like that these are the same on the outside. They'll be different on the inside."

Ian raised an eyebrow at her, but he took the journal from her, brought it to the register, and paid.

*

When the Jeep pulled into the O'Brians' driveway, the sun had set. Orange fire still streaked the sky. Her own house was dark, but the lights in the O'Brians' house were on.

Ian didn't seem concerned about anyone seeing the two of them. He met Diana on the passenger side, put an arm around her, and sauntered up to the front door. He made no effort to be quiet as he turned the key in the lock and flicked the light on in the entry hall.

When he led her into the O'Brians' long kitchen, Diana expected him to hustle her upstairs in the dark. Instead, he dropped a quick kiss on her lips.

"Wait here." He disappeared through the swinging French doors. Feet thudded up the stairs.

Okay. She'd wait. Ian seemed to be making a habit of telling her to stay put while he ran off to do God knows what. Brushing her bangs off her forehead, Diana looked around the kitchen.

Everything was in place. Plants lined the windowsill above the sink, the granite counters shone, the ceramic cookie jar with the broken lid sat on top of the fridge, and a large photo of the twins, posing in basketball jerseys, hung by the doors.

The last time she'd been in here, she and Ian had just confessed their love to each other, Brendan had gotten rid of two dozen pool party guests and given them his blessing, and the three of them had cleaned up the gigantic party mess. Everything had felt easy and right and uncomplicated.

Tiptoeing to the doors, she peered into the dining room.

"Brendan?" she murmured. He probably wasn't home. Other than their good-morning hug ritual and the one conversation in the Jeep, she hadn't seen him around.

The fridge hummed. She remembered how the stainless steel had felt against her back, with two pairs of male hands slipping inside her bikini.

TV sounds came from the den, along with Mrs. O'Brian's laughter. Eyeing her black and white polka-dotted dress, Diana tried to adjust the straps, tugging in an unsuccessful attempt to hike up her neckline. No way around it: her dress showed off her breasts.

She wandered over to the fruit bowl on the counter and picked up an apple. The blush of red on green deserved its own poem.

Had her cheeks been that red the first time Brendan kissed her? Had her face burned that bright the first time she'd asked Ian to fuck her? Or had she been too loosened up with alcohol, too swept away in living out her fantasy, to turn crimson at all? Had she been as flushed as her tight red dress when the twins had taken her to the club and she'd ended up in a stranger's incense-scented bedroom? Would a time come when absolutely nothing made her blush?

She reached inside her tote bag, still hanging on her shoulder, to thumb through the loose pages of her old journal. Then she dropped her tote bag on the table, along with her plastic bag from the bookstore.

Ian reappeared with a stack of books. She caught a couple of the titles — *Business Fundamentals, Organizational Behavior* — before he tossed them on the kitchen table with a resounding thump.

"Hey guys, I'm home," he called carelessly. "Diana's here. Come say hi."

The TV sounds stopped.

"What?" she hissed. "What part of this is sneaking?"

"Watch and learn," Ian said out of the corner of his mouth.

Mr. and Mrs. O'Brian came through the swinging french doors. Their faces brightened.

"How wonderful to see you, dear!" Mrs. O'Brian exclaimed, giving her a hug. Diana returned the greeting, her stomach doing flip-flops.

"It's been too long." Mr. O'Brian added. "Ian here can always use your civilizing influence."

"Diana's here to help me catch up on my business classes." Ian gestured at the pile of books on the table. "You know the ones. We're gonna study in my room."

"Well, that's great." Mr. O'Brian looked surprised. "Very nice of you to help Ian out, Diana. We know you're busy. Your mom's told us all about what you're up to this summer. Very impressive." Two pairs of eyes went to the plastic bag on the table.

"You went to a *bookstore?*" Mrs. O'Brian asked. "Together?"

"We needed to prepare." Diana kept her voice off-hand.

"Yeah, Diana had to teach me how to read first." Ian slung an arm around her shoulders like he just needed a place to rest it, and she bit her lip to keep from laughing. "All better now. See, Mom?" He grabbed the top book off the table and pointed to the word *Fundamentals*. "That says 'cat.'"

"Ian, your situation is not something to joke about," Mr. O'Brian began, but Mrs. O'Brian did laugh.

"It's so good to have you over again, Diana," she broke in. "And Ian home in the evening? That doesn't happen too often." She bustled to the fridge. "We haven't seen you with the twins for a couple weeks! Ian, where's your brother?"

"Doing Brendan stuff."

"Really? I would have expected him to be here too." Mr. O'Brian's voice was hearty, but Diana didn't blame him for being confused.

Ian shrugged. "He doesn't need the academic support."

The silence that followed was so short, Diana wouldn't have caught it if she hadn't been paying attention.

"Would you like something to drink, dear?" Mrs. O'Brian asked brightly. "Soda, lemonade? We have cherry Coke. I remember how much you and the twins loved that when you were kids."

"I'm fine, thanks," she began, but Mrs. O'Brian was already rooting through the fridge.

"I can't tell you how much we've missed having you over. You and the boys were so close when you were little." Bottles clinked. "I never thought we'd see you with just Ian, though. You always wanted Brendan too." Mrs. O'Brian smiled over her shoulder. "Dennis, remember when Ian broke his collarbone falling off the roof?"

"Do I ever." Mr. O'Brian shook his head.

"Diana came over with a plate of M & M cookies that she'd baked. I'll never forget it. She felt so bad that Ian was grounded, she even tried to argue that it wasn't his fault. And you wouldn't take no for an answer, either," she added to Diana, pulling a can from the fridge. "But when I told her Brendan was down the street getting Slurpees, she refused to come in! She just gave me the cookies and ran back to her house. It was the cutest thing." Mrs. O'Brian looked down at the can of cherry Coke in her hand. "Ian, get Diana a glass. Be polite."

"Already did." Ian nodded at the counter. Startled, his mother picked up the glass waiting there. "First I've heard of that little story." He smirked at Diana. "You ran away, huh?"

She flushed. "You got the cookies, right? So what's the problem? Thanks for the Coke," she added, accepting the glass.

"You're welcome to study at the kitchen table." Mr. O'Brian looked meaningfully at his son. "Lots of light out here."

"Nah." Scooping up the books and bags on the table, Ian put a hand on Diana's back, guiding her toward the swinging kitchen doors. "Too distracting, right, Diana?"

Her heart was pounding again. "Definitely. I know I'd just want to raid the cookie jar."

"Yep. You'd eat them all too, and you wouldn't share. Thanks, though," he added to his father as an afterthought.

"Dennis." Mrs. O'Brian's voice floated out as they walked through the darkened dining room, though she was trying to whisper. "There's nothing to worry about. You know how the twins are about Diana."

"I know how Ian is about women," Mr. O'Brian grumbled. "And I know when the twins were in high school, a lot of girls went through that bedroom. Even with Brendan trying to keep him on track."

"Yes, but this is *Diana*."

Chapter Six

The trip upstairs was quiet. Ian switched on the hall light at the top of the stairs. When Diana took his hand, he gave her a squeeze, his warm palm sending flutters through her body as they walked along the polished wood floor. The door to Brendan's bedroom stood open a few inches, darkness beyond.

"Where's your worse half really?" she asked.

"Making mayhem."

"Seriously?"

"Probably. I don't know what's up with Brendan anymore."

Worry curled through Diana's stomach. "That's not right. I get that you don't want to be attached at the hip, but this is Brendan."

"Sweetheart." Ian stopped in front of his closed door and looked down at her. The light above him was burned out, and his face was shadowed from the side. "Aside from us getting together, the biggest thing that came from sharing you was Brendan learning to mind his own business, and me learning I didn't need him in my business."

"But—" she began.

"But what?"

"Remember what you said, when you climbed in the window and made me guess who you were? *He knows I always have his back, and I know he always has mine.* That isn't something you just walk away from."

Ian's lips flickered in a half-smile. "How would you know?" His hands circled her waist. "You're an only kid."

"All the more reason why you don't walk away from that. I was so grateful for you guys being my big brothers when we were kids, even though you gave me a hard time. I've always wanted a brother or sister."

"I know," Ian said quietly.

"How?" Diana stared at him. "It's not like I was spilling my guts to you while you were dumping ice down my shirt. Brendan always looked out for me, but I didn't open up to him either."

"A long time ago — say, me and Brendan were nine. So you'd be seven. Little." Ian smirked at her. Diana glanced toward the stairs — the TV was back on — and blew a loud raspberry into his neck. He laughed. "Your mom was yelling across the yard for you to come home and clean up your room 'cause your cousins were coming to visit. You were so excited, you were jumping up and down. It was so cute. When you went home, I was like, 'Awww. Poor little baby Diana. Sucks to be an only kid. Must be why she hangs around our house all the freaking time.' I was being a jerk, but Brendan got it. He looked at me, all serious, and said, 'Okay, we'll be her brothers. We'll always be her brothers, no matter what, for the rest of our lives.' And we shook on it. It was one of our agreements."

"You never told me."

Ian shrugged. "I figured we didn't need to, because you'd know. I heard you say we're like your brothers."

"But for the rest of our lives— If you make agreements that involve other people, it's nice to let them in on it."

"Sometimes." Ian gave her a crooked grin. "But me and Brendan, we're done with agreements."

"Completely?"

"As far as I'm concerned."

"Does he know that?" she asked softly. "Or is that last agreement a one-sided one?"

Ian opened the door to his bedroom. "He knows. Let's talk about something else, baby."

Moonlight came through the open windows. As they walked in, Ian dropped his business books and her bags on the desk. He shut the door behind them.

Posters plastered the walls and ceiling, like she remembered. Sports, heavy metal, punk. On the low bed was the shape of Ian's sleep: sheets half-pulled from the mattress, blankets hanging off, pillows scattered everywhere. When he pulled her close, she pictured him dreaming: one sleek arm flung out, the other hugging a pillow, muscled legs tangled in the sheets.

"Fine. New subject." She ran her palms up his chest. God, Ian felt good. Warm, solid, right. "Should I be insulted that your parents don't think you see me as sexy?"

Then she gasped when hands brushed her breasts.

"What was that, Diana?" A tongue traced her ear, and she swallowed a moan. "You were saying something."

Heat trickled down her neck, from her earlobe to her breast. Ian was working his hand into the cup of her bra, rolling her nipple between his fingers. His other hand tugged the zipper on her dress.

"I was saying—" her voice fizzed out.

"You were saying, can anyone think I don't see you as the hottest, most delicious, most fuckable girl in the world?" He licked her collarbone, driving a moan from her mouth. Heat swirled through her body. She thrust her fingers into his hair.

"Maybe not," she gasped.

Oh. Oh. Yes. Ian's pinches on her nipple were driving her crazy. Blood rushed to the sensitive skin. Her lips ached to kiss him, and fire licked between her legs.

But going straight to sex after that discussion of agreements outside Ian's room — she pulled back, gripping Ian's hair.

"Your pinup girl is watching us." Across the room, the curvaceous brunette frolicked by Ian's bed, one figure amid the posters up and down the walls and across the ceiling. Faces and words everywhere.

"Oh, her? That 'cause you're turning her on." A hard bulge brushed her belly. Her dress gaped open in back, held up only by the straps. Ian's fingers were unbearably exciting on her nipple, rubbing and pinching it into taut need.

"And all your posters," she breathed. "We're not alone."

"Mm-hm." Teeth nipped her neck. She muffled a yelp as a warm tongue soothed her skin. "They all want to see you get fucked 'til tomorrow."

"Ian," she moaned, trying to keep her voice down. "I have an awful poem to read you. I'm supposed to help you study. If you take my dress off, none of that is going to happen."

He laughed softly. "Who said anything about studying?"

"You did. I know you weren't joking about your college classes and catching up." She was probably ruining the mood, but she pressed on. "Your dad said something about your situation—"

"Right." When Ian pulled her sleeves down her shoulders, she stifled a cry of need. "You know everything, baby, but do you know about business fundamentals? Because trust me, you don't want to."

"If you give me the book to read, I'll understand it," she insisted. "It'll take me one night." Ian moved back, startled. "I'm just being honest. I can help you."

"No, babe." His voice was low in her ear. "It's not your damage. It's mine. I'll handle it."

"Fine." She caught the surprise on his face, her dress half-off, and twined her arms around his neck. "What, you thought I'd keep pushing? You just said you'd handle it. I believe you. Also, it sounds boring." She scratched his bare arm.

"Fuck yes, it is. So let's not talk about it anymore." He shook his head like he was flinging off water. A demanding mouth met hers. "Can you read me your poem naked?"

"We can try." She pushed him back, nerves surging through her body.

When she let go of Ian, her dress fell around her hips. He eased the polka-dotted fabric down, squeezing her full curves. One finger slipped into the waistband of her panties. She couldn't stop running her palms over his chest.

"Pink. Lacy. Hot." He tweaked her panties, pulling the silky material away from her body. "You want to read your poem to me with these on, or off?"

"On," she said, on an impulse. She'd be naked enough, reading her rough draft out loud to him. "But I want you to strip."

Ian yanked his shirt over his head and unbuttoned his jeans with one flick of his wrist. His zipper parted, revealing a plaid waistband. He held her gaze as he shimmied his jeans and boxers down together.

"You're staring," he teased, but his voice was husky. He kicked his jeans off and dropped them on the floor. "No surprises. You've already seen it all."

She had. But how many times had she gotten the chance to really look at Ian, undressed, with no distractions? He was tall, broad, sleek, alive with animal grace even when he stood still. Every line flowed to the next. Her eyes followed a path from his face, intense with anticipation, over the rugged terrain of his torso to his cock, a thick stalk curving toward her.

"I like seeing it all," she said softly. She took a deep breath for courage. "Now sit on the bed."

A slow smile spread over Ian's face. He sat down on the bed, the lamplight highlighting his broad chest and shoulders, his body expectant.

Going to the desk, Diana felt in her tote bag for her journal. She tore out the last page. Quickly, she folded the poem into a paper airplane the way Ian had shown her when they were kids.

She sailed the poem across the room to Ian. He caught it deftly. Sinking down on the bed beside him, she cleared her throat.

"Listen, I just scribbled this yesterday in the lab between switching temperatures on things. I haven't revised it yet. It probably really is terrible."

"Let go of that." He drew a line over her collarbone, easing her onto the bed to lie close to him. "If you wrote something good, I want to hear it. If you wrote something bad...I really want to hear it."

She flattened her palm on his warm stomach, feeling the ripple of his abs. "Okay. For you. Can you turn off the light?"

He stretched out an arm to switch off the lamp. Fitting her body to Ian's, she began to read by the moonlight from the window.

In a whirl
So fast
I can't get off
I'll never be off, no matter
How much I try
How high I jump
How far I run

When I leap, it's to you

Fever flares
Motor revs
Fire sears
Pedal pumps

Too fast
To think
Too fast
To know
Can't see, can't hear, can only feel

Each word dropped into the dark bedroom, spreading ripples. When she finished reading — nothing.

"Diana." Ian finally spoke. "We don't have to do anything tonight if you don't want to."

"What do you mean?" She sat upright.

"You were talking about…running." His voice was careful. "Trying to get away."

"I didn't mean it like that," she protested. "I'm saying that what I feel for you is so big that I can't outrun it or overcome it. I don't want to."

"You said everything was going too fast."

"I like it that way."

"I know, and you've always been so hot and into it, but then you read this —" he tapped the poem in her hand — "and I'm thinking about how you went from nothing to me and Brendan in the treehouse, and us getting together, and being so wild and crazy out of nowhere…"

"It's not out of nowhere," she protested.

"Okay, it's not." He smiled faintly. "You had the dirtiest, craziest fantasies, but they were all in your head for the longest time, right? I don't want you to feel like it always has to be about sex with us."

"You don't want me to feel that way," she repeated. "Why don't you tell me how you feel?"

"I guess I'm saying that I don't want to feel that way."

"Thanks." With one fingertip, she traced his lips. "I know that's not all there is."

What would it be like if they didn't have sex? Her curiosity intensified as his breath stirred her hair.

"What if we do things but we don't have sex tonight?" she murmured.

She caught Ian's smile in the dark, a flash of white teeth. "What kinds of things?"

She was feeling her way, without knowing what lay around the corner. Ian was right. She hadn't just dashed around the bases with the boys next door, she'd blown up the ball field. She'd been so hungry to experience the touch she'd been missing, so eager to cut through the awkward moments of figuring someone else out. Two someones.

Ian rubbed her back as they lay together, the barest inch of space between their bodies. His touch was gentle, but tension coiled his arms. Hard flesh brushed her stomach. He was holding back. Knowing Ian, that didn't come easy.

Her lips still felt the words of her poem, and her ears still echoed with every sweet and dirty word he'd ever whispered to her.

"Can you put your mouth on me?"

His eyelids flickered, but he kept the distance between them. "Where, baby?"

"Start at the top."

Grasping her waist, he rolled her onto her back. The twist of sheets and blankets rubbed her skin. His face came closer and closer, moonlight outlining his brow and cheekbones.

Kisses dropped on her hair, then her forehead. Lips touched each eyelid and her nose. Her breath quickened when warm hands cupped her cheeks. The kiss that landed on her lips was so innocent, it didn't even occur to her to open her mouth.

"You're such a nice kisser," she whispered.

He grunted softly. "I've never gone this slow."

"Not even for your first kiss?"

"What are you talking about? This is my first kiss." He gave her another, lips still closed. This kiss lasted longer — soft, sweet.

"Oh..."

"You like it?" A dimple flickered in the cheek lit by moonlight. "Am I doing a good job?"

"You're...amazing."

It wasn't easy for her either. Her hands itched to grab Ian's ass, pull him down, and urge him toward her eager pussy. He was keeping distance between them, but every time his cock nudged her skin, it was obvious how hard he was. She rubbed his back instead, running her hands over his sides.

"You feel so good," she giggled. "I like making out with you."

"Me too. I've always wanted to kiss you. When we were kids, sometimes I thought about sneaking up and giving you a kiss. Then I'd put a fake spider down your back, for insurance."

She snorted with laughter. "Why didn't you?"

Ian's lips trailed over her jaw and down her neck. "Because I thought you wouldn't want me to."

"I would have been so shocked, I don't know what I would have done."

He kissed her throat. She gasped at the graze of his lips and tongue. This…this was not innocent. Not a first kiss. When he tasted the hollow between her collarbones, she threw her head back, surrendering to his tongue.

She couldn't wait. There was no way she could handle Ian's slow path of kisses downward, over the fresh patch of sunburn on her chest, wondering if he would ever reach her breasts. But God, if Ian of all people was being patient, she'd try, too.

He nuzzled the very tops of her breasts, kissing them where they began to swell out, and she gripped his waist. It took every ounce of willpower not to arch her nipples toward his mouth.

"Please," she whispered. "Touch my breasts, babe."

He looked up, surprised. "But we're just making out. We're doing innocent little kisses. You really want me to go that far?"

Jesus, whatever game Ian was playing, it was pulling her in. Her nipples puckered, her body tingled.

"We're also naked."

"Oh." He looked down at her bare curves, then his bronzed muscles and pointing cock. "What do you know. I am. You're not, but

94

close enough."

His mouth closed around her nipple. A rough hand cupped each breast.

"Mmmmm," he hummed, the sound all pleasure.

"Oh God." Diana jerked upward, then relaxed as Ian sucked. He massaged her breasts, letting her nipple go with a soft pop.

"Do you like having your tits touched for the first time?" he whispered.

"I love it."

"Everything you thought it would be?"

"Better," she panted. "Is it your first time too? Because you really know what you're doing."

"You make it easy." Warm lips and tongue slid down between her breasts. Ian was kissing her stomach, his breath hot. "More?"

"Yes…"

His tongue traced line after line below her belly button, the strokes ticklish and arousing.

"Ian, lick me," she moaned.

"I thought that's what I'm doing."

"Go lower."

"You want me to lick your pussy?" He gave her an astonished look. "That's so bad, Diana. We're supposed to be going slow. You're ruining all my innocence." He slipped a finger in the lacy waistband of her panties. "Convince me. You're the one who's good with words."

Jesus. "You turn me on like nothing else," she whispered. "Everything about you. I want to get tangled up in you and lock together and drink you in. I love that we've known each other forever but we're just starting to know each other, and…you get me so, so wet. You're so right. I need you, Ian."

"Fuck," he muttered. "You've convinced me. I just want to eat you up."

Hands slid up her thighs, spreading them. Her panties were

soaked now. He peeled off the pink lace. The lust in Ian's eyes made her gasp, and she thrust her crotch toward his face involuntarily.

"Yes—"

He sucked on her thigh. The posters on Ian's ceiling blurred above her. The pale softness of her skin, gleaming in the moonlight, anchored by his large hand and so different from his hard bronzed body, just seemed to feed his appetite.

"Mmmmm," he growled. Diana grabbed his hair as he licked and sucked his way up her sensitive skin. Her breathing quickened, but she tried to hang on. She tried to let Ian take his time.

When he kissed the crease where her thigh met her crotch, a snarl split the air. That was her. She'd made that noise. She was still making it. And—

A swirl teased her clit. Her juices trickled down her ass. She was so aroused, spread out naked beneath him. He tongued her slowly, exploring her secrets.

"Ian…" her voice wavered.

"You like this?"

"Yes, yes, yes."

"Good. I like it too." His voice was soft and raspy. "I could eat you out all night. You have the most delicious little cunt I've ever tasted."

Pleasure wound around her as his tongue played over her swollen clit. Ian's fingers were splayed on her thighs, holding her down. Pressure at her opening made her moan and lift her hips. He massaged her entrance, but he didn't penetrate her.

She was ready to beg, ready to breathe the word *more*. *Please. I need you, Ian. I need you right now, I need more, I need it all.*

But what would happen, for once, if she didn't ask for more?

What would happen if they stayed right on the edge of this moment?

The exquisite sensations of being lightly stroked took over. When he sucked on her clit, the pleasure flattened her into the bed.

A slow, slow wave rolled over her body, starting at her thighs, gathering strength as it poured over her pussy. It curled at her stomach and crested at her breasts, tightening her nipples to pure desire. Another wave came, stronger, foaming. The third wave washed her away.

"Ian, I'm coming," she gasped.

He didn't stop sucking on her clit. Each delicious spasm felt like an hour, clenching and expanding all the way through her body. How was he so patient? How could he massage her opening so lightly—

"Ooohhhh," she groaned. He was just going to continue, wasn't he? He'd keep sucking and licking and stroking with no end in sight, ever.

He lifted his head. "More?"

"Yes," she pleaded.

"So demanding." He held her legs open. "First we're just kissing, then you come, and then it turns out one isn't enough for you."

She clutched his thick hair. "I guess I'm the bad influence."

"Damn right." His hands slid to her arms, tugging her up, rolling her on top of him in a crazy tangle of limbs. "Sit on my face."

"What?" she breathed. A fresh wave of want rolled over her body.

"You heard me, bad girl."

Flushed, she rose on her knees, kneeling over Ian. The bars of moonlight and shadow through his window played over his shoulders, his carved pecs, the soft patch of hair on his chest. She kept space between them as she crawled up the bed. Bracing her knees on either side of his head, she took a minute to look down at the male face between her legs.

Eyes dark with lust met hers, and a half-smile that barely hid the raging hunger behind it.

An animal lick swiped her juicy center. Pure heat swirled inward to her core. She felt so bare, so wanton, so obvious in her desires, poised above Ian like this, that her knees buckled. She clutched the wall above the bed to hold herself in place.

A pinch on her ass made her yelp.

"Down, girl." Ian's eyes glittered. Reflexively, her legs relaxed and she sank onto his face. Her soft folds met a hot, insistent tongue that flicked her clit until she trembled.

"Ian," she whispered. "I'm getting your face so wet."

Hands squeezed her ass, lifting her just enough to free his mouth. His feral grin made her body throb.

"That's the point."

Her thighs shook as he slathered her pussy with lick after lick. She was close to coming again. Just as she was about to tip over the edge, Ian pushed her up.

"On your back."

She cried out, trying to lower her clit to his tongue, but Ian had her thighs in a firm grip. Dazed, she climbed off him and rolled onto her back. Above her, Ian opened her legs again.

"Quiet, Diana." His deep voice made her shiver. "Unless you want my parents to know we're being very, very bad."

She grabbed a pillow and buried her face in it.

Lips closed over her clit. Her pussy clutched his fingers as he worked them in. Ian was massaging firmly, deliberately — not inward, but upward.

"What are you doing?" she whispered. He was focusing on one spot inside her, pressing hard, and it felt…incredible.

"Do you like that, baby?"

"Yes…"

"Then just let it feel good."

His fingers curled inside her, and each cry deepened to a moan. She bit the pillow. Jesus, it was exactly what she needed, and she felt so full, so heavy with desire, so sensitive to every touch… Ian's tongue and fingers were about to make her explode.

"Oh God, oh God, oh God," she burst out.

"Yes, baby," Ian hissed. The force kept increasing. He pressed harder and harder. "Flood my face. Give me everything."

She could. She would. She wanted to.

Heat flashed through her body as she came. She was kicking, overwhelmed, out of control, wet as hell. Through her thrashes, Ian kept going.

"Oh God— I— okay. That's enough."

He pulled back and kissed both her thighs. Then he looked up at her with a smug grin, his lips shiny with her juices.

"Slow enough?"

"Yes." She collapsed in his arms. Ian held her close, his cock against her ass, his breath hot on her neck.

He really was holding back. Sudden urgency lit up her body.

"What do you want? What kinds of things?" she asked.

"Same. Use your mouth."

The order, soft as it was, sped her breath up.

Thighs aching from being held open, her pussy throbbing, she climbed off the mattress and knelt on the rug between Ian's spread legs. She kept her eyes on his, watching every flutter of his eyelids and grimace of need, as she wrapped her fingers around his cock.

"You're so beautiful," she breathed. "I love your cock, Ian. I really love it." She couldn't get enough of saying "love" to Ian, whenever she wanted, just like that.

He groaned softly, rolling his hips to push his shaft through the circle of her hand. "It loves you, baby."

As she leaned forward to take him in her mouth, Ian's hands closed over her head.

Yes...he tasted so good. She hadn't been in love with the taste when she first sucked the twins' cocks, though it was exciting to know she was doing it. A few weeks in, the experience was entirely different. She didn't mind her aching jaw. She didn't wonder how long it would take Ian to tip over the edge and cum in her mouth. The trickle of dew from his head just spurred her to lick faster.

"That's it, Diana. Lick me like that, sexy. Cup my balls and roll them a little bit." Ian's voice was down to a rasp. "Mm-hm." He broke off in a grunt, then caught his breath. "Give me head just like that. You're so good at sucking my cock, you bad girl."

She swirled her tongue over the underside, then let her warm mouth sink down on Ian's shaft. How far could she go? How much could she drive him crazy?

Ian was panting over and over now, one hand wrapped around her hair, the other hand resting firmly on the back of her neck. Every pull on her hair sent a current straight to her throbbing nipples. Need gathered between her legs. The rug pressed against her knees.

Intensely curious, she let her throat relax, taking Ian deep into her mouth as she fondled the softness of his balls.

"Oh, Jesus." Ian's voice was almost a prayer.

God, it was nearly more than she could handle, but it was so very right to be opening to Ian like this. She'd read him her most private words. He'd listened. She wanted to do something else with her mouth now. Breathing through her nose, she focused on allowing him in. His plump head nudged her throat, twitching with each brush of her tongue.

"Diana. Love." His fingers combed roughly through her hair. "Keep that up and I'm gonna come."

Pulling back with a slurp, she panted for breath. Hazel eyes, glazed with need, looked down at her. Ian let her hair go.

"Are you okay? 'Cause—"

In response, she took his cock between her lips again and sank down until her face was buried in his warm crotch. His thatch of hair tickled her nose as she breathed in his musky scent. Ian felt huge in her mouth. She curled a hand around his balls again, caressing the soft skin.

"Fuck." Hands gripped her hair. His voice was rough and dirty.

"Suck me, baby."

How was she going to do this? She had no idea, but she wasn't stopping now. Her mouth was full, her throat was full. Ian was all around her, inside her, absolutely everywhere. The room tilted, everything soft and disoriented, his flannel sheets rubbing her aching nipples.

"Yesssss. Just like that, you hot little slut. You know how," he grated.

She had to pull back when he came. She wanted Ian's warm cream on her tongue, but she needed to breathe. The first jet landed on her lips. Quickly, she took him back in her mouth, sucking as he spurted and cursed under his breath and fisted her hair.

God, he was coming hard. She breathed with him, feeling his excitement, until his thrusts slowed and his hands relaxed their grip.

"Holy shit," he whispered

She wiped her mouth with the back of her hand and coughed. Then she laughed. Jesus, her eyes were actually watering.

Ian helped her back onto the bed and handed her the glass that had been waiting on the desk.

Stretched out next to him, she sipped her cherry Coke. If cocoa in the Jeep had brought back winters with the twins, the sweet fizz on her tongue brought back grass fights and lazy bike rides.

"You okay?" a whisper came in her ear. She took another drink.

"You burn me up." She'd meant it to come out teasing, but her husky whisper sounded all too serious.

"Water?" Ian looked concerned. She shook her head. He kissed her throat. "Poor baby."

"Mmmm." She took another sip of Coke, then handed it back to Ian. He tipped his head to chug the rest. "Don't even think about challenging me to a burping contest."

"No contest. You're too much of a lady."

"You wish." Drops fizzed on her skin and she gasped in surprise.

Ian was shaking the last of the cherry Coke over her breasts and belly. Before she could grab the glass, his tongue followed.

"Now you're playing dirty."

Teeth nipped the soft skin of her belly. "You just taste so good. See what happens when we 'don't have sex?'"

"Oh well," she giggled. "We'll hold off someday. Maybe when we're old."

Ian's mouth stopped moving.

Jeez, where had that come from? Getting old together? First they had to make it through the summer. She hoped she hadn't scared him.

His arms tightened around her in a rough squeeze. "I love you."

"Always," she whispered.

Downstairs, the front door opened and closed. A familiar deep voice came from the living room: Brendan, saying hi to his parents.

"Did you know Diana's here?" Mrs. O'Brian exclaimed. "She's helping Ian study. They're up in his room. I'm sure she'd love to see you."

"Might be a good idea to poke your head in," Mr. O'Brian added. "Make sure Diana isn't buried in a pile of fake spiders. It's been a little too quiet."

"Nah." Brendan chuckled. "Di's keeping Ian in line. Count on it."

"You're not going say to hi?" Mrs. O'Brian sounded surprised.

"'Course I am." Footsteps sounded up the stairs. There was a light tap on the door.

"Don't come in," Ian mumbled. "Massive amounts of studying going on."

"I figured. "

"Hi, Brendan," Diana called.

"Hey, Di. Is Ian being good for you?"

"As good as he'll ever be. Which is to say, very, very, good." Ian sighed and rested his head against her shoulder.

In the silence that followed, Diana wanted Brendan to come in.

What for, she wasn't sure. She and Ian had gotten about as private and intimate as two people could get, and Brendan had his own life.

"I'll leave you to it."

Footsteps sounded down the hall and ended with the soft click of Brendan's door.

Chapter Seven

Back when they were kids, storming the neighborhood and pulling stunts, the twins had made their "agreements." Diana knew the good twin-bad twin agreement was the biggest, but it was one of many. Someday, she might learn about them all. Probably most were forgettable, like who got the bigger cookie in kindergarten, who got the shower first in high school.

Now, she and Ian had their own agreement: taking turns planning dates. The destination was always a secret. No matter how awkward the other person felt, they had to give it a fair try. If and only if they couldn't handle it, they'd speak up.

Over the next few weeks, through one of the hottest Junes on record, they trusted each other to provide a surprise. Once Diana made it clear she was open to Ian pulling her out of her comfort zone, again and again, he began to relax and let her do the same for him.

Taking turns with dates gave her a little thrill. She never knew how Ian would react to the places she took him, or what he'd do to surprise her.

He taught her to shoot pool; she took him to the independent movie theatre downtown. He took her hiking up to the lookout point. She took him to a sidewalk cafe to sip wine, purchased with the fake ID she'd wheedled him into helping her get.

In between, she met him at the gym, put in her time at the lab, scribbled poems in her new journal, and tried to make time for her friends so she wouldn't be tempted to stay in a bubble that just held her and Ian.

So her excuses to her parents wouldn't be total lies.

Late nights found them in the Jeep or her backyard, skin sweaty and slick, making noise in the car or silently cresting on the grass.

Mostly, it worked out fine. Better than fine. Outstanding, in fact. But she never saw Brendan except in the morning before work, and he and Ian didn't seem to be spending much time together. As caught up as she was in Ian, it bothered her.

One morning, heavy and sticky with clusters of clouds overhead, Brendan gave her the usual big-brotherly hug in his driveway.

This time, she leaned into the hug, resting her head against his chest. Her arms didn't want to leave his back. He gave her an extra squeeze.

When they both let go, she asked, "How are you?"

"I'm good."

"Really, how are you?"

"I'm still good, cutie." He flashed his dimples.

"What have you been up to?" she prodded. "How's work? How's your summer going?"

"Work's going well. The summer's great. Everything's fine, Di."

"The three of us should hang out," she blurted. "You, me, and Ian. Like we used to."

Brendan raised an eyebrow. He rested a hand on her shoulder. "And do what?"

"Anything. Go see a movie. Get something to eat. Play some pool. Did you know I have hidden pool talents? I can actually hit the ball with the cue." She stretched up to whisper in his ear. "I have a fake ID now. My idea. Ian helped me get it."

Brendan's mischievous grin told her everything would be fine. The three of them might get into a scrape, but they'd handle it together instead of Ian taking the blame and Brendan shouldering the cleanup. The twins would have each others' backs, but better — their bond stronger, not weaker, because of her.

God, she wanted that. She wanted it so badly, she could taste it.

"Ian's taking care of you." Brendan's voice burst her bubble. "I'm glad."

"I want to play pool with you, Brendan. I bet you're really good." She leaned on the handlebars of her bike and looked up at him, trying to be persuasive.

"When you look at me like that—" He chuckled and touched her waist. "Maybe someday, cutie."

"But I want to see you, and I want you guys to see each other."

Now she was feeling really young, practically pleading. *Pleeeeease, Brendan? Say yes.* The *cutie* wasn't helping matters.

Hazel eyes moved over her face, the basketball hoop nailed above the garage, the Jeep parked in the driveway, and the patch of green lawn leading to the landscaped backyard.

"What are you doing July fourth?" he asked.

"I don't have plans yet."

"Mom and Dad have their annual barbecue."

Diana wondered where this was going. "I know. The barbecue I've avoided since the shitty year away."

"You mean, when you moved away in middle school?" Dark lashes blinked at her. "That was a shitty year?"

Right. She hadn't told Brendan anything about that year — only Ian. All Brendan knew was that she'd had some bad experiences. And that she didn't trust guys as a result.

"It was rough. That's why I came back so shy and scared. People were mean at my new school, and they picked on me because I, you know…blossomed early."

The words came out so easily, they shocked her. She'd built brick walls around that year, but telling Ian had loosened all the mortar.

"I'm sorry, Di," Brendan said gently.

"Thanks. You're the second person I've told. It's a lot better now.

You're part of the reason why."

He kissed her cheek. It was a light kiss, but his hand on the back of her head, the whiff of cologne, and the brush of his lips on her skin made goosebumps rise.

"Glad I can be the reason something's better."

"Of course you are," Diana protested. "So many things are better because of you."

Brendan shrugged.

Did he really think they weren't? Of course, she'd been upset with him not so long ago. She'd resented the blame Ian had taken for Brendan, the talking Brendan had done for Ian.

Me and Brendan, we're done with agreements.

"You were talking about July fourth," she said quickly.

"Come over." He smiled at her. "The three of us can hang out, like we used to."

At the O'Brians' annual barbecue. She'd gone every year as a kid. She'd scarfed down too many hot dogs, Brendan had taught her to play ping-pong, and Ian had reliably stolen her dessert, year after year. And once her family moved away, then moved back, she'd stubbornly buried herself in her bedroom with a pile of books while grill smoke curled above the O'Brians' backyard and her parents pleaded with her to come say hello, just hello, to the twins and their parents.

"Hasn't it been forever since you and Ian went to your own family's barbecue?" she asked. "Even when I didn't go, my parents gave me the rundown."

Brendan patted her shoulder.

"Yeah, me and Ian usually do our own thing on the Fourth, together. But this year, he's going to want to be with you. And let me guess, you're not going to tell your parents and go off alone with him all day. So the three of us can hang out, just like we used to. Swim in the pool, have a low-key good time. Then you guys can watch the fireworks in the evening, or—" Diana raised an eyebrow at him, and he laughed, holding up his hands. "—or whatever you want."

Low-key. She and Brendan obviously had different ideas of the concept. The O'Brians' barbecues tended to be crowded and noisy. Sure, they weren't as intimidating as a pool party with thirty drunk college students, but the backyard would be packed with everyone in the neighborhood.

Maybe that's what Brendan wanted — a busy get-together, during the daytime, with lots of people around to take the pressure off.

But what pressure was there? Why should there be pressure at all?

"Okay. Just like we used to. You'll help me with my Ping-Pong game, and I'll give Ian hell when he tries to steal my dessert. You'll tell him we're doing this?"

"Why don't you." Brendan's dimples showed, but there was a shadow in his eyes. It bothered her.

"Of course I will."

"Have a great day, cutie. Be good." He tousled her hair and walked to the Jeep.

Diana waited, her hands resting on the handlebars, until Brendan settled in and closed the door. Then she sped off, pedaling fast, to make up for lost time.

*

The storm moved in that evening. Clouds had darkened the sky all day, but the first crack of thunder didn't come until after the sun set.

Diana was lying with Ian in the Jeep at the lookout point, trading soft conversation as her sweaty skin rested on his. His arm was slung around her waist. She was teasing him about his outie belly button, while admitting she'd always had a thing for it, when lightning split the sky.

A boom followed, then pelting rain.

Ian kissed her temple. "Looks like no one's camping out in your backyard tonight." A few drops of rain blew through the cracked-open windows.

"I guess not." Disappointed, she stretched, enjoying the slide of skin on skin, then bolted upright. "Oh, shit. My record player. It's out in the backyard."

"Call your parents." Ian reached lazily for her purse. "Ask them to bring it in."

Dialing her home number post-sex with Ian, naked in his arms, was beyond awkward. But she really was worried about her record player.

"Diana, where are you?" her mother demanded when she picked up.

"Why do you ask?" she parried.

"Honey, you know Dad and I trust you, but that's not the answer I want to hear."

A hand played over the full curve of her breast, tickling underneath, and she slapped it away.

"I'm with Marissa, Mom. Everything's fine. Can you bring in my record player before it gets ruined? It's in the backyard. My sleeping bag, too."

"Stuart!" her mom called. "Can you bring in Diana's record player? No, I don't know why she insists on having it outside either. Or why she sleeps outside when she has a perfectly good bed. Don't forget her sleeping bag. *Teenagers.*" Her voice came back on the line. "Make sure you get a ride home, honey. Walking or biking in this storm, or even taking the bus, is not a good idea."

"Thanks," Diana said drily. Ian was running his fingers over her stomach, just shy of tickling. She sucked in her breath. "You're going to keep up these reminders when I go to Yale, right? I might not survive the first week."

"You're our only daughter," her mother sighed. "We worry. It's different with boys."

"Right. When boys bike in a storm, they don't get wet."

"Please just be careful."

"I will, Mom."

"Dad and I are going to bed. Don't stay out too late."

"I won't, Mom."

She hung up. Ian smirked at her.

"Watch out, little girl." He pinched her nipple. "Can't get wet or you'll get in trouble. I better take you home."

"You're disgusting," she wheezed through her laughter. She dried off with Ian's towel, then sorted through the pile of clothes on the floor of the Jeep to find her dress and underwear. "When did your parents stop worrying about you and Brendan?"

"Brendan?" Ian shrugged, pulling on his boxers. "When he was five. Me, never."

"But they don't keep tabs on you."

"Yeah, they gave up awhile ago. I wore them out." He flashed a jaunty grin. "It'll all change when you get to college. Your parents will ask for updates, but you'll be able to do whatever you want."

Whatever you want. Brendan had said the same thing, back when they were all in high school. She'd wanted a lot then, and she hadn't known if she would get any of it.

Now she had so much. But college seemed far-off and unknowable, and she didn't know what she'd want when she got there.

She caught Ian's shoulder and kissed him before he got in the driver's seat. She didn't want to think about being apart from him.

By the time Ian dropped her off, the rain was falling in sheets. Lightning forked the sky in bright bursts, and thunder came close on its heels. Diana dashed into her house and up the stairs.

It felt strange to be getting ready for bed in her room, after sleeping outside for the past month. She left the window open for some fresh air, though rain threatened to spatter her desk and the huge tree outside tossed in the wind. The screen was back on her window. Once she'd dragged the sleeping bag out to her backyard, there wasn't any reason for a twin to climb into her bedroom in the dark of night.

Stripping off her damp clothes, she wriggled into a short white slip that did double duty as a nightgown. Then she rustled through her underwear drawer for a light blue thong. She paused, the scraps of lace dangling from her hand.

Ian had fingered her in the Jeep before plunging in, giving her the kind of quick, explosive orgasm that left her wanting more. Usually, when he fucked her after making her come like that, his deep strokes, her own thrusts, and their hard kisses were enough to satisfy her.

But her pussy ached now, needing attention. The storm was making her restless.

She tucked the thong back in her drawer, turned out the lights, and sprawled on the bed. One hand went between her legs to cup her mound; the other slipped into her nightgown to pinch her nipple.

God, her pussy was so wet and hot, so eager for touch, her nipple so puckered and sensitive. Her clit needed to be circled while she thought about Ian taking her. She felt his hard weight on top of her, the first delicious shock of his cock opening her up.

But she couldn't get off. No matter how much she stroked and teased her clit, caressed her breasts, slid her fingers inside her own tightness, no matter how much the cracks of thunder reverberated through her body, she hovered on the edge.

Ian was with her, breathing hard, whispering dirty words, heavy and hot...then he'd disappear. They were together in the summertime, blissful, seeing each other every day...then she was catapulted forward two months to college, away from him.

And dammit, Brendan was flickering in and out of her vision, lying next to her as she rubbed her clit, resting an encouraging hand on her thigh. She just wanted a word of reassurance from him, a soft whisper telling her everything was okay so she could come now. But

111

every time she asked for it, he vanished.

Finally, frustrated, she rolled onto her side with her hand wedged between her legs. All through high school, she'd had lots of experience lying awake late at night. Thoughts tossing, stomach lurching, focused on a physics test or the hopeless crush she couldn't talk to or the college applications she'd sent out.

Usually, touching herself calmed her down. She'd disappear into a fantasy world where Diana Cooper was all confidence. Openly hot. Doing whatever she wanted with all the boys she wanted to do it with.

Now that the fantasy had become reality, reality was intruding on the fantasy. She couldn't lose herself anymore.

Burrowing under the covers, she breathed in and out like Ian had taught her to do at the gym during tough stretches and weight lifts. In through her nose, out through her mouth. One deep breath after another, focusing on nothing except the next breath, until her eyelids went heavy.

*

She and the twins were kids, speeding through the neighborhood on their bikes, the wheels hardly touching the ground. Brendan ahead of her like always, but not too far, so he could keep an eye on her; Ian far ahead, popping wheelies, a bump away from soaring into blue sky or eating pavement. As she pedaled faster and faster, she gained ground on them, flying past Brendan first.

"I've never passed you before," she squealed, giddy with excitement.

"Keep going, Di," he urged. "Don't stop. Faster. Go. Go. Go."

Brendan wasn't usually pushy like this. Encouraging, but pushy? Brendan? No. But his voice drove her on.

Her legs pumped faster. She was panting, wind whistling past, blowing her bangs off her forehead. Close to Ian now, gaining on him, passing him.

"Look at me!" she crowed. "Look, Ian! Are you looking?"

She glanced back over her shoulder, just to make sure he saw her moment of glory.

The bump that came shook her body. She flew into the air, over her handlebars, both twins staring at her, and landed with a thud.

She was naked, eighteen and grown-up, flat on her back on Ian's bed with all his posters looking down. A boy crouched over her — no, a man. Strong hands pinned her shoulders to the mattress.

"Oh yeah," he whispered. "I'm looking."

A hot tongue grazed her nipple. Her body seized up as she stared at Ian's face above hers. He hadn't moved.

"Brendan?" she gasped.

She felt for his solid frame close by. Her hand moved through air. But when she followed Ian's gaze, lust-drunk, she saw his brother's head above her breasts.

Need coursed through her as Brendan sucked her nipple into his mouth, licking the puckered skin so softly she could barely stand it. Another mouth marked a much harder path down her body.

When she reached for Ian, he was air, just like Brendan. She couldn't touch him, couldn't grasp his shoulder or stroke his hair. But her skin felt every bruising kiss.

She groaned with frustration as Ian opened her thighs. His tongue was fire. Pure heat, pressed into her center. Pushing inside her, a single flame. And God, Brendan's tongue on her breasts, licking every slope of the soft mounds, was water, soothing her so Ian didn't incinerate her.

No. Not water. Not anymore. He was blowing on her skin, cool streams that made her nipples contract and her cunt buck desperately against Ian's ember of a tongue. Brendan was air, and air only fanned flames.

"O-o-o-oh," she sighed shakily. She was soaring again, and she didn't know where she'd fall. "Oh God…"

"Keep going, Di." Brendan lifted his head, and her grab to pull him back was like clutching at mist. But his pinch on her nipple — that echoed through her whole body. "Don't stop. Faster. Go. Go. Go."

She was panting, wind whistling past, blowing her bangs off her forehead. When burning fingers met her clit, she arced and flew. Shaking, shuddering, crying out, falling.

Her heavy lids opened.

Dark. It was dark in her bedroom. Branches rattled against her open window, and rain spattered the screen. She was alone, soaked with sweat and arousal, her pussy spasming in an achingly intense orgasm even though she hadn't touched herself. Her sheets were plastered to her curves. A burst of lightning lit the sky.

"Please," she whispered. "Please both be here. Be together." Her hand went between her legs. Her clit was a point of concentrated desire, slipping under her fingers. "I don't care how. Any way that works."

Burying her face in her pillow, she gasped as pleasure rolled over her body. When she felt both twins inside her, hard and hot and moving, she cried out, peaking again.

As her breath slowed, she collapsed on the bed.

The rain was slowing too, getting lighter. After watching it run down her screen for a few minutes, Diana climbed out of bed, rubbing her eyes in disbelief.

She'd come in her sleep. That had never happened before. She wouldn't have believed it, if she hadn't experienced it.

Obviously it had been a dream, for Ian to get his tongue inside her like that.

Tiptoeing to the bathroom in the dark, she splashed cold water on her face and cleaned up as quietly as possible. She slipped on her robe and belted it tightly.

A board creaked on the way back to her room, and she froze. Every step felt like a secret. Finally, she unclenched her hands and made it back to her bedroom.

Pulling her old red journal out of her tote bag, she turned on the desk light and settled into the wooden chair. She'd spent hundreds of hours in this chair, working her way to the top of her high school class. But she hadn't sat at her desk since graduation day, when she'd rewritten her valedictory speech from scratch after Ian climbed in her window.

A few drops of rain speckled the desk, but the storm was over. Books were piled neatly on one side. Her laptop sat on the other side, barely used. Her purse hung over the back of her chair. She found a pencil and turned to the poem she'd written for Ian.

Crossing out a line in the middle, she rewrote it. She drew an X through the ending, erased it, then tapped her pencil on the last three words, doodling random swirls in the margin.

Keep going, Di. Don't stop. Faster. Go. Go. Go.

She'd really thought that if she repeated "Brendan equals brother" enough, he'd become exactly that, with no lingering feelings. Those feelings didn't have a name, the territory that was more than lust, but less than love.

That territory lay miles away from what she felt for Ian. That comment she'd made about being old together — Jesus. She clapped a hand over her mouth, remembering her surge of surprise, Ian's silence, and his rough hug.

She'd showed him her poems. She'd never felt so bare in front of anyone in her life.

Closing her journal with a thud that made the loose papers crackle, she took off her robe, put on her most boring bra and panties, and found a clean T-shirt and a skirt that was full enough to bike in.

She pulled her purse off her chair and found her phone. She had years of experience with unfulfilled fantasies. This was just one more. Dreaming about the twins was smoke — something to blow away, not something to chase.

Phone in hand, she tapped out a text.

You awake?

A pause, then: *Hell yes. What are you doing up, woman? There's no studying to be done in summer, did you get the memo?*

Good. Marissa was a night owl. Diana had counted on her being up.

Chapter Eight

Empty streets gleamed under streetlamps, washed clean by the storm. Diana pedaled over the pavement, fast as she dared. She hadn't risked taking one of her parents' cars and waking them with the sound of the garage door. Then the questions would start, and she wasn't in the mood for the most basic questions.

But as she biked, her dream spun through her head like an out-of-control movie reel. Deliberately, she slowed her pace and focused on the wet world around her. After midnight, slicked with summer rainfall, the familiar neighborhood looked changed. Eerie, yet peaceful. Other than one car passing by, she was alone.

When she pulled up to Marissa's house, she caught a flash of rainbow-colored hair. Marissa stood by the back gate, beckoning to her. Dandelions dotted the unmown front lawn. She walked her bike past the side of the house and left it against the gate.

Marissa's one-story house was the quietest she'd ever seen it. All through high school, this had been the gathering place for parties and study sessions. Marissa's mom traveled for work, and as long as her daughter got good grades, she gave her a long leash.

The backyard was still and hushed in the storm's wake. Strands of twinkle lights illuminated the leaning boards of the fence. Raindrops glimmered on the grass and trees, and fraying lawn chairs lay on their sides from the wind.

"The hammock's dry." Marissa pulled a blue tarp off the rope hammock in the corner of the yard. "Want it?"

"Let's." Diana settled into half the hammock, leaving space for Marissa, who raised her eyebrows.

Right. She'd never been the cuddly type. *Least huggy person ever,* Janelle had said. Until recently, that had been true.

"Sure." Shrugging, Marissa got situated next to her. "Let's smush. Ooh, you're squishy, and I mean that as a total compliment."

Diana snorted. Lying with Marissa in the swaying hammock, she watched the faint wind play with the tarp while Marissa lit a joint and turned the end around in the flame.

"I couldn't sleep," she said.

"Yeah? Did you have that dream where you're not really done with high school? You have to dissect one more frog, or you owe a shitload of library fines? 'Cause I've had that dream three times since graduation."

"Me too, at least once. But no, different dream tonight." Diana hesitated, then took the plunge. "A sexy dream."

"Whoo!" Marissa cheered. "It's about time. Details, please."

"Uh…" She blushed and laughed. "Two guys."

Marissa let out an approving whistle. "Damn. And you were the girl between them? Or you were watching them get it on? Or were all three of you going at it?"

Smoke rose over them, drifting into the trees. Heat trickled down her neck. "I was the girl between them."

"Well, that is the dream. Don't we all want that."

"Really?"

"I'm not saying every woman does, but I sure do, and when I think about it—" Marissa lowered her voice to an exaggerated whisper. "I start with your neighbors. I know you don't see them that way, and it's never going to happen anyway, so try not to visualize it too hard."

"Mmmph," Diana said noncommittally. Could she tell Marissa? Once the truth was out there, she could never take it back. It wouldn't be a secret, hers to control. "Would you ever want it to be real, or just a fantasy?"

"I don't know." Marissa waved the joint lazily in the air, tapping ash over the side of the hammock. "I'd have to really trust both the guys in real life, and they'd have to be comfortable getting naked in front of each other, and there would probably be awkward coordination issues. Not to mention the potential for jealousy. Like, Shaun and I aren't anything official right now, but I would never mention this to him."

"Real life is more complicated than fantasies." Diana looked down at the moving ground as the hammock swayed. The grass was long and soft.

Marissa took a deep drag. "You're not a virgin in any way now, are you?"

"No." Diana trailed her fingers over the tips of the grass. "Not in any way."

"Then here. Let me corrupt you some more." Marissa handed her the joint.

Diana inhaled a bitter mouthful of smoke and leaned over the side of the hammock to cough.

"Smooth." Laughing, Marissa kicked at the rope.

"Not all of us are experts at smoking up." Diana handed the joint back, gulping fresh air. "I haven't exactly made it a habit since the last time I tried it, which coincidentally was also in your backyard."

"Okay, good."

"What do you mean, good?"

The hammock rocked gently. When Diana turned her head to Marissa, she was looking up at the stars.

"All of sudden, like out of the blue, you're doing things that I haven't. I think there's more you're not telling me. Who's going to be my most innocent friend?"

Diana was too surprised to answer right away. "You liked that about me? You were just talking about corrupting me some more."

"Kind of. You had your shit together and you were staying pure. It was reassuring."

"Trust me, it didn't come from any deep beliefs." She accepted the joint and puffed, imitating the way Marissa blew out a stream of smoke. "I was scared, that's all. Scared of boys, of everybody."

"How'd that change?"

Diana began to giggle. "Some nice people helped me out."

"People?" Marissa looked stunned. "Did you just use the plural?"

"Uh-huh."

"Shit, Diana, how many guys are you talking about?" Diana laughed harder, rolling her head against Marissa's. "That's what you're saying, isn't it? Is it just guys? Have you been with girls too? Am I losing my mind?"

"You're not losing your mind!" She gasped for breath.

"Oh my God." Marissa gave the hammock a push, making it swing crazily. "I'm freaking out."

"Don't freak out. The guy I told you about is the only guy now. He's all that matters."

"I don't even know what to say."

Diana linked her fingers with Marissa's, squeezing to calm them both down. "It's okay. You don't have to say anything. You're still my wildest friend." Except the twins, who didn't fit the friend box. Not either of them, not anymore.

"I'm not that wild, babe. You haven't seen wild."

"Actually, I have," Diana murmured.

"Who are you?" Marissa blew out smoke and looked at her through the haze. "Like, seriously, who are you?"

"I'm still figuring that out."

"Aren't we all."

"But I'm not Saint Diana."

"None of us are. I still love you. You'll always be the patron saint of nerds, no matter how much anal lube you carry around."

Diana snorted. Her head felt heavy now, but it was expanding at the same time. It was strange, but nice. She rested her forehead against Marissa's shoulder. It was so peaceful to swing in the hammock together, pushing back and forth. Marissa was humming a song. She joined in, but damn, she was feeling sleepy. Marissa's long hair brushed her arm.

"Ian says your hair is three different colors," she mumbled, "but I think it's four colors."

"Who?" Marissa murmured. "Who says that?"

Shit. "Oh, just people."

"They're wrong, babe. It's four."

"I should go," Diana giggled. "It's really late."

"Stay over. Or I'll drive you home."

"Nuh-uh. You're high and I have my bike. I have to get up early for work."

"Yeah, like you aren't high too, Ms. Second-Time Smoker." Marissa rose on one elbow. "It doesn't take much for you. I'm not letting you bike home alone at two am."

"I like it! I like the risk."

"I'm going to ask again: who are you?"

Marissa managed to convince her that she was fine to drive. Diana left her bike just inside the back gate, because there was no way it would fit in Marissa's two-door hatchback.

"I'll set my alarm early," Diana yawned, as they passed quiet houses and flickering streetlamps. "I'll jog over and get my bike before work."

That got a sidelong glance. "You jog now?"

"Yep. I go to the gym every day, can you believe it? So I'll just get up super early. You're not that far."

"Uh-huh." Marissa steered the car into Diana's driveway. "You do that. Good luck."

"Thanks." Diana gave her a drowsy hug. "You know I love you, right? I know I don't usually say things like that. But I do."

"Yeah, yeah, I know." Marissa laughed. "Next time you can't sleep 'cause you had a dirty dream, my backyard is your backyard."

Diana blew her a kiss and climbed out of the car. Opening her front door as noiselessly as possible, she tiptoed inside her unlit house. As she headed into the kitchen for a bite to eat, or possibly all the pretzel sticks and peanut butter in the world, she met a dark shape in front of the open fridge.

"Dad?" she giggled.

"Diana?" Her father, in pajamas, blinked at her. "What are you doing up?"

"Just getting some food," she said dreamily. "You too?"

"Yes. Is everything all right?"

"Everything's fantastic." She drifted to the pantry, found the pretzels, and stuffed a handful in her mouth. "I just got really hungry. I'm going back to bed now. 'Night."

Her father gave her a strange look, but it didn't matter. In her room, she sleepily got out of her clothes and stretched out in bed. She felt so relaxed now, and there was nothing to worry about. All she needed was sleep. Dreams were just dreams.

*

Sunlight, streaming through her window, woke her the next morning. She blinked, yawned, and tried to bury her face in the pillow for another minute of precious sleep. But the bright gold of the sunlight, the heat already rising in her room, forced her eyes open all the way.

Shit. She leapt out of bed and pushed aside the pile of clothes she'd dumped on her desk just hours before. Her purse lay underneath, her phone inside. She'd never set an alarm, she'd just passed out, and it was already 8:23. Seven minutes to get ready before she hopped on her bike to make it to the lab on time — except her bike wasn't here.

Frantically, Diana threw on fresh panties, hooked herself into a bra, and shimmied into a green checkered dress — the same dress, she remembered, that Ian had eyed her in at the grocery store right after the twins got home from college for the summer. He'd smirked, she'd blushed, and she'd dashed off to hide in the produce section. That was, what, less than two months ago? Seemed like another lifetime.

In front of the mirror, she adjusted the high collar and unrolled the elbow-length sleeves. Librarian-on-crack all the way, or maybe somebody's grandma. She was cool with that. All of last night was coming back. Dreams teased her mind, desire slammed her body, and right now, that needed to go.

Hastily, she brushed her teeth, combed her hair, and raced downstairs. The kitchen was empty. Both her parents had left for work. Should she call a cab? Would it matter if she was late twice in a row after being punctual all month?

Yes, it would. There was a meeting this morning, and fuck if she'd walk in late in front of everyone, after she'd overheard grumbling at lunchtime about a high school graduate taking a job undergrads should have had.

She found herself outside on the driveway, blinking in the sunlight, phone in hand.

"Hey, cutie," called a masculine voice. "Everything okay?"

Brendan was strolling across her front lawn. The Jeep stood behind him in the O'Brians' driveway.

"I — kind of screwed myself over," she muttered.

"I was wondering. I didn't see you out here like usual." He stopped in front of her, crisp and clean in a button-down and tie, his hair freshly cut. "How would I start my day without our hug?"

Diana studied him. Brendan was giving her the same indulgent smile he'd given her friends at graduation. He clearly saw her as a little sister now. She was being an idiot, making something out of

123

nothing, when nothing was all there should be.

But Brendan had been inside her. You don't just forget that.

"You tell me," she responded, edgy. Her body still buzzed from the dream. "How would you start your day? Would you be able to manage it?"

His smile was white, his dimples deep. "Hope I don't have to find out. What's going on?"

"I— went to a friend's house late last night. She gave me a ride home and I left my bike. I was going to jog back and pick it up this morning, but I overslept..." God, this shouldn't be awkward, but it was. "Can I get a ride with you?"

"No problem." He beamed at her. "Hop in."

In the Jeep, Brendan was back to his usual chatty self, telling her all about the great girl he was seeing at work and how the four of them should do a double date. It was either the best or the worst thing to hear right now. Probably the best. At least he wasn't being huggy or ruffling her hair.

"I thought you weren't into relationships," she broke in.

"I'm not." Brendan raised his eyebrows. "This is just for fun, cutie."

"And relationships aren't fun?"

He shrugged. "I'm not saying they're bad. It's nice to be with a special someone. But your options just aren't the same."

"Plus everyone's special to you if you're Brendan," Diana added, sharper than she'd meant.

"Is something wrong?" His voice softened.

She took her glasses off and rubbed her eyes. They'd pulled up in front of the lab. "You know the nice thing about living in a shell? Things don't get confusing. Or messy. Life is confusing sometimes."

"Yeah." Brendan leaned his head back against the seat. "It is."

"For you, too?" Diana blinked. "Did you really just admit that you get confused?"

He straightened up and flashed his dimples. "I hear it happens. Or so people say."

"Don't do that."

"Do what?"

"Turn up the charm when I'm talking to you. Remember when you said I could tell you anything? Same goes for you."

Brendan held her gaze. Long enough to see the starbursts of green and brown in his eyes, and how they differed ever so slightly from Ian's. Leaning in, he kissed her cheek. Damn the way her body tightened when he did it.

"Have a good day, cutie. Next time you leave your bike because you're smoking up somewhere, text me. I'll give you a ride."

"How'd you know?"

He laughed and waved her out.

Chapter Nine

The parking lot was huge, unfamiliar, and half-filled with cars. As Ian pulled the Jeep into a spot, Diana eyed the arena looming against the dark sky.

It was Ian's turn to take her out. July fourth was tomorrow, and a few early fireworks already crackled in the distance.

"We're going to watch sports?" she asked nervously as Ian put the car in park. He'd almost stuck to the speed limit on the way over. She had to admit, Ian's driving was a lot more careful these days. But a feeling charged the air, a feeling she couldn't name.

He grinned and leaned over for a kiss. She gasped when he bit her lower lip.

"No questions, remember? You made the rules. Just keep an open mind, Diana. You look good tonight."

"Just good?"

The parking lot was putting her on edge, making her stomach flutter. Streams of people, almost all men, prowled toward the arena under bright stadium lights. With this much testosterone flooding the open lot, she could barely imagine what it would be like inside.

"Sexy as fuck. Burning up the car." One finger slipped into the sweetheart neckline of her dress, leaving a trail of fire over her creamy cleavage.

"Just tonight?" She really was stalling now.

"Twenty-four hours a day." When Ian worked his finger between her breasts, she tensed with need. His eyes half-closed as she slid her hand up his leg, over well-worn denim, to cup a very hard bulge. "You're a little tease, Diana," he breathed. "It's almost like you want me to do something about it."

Jesus, Ian's hand was inside her bra now, coaxing her nipple to a tight bud. If she tried, she could distract him. Get him hot and bothered enough to drive to the lookout point instead of taking her into the arena bristling with guys.

Could she? She'd never actually tried to seduce Ian, or anyone else. She hadn't needed to.

But it didn't feel honest. Why use sex to get her way? She didn't need to be afraid of the arena. She was here with Ian. She'd promised to keep an open mind. She trusted him.

As she stepped out of the Jeep, Ian was already around the car and at her side, dropping an arm over her shoulders. She tried to match pace with his long stride. As they passed more and more people — more and more guys — she caught the sidelong glances. Men were checking her out. She'd begun getting used to eyes on her, but these were so...open.

The stares took her back to that Saturday night with the twins, less than a month ago, strutting between them to the club while heads turned. Tonight, she was wearing a white sundress with blue flowers instead of the clingy red dress, more sweet than sexy, but the attention made her face flush and her stomach lurch.

Heads also turned to Ian, in a "right on" kind of way. Ian's possessive arm around her shoulders sent a clear message. And that, right there, spelled a world of difference from the club night.

The crowd was thick and rowdy when they walked into the arena. Guys were shouting, punching their hands. Rumbles stirred the clusters of people.

"Ian?" Diana gripped his hand. "What the fuck is this?"

"It's okay, baby." He squeezed her palm. "Stick close to me. Let's get our seats."

They made their way through the outer corridor to a door and up some stairs, where they had to climb over three obviously drunk twenty-something guys to get to their seats. Diana perched on the edge of her seat, looking around, her heart beating fast. Everything about this situation was new. She'd always put as much distance as possible between herself and any kind of athletic event. Rows of seats, rapidly filling up, surrounded a roped-off ring.

"Boxing?" she yelled over the noise in the room. "This is what you're taking me to watch?"

"Just give it a try." Ian grinned at her.

Diana grabbed his hand again. Bottles and cans were everywhere, and an alcohol-fueled wave rolled over the crowd. When two stripped-down guys stepped into the ring, muscles bulging and faces growling, mayhem broke loose. Shouting, pounding, screaming. Diana felt lightheaded.

She forced herself to watch as the punches began. Cheers met each blow. When she glanced at her boyfriend, the wild look in Ian's eyes was all animal, totally riveted on the fight. She'd seen that look before. Directed at her, when he was buried deep inside her, or about to be. Crouched over her bare curves, ready to fuck her with everything he had.

Seeing that primal energy pointed elsewhere — at two guys duking it out in a ring — made Ian seem very far away.

"Babe?" she shouted in his ear. "Are you there?"

"Oh yeah, I'm here. Woo!" He jumped to his feet, pulling her up. "Get him!"

Jesus. She was trying, really trying to get into this. At least, to see what Ian saw. It was obviously doing a lot for him.

"Damn." He let out a loud whistle as a glove smacked a face. The crowd roared. Diana winced.

"How can they do that?" she yelled. "Do you know how many brain cells can be damaged from a blow? One concussion—"

"Don't think, Diana," Ian yelled back. "Just feel."

The ending of her poem for Ian rushed into her mind.

Too fast

To think

Too fast

To know

Can't see, can't hear, can only feel

She did feel, with Ian. She felt everything. But she didn't want the energy in the arena. When a fist smashed a jaw and a head bounced back, she clapped her hand over her mouth. Her free fingers found Ian's arm and squeezed, hard.

"Diana?" His eyes, wide and dark, focused. "Shit. You're not okay." Large palms cupped her face. He turned away from the fight. "Say something. Do you need to go outside?"

"No." She swallowed. "I'm okay. This is just — a lot."

"Too much?" Emotions warred on Ian's face, pulled between the fight and her. As he blinked, his face cleared. His hands on her face felt warm and steady. "Say the word and we'll leave."

"I promised to trust you. I can do this."

"No, I knew this was a long shot. I thought maybe you'd be curious. We don't have to stay."

"You paid for tickets. I can tell you're really into it."

She shouldn't be surprised. Ian had always been extreme. Competitive at sports, finding scrapes, pushing the limits. She'd learned as a kid that the only way with Ian was *fight back, fight harder.* But all the pranks, the rule-breaking, the rebelling — the person who got injured in those escapades was always Ian.

"You hate this." His voice cut through her thoughts. "You're freaking out."

"I'll stick it out," she yelled over the uproar. Something dramatic had happened in the ring. One guy was getting up from the floor. "This matters to you. I want to understand what you get out of it. If it's too much, I'll go out there and wait for you until it's over." She pointed up the seats to the exit.

Ian shook his head forcefully. "This isn't a place for you to be alone."

She saw his point. "I want to feel what you feel."

He leaned close and pressed his forehead to hers. The din of the arena dimmed.

"Diana, you don't have to prove yourself every fucking minute of the day. You're not gonna earn an A for doing the things you don't want to do. I'm not making you a good girlfriend report card. It's okay. You don't have to feel what I feel. You shouldn't."

"What do you mean?"

Ian took a breath. "Just trust me on that." He squeezed both her arms.

Diana glanced at the ring, then at Ian's serious face.

"Can we step outside for a minute?"

"Yeah, of course."

Taking her hand, he led her up the stairs and out the nearest door to a quiet spot in the outer corridor. Diana leaned against the wall, cool concrete meeting her sticky skin. Ian loomed over her.

"Jesus, you're pale," he muttered.

"I'm always pale." She tried to laugh.

"Used to be, you mean. You've been out in the sun this summer, probably for the first time in about five years. Getting the cutest freckles." He traced a line down her nose.

"You're just distracting me," she murmured.

"Yep." Ian gave her a little smile, but his face was flushed. Sweat glistened on his forehead. When she touched his wrist, his pulse throbbed against her thumb.

"The first time I was here," he said abruptly, "me and Brendan came together. We were thirteen, and we told our parents we were going to the movies. This was after you moved away. I don't know if they would have cared, but we were so used to making shit up, that's what Brendan told them. We got a ride with someone older. We got here, and Brendan wasn't into it. He liked the thrill, but after we did it once, he was like, okay, on to the next thing. What's our next stunt? Brendan's not big on fighting. But I kept coming back alone. I'd find a ride and sneak out. I liked watching the fights by myself. He knew, and he covered for me, but he didn't like it. It bugged him that I had a thing I did alone. He never said so. But I knew."

Diana's head tipped back as Ian cupped her cheek. "I thought you didn't keep tabs on each other."

"Sure, in college, although we've been together more than apart." *Until now,* Diana added silently. "But in high school and before that, fuck yeah, we were always together. Except for this place."

"You love coming here and being alone."

"I love coming here and I wanted to show you."

"Then let's stay," she said quickly. "I can handle it."

A crooked smile tugged his mouth. "No big deal. Like I said, it was a long shot. We don't have to like all the same things, baby. We're never going to."

"What keeps you coming back? Don't you want to do it instead of just watch?"

"Do what?" Ian's voice was very quiet now.

"Let it all out. Be yourself. Lose control, instead of being the person everyone expects you to be, including your brother. Playing the part everyone expects you to play. Even if you're the bad twin and the rebel, that's locked you up so tight that in the end, you've just played by the rules."

Ian's eyes widened. In the space before his answer, she heard scraps of conversation from passersby, a loudspeaker announcement, a muffled roar from inside the arena.

"If you think that's about losing control —" he jerked his head toward the stadium door — "you don't understand boxing."

131

"I know it's not," she said impatiently. "I'm talking about you and why you come here. You've seen me let go. You've told me to fall apart, and I have. But you're holding back. I'm not talking about drinking or doing drugs or crashing your car or being crazy out in the world. I'm talking about you," she took a deep breath, "and me."

"You don't want to see me lose it, Diana."

"Oh, I so fucking do."

His fingers tightened on her arms.

"You're so soft," he muttered.

Diana sucked in her breath. A shadow clouded his eyes. Animal lust. She'd seen it before, God knows she had. But no matter how dirty he'd talked, devoured, fucked, there'd always been some self-control.

Ian's darkening eyes, his handsome face relaxing as he gripped her arms, told her the control wouldn't be there tonight. His growl sent desire winding between her legs.

"And you're so hard," she breathed.

She pushed her hands against his T-shirt. His pecs fit her palms. Her heart rocketed through her chest. Impulsively, she pulled his hand there to feel her pulse.

Ian blinked. For an instant, the fog of lust cleared.

"If you don't like it, you have to tell me to stop." His voice was thick. The air around them was thick. She was dizzy with the promise in Ian's deep rumble, wedged between his body and the wall. "Because otherwise, I won't stop."

"I'll tell you." Her throat was dry. Talking was harder now.

A firm leg prodded her thighs, opening them, pushing in the blue and white flowered material of her dress. A cock pulsed against her belly. Hands dropped to her hips, squeezing, and his hazel eyes filmed over again.

"So soft everywhere," he grunted, like he was talking more to himself than her. His gaze on her body, his fingers on her curves — he wasn't trying to drive her crazy. He was taking greedy pleasure in

132

looking, in touching. In having. Taut need arrowed though her body, and she jerked under his touch. "What I want to do to you…"

"Show me," she whispered.

"You really want this?"

"Show. Me."

Ian pulled her from the wall, planted a hand on her back, and walked her swiftly down the stairs. His palm burned through her dress. She hurried to keep pace with his long stride. In two minutes, they'd left the hustle of the arena behind and were in the Jeep.

Twisting the keys in the ignition, he floored the gas before she'd buckled her seatbelt. The Jeep shot backwards, then roared out of the parking lot. Diana grabbed the handle above the door.

"Jesus, Ian," she half-laughed, half-gasped.

"Where are your parents?" His voice was low, unrecognizable. A slow finger traced her thigh.

"Out. At an event somewhere."

"Good. I'm gonna take you in your room."

She shivered. "Can you wait that long?"

He laughed softly. "Don't push me, baby. I don't think you want to do that."

"I do, actually."

"Don't."

Diana shuddered at the word. Ian's face was dark.

His finger burned a path across her creamy thigh to slip into the softness between her legs. She bit back a moan. He threw a glance her way as he stepped on the gas.

"Are you holding back, bad girl? Are you keeping quiet with me?"

"You said not to push you." Her breath was coming in pants as Ian insistently squeezed her crotch. But she put a little tease back in her voice. "Can you handle me, Ian?"

"You're going to find out. Now do all the fucking moaning you need to do, you hot slut, because this is only a warmup."

Her thighs clenched around Ian's wrist, hugging his hand. God, her panties were already soaked, but Ian's crude words made her nerves hum. He'd talked dirty to her plenty of times, and she'd loved every profane whisper. She'd started getting the courage to do the same with him. But this was rougher. More indecent. More…animal.

"Oh Jesus—" she burst out. It turned into a long groan as Ian pressed her clit through her slippery panties. More fingers explored her pussy, pulling aside the thin silky strip of her thong. When one fingertip found her juice-slicked entrance and pushed inward, she yelped, opening her legs to Ian's touch.

"You need to drive," she managed.

"I'm driving all right."

His finger worked deeper into her tight warmth. Dear Lord, his firm rubs on her clit, right on the precipice between pleasure and pain, sent pulses of heat through her crotch and thighs. She couldn't wait for her bedroom, she had to feel him too… She ran her hand swiftly up Ian's leg to capture the raging erection in his jeans.

"Don't touch," he ordered in a strangled voice. She stared at him. "I touch you. You don't touch me."

Slowly, she uncurled her fingers. She clutched the seat instead.

When they roared into their neighborhood, Ian slammed on the brakes in front of the O'Brians' house and parked in his wide driveway. Thank God both their houses were dark. As soon as she stepped out of the Jeep, strong arms scooped her up.

"Fuck," she gasped, laughing as Ian carried her across her front lawn. But Ian wasn't laughing.

"Give me your key," he grated at the front door.

Trapped in his arms, aroused from his attention in the car, she got her purse free and found her keys. She hung on to Ian's neck as he unlocked her door and kicked it open, then shut, behind them. He took the stairs two at a time, holding her tight. She jounced in his grasp, breathless.

134

In her room, Ian threw her on the bed. The breath was knocked out of her as she bounced on the soft mattress. Impatient hands unzipped her flowered dress, ripped off her bra, tore off her panties.

"Cute little dress," he muttered. "Looks good on your hot body. Looks better on the floor."

Diana reached for his shirt, but he pushed her back down. She'd never seen Ian lose his clothes so fast. Lust distorted his face.

On all fours, crouched over her, he caged her in with his hands and knees. She tried to lift her head to meet him, but he seized her hair. Lips and teeth bruised her mouth with kisses. Suction on her neck made the bed drop out from under her. When pressure met her breasts, she gasped. Strong hands squeezed her generous swells. Diana moaned, arching her back to rub her nipples against his palms, but Ian straddled her, pinning her down.

"Jesus fucking Christ," he ground out. "These tits. I want to eat them."

She would have laughed, but she was far past laughing, spread out naked beneath him. She was past talking. She was so vulnerable as Ian fondled her breasts, pinching her rosy nipples into aching peaks. His hands were everywhere, possessive and hot and moving so swiftly she could barely keep up.

"Then eat them," she panted.

Heat met her hard nipples, one then the other. Ian's hands and mouth were a blur. But wait — something was happening, an intense sensation at the curve of one heavy breast. He was sucking the underside, hard, while he pinched her nipple.

"Yes..." When she yanked his hair, Ian's sucks became greedier. "Ian, Jesus—"

He pulled back, his eyes glittering. "Oh yeah. You'll see it tomorrow, little girl. A secret for you and me."

"Let me touch you—"

"I'm not letting you do anything, baby."

She was shaking, scared and excited at the same time, and very aware of how much stronger Ian was. One hand felt roughly between her legs, palming her sopping pussy. Pressure at her entrance made her moan. Instinctively she opened her thighs, and fingers filled her cunt.

"Ian... Oh God..."

He muffled her cries in a dominating kiss. There was no other word for it, no other way to describe how Ian's lips took hers. When he let go, her mouth throbbed.

"This isn't fair."

"Who said it was fair?"

"It should be," she gritted, and did she even know what she meant?

"Who ever said love was fair, Diana?"

Ian's hand left her pussy. His eyes were dark and wild, his hair a mess. She tried to pull him back. Instead, tangy warmth met her tongue. Ian was pushing his fingers into her mouth. She gasped, taking them in.

She'd licked her juices off Ian's fingers countless times, but this was different. He was fucking her mouth, barely giving her time to taste her cream and the salt of his skin. His handsome face was glazed with animal lust.

This was torture. She couldn't wait. She needed his touch between her legs again, finding out her secrets, knowing her most private place. As she frantically sucked his fingers, her own hand slipped over her folds to rub her eager clit.

A sharp pinch on her nipple made her bite down. Ian pulled free and pounced on her. Diana squirmed under the sudden weight.

"Mine," Ian growled. "My pussy. Don't touch."

"Then do something about it, you bastard," she panted.

The next thing she knew, his head was between her legs and a burning tongue slurped up her cream. Lips closed on her clit, sucking hard on the swollen bud. Her hands fisted in his thick hair, pulling with all her strength. He grunted, his sucking even hungrier, his tongue greedier for her juices.

When her back arched, he gripped her soft thighs, digging into her flesh. Jesus, the discomfort of being held down and the pleasure of Ian's lips on her clit made her scream out loud.

"Oh yeahhhh," he muttered. "Scream for me, Diana. I'm going to make you scream even louder."

The window was open. Everyone would hear her, everyone would know— and Ian's lips and tongue were relentless. She didn't care anymore. Right now, she wanted the world to know.

His mouth sent sparks through her pussy as he sucked with white-hot intensity. Juices ran down her ass, soaking the sheets. Hands ravished her hips and thighs, pinching and possessing, until her cunt quivered around sudden fullness.

"Ian, please—"

His fingers flexed inside her. Heat ran all over her swollen lips, wet core, and tender clit, over and over. He was moving too fast for her to grab his hair, to lift her hips, to do anything at all but come.

She arched her back, motionless. Ian's fingers and tongue never stopped stroking. Sweet Jesus, he was pulling her orgasm out of her. Taking her as she came. And she was giving herself to Ian with every clutch of her pussy, squeezing down on him with pure desire.

When he withdrew, anger pricked her body. It made no sense, but she glared up at him.

"Turn over," he gritted. The low command made her shiver.

"Make me," she tossed at him.

He grabbed her, wrestling her soft curves. She fought back, biting the swell of his shoulder, clutching his powerful arms, raking her nails down his back with all her strength.

Why was she fighting? She wanted Ian to take her. He knew it. She knew it. When he flipped her over, the bed shook.

"Bad girl." Blunt flesh pushed against her cunt. "Fuck, you're wet."

One arm pulled her to her knees. Palms spread her cheeks. She gasped when his cock speared her. He sank in and held her firmly against him.

"Sweet baby," he rasped. "So tight. And burning hot."

A smack on her ass drove the air out of her. Yes…she wanted more, she wanted Ian to really spank her…but before she could speak, he began to move.

"Oh God— oh God—" Her breath left her mouth in gasps. From behind, Ian thrust again and again. Every pulse of his shaft was delicious agony. She tried tilting her hips toward him, but one hand squeezed her waist and the other had a tight grip on her hair.

"I'm gonna fuck you all the way through, Diana," his low voice rasped. "Mine."

She moaned at the hard flesh piercing her cunt. The rocking bed, the creaking mattress, the hand grabbing her swaying breast — everything was happening so fast. His cock was smooth, slick, alive, plunging deep. Her dark room spun around her. She clutched her sheets, her thighs spreading wider. When she buried her face in her pillow, tears bloomed on the fabric.

"Ian —"

"So wet," he groaned. "Such a sweet little pussy all for me."

She was. She was so wet. His arm circled her waist, tense and muscled. With every pinch on her nipple, pain and pleasure flared. His hand left her breast to spread her pussy open. When fingers surrounded her clit, she spasmed around Ian's cock, jerking in his firm embrace.

"Yeah," he grunted. He massaged the sensitive bud, rubbing faster and faster. Heavy arms and legs caged her in. "I'm fucking you, baby. There's nothing you can do except come on my cock."

She cried out. Ian's strokes were demanding. Insistent. Owning. His fingers were relentless on her exposed clit. As she tried to move against him, her pussy contracted, clasping him in a long, helpless orgasm.

"More..."

His breath burned her neck. "You're gonna come as long as I want you to. You're hot. You're fire. You're going to explode."

She was already exploding. Pleasure rushed her body. She pressed her face into the pillow, the soft cotton her only anchor.

No. Ian was her anchor. Molded to her, holding her against him, fucking her ferociously.

"Mine," he hissed.

"Mine." Diana tried to push back, but his tight embrace trapped her. He felt enormous from behind.

"Mine." He emphasized the word with a hard thrust.

"Mine." Now she could move, just barely, and the friction made her silken cunt ripple around him.

"Fuck. Diana. You're mine. Mine. Mine." Each syllable was punctuated by the sharp sweetness of his cock sinking deep.

"Yours," she whispered.

Ian groaned, his body tightening. He seized her hair again. Grunts of release overlapped her cries as he came in long strokes, spurting inside her.

Afterward, he stayed buried in her cunt. Their ragged breathing smoothed out. A breeze from the window stirred damp hair on sweaty skin. The fullness eased off as he withdrew and lay down next to her.

Her knees buckled. She slumped into strong arms.

"Ian?" she whispered.

"I'm here."

Dazed hazel met hers. Her head flopped onto his chest. His skin was sticky with sweat, or was it hers?

Downstairs, the garage door opened. Her heart beat faster, but she was too exhausted to move. She was completely entwined in Ian's long arms and legs.

"Diana, honey?" her mother called into the dark house. Ian's arms tightened around her.

"She's not home, Julie," her father said. "She told us at breakfast she'd be out with her friends again tonight."

"She's never home anymore," her mother sighed.

"She's having fun. She should enjoy herself."

"I know." The garage door rumbled closed. "She was so serious in high school. But I'd like to have just a little of her before she leaves."

"So tell her. Make some time together."

"All right. Here's something from Yale in the mail." There was a pause.

"What is it?" her father asked.

"I worry about her going to college, Stuart. She's just so…innocent. What does she know about the world?"

"Diana has her head on straight. She's going to accomplish great things," her father said reassuringly. "She plays it down, but I hear she's impressing everyone in her lab."

Ian shifted next to her. Diana opened her legs, letting him wedge his thigh between them. Her body throbbed from his rough treatment. Her pussy ached from his primal thrusts. He stroked her hair, his fingers gentle where'd they'd been brutal just minutes ago.

"Of course, I wouldn't expect anything less." Clinking sounds came from downstairs — her mother, bustling around the kitchen. "I should prep the coleslaw for the O'Brians' barbecue tomorrow." Her voice was brisk now, the worry gone. "Brooke said the twins will be there. I keep hoping, with Diana and Brendan…well, that they'll see more of each other. I've told him he's welcome here any time."

"Brendan's a nice enough kid." Her father sounded dubious. "But between you and me, I don't think he's smart enough for our daughter."

A snort from Ian vibrated his chest against hers and puffed warm air into her hair. She shook her head, too spent to talk.

"Brendan's smart," her mother protested. "And very accomplished. He's involved in so many things, even his parents can't keep track of everything he's up to. Maybe he doesn't have the time. He's got his internship, volunteering for the mayor, training for basketball season, and who knows what else. Oh, and keeping his brother out of trouble, of course."

"Is he? Keeping his brother out of trouble, I mean."

"He seems to be. I keep hearing that Ian's so much better now. He isn't rolling across the doorstep at six am or stumbling around with a hangover at noon." There was a shudder in her mother's voice. "No speeding tickets, no pileups. Brooke said he's even studying to make up the classes he flunked last year. Thank God. His parents about tore their hair out when he went on academic probation. Of course when it happened, he acted like he didn't care."

A low rumble stirred Ian's chest against her cheek.

So that was the "situation" his dad had brought up. Why hadn't Ian told her? Flunking multiple classes — she knew people did it, but it was hard to wrap her head around it. Especially when grades had come first for the past seven years.

She lifted her head to look at him, but he turned away.

"It doesn't matter to me," she whispered. "I know who you are and what you can do."

"Well, that's good news." From downstairs, her father's voice was doubtful. "I'm sure the O'Brians appreciate the reprieve."

"We'll see how long it lasts. You just wonder where that boy would be without his brother."

Her parents' voices floated up the stairs, getting closer, then fading as they went into their bedroom and closed the door.

She lay there with Ian for long minutes. Moonlight striped the bed, filtered through the branches of the huge tree outside her window, as his chest rose and fell in time with hers. Her hand found his shoulder. As she slipped into sleep, he kissed the top of her head.

Movement startled her awake. She reached for dew-drenched grass to remind herself that she was outside, the way she always did when she woke during the night. But her hand met a male body, shifting position, and when she kicked involuntarily, she felt blankets and heard a soft grunt.

"Ian?" she whispered. "Don't go home."

He pushed back the comforter, unfolded his body from her embrace, and stood. Silhouetted in front of the window, he tucked her comforter around her.

"Get some rest," he said hoarsely. "You'll sleep better alone."

"Stay the night." Her voice was husky. "Let my parents find you in my bed in the morning. I don't care. Tell them you're Ian, not Brendan."

"Really?" Ian's eyes, framed with dark lashes, were fixed on her. "Really, Diana? That's how you want it?"

"Yes. I'm sick of secrets."

He bent to kiss her. His lithe body, outlined in moonlight, seemed shaky. She glimpsed the scratches she'd left on his shoulder.

"I love you." His voice was gruff. "And that's not how I want it."

"I love you too." There were no other words.

Diana watched through half-closed eyes as he pulled on his clothes. When he pointed to the window screen, she nodded, and he took it off. He picked up his shoes and dropped them one after the other out the window. Two soft thuds sounded on the ground below.

Climbing easily onto her desk, he maneuvered through the window frame and out to the tree. Then there was only the soft sound of branches rustling in the night.

Chapter Ten

At six in the morning, Diana dragged herself to the quiet kitchen to make Rice Krispies treats for the barbecue. They'd been her own Fourth of July tradition before she started hiding in her bedroom, one of the first dishes she'd learned how to make. She'd beamed with pride when she carried the plate of treats over to the O'Brians' for the first time, basking in Brendan's compliments and racing after Ian when he swiped half of them.

Of course, when she was a kid, she hadn't been rolling out of bed at the crack of dawn to make dessert. But today her body hummed, her crotch throbbed, and no way was she staying under the covers. After she patted the Rice Krispies treats into the pan, she had time to gulp a pot of coffee, shower off the sweat, and dab makeup over the hickeys on her neck before any sound came from her parents' room.

Wet hair clinging to her cheeks, she stared at the steamed-up mirror and cupped her breast to see the rosy mark Ian had left on the underside. He'd sucked like he was starving. That raw hunger made her shudder in the warm bathroom.

Hours later, when she met up with her friends for a picnic lunch in a park, she fought to focus on the conversation.

The picnic had been her idea. Wrapped up in Ian, she'd felt pangs of guilt. She was flat-out neglecting her friends, wasn't she? Making excuses, lying about what she was up to. They were used to her blowing them off to study, and they paid her back with teasing. But school was out. Over. Done.

Her thighs still felt the push of Ian's hands. Her pussy still felt the lashes of his tongue. Her body buzzed so loudly with the force of their fucking, everyone at the picnic table had to feel it too. And every single hot thought racing through her head was about losing control. To Ian, to — oh God — Ian and Brendan together, even to total strangers that crazy night at the club, pulling her clothes off eagerly.

Love. She was definitely in love. No question about it. When she'd daydreamed about love before the boys next door made her an offer, she'd figured it would be glorious. Someday, she and some nameless, faceless guy would hold hands and skip in the sunshine and browse through bookstores and have plenty of hot sex.

Now she was learning: love wasn't always soft and sweet. As down and dirty as her fantasies had gotten in high school, she'd never crossed them with loving someone. In her mind, she'd fucked just about every boy in her class on every available surface. But she hadn't laid herself bare for them, and she wouldn't have wanted to see them bare for her.

What she felt for Ian was so huge and raw and overwhelming, her skin was about to burst. When Marissa showed up late and gave her a hug, she jumped.

"What is it?"

"Stuff," Diana whispered.

"Is it the boy?" Marissa whispered back.

"Yes. It's the boy."

Ian wasn't a boy, not anymore. Not to her. He was a man. Being a woman, with a man, was a lot to wrap her head around. Sweet Jesus, he'd fucked her hard.

"Is it more than you can handle?" Marissa squeezed her hand.

"I can handle it."

Her shoulder pressed against Marissa's, the solid contact helping her breathe. She needed to talk. She needed to tell someone about being overwhelmed, someone who wasn't Ian. But if she couldn't start the story at the treehouse, could she start anywhere? She was sitting on a wooden bench leaning against one of her best friends, but would Marissa listen with an open mind, or would she hear the words "Ian O'Brian" and lose all her shit?

A familiar face floated across her mind — bright hazel eyes, broad dimpled smile, chin with a cleft.

Brendan would understand. She could be totally honest with Brendan, about everything. He'd been there, done her. Seen her let go, urged her further. *Deeper, Di. Harder. More.*

She grabbed the splintery table with one hand, dizzy. If she just found a minute alone with him today... God, no, that wasn't a good idea.

"Are you two done having a moment?" Janelle waved a hand in front of her and Marissa. "Because there are decisions to be made about food."

*

Gray-blue smoke hung over the O'Brians' backyard. The barbecue was already in full swing, and the landscaped lawn and patio pulsed with noise and people.

Heat shimmered in the air. Diana followed her parents through the gate, carrying the Rice Krispies treats she'd made that morning.

Her ladybug-printed dress — the first real purchase she'd made with her summer job paycheck, after replacing the glassware and putting half in savings — showed a peek of cleavage and fit like a glove. It didn't just outline her curves; it flaunted them. If Ian thought her usual style was librarian-on-crack, this was librarian on the red pill he'd held out to her, that night at the club, like a dare on his palm.

Find out with me.

She was finding things out, but Jesus, did she understand anything about what she was learning?

As the gate creaked closed behind her, she scanned the bustling yard for two tall tanned frames, two pairs of muscular shoulders, and two heads of brown hair. Both twins stood in the center of the patio, surrounded by people.

Half the neighborhood was milling around the pool and patio, along with a generous helping of the twins' friends — the same people, barely dressed, that Diana had watched enviously from her window that hot May weekend when everything began.

Now the beautiful people were starting to look like regular people. She recognized the guys who'd spent half of high school in the O'Brians' driveway with their shirts off, the girls who'd stuck to the twins' sides in the halls.

But what the hell were they doing here? Brendan had promised her a low-key afternoon, just her and the twins hanging out at a family barbecue. Wholesome, innocent — and the three of them. The twins' friends weren't supposed to play a part in it.

Mrs. O'Brian hurried up, giving hugs and kissing cheeks. Diana smiled through the greetings. As the conversation turned to her mom's secret coleslaw recipe, she slipped off to the dessert table. Setting her plate down by piles of brownies and cookies, she tore away the plastic wrap.

A bare arm brushed hers. A muscled body bumped her hip.

"'Scuse me." Ian gave her an unapologetic smirk. But the shadows under his eyes — those were all her fault.

"You're excused." Her throat was dry. Ian was warm, even feverish against her side. Shirtless, not wearing much else. His boxers peeked above his low-hanging shorts. He snagged a Rice Krispy treat and held it to her lips.

"You should eat one before everyone rushes the table. I remember when you used to bring these. They always went first."

She hadn't been able to eat all day, but she bit into the sticky square. She wanted to kneel in front of Ian on the bricks, beg another bite, lick marshmallow off his palm, yank down his shorts…

Jesus, as dirty as her mind had been in high school, this was another level. Deeper and stronger and out of her control.

Past the table, a smiling twin stood in the middle of a group, laughing easily at someone else's joke.

I need you, Brendan, she thought at his broad back. What she felt for Ian went way past need. And thank God Brendan had a shirt on, because she did not need to see both twins half-naked right now.

"The way I remember it, they disappeared because you ate most of them," she murmured to Ian. "Plus, you stole mine and made me chase you for it."

"'Course I did. You would have cried if I didn't." He offered her another bite and flashed his dimples. But his eyes were dark, as dark as they'd been the night before, the rings of hazel almost hidden by black.

"Diana!" Her mother bustled over. "The DiStefanos want to hear all about Yale. Go talk to them."

"I haven't started there yet," Diana muttered. Normally, she'd do the polite thing and trot over anyway. Always the good girl. But she stayed put. "I can tell them about it at Thanksgiving break."

Mrs. Cooper raised her eyebrows. "They're dying to hear whatever you have to say. Hello, Ian," she added less enthusiastically, eyeing the Rice Krispy treat an inch from her daughter's lips.

"Oh, hey, Mrs. Cooper," he drawled. "Diana's hungry. I don't think you're feeding her enough."

Mrs. Cooper smiled brightly. "You look—"

"Exhausted," Mrs. O'Brian filled in, joining them. "I'm not going to ask what you've been doing, because I know we won't get an answer."

"Working out. Drilling. All good stuff." Ian bent to kiss his mother's cheek, popped the rest of the Rice Krispy treat in his mouth, and strolled off. Looking over his shoulder, he caught Diana's eye and pointed to his full mouth. "Yum."

Mrs. O'Brian put a hand to her cheek. "Did you see that?" she exclaimed. "He's been so affectionate recently. At home, he'll just come up and give me a hug. The last time I got a hug from Ian — it must have been high school graduation. Of course, Brendan has always been such a sweetheart, but if Ian hugged me once a year, I was lucky. He looks so tired, though. It worries me."

"All that partying is taking its toll," her mother tsked. "I'm surprised Brendan doesn't keep him in check."

"Well, we certainly can't." Mrs. O'Brian shook her head. "But he seems to be turning things around. We see him studying, and I don't think he's drinking like he used to. I don't know why, but it's coming from somewhere. Dennis says we need to buckle up for a huge explosion, but I have hope. I've always had hope for Ian."

"I'm going to say hi to the DiStefanos," Diana said quickly. "Mom said they wanted to talk to me."

"Of course. Help yourself to a drink on the way," Mrs. O'Brian offered. "The cooler's by the grill, and we have too much food like we always do. Dennis is keeping the beer out of sight," she added to Diana's mother, rolling her eyes at the twins' friends. "We didn't expect so many of them to show up, but Brendan promised they're just stopping by."

Diana bent over the cooler, sifting through the ice. She welcomed the cold sting on her palm.

So the twins' friends were at the barbecue because of Brendan. Was he avoiding her and Ian? And here she'd been hoping to talk to him. She wanted to grab him, shake his shoulders, ask what his deal was and get an honest answer.

"No matter how much you scrape the bottom, you're not going to find beer," a male voice said.

Diana straightened up from the cooler and turned to see one of the twins' friends, blond and broad. It took her a second to realize: he was flirting.

She cleared her throat. "That's okay. I'll just get a club soda."

"Aw, that's no fun. Let loose." He grinned at her.

She remembered this guy. She'd seen him in high school with the twins and their pack of jock friends, taking over the front lawn and shouting down the halls. Kent or Keith or Kevin somebody. Here he was, giving her a confusingly puppyish smile. Maybe the ice princess shell had really cracked.

"O'Brian's rounding up the alcohol," he went on. "Dude has a nose for it, wherever it's hidden. You know him? I haven't seen you around here."

O'Brian. Was that Ian or Brendan? The nickname reminded her that the twins had a whole life she didn't know about. But she knew the real Ian and Brendan, dammit. Didn't she?

"Yes, I know him," she said firmly. "I've known the twins forever. We grew up together. I'm Diana."

"Nice. I'm Keith. They've talked about me, right?"

"Definitely. All the time." She began to giggle. "I can't get them to stop."

Sudden cold against the back of her neck made her jump.

"Ian!" She glared over her shoulder at an evil grin.

"Whoops. Just checking that this is cold enough." He held up his hands, a can in each, and nodded to Keith. "Beer."

"Beer," Keith repeated. "Alcohol calls." He turned to Diana. "You sure I can't get you some?"

"No thanks," she murmured. "I'm all set."

"Come on." Ian tossed a can at Keith's chest and walked him toward the grill. "There's more where this came from."

Diana watched him go, unable to tear her gaze from his sculpted back. As far as she knew, Mrs. O'Brian was right. Ian hadn't had much to drink since they got together. Definitely not with her, other than the wine they'd sipped at that sidewalk cafe. She hadn't needed to taste that wildness either. Being with him was intoxicating enough.

Seeing him half-naked across the patio, unable to touch him or even admit to anything going on, was driving her crazy. How much longer could this continue? She needed to walk over to her parents and tell them the truth, right now. But she stayed where she was.

Over by the grill, Mr. O'Brian came up to Ian, gave his son an exasperated look, and held out his palm for the beer. Ian shook the can, obviously empty now, and handed it over with a jaunty smile. As his father launched into a lecture, Ian nodded agreeably, then sauntered over to the grill and picked up the tongs. He waved a hand at his dad to signal that he was taking over flipping duties, gesturing toward the table loaded with food and the people milling around the backyard. Mr. O'Brian looked pleasantly surprised.

"There you are, Diana!" Mrs. DiStefano was standing in front of her with a big smile. "I was just telling your mom that we have to hear all about Yale. You must be so excited."

"Thanks, I am," she murmured. She twisted the cap off her club soda. Someone draped an arm around her shoulders.

"Are you finding everything you need, Di?"

She nodded, blinking up at Brendan's dimples. She probably looked lovesick, and the gleam in his eyes told her what he thought of it.

"Hi, Mrs. DiStefano," he added. "It's so good to see you."

"You too, Brendan. Always a pleasure." Mrs. DiStefano looked with interest at Brendan's arm around Diana.

The charm was practically rolling off him, Diana thought. She eyed the line of his jaw, then his broad chest, hidden by his light blue polo shirt. If she could flick a switch there to turn off the charm, she would.

Mrs. DiStefano was asking about Yale again. Diana summoned up every fact she remembered from her visit last fall. Brendan filled in with helpful comments, because of course he'd been to the campus for some reason. As Diana glanced toward the grill again, Ian's eyes went to her like a magnet.

She tensed. Brendan must have felt it, because he rubbed her shoulder.

"And Brendan, I hear *so* much about what you're up to," Mrs. DiStefano exclaimed. "Not as much about your brother, but I hope no news is good news. I swear, I'm still scrubbing the slime out of my mailbox from that giant slug he left in there, and I don't know how many years ago that was."

Diana cleared her throat. Looking up at Brendan, she did her best to bore holes in him with her eyes.

Brendan hesitated a split second, then gave Mrs. DiStefano his most rueful expression. "I'm so sorry, Mrs. DiStefano. I was the one who put that slug in your mailbox. I was being a dumb kid."

"You?" Mrs. DiStefano looked shocked. "I can't believe that."

"Really. I was five and I thought it was funny." A very small quirk at the corner of Brendan's mouth told Diana he still thought it was funny, but it quickly smoothed out. Regret radiated from his face. "I shouldn't have done it. I'm sorry."

"Oh, don't be, Brendan." Mrs. DiStefano gave him a bright smile. Diana had a feeling Brendan had gotten a lot of those smiles from the moms in the neighborhood. "It's sweet of you to cover for your brother, but you don't have to do that. It was such a long time ago. And anyway, what about our rear bumper? And our left tail light? Are you going to say those were your fault too?"

"No." Brendan looked embarrassed, which Diana was pleased to see. "That was Ian."

"Exactly. I hope he shapes up soon, for your parents' sake if not his own."

"Ian's fine the way he is," Diana began, but Mrs. DiStefano was speaking over her.

"Good luck at Yale, Diana. I hope you make the most of it."

"Thanks. I'll try."

"I promised Di a round of ping-pong. Great to see you, Mrs.

DiStefano. Happy Fourth." Brendan walked Diana away with a hand on her back.

"Did you have something to do with the DiStefanos' car?" she whispered as they approached the ping-pong table. It stood by the fence, away from the people thronging the pool and patio.

Brendan ran a hand over his hair. The gesture was so much like Ian's that she had to stop herself from brushing the hair off his forehead.

"I was in the Jeep. Ian was drunk at the wheel. I'd had a few."

"I see."

He shrugged, apology on his face. "Di, I tried just now."

"Try harder." Diana crossed her arms.

Brendan's eyes widened. She'd bet every dollar she was paying for the broken glassware that no girl had ever told Brendan to try harder before.

Taking the paddle he gave her, she turned it over. Ian was still busy at the grill, his bronzed chest smudged with charcoal. A few girls clustered around him, trying for his attention. But his gaze flicked away to meet Diana's, and the hot want there almost knocked her over.

Hiding. She was so sick of hiding. Dammit, she didn't want secrets anymore. She'd done so much already, but this...

She glanced at Brendan, bouncing the ball against the table with his paddle, his eyes amused again.

"You guys are so in wuv, you make me want to vomit," he said.

Diana snorted with laughter, fumbling the ball when he served it to her.

"Do it by the fence, okay? Far away from me." She sent the ball back to him. "Why are all your friends here? I thought the three of us were going to hang out."

Brendan shrugged. "Sorry. I told one or two people to stop by later before we go out. They came early, they brought a bunch of other people. You know how it goes."

She didn't, actually, but now wasn't the time to point out the differences between her and Brendan's social life. Did he not want to spend time with her and Ian? Was this the Brendan version of saying no?

She smacked the ball across the table, keeping an eye on the patio.

Ian was waving a barbecue fork around. He poked it toward one of the girls hovering nearby, and she jumped back with a screech and a laugh. But a second later, his eyes went back to Diana.

"Di," Brendan began. "This past month — Ian's been the happiest I've ever seen him. You're making him really happy."

"I'm really happy with him too." She was also fevered. On Fire. In a daze. "Have you ever felt like you, I don't know, just want to smash into someone and bury yourself and get all smushed together with them?"

Brendan raised his eyebrows. "No."

"Never?"

"Nope. Not at all. Sounds like you do."

"You do know I wouldn't talk about this with anyone else, right?" Ian kept drawing her gaze.

"I know, cutie." Brendan's voice was a little too patient. The ball bounced off the corner of the table. "Eyes on the ball."

"Don't tease me." She snatched up the ball from the grass and batted it towards him.

"Why not? He's still Ian who puts his laundry in with mine and leaves his dirty dishes in the sink."

"Uh-huh," she said distractedly.

Some kids from the neighborhood were swarming the grill. Ian motioned them to the front of the line and filled their plates. He was making faces at them, and their shrieks of laughter carried across the lawn.

"Aw, he's making those kids laugh," she sighed.

"Di." Brendan aimed a pointed look at her cleavage.

Oh shit, her ladybug dress had pulled away from the swell of her breast. One of the hickeys from Ian was peeking out. Fast as she could, she adjusted the tight fabric and scrambled for the ball again. Her breast throbbed, as much from Brendan's gaze as from Ian's mark.

"Rough night?" Brendan's dimples showed. Hazel eyes flicked to the heavy curves of her breasts again, less obviously, as if he didn't mean to look this time.

She blushed, very aware of the solid body of her boyfriend's twin at the other end of the ping-pong table. "You didn't hear all the details?"

"I didn't hear any of the details. Ian doesn't tell me things anymore. Especially about you. I guess we have some secrets from each other now."

"That's good, right?"

"It's the way it is."

Quiet fell. The only sounds between them were the bounce of the ball on the table and the clack of the paddles. Someone cranked up the music on the patio.

She wasn't looking away from Brendan now. Across the table, he raised an eyebrow at her.

I'm sorry, she wanted to say. Or, *you know what, Brendan? It is a good thing. Because you and Ian are two separate people. Or, Ian didn't give you any details, but I need to. Or...*

"Please don't tell me my top was pulled down this whole time," she blurted out.

"Okay, I won't tell you."

"Brendan..."

"It wasn't, Di. Don't worry."

The ball flew off the table toward the fence.

"Ugh, I'm sorry. I'm not paying attention." Diana knelt on the grass to find the ball. Brendan reached for it at the same time.

"No, my fault."

"Wait." She put her hand on his shoulder as they crouched on the grass. It was such a basic gesture. So simple. Brendan had probably rested his hand on hundreds of shoulders. But for a girl who wasn't a toucher, whose friends were still surprised when she grabbed them in a hug, it wasn't a simple gesture. It meant something. She didn't know if Brendan would understand that, but he looked down at her hand, then at her face, he had a funny expression.

The ping-pong table hid them from view. Brendan was close enough for her to whisper.

"I need to talk to you."

Brendan looked startled. "Anytime."

"Now. Alone. Please, Brendan? Don't brush me off this time."

Hazel eyes blinked, then cut to the people milling around the grill and the bodies thronging the pool.

"Go inside," he said softly. "We can talk in my room. Now, alone. I'll meet you in a few minutes."

"I— okay."

She swallowed a dozen things she wanted to say, threw one last glance at Ian flipping burgers, and headed for the O'Brians' back door.

Chapter Eleven

Diana's dress clung to her sweaty curves as she climbed the stairs. Brendan had taken charge again as naturally as breathing, she thought. And she'd followed his directions just like that. It hadn't occurred to her to argue.

She was alone in the house. The laughter and music of the barbecue were muffled.

At the top of the stairs, she turned right and pushed on the slightly open door.

Late afternoon sunlight streamed through the windows. Brendan kept his room neat and clean. The room was bigger than Ian's. This was the bedroom the twins had shared as kids.

Diana stopped in the corner where the bunk beds used to be.

Long ago, during a thunderstorm, she and the twins had built a blanket fort on the bottom bunk and whispered ghost stories over flashlights. At the most chilling moment of the scariest story, Ian had breathed down her neck like a monster. She'd screamed and tackled him, going straight for his armpits.

Ian had been aggressive — no surprise there. *Fight back, fight harder,* she'd kept telling herself, until they tumbled out of the blanket fort and Brendan called a truce. But it had come as a surprise that Brendan wasn't ticklish. At all.

Rows of trophies sparkled on the shelves over Brendan's dresser. Sports posters decorated the walls. A mini basketball hoop hung on the door above a UConn pennant.

Pausing by the full-length mirror, Diana smoothed her windblown bangs and eyed the deep line of her cleavage. She really was poured into the ladybug dress. The printed fabric covered her skin, and the hem hit her knees, but nothing was left to the imagination. No wonder that guy Keith had been hanging around like a hopeful puppy.

As she pressed her hands to the mirror, she felt Ian's mouth on her breasts, sucking each of her nipples to swollen hardness, devouring her skin. Ravenous, consuming her with sheer desire.

What would he say if she told him she was overwhelmed? That she loved last night, she didn't regret it, but she was so raw with feelings for him that she had no idea what to do? How did you put that into words? He'd been vulnerable afterwards. She'd seen it. Stripped as bare as she was.

She glanced at the closed door. Brendan would have a clear head. He'd probably tease her, but that was part of being a big brother. It would all be better after she talked to him.

Taking a deep breath, she walked over to the desk to look at Brendan's photos. They covered the wall in a collage. The twins were everywhere: shirtless, wearing tuxes, in their basketball uniforms, streaked with paint at someone else's game. Always together, always confident.

Her own face caught her eye, though she barely recognized herself in the blue cap and gown. She touched the picture Marissa had taken of the three of them at graduation.

Her cheeks were flushed, her eyes were bright behind her glasses, and her smile stretched from ear to ear. Her graduation cap was crooked as the twins sandwiched her. That was Ian on the left, a half-smile on his face, the faint shadow of a hickey on his neck, and his hand invisible behind her back. Her ass remembered his pinch. Brendan smiled broadly on her right, an affectionate arm slung around her shoulders.

And later that night, the two of them in her bed, inside her together…

Mixed in with the college photos were high school pictures: Brendan and Ian lifting weights, posing with gorgeous girls at prom, in motion on the court.

Diana stopped on a shot of the twins outside the school auditorium. Brendan wore a white dress shirt and striped tie. His face was clean-shaven, his arm around his brother. Ian wore a black hoodie, his jaw stubbled, his eyes bloodshot.

Both twins had the same half-smile, like they shared a secret. A lot of secrets.

Diana remembered that spring day near the end of her freshman year. Brendan was running for student body president, and everyone knew he'd win. She'd stared at him as he gave his speech, drinking in his handsome face and athletic body. She'd burned with envy at his total assurance. She'd missed him more than she had in a long time.

And, as she squeezed her knees together, feeling uncomfortably warm, she'd scanned the auditorium for Ian.

He sat in the front row, sprawled across three seats, a huge smile on his face as he watched his brother. He looked entertained, sure. But he also looked proud.

As Diana followed the edges of the collage, the pictures went back even further. The twins were twelve and riding their skateboards. They were ten and waving water pistols. Then she spotted a girl's heart-shaped face.

Wide blue eyes looked out from under dark bangs, and a kid's crooked grin — her grin — beamed fearlessly at the camera. She was bouncing between the twins on their trampoline, pool water dripping from their swimsuits.

Had this picture been on Brendan's wall all through high school? College? Or was it more recent?

She turned away. The striped student body president tie lay on the desk chair, the only mess in the room.

A poster above the bed made her grin. *Believe you can, and you're halfway there.* So Brendan.

A tall floor lamp stood near the bed. Inside the lampshade was a shadow.

Curious, Diana walked over to the lamp. When she reached inside, her fingers met plastic loops. She stared at what came out in her hand. Then she burst out laughing.

Handcuffs. Dangling from her fingers, made of that pale green glow-in-the-dark material. This was a joke. It had to be. For a costume, or something.

But Halloween was months away. And it was too easy to picture Brendan walking toward her, a persuasive smile on his face, holding those handcuffs.

She shook her head hard to clear it. Yet suddenly she felt herself lying on the big bed, Brendan's bed, hot and aroused, her bare curves on display, her arms stretched above her head. A naked twin knelt over her in the near-darkness. All she saw was the outline of his muscled body. Cuffs closed over her wrists, one at a time, with a soft but definite click.

"Ian?" she whispered. Fuck, her eyes were actually closed, and she'd said his name aloud. "Brendan?"

Not telling.

She knew the intimate tease in that low voice. Didn't she? Oh God, this was crazy. She strained at her bonds, her back arching. Ian — yes, it was Ian, it had to be — was running his hands all over her breasts. Squeezing the full swells, whispering the filthy things he was going to do to her.

And Jesus, more touch opened her thighs, gently but firmly. Brendan was stretched out next to her, his soothing hand on her cunt, stroking her swollen clit over and over. And the two of them were doing whatever they wanted with her while she ached for release...

Beg, Ian breathed. *Beg for what you really want.*

Steady footsteps sounded in the hall. Lightheaded, she slapped the handcuffs back inside the lamp, just as Brendan walked in the door. His amused expression turned her face even hotter.

"Glow in the dark?" she sniffed. "Really? I thought you had class."

Brendan chuckled, but his eyes flickered over the flush on her skin.

"You're as nosy as Ian is. No wonder you guys are perfect together." He took the cuffs out of the lamp and handed them back to her. "Here. Have a look."

"They look uncomfortable." She busied herself examining the cuffs, turning them over and trying out the mechanism that opened them. "Who would want to wear these?"

"No idea." Brendan's look of wide-eyed innocence could have belonged to his brother. "Maybe someone who likes being uncomfortable."

Her legs turned to jelly.

"Who would want that?"

Brendan's teasing voice floated past her ears. "Someone who likes being pushed. Someone who can handle more than she thought she could. Someone who wants to let go."

Jesus. Instinctively she reached out to him for support, and he put a hand on her back to steady her.

"You can get softer ones." Brendan sounded normal again. "You might like those better, Di." He took the cuffs from her and held them up to the light, like this was just a friendly chat with a big brother who dispensed kinky advice. "Wanna borrow them?"

She swallowed. "I— no. That's okay."

Brendan looked surprised. "You trust Ian, right?"

"Of course."

He grinned. "He'd probably let you put them on him, if you wanted to. He'd do a lot for you. You don't have to be scared, Di. It's really fun."

"Easy for you to say." Her face flamed. "Nothing scares you.

You're not even ticklish. And I'm a hundred per cent positive you're not the one wearing the handcuffs, so don't tell me about being scared."

Brendan's smile disappeared. "Do you have a problem with that?"

She crossed the room, restless and prickly. She'd felt raw all day. Overwhelmed, sick of secrets, desperate to keep them. Feelings were beating inside her, dying to get out. Her boyfriend's twin, standing there by the bed with his glow-in-the-dark handcuffs, made her want to snap.

"You always have to be in control," she burst out. "Don't you? Everything has to go your way."

"Not everything." Brendan watched her, his eyes alert.

"You asked a few people to 'drop by' today instead of hanging out with me and Ian. Because for whatever reason, you don't want to do that."

"I'm talking to you right now. Alone, like you asked."

The edge in Brendan's voice made her want more. Jesus, wasn't it enough that she'd pushed Ian to lose control? Her stomach was knotting, pressure hot behind her eyes.

"Okay. Thank you. So when are things going to change? Ian's trying, but you're not."

Hazel eyes widened. "What are you talking about?"

"The good twin-bad twin bullshit."

"It's not bullshit."

She ignored his warning tone. "It absolutely is. Tell the truth for once."

Brendan walked over to the desk and looked out the window. Blowing out a breath, he turned to meet her eyes. The charm was back, curving his lips in a winning smile.

"I just 'fessed up to putting a slug in the DiStefanos' mailbox. What more could you want?"

"Yeah, but you still think it's funny."

"Come on, Di. It was a giant slug. Of course it's funny." Brendan's dimples invited her to share the joke. "We were fucking five years old. It's in the past. Let it go."

"Says the boy whose wall is covered with old photos."

Brendan folded his arms over his chest. She'd used the wrong word. Brendan wasn't a boy any more than Ian was.

She pressed into the silence. "I looked at your pictures before you came in. You were so busy being wonderful. Did you really do his homework in high school? Because that is fucked up."

"Yes, Diana. I helped Ian in high school." Brendan was speaking very slowly. The space between them stretched tight. Those three feet felt like a rubber band, pulling her closer to Brendan and shooting her away. "You know why? Because Ian has trouble in school."

"I know that," she snapped. "Maybe he would have pulled it together on his own. He's doing that now."

"Because he gives a shit. He didn't then. He wasn't thinking about the future. Someone had to."

"So when you're not hanging on to the past, you're controlling the future? Do you ever just deal with the present?"

Brendan's mouth opened. Staring at his face, the tension bunching his muscles, she knew she'd pushed him to the end of his fuse.

"You don't know what you're saying, Diana. You think you understand the situation and how to handle it, but you don't. You're young, you're so fucking naive, you think everything is black and white, you're shit-smart but you know nothing about the world or anyone who's different than you, because you basically locked yourself in your goddamn room and lived and breathed school for six years and now you come out expecting to do everything."

"Brendan?" she gasped. She didn't believe her ears. "Fuck you. You said I could do anything when I graduated. Was that another line?"

"I've never fed you a line, Di." Brendan's voice was quiet now, vibrating with anger. "I've never lied to you. You think Ian's this victim, playing a part he never wanted to play. Would you believe me if I told you he was into it? That it was real?"

"It's not all of him."

"No, it's not. But it wasn't fake, either. He cut class because he wanted to, he smoked shit because he wanted to, he screwed more girls than even I can count because he wanted to."

"Okay." The room wavered around her. "I get it. You can stop now." She whirled toward the wall and covered her face with her hands.

"Jesus. Jesus Christ, I'm sorry." Brendan was in front of her, holding her shoulders. "I'm sorry, Di. I shouldn't have said that."

"No, I told you to be honest." She couldn't take her hands off her face. She couldn't breathe. "It's my fault."

"I went too far. That was shitty of me. He's always wanted you."

"I don't want to fight with you," she whispered. "I've never seen you lose your temper before."

Brendan laughed briefly. "That's because I don't."

"I just—" She let out a shaky breath. Then she grabbed him in a hug, hard.

Brendan was going to think she was crazy. But his arms went around her, pulling her close.

"It's not just that," she said into his chest. "It's everything."

"Shhh. Shhh, it's okay," he soothed. His voice was still urgent, but he rubbed her back in circles, her neck. She squeezed his waist, wanting the solidity. "Whatever it is, it's going to be okay."

"Can I tell you?"

"You can tell me anything."

"Ian took me really hard last night," she whispered.

For a minute, no one spoke.

Then — oh God. That was a definite throb against her belly. She kept her face pressed against his chest, not daring to react to the sudden erection between them.

Brendan stopped rubbing her back. He eased his body away from hers.

She forced herself to look up at him. *Please just be my big brother right now,* she thought, as hard as she could. *I need you to keep hugging me.*

"Don't let go," she said out loud.

Slowly, Brendan's hand flattened on her back. He held her carefully, like she was a time bomb about to detonate.

"Did you want Ian to take you that way?" he asked softly.

"Yes."

"Did you like it?" Brendan's hand moved into her hair.

She swallowed. "Yes," she breathed. "I liked it. Did he say anything to you?"

Dimples flickered in and out. "I saw the scratches on his back when he went to shower this morning. That was you, wasn't it, Di? It wasn't just Ian being rough. You were giving it right back to him."

"Yeah." The word came out on a long breath. "I started it. He took me to that boxing arena you guys sneaked off to when you were thirteen. The one he kept going back to." Brendan's startled expression reminded her that had been the twins' secret, but she rushed on. "I asked him to let it all out and show me everything. And he wanted me to lose all control. If we could have devoured each other, we would have. It was so much…it was so intense…oh God." She buried her face in Brendan's chest and squeezed her eyes shut. "I came so hard it scared me," she whispered. "I know it sounds crazy. But I don't know what to do. I can't talk about this with anyone but you."

Jesus, Brendan was rock-hard. His powerful arms circled her, his fingers tightened in her hair. And fuck — her heavy breasts pressed against his chest. She should step out of the circle of his arms, right now, but she stubbornly stayed in the hug.

Her eyes locked on his. "I love Ian so much, I don't know what to do sometimes."

"Yeah," Brendan said quietly. "Same."

Diana stared up at him. "I don't want things to be different."

"They already are, Di. It had to happen."

"Exactly." She rested her cheek against his chest. From the side, she saw herself in the mirror, in the embrace of a twin, making her head spin. "Everything's changing. So much has happened, and it's all so fast. It's good, but— I'm completely overwhelmed."

When she looked up, she met hazel eyes, as full of secrets as in the high school election photo on the wall.

"What do you want, Diana?" He pulled her head back, just a little, fingers twined in her hair.

Dear God, she'd expected Brendan to tell her how to handle last night. No, she'd hoped he would.

"I want things to stay the same for awhile," she murmured. "I want to go back and take all the best pieces from the past and bring them into now. I want the rest to disappear. I want everything to be better than it used to be."

"I want that too." Brendan held her gaze. Diana tried to relax into his touch, to forget about sex for two damn seconds, to be close. "But it's not possible."

Brendan's voice was still soft, but oh Jesus, the bulge pressing into her stomach was so hard.

"Can we get Ian in here?" Her throat was dry. "Because the three of us need to talk."

Through the bedroom door came the thuds of feet pounding up stairs. Voices carried down the hall, yelling and laughing — the twins' friends. Diana sprang back as Brendan dropped his arms.

"Fuck," he muttered. She could have sworn the other O'Brian brother stood a foot away from her, struggling for calm. She pulled damp hair off her neck, trying to breathe.

"Where'd B go?" someone hollered from the stairs.

"Betcha he's in his room with a girl. Let's break the door down."

Lightning-quick, Brendan pitched the handcuffs into the closet, pulled the door shut, and dashed back to give Diana's shoulder strap a firm tug upward. She hadn't even noticed it slipping down.

"Make them leave," she whispered. "Just get Ian."

"No time." Brendan swiped a hand over his hair. "It'll be fine. We'll talk later, I promise. Act normal."

"How do I do that, again?"

Brendan just patted her on the back, in a way that lived somewhere between brotherly and very much not.

The doorknob rattled. More voices filled the hall, along with Ian's laughter. An hour in the same place with no contact had driven her crazy. She needed to hold Ian's hand, feel his arms around her, get her head on straight. She needed to go back to Brendan as big brother — nothing more, nothing less.

As the door flew open and people poured in, Diana went straight to Ian. She hoped the twins' friends were too drunk to notice or care that she was the girl in Brendan's bedroom. She caught Ian's startled expression before she wrapped her arms around him like they'd been separated for a week. Standing on tiptoe, she gave him a good, long kiss. His shirt was still off. His bare back was sticky, sheened with sweat.

"Oh, so *that's* how it is," she heard Keith say.

Ian held her in the kiss a minute longer. When they separated, he glanced from her to Brendan, who was ushering everyone into the room with a big smile like he'd expected them to drop by.

"Everything okay?" he asked in a low tone. Diana nodded. Later, they'd talk. She wanted to believe Brendan so badly. Ian cupped her chin. Then a grin split his face. "Uh-huh," he said to Keith. "That's how it is."

Brendan's bedroom was suddenly very full, overflowing with the twins' friends. And everyone was looking. At least a dozen pairs of eyes were focused on her and Ian, mid-passionate reunion.

"Sorry, who are you?" one of the girls asked.

"Yeah, who's this, O'Brian?"

"I'm Diana Cooper. I live next door." Diana tried a smile. Even if she didn't know who the hell she was right now, one thing she could be sure of: she was herself.

"Hey, I remember her," another girl exclaimed. "She was valedictorian this year. My little brother was in her class. I'm Taylor," she added to Diana. "You're going to Yale, right? What are you doing with this lowlife?" Taylor pointed to Ian.

"She's my girlfriend." The grin hadn't left Ian's face. One solid arm draped over her shoulder. *Girlfriend.* The word made Diana fizz with nervous excitement from head to toe.

"Seriously? Valedictorian, Ivy League chick, with someone who doesn't know what school is? Is this a joke?"

"It's one of O'Brian's pranks, Tay." The guy who was speaking hooted with laughter. "How much did he pay you to go along with it?" he asked Diana.

"Not enough," she replied. The laughter made her breathe easier.

"You shit!" Taylor whacked Ian across the chest. "When were you going to tell us? B, did you know about this?"

Over by the closet, Brendan smiled easily. "Yeah, I knew. I've known for quite a while."

A glance between the twins caught and held. Then another girl came up to Brendan. Putting her arm around him, long hair swaying, she whispered in his ear. Diana looked away before she pictured those glow-in-the-dark handcuffs on someone else's wrists.

"I was going to tell you guys sometime." Ian whistled innocently and squeezed Diana's shoulders. "Maybe in six months. Diana spilled the beans."

She smiled brightly. "I guess I couldn't hold back anymore."

"Six months?" the prank guy muttered under his breath. "O'Brian's

optimistic."

"He looks really happy, Hunter," Taylor whispered. "And she looks like she can keep him in line."

"Yeah?" Hunter looked Diana over, obviously sizing her up.

"Guys, I can hear you," Ian said. He looked like nothing could touch him. "So can Diana."

She shrugged. "Hear what? I don't hear anything. Except how much your friends love you and their high opinion of you."

She was relieved to see smiles. People rearranged themselves, settling onto Brendan's bed and and the floor. Introductions were made, and she tried to keep track of a dozen names.

Ian guided her to a spot on the bed. As they settled against Brendan's pillows, he pulled her close, grinning at her like they hadn't gone together to a dark and wild place the night before. Maybe it was gone from his system. He'd let out the beast, and now she was left holding it.

Brendan opened his closet — no sign of the handcuffs — and deftly moved out a whole row of trophies to reveal a gleaming collection of bottles. Diana blinked at the stash of alcohol. Brendan's closet was as well-stocked as a liquor store, down to the mini-fridge in the corner and the stack of red plastic cups.

Out of the corner of her eye, she saw Alyssa, the girl who'd whispered to Brendan, motion him away from the bottles. She put her hands on his broad shoulders and pushed him into the desk chair. He smiled tolerantly and sat down, letting her perch on his lap.

"So where'd your graduation speech come from?" Taylor asked. She leaned toward Diana. "I'm not kidding, it really spoke to me. I could tell you'd lived what you were talking about, the whole 'try something that's just not you,' even though you looked like such a straight arrow."

"Thanks." Diana laughed and laced her fingers through Ian's. She needed to be alone with him, she needed to be alone with him and

Brendan, she needed to be alone with herself... "Honestly, Ian helped. I wrote it for him too."

"You did?" Taylor looked from Diana to Ian with a knowing smile. "She did?"

"Brendan helped too," Diana added quickly.

Brendan waved her away. "Nah. It was all Di and Ian."

Diana eyed him as he absently rubbed Alyssa's back. Brendan was drawing the same slow circles he'd drawn on her own back a few minutes ago, with none of the urgency. She wondered if Alyssa meant anything to him, if any of the girls Brendan had been with meant anything. If his gut had ever twisted for someone, if his heart had ever ached for someone.

Hunter grinned at her. "So is O'Brian wearing you out? You know he has a rep with the ladies. And that rep includes walking funny the next day."

Taylor gave his shoulder a shove. "You're so nasty."

Ian's arm tightened around Diana, and he gave Hunter a clear look of warning. The protection was nice, but did she really need it?

Diana shrugged. "Who looks more tired? Him or me?"

"Him. Definitely him." Hunter roared with laughter. "So what do you do when you're not wearing O'Brian out, Yale girl?"

She wished she could think of something cool and flippant to say, but all that came out was the truth. "I work in a bio lab."

"Doing what?" Everyone was looking at her now.

Diana pushed her hair behind her ears. "I run polymerase chain reactions. It's a way to make copies of a piece of DNA. It's really boring," she added quickly. "I just put test tubes in a machine and watch it all day."

For a minute there was dead silence. Then Taylor burst out laughing and grabbed Ian's arm.

"How'd *you* get *her*?"

Ian shrugged. "She likes my pretty face."

"You understand what I do," Diana protested. "We were talking about it the other night."

"O'Brian's good at faking it." Keith leaned over to pat her shoulder. Diana itched to swat his hand away.

"Which O'Brian do you mean?" she retorted. "'Cause Ian doesn't fake it."

Low chuckles and *oohs* ran around the room. Amusement showed on some faces, confusion on others. Even with the alcohol-loaded closet, Diana had been wondering how many of the twins' friends were in on the good twin-bad twin game. Now she had her answer: some, but not all. She caught Brendan's raised eyebrows as he met her quick glance.

Keith held up his hands, abashed. At the same time, Ian's pinch on her thigh made her twitch, while Brendan said affably, "Keith, come over here. We found some old yearbooks. You have to see this."

Keith went. The conversation shifted.

"What?" Diana whispered to Ian. His hand still rested on her thigh.

"Sweetheart." His low voice brushed her ear. "Take it easy."

"Do you *want* your friends to think you're dumb?" she whispered fiercely. Ian blinked. "Sorry. That came out so wrong."

"I want to see you not get in a brawl with Keith. Dude would sustain serious damage if you really lost your temper."

"Come on." She breathed a little easier. "You don't want to see that?"

"Never mind, I'd buy tickets. Front row." He nuzzled her ear.

"You can have tickets for free. But I only want to brawl with you." She squeezed his hand, grateful that Brendan had managed to distract everyone.

"That's more like it. Now? My room?"

God. Her body buzzed. She wanted to. But the knowing smiles on some of the faces, watching her and Ian sidelong, kept her from dragging him across the hall, into the privacy of his bedroom, and begging him to fuck her senseless.

"Later," she whispered. "Tonight."

Ian gave her the crooked smile that made her insides turn over. "You're the boss."

"Me? Uh-uh. You are."

"Not even close."

Brendan had opened his laptop and turned on some music. It filled the bedroom, mellow enough to let everyone talk, but a definite presence. Pulsing, filling the space with steady guitar.

Fortunately, she and Ian weren't the center of attention anymore. A handful of other people sprawled on the bed with them, trading gossip and talking about evening plans. Keith, Taylor, and Hunter were pawing through yearbooks and watching old videos on their phones, calling out high school memories as if they'd happened yesterday.

Brendan was completely focused on Alyssa, talking in low tones. His hand, toying with her long blonde hair, looked a lot less like just friends and a lot more like foreplay. Diana tried to ignore them, but she couldn't shake the feeling that the girl on Brendan's lap could be anyone.

"Diana?" A voice echoed down the hall — her mother's. "Are you up here, honey? Dad and I are leaving—"

Brendan's door, already open a crack, pushed open further. Mrs. Cooper stopped short, her eyes widening.

Diana froze. There was no disguising the way her bare leg draped over Ian's as they lounged on Brendan's bed, or how he was intimately playing with her fingers. There was no question which twin was entwined with her, shirtless, his hair messy, or which twin sat alert in his desk chair, fully dressed, his lap empty now.

Mrs. Cooper swiveled from Diana to Ian to Brendan, her mouth an O of shock. Brendan was already getting up. He must have reacted as soon as the door opened, because Alyssa stood to the side, giving

Diana a sympathetic look.

"Mrs. Cooper," he began smoothly, "I'm so glad you came in. Diana is—"

"—coming out to talk with you," Diana said over him. "Privately, Mom? In the hall."

A few snickers ran around the bedroom. She ignored them as she climbed off the bed. Ian got up too, and she shook her head slightly at him.

In the hall, her mother didn't try to keep her voice down. "Diana Cooper, did I just see what I thought I saw?'

"Yes, Mom. You did."

"Ian. You're...with Ian."

"Yes."

Mrs. Cooper's mouth opened and closed a few times. "When, exactly, were you planning to tell Dad and me?"

"Soon. Really soon." Diana pushed her bangs back. "I'm sorry."

"How long has this been going on?"

"Like this — a few weeks. Before that — all our lives. I just didn't know."

Mrs. Cooper took a deep breath. "I'm trying to stay calm, Diana. I'm really trying to stay calm."

"Mom, there's nothing wrong."

"Look. I know the twins are old friends," her mother began carefully. "And it's wonderful that you reconnected with them...both. But getting involved with Ian— Honey, he has a history. Years and years of bad behavior. He's not good for you. And God knows it's awkward when we're such close friends with his parents—"

"Mom, no. That's not true. Ian's just...so good." This wasn't easy. Her face was hot, and sweat pricked under her arms. She struggled to put everything she felt for Ian — the intensity, the need, the want, the rightness — into words. "He's incredibly loyal and caring and strong and he loves his family, and he's smart and hilarious and always wants to try new things, and I'm the happiest I've ever been with him, and I just...really...love him."

"Love who?" Her father's voice made her start. As she turned, it became obvious this wasn't a cozy Cooper family moment.

Mrs. O'Brian hovered nearby, holding a bowl of fresh salad, looking hopeful. Mr. O'Brian stood behind her at the top of the stairs, a broad smile on his face. Blood rushed to her cheeks when she saw both twins outside Brendan's open bedroom door. She hadn't even heard them come out, and of course everyone inside the bedroom was craning their necks to watch. Ian was trying for a casual lean against the doorframe, but his neck was red. Brendan's encouraging smile just made her own face hotter.

"That guy." She pointed to Ian. Literary magazine editor-in-chief, winner of two national writing awards, more poems in her journal than she'd ever admit to writing, and language had failed her completely.

Silence reigned. Ian cleared his throat.

"Diana's great, Mrs. Cooper. Mr. Cooper." He nodded to both her parents. "I've thought so for a long time."

Suddenly, everything was happening at once. Mrs. O'Brian threw her arms around Diana, as misty-eyed as if she and Ian had just announced their engagement. Mr. O'Brian clapped Ian on the back, his grin an echo of Brendan's. Diana's father asked, "How long, exactly, has this been going on?" And her mother tried to smile while casting some very misgiving looks at Ian. Her gaze turned pointedly to Diana, then Brendan. The message was clear: *Are you sure you've got the right twin?*

"Mrs. Cooper, I'm completely to blame." Brendan spread his hands with a conciliatory smile. "I'm the one who set them up. I just thought they'd fit so well together."

"Tone it down, Brendan," Ian muttered out of the side of his mouth. Quiet enough for just Brendan and Diana to hear.

"Brendan?" Mrs. Cooper demanded. "You're responsible for this? Diana, what is going on? Just a few weeks ago, Brendan was in your bed because you were having nightmares, which by the way, we still haven't discussed, but only because it was Brendan—"

"Brendan was in her bed?" Her father's jaw dropped.

Diana clamped her lips down on an unholy burst of laughter. The twins exchanged a swift glance. Mr. and Mrs. O'Brian traded matching glances that made it clear they knew exactly which twin had spent the night in her bed, and thank God they looked more amused than upset.

"It was a special situation, Mrs. Cooper." Ian's voice was as smooth now as when he'd impersonated his brother. His blush had faded. He dimpled at Diana's mother, his handsome face all apologetic assurance. Diana unhooked her glasses to rub her eyes. Seeing Ian take on Brendan's body language — it wasn't the first time, but it still made her head spin. "Diana's told me how much she appreciates that Brendan's like a big brother."

Mrs. Cooper blinked a few times. "Which is why I hope Brendan's around to keep an eye on things."

"Yes, Mom." Diana crossed her arms primly. "Brendan chaperones all our dates. We drink milk and watch cartoons, just like old times. And then he puts us down for a nap."

"Diana," her father began warningly. Her mother looked stunned, like a different Diana had taken her daughter's place. Ian coughed the fakest cough she'd ever heard into his hand, and Brendan's very broad smile told her he was hiding a burst of laughter. A few snickers floated from Brendan's bedroom. Mr. and Mrs. O'Brian just kept beaming.

"Sorry." Getting mouthy with her parents wouldn't help her case that Ian was doing her a world of good. "Really, I'm sorry that I didn't tell you. But I'm not sorry about Ian. Not at all."

"Ian really is a good boy, Julie," Mrs. O'Brian said reassuringly, putting an arm around Mrs. Cooper. "We've always hoped the right girl would bring out the best in him."

"Yes, of course." Diana's mother glanced from Ian, hands in his pockets, to Brendan nodding agreeably, then back to her daughter.

"You're a good boy, Ian," someone yelled from the bedroom. "You're the best boy." It sounded like Keith.

"Well, we have some talking to do. Quite a bit of talking." Her father nodded to everyone. "We should be getting home. Thanks for a great barbecue, as always."

Dammit. Diana seethed as her parents shepherded her out, calling goodbyes to the O'Brians. There was nothing she could do, except hold Ian's gaze as they left the hall. Brendan stood next to his brother, a hand on his shoulder.

"We don't need to be worried, do we, Stuart?" her mother asked on the way downstairs, in a tone that tried and failed to be a whisper. "They've known each other since they were babies. She'll get this out of her system and leave for Yale."

"Mom," Diana hissed. Everyone upstairs had heard, she was sure of it.

Her father, oblivious, gestured toward a window to the two backyards, side by side. "I'm just glad there's a seven-foot fence."

Chapter Twelve

Diana expected her own personal fireworks display once she got home with her parents. Instead, everyone was very quiet, which was worse. The three of them sat down at the kitchen table in ominous silence.

"All this time," her mother finally burst out. "All this time, you've been telling us you were out with your friends every night. Was it always a lie?"

"I've been with my friends too," Diana muttered. "But yeah, I've been spending time with Ian."

"Why didn't you tell us?"

"Because I knew you'd react like this."

Her mother threw up her hands. "When you came home late that one night, Dad said you didn't seem like yourself, but we thought we were imagining things. He got you high, didn't he? He's giving you drugs."

Jesus. She clutched her hair, then pulled off her glasses and skidded them across the table.

"You can call him Ian, okay? You can say his name. I really was with friends that night. I was making my own choices. Ian wasn't there. He had nothing to do with it."

"Your friends?" Her father looked at her in disbelief. "Your school friends? You were smoking pot with them?"

"Not *Marissa*," her mother broke in.

Diana fiddled with her glasses, then put them back on. The last thing she wanted was to get anyone in trouble. But this was so ridiculous.

"We were hanging out. I took a couple of hits. It's fine. We're adults."

"No, you're not," her father said.

"All this time, we thought there was nothing to worry about—" her mother began. "We've given you freedom because we thought you would never get in trouble."

"*Now* you're upset?" Diana exclaimed. "Where were you when I was in sixth grade?"

Her parents glanced at each other.

"What happened in sixth grade, Diana?" her father asked.

"Nothing that was my fault," she mumbled.

An uncomfortable silence hung over the table. Her parents' gazes were fixed on her, and she stared stubbornly back. Finally, she couldn't stand it anymore.

"Please just trust me. I'm eighteen. I know Ian, I know myself, I know what I'm doing."

Her father coughed. "*Do* you know Ian? Of course, you grew up together. But you painted a very rosy picture of a boy who's reckless. Impulsive. Maybe even dangerous. A troublemaker who's never taken anything seriously. Of course, he's an excellent athlete. But the attitude, the grades, the partying, the pranks, all spell bad news. Though actually—" Her father's voice warmed. "I heard about one prank that was really a feat of engineering, and very impressive to actually pull off—"

Mrs. Cooper shot her husband a warning look, and he trailed off.

"When Ian was growing up, he broke a different bone every week." Her voice rose. "In high school, he was with a different girl every week. I'm sure it's only gotten worse in college. You have focus, Diana. You are going places. So is Brendan."

"Mom, don't even," Diana interrupted.

"You need to think long-term. Everything you've worked so hard for, all your accomplishments—"

"Ian's accomplished." She glared at her parents. "You know what he does every day? He gets up, goes to the gym, and works out. Then he spends eight hours helping people get stronger. And he's really, really good at it. He's made my life better. He's serious about what he does, he's serious about sports, he's trying to turn school around, he wants to be the best he can be."

"Because of Brendan," her father said firmly. "We've heard this from his parents, over and over. Ian has always been hanging by a thread. He wouldn't have graduated high school without his brother; his parents are sure of it. If it weren't for Brendan, where do you think Ian would be?"

"Oh, I don't know," Diana snapped. "Maybe student body president. Maybe voted most likely to succeed. Maybe working for the effing mayor. And by the way, Brendan doesn't own Ian."

Both her parents stared at her. She blew out air and drummed her fingers on the table.

"Never mind," she muttered. "That's just stupid high school. It's all over and none of that matters."

Was she still mad at Brendan? If they hadn't been interrupted, if he'd gotten Ian in there for the three of them to talk... She had no idea how that conversation would have gone. The opportunity was probably lost forever now.

She crossed her legs, unwilling to break the silence. Her arms too, while she was at it.

"That's a very low-cut dress, Diana," her mother had to remark.

Jesus. Yes, her arms were crossed, and a deep valley of cleavage disappeared into the tight top of her ladybug dress. She wasn't even going to glance her dad's way right now.

"That's right, Mom. I have boobs. I'm tired of pretending they don't exist."

"Diana!" her mother exclaimed. Her father coughed more loudly. Her own face was hot now, but she made herself look him in the eye. She looked both her parents in the eye.

"You need to let me do this," she said quietly. "I love Ian. We're good together. And I like Brendan a lot," she added hastily, as her mother tried to break in, "and we would not be good together."

"It's not your responsibility to fix Ian," her dad begin.

"Nope. It's not. Ian doesn't need to be fixed."

"Sweetie." Her mother's voice softened. "We just want to make sure you're going in with open eyes. You're very inexperienced. You've never had a boyfriend. Unless there's more you're not telling us."

"No, Mom," Diana murmured. "Ian's my first."

Heat seeped through her skin, bringing back two male bodies surrounding her in lapping water. Bare toes digging into bark, blankets cushioning her back, trees rustling all around. Gasping when Ian took her virginity, her hands clutching his shoulders. Brendan cradling her head in his lap, then persuading her to let him in deep.

Inexperienced? She'd done more than her parents — or anyone — could ever know. But it had all happened so fast.

"Please believe me," she said quickly. "Ian's good to me, he's good for me, I'm good for him. And yes, I do know him. Maybe better than anyone else. Even Brendan."

Her parents glanced at each other, sighed, and shrugged.

"Well, if that's all settled—" Diana pushed back her chair.

"Why don't we spend a nice family evening together," her father said firmly. It wasn't a question.

"You're never home anymore," her mother pointed out. "You only have a few more weeks before you leave for Yale."

"Seven," Diana said under her breath. Now wasn't the time to argue. College seemed too close and too far away at the same time.

Determined to make the best of it, she popped a bowl of popcorn, settled on the couch in front of the TV between her parents, and sat through a movie with them.

A drama, or maybe it was a comedy. Or a musical, or a freaking cartoon, or a silent film. Her thoughts were everywhere but the screen.

When she looked down at the bowl in her lap, a few kernels lay at the bottom. Either she'd eaten all the popcorn, or her parents had. As soon as the show ended, she couldn't sit still any longer.

"This was fun. I'm glad we had some time together. Let's do it again soon." She stood and grabbed her purse. "I'm going for a bike ride now."

"So that's what you call it?" her mother sniffed. "What are you really planning to do?"

"Mom, the bike's name isn't Ian, I swear." The second the words left her mouth, she prayed her parents would hear them as completely innocent. "If I were heading out to meet him, I'd tell you. I don't have anything to hide now. Look, I'm leaving my phone at home." She felt in her purse for her phone and dropped it on the kitchen table. "I just need to breathe."

"Diana, I really think—"

"Let her, Julie," her father said suddenly.

Diana glanced at him, surprised by the support. "Thanks, Dad."

She stretched up to kiss his cheek. He nodded and shooed to the door. Impulsively, she hugged her mother too.

Mrs. Cooper held up her hands in a gesture to wait. "Diana, I realize we've never talked about boys or...ahem. Boys. There are things we should discuss, honey. If you have questions..."

"Mom, don't worry. I already know everything."

"She'll be fine," Diana heard her father say as the door closed. "Let her stretch her wings."

Outside, she pedaled past the neighbors' quiet lawns. Maple trees rustled overhead. Her ladybug dress was hiked up around her thighs. The breeze blew her hair straight back.

Standing on her pedals to coast down a hill, she felt her muscles stretch. What the hell did she know? A lot. Nothing at all. She remembered telling Ian, that first session in the gym: *I had no idea what I was doing.*

"I still don't," she said out loud.

Fireworks lit the velvet sky in bursts. Crackles punctuated the air as she biked in circles around the neighborhood. It felt good to be outside, alone and moving over the pavement.

Whatever had happened between her and Brendan in his bedroom was lust, nothing more. Nothing to take seriously. She loved Ian, really loved him. What she'd told her parents didn't begin to do that feeling justice.

That love was out in the open now, hard as she'd tried to protect it. Having it exposed just made her want to protect it more. She was so vulnerable after stripping down with Ian last night, she'd responded to Brendan, and—

Maybe Ian didn't need protection. Maybe she didn't either.

When her legs throbbed and she'd followed every street in the area, she pedaled back up the hill. Her pulse quickened, and she'd tired herself out on the ride, but the climb was easier than it used to be. The training with Ian was paying off. Her body was still soft and curvy, but stronger. She liked it.

Back home, she tiptoed into the dark kitchen. Her parents' muffled voices drifted down from upstairs. The microwave clock said a few minutes past ten.

Her phone was quiet. That was okay for now. She'd let it be. She didn't want to be that person who couldn't last two minutes without texting her significant other. But her body ached for Ian, and the ache threatened to overwhelm her.

Leaving her phone on the counter, she slipped out to the backyard.

*

181

Night breezes whispered as Diana stretched out on her sleeping bag. She hadn't bothered to take off her dress. Tiny dots starred the velvet sky, and soft music unwound from her record player.

Every so often, a low boom met her ears, and a shower of sparks brightened the darkness. The sound of splashes drifted over the fence.

Ian liked to swim at night. A few times, she'd joined him after everyone else was asleep, but she didn't begrudge him the alone time. She understood, maybe more than anyone else, and thank God Ian understood she needed to be alone sometimes too.

But after snarling "mine" last night, pretending there was nothing between them today, meeting the twins' friends, her mom bursting into Brendan's bedroom, and her father's comment "I'm just glad there's a seven-foot fence" — Ian deserved a surprise.

Standing, she peeled off her ladybug dress and let it fall on her sleeping bag. Her bra came next. She wriggled out of her lacy thong panties and kicked them away.

The grass was soft under her toes. Before she lost her nerve, she ran toward the fence.

Oh God. She was naked. Outside. At every jog, the bounce of her breasts reminded her, not to mention the air rushing around her bare skin.

Please let the spot still be here....yes. At the end of the fence, behind the bushes, lay a pile of rocks and extra boards. She and the twins had used it to climb back and forth when they were kids, and her parents had never bothered to clear it away.

Clambering onto the rocks, she grabbed the top of the fence and dug her toes into the boards. This would never work if she hadn't been training with Ian. So crazy, trying to climb the fence naked, but she was halfway up now and there was only one way to go. The top scraped her knees, but she made it over and dropped onto the O'Brians' lawn, panting and laughing and totally bare.

The laughter died on her lips when she saw two sleek male bodies in the pool. Pool toys bobbed on the water.

Crouching on the landscaped lawn, Diana crept close to a tree. The trunk wasn't big enough to conceal her, but if she didn't move, the twins might not notice. She'd stay here until they went inside, then climb the fence and text Ian.

She was spying, she knew. No better than when she'd watched the twins through her bedroom window. But the urge to see them together, in an unguarded moment, won out.

The muscled back streaking through the pool had to be Ian. The strong arms doing a steady breaststroke — Brendan. But the next minute, Ian grabbed the plastic raft nearby and flipped onto it in a lazy float. His swim trunks clung to his body.

"Aw yeahhhh." The edges of his deep voice were blurred. "This is it."

"As good as it's gonna get, huh?" Brendan's quiet chuckle might have been Ian's, but the lanterns strung on the patio highlighted the cleft in his chin.

"No, it's just gonna get better. And better. Unless Diana's parents decide to lock her up." Ian's words were definitely slurred.

"She told them what's what, bro. She's come so far. You've got nothing to worry about."

"Don't say you're so proud of her." Ian flung one arm back, his eyes on the fireworks exploding overhead.

"I am so proud of her. You are too, I can tell." Brendan swam to the side of the pool with easy strokes, picked up a beer bottle, and took a long swig. "You remember the first time? She was sweet. So shy. Just waiting to get wild."

His reminiscent smile sent goosebumps across Diana's skin. She shifted position on the grass, as quietly as possible.

Ian laughed, kicking off the side of the pool as the raft drifted close. "Are we talking about the same person? 'Cause I don't remember my girlfriend being shy with us, that time or any time."

Diana shivered at his words. Fresh-mown grass imprinted her knees. The constant breeze teased her nipples. "I remember a girl who was sick of playing the stone-cold fox and jumped at the chance to be herself."

"Remember anything else?"

Ian stretched out his arm. Brendan handed him a half-empty bottle. Tipping his head back, Ian drained it and tossed the bottle onto the grass.

"I remember thinking this wasn't real. Being inside her. Holding her. Sometimes I still think that."

"It's real," Diana called out impulsively.

Two heads swiveled to the back of the yard. She was kneeling in the shadows of the big trees, away from the patio lights, but she was naked and pale and it was only a matter of a second before both twins were staring at her.

Oh God. There was nothing to cover herself with, nothing to hide behind. Nothing for her to focus on, except the identical expressions of shock on two male faces.

Fuck, she was so exposed, her skin flamed from head to toe, and there was only one way to solve both problems. She stood up. She ran. Grass springing beneath her toes, she left her glasses on a chair and took a flying leap into the pool.

Water surrounded her. She blinked drops from her eyelashes. Male bodies closed in on both sides, crowding her.

"Hey," she breathed.

"What the fuck, Diana?" Ian's face was incredulous, his hands firm on her hips.

Brendan said nothing, but his pleased smile widened. He tucked a strand of wet hair behind her ear.

"I wanted to surprise you." She wriggled when Ian pinched her ass underwater. "I didn't know you were both out here."

"You want me to leave?" Brendan turned in the water.

"No," she said quickly. "Don't let me interrupt."

"You already have, baby." Ian's strong arm surrounded her. That was definitely another pinch on her ass. One hand clasped her head, pushing down.

"Ian!" she screeched, breaking free and sending an enormous splash in his direction as she kicked backwards. "Do that again and you'll regret it."

"No regrets." He plowed toward her with an evil grin.

A muscled arm wrapped around her soft bare stomach. Brendan pulled her out of the way and up against his body.

"Ian, be nice to your girlfriend," he called. His breath brushed her ear as he leaned close. "He's kind of drunk, Di," he whispered.

Diana twisted to look at Ian, whooping his way across the pool. Behind him, empty beer bottles lined the patio table.

"Those can't all be his," she whispered back.

"Don't worry." Brendan flashed her a dimpled smile. "Some of them are mine."

Before she could answer, a splash soaked her face.

"Ian, you asshole!" she shrieked. Dripping, barely able to see, she grabbed at the air. Her hair was plastered to her face. Her hands closed over broad shoulders, sleek and wet. "You're going down."

Two deep voices played around her ears. "Nice try" and "It's me, Di. Don't push."

"Oh, Brendan! Oops." She pushed down hard on his shoulders.

"Hey!" At Brendan's startled voice, she and Ian both dissolved into laughter. She was relieved to hear Brendan laughing too.

The next thing she knew, water churned around her. A hand squeezed her waist, another hand grasped her arm. A third hand wrapped around her hair. They were out in the middle of the pool, too deep to find her footing.

"You guys…" She blinked away drops of water, trying to see in the velvet night. "Play nice. Play fair." Her breath came in gasps between bursts of laughter.

"You started it." Ian's teasing voice tickled one ear.

"You should have listened to me, Di." Brendan's patient voice *brushed* the other. "I told you not to push."

"Maybe I'm not so good at doing what Brendan tells me any more," she giggled. Everything seemed very funny. "How about you do what I tell you?"

No one answered right away.

"Me or Brendan, baby?" A large hand slid over her ribs, tickling under her arm. She writhed and kicked. "Or both of us?"

"Brendan first." Both twins were moving swiftly around her in the water, and Jesus, she was caught between them. She wasn't sure whose hands were where. As she treaded water, her palm connected with a wet chest.

Yes...that was Brendan in front of her, his hand still wrapped around her hair. The lights from the patio deepened his dimples and the cleft in his chin. "C'mere. I've never seen your hair messed up. In my life."

Ian chuckled. "She has a point, bro."

Diana's body tightened when he squeezed her generous breast. It was underwater — but she was so close to Brendan — and fuck, completely naked — and this was all just innocent horseplay, right?

"I don't get messy." Brendan shrugged.

"Oh really?" Diana buried her fingers in his wet hair and tousled it gleefully.

Ian shook with laughter. Brendan's eyebrows lifted. Hands grabbed her, tickling her bare skin.

"Brendan! Not fair! I'm going to get you back so good..." She dug her fingers into his sides.

"Nope." Brendan whispered. "Not ticklish. But I remember how ticklish you are, Di." She thrashed between the twins. "Here..." He tickled under her arm, and she clamped her arm down on his hand, only to feel him slip out. "And here…" He tickled her belly, and she kicked. "And definitely here." Large fingers teased the sensitive skin behind her knee.

She tried to grab his hair and pull. Oh God, she was burning in the cool water, but that didn't have to matter, did it? Couldn't they play like innocent kids for now?

Fuck, her nipples were tight and rosy, her breasts totally exposed as she wriggled between the twins. And Ian was being no help at all, guffawing with laughter, wrapping one strong arm around her waist to hold her in place.

"I hate you, Ian," she panted.

"Aw, just me?"

"I hate Brendan too."

Brendan crooked her leg to tickle higher, and dammit, Ian just held her in place. The movement parted her thighs.

"Oh, no." Brendan smiled down at her as she wriggled. "Don't hate me, Di."

Water swirled between her legs, doing nothing to quench the fire building there. Brendan's fingers eased up on her tender skin just enough to make her gasp. She hoped neither twin heard.

"Oh my God— okay, Brendan— enough."

He let go. But two hard bodies kept brushing against her and she was laughing too hard to breathe. Her only option was to send a giant splash toward Brendan and take satisfaction in seeing him spluttering. Then Ian. Then…

A firm tug on her hair cut off her laughter, just as someone grasped her shoulders and spun her around.

"Ian, don't even try," she began.

"Not gonna dunk you, baby." Hot lips closed over hers. Instinctively, her mouth opened to Ian's rough kiss. The taste of beer on his tongue turned her on more than it had any right to. And her wet hair was still in someone's hand — Brendan's. She felt the light

187

pressure all the way up to her scalp.

"Drink with us, Di." Brendan's voice was so coaxing, like this was the most reasonable suggestion after she'd jumped naked into their pool. His hand went to her neck, stroking the spot just above her collarbone that was especially sensitive. God, Ian had sucked hard there last night while her bedroom spun around them, and she'd covered the rosy mark with makeup before seeing her parents, and the makeup must have washed off in the pool. Brendan pressed against her skin just enough to make it clear he'd guessed all this. "You need to get ready for college. Build up some tolerance, 'cause you don't have any."

She was already buzzed, warmth spreading through her limbs as water surrounded her bare skin. Drinking with the twins tonight — it was the best worst idea possible.

"No. Uh-uh. No way," she giggled. "Not after you tickled me like that. And I haven't gotten drunk since that night."

"Which night, baby?" Ian nipped her neck. His heart, beating faster against her back, told her he didn't need to ask.

Brendan slipped an arm around her. "Don't worry, Di," he murmured. "I won't tickle you again. Friends?"

"Friends."

"Good." Brendan massaged a path down her back. Her breath caught in surprise, and she glanced at Ian. The hazel gaze that met hers was all challenge.

"You know. That night." She broke off when Ian's teeth scraped her neck. A large hand cupped her bare ass, and she didn't know if it was his or Brendan's. "The club. The insanity. The— oh God." The hand squeezed her round flesh, kneading it. "The orgy," she breathed.

"Oh, *that* night." Ian's voice was loaded with tease, the edges fuzzed. "You mean, when you let a girl you didn't even know lick your sweet little pussy while you sucked Brendan off? And you made another girl come while I fucked you? That was so bad, Diana. You need a spanking. Can't believe I haven't given you one yet, for being such a slut."

She gasped with shock and arousal. When she looked over her shoulder at Brendan, his hazel eyes were intent.

"That's part of you, isn't it, Di? We were just bringing out what's there." He cupped her cheek understandingly. His mouth was almost close enough to kiss.

"Ye-e-es." She was dizzy with lust. "But I don't need it all again. Not the girls. Not the fight afterwards." A whimper left her mouth when the male hand exploring her ass slipped between her legs. Ian, definitely Ian. "I don't ever want to fight with either of you again," she whispered. "I don't want you guys to be mad at each other again. I—oh fuck!"

Her mound was being stroked, her thighs tickled. And she was shamelessly parting them, needing to rub her lush cunt against Ian's hand.

"It's okay, Di," Brendan murmured soothingly. More touches caressed her ass, and a warm palm cupped her belly. Jesus, in the swirling water, she couldn't tell which twin was stroking her where. "Don't worry. It's all okay. No more fighting."

"Promise? Please—" Thick fingers slid inside her pussy, and she quivered around their probing touch. "Ian! You're inside me."

Flushing hot, she glanced at Brendan. He just gave her a big-brotherly grin and ruffled her hair. But his hand, massaging her back, was slow and sensuous, and lust smoked from his eyes.

"Surprise." Ian licked her ear. His fingers eased out to rub her clit. "Want me to stop?"

"No-o-o… Don't stop."

He grunted, opening her swollen lips again. And dear Lord, Brendan was watching everything from close range, arousal written all over his face as he stroked her hair, his other hand firm on her waist underwater. With every gasp and twitch she gave from Ian fingering her, his brother squeezed her waist a little tighter.

"Brendan…" she whispered.

"Just feel it, Di." He ruffled her hair again. She groaned, relaxing around Ian's fingers, then tightening again, and heard his hiss. Jesus, this was so crazy, and as her breath sped up and she turned to look pleadingly into Brendan's eyes, he leaned close to murmur in her ear, "Is Ian going deep, baby?"

"Yes…"

"Good." His voice was so reassuring that she moaned out loud. "Let him give you what you need. We know you need a lot, sweetness."

"Oh God, oh God," she whimpered. "Yes."

Ian squeezed her cunt. "You told my brother about you and me last night, didn't you? You wanted him to know."

"Yessss," she gasped. "I—"

Her pussy was so full, fingers twisting inside her again and again, hot and slippery even as pool water lapped her legs. She bucked toward the invasion, welcoming it, begging for more.

"You guys," she panted. "I'm going to come."

She glanced back at Brendan. A beaming smile broke across his face. "Mm-hm, Di," was all he said.

"Fuck yeah, you are," Ian growled. His other arm wrapped tight around her lush curves, pulling her up against hard muscle. More fingers slipped into her wet valley, surrounding her swollen clit. "You're going to come right here for us."

"Reach up," Brendan coaxed. "Wrap your arms around my neck."

Confused, she stretched her arms up and behind her to twine around his neck. Her whole back arched, thrusting her heavy breasts toward Ian. He groaned. When she looked over her shoulder, hazel eyes, bright with arousal, roamed approvingly over the water running down the pale swells and large firm nipples.

"Just like that. Gorgeous, Di. You have such beautiful tits." His voice was lulling. Hypnotic. "Such beautiful, naked tits."

"Please—" she gasped. Ian's fingers were everywhere between her legs, pressing her clit, penetrating her satiny entrance, massaging her lips. Brendan's gaze stroked her bare curves. If he reached out and touched her breasts, oh God, she'd let him, she didn't know what she'd do, she'd completely lose it, she'd come right here...

Instead, a warm palm cupped the slight curve of her belly. Brendan rubbed her stomach gently, his hand above his brother's.

"Oh Jesus," she groaned.

"Feels good, doesn't it?" Brendan smiled at her.

"That's right, baby," Ian's heated whisper made her sob with need. "Don't hold back, Diana. Don't even try."

"Promise." She teetered on the verge of a blinding plunge of pleasure, but she had to say this. "Promise me we won't fight again."

"Promise, Di," Brendan said immediately. He gave her stomach an intimate squeeze. She moaned, her pussy contracting around Ian's fingers in a long spasm.

"Promise." Ian's voice was so low she barely heard it beneath her cry of release.

Pleasure spun outward, sweeping over her, blotting out the lights on the patio and the bobbing water and the firm bodies keeping her in place.

"Mmmmm." Brendan's sigh made her cry out again. "So good, Di. You're such a good girl. Every time you let go a little more..."

"Keep coming, Diana." Ian's rasp just made her burn hotter.

"Please— Oh, please—"

Brendan stroked her stomach. "I know, baby. You need to be fucked, don't you? You miss Ian when he's not inside you. You want him there all the time." A warm hand cupped her face.

"Yes." It was all she could say.

"Fuck, Diana," Ian groaned.

"Tell us, gorgeous."

"I do," she gasped. "I want Ian inside me all the time, all the way... And, oh fuck, it's scary to want someone that much...to love someone..." She was coming again, half-floating in the pool, and she felt like she was losing her mind. "Ian...Brendan..."

"I know, baby," Ian breathed in her ear. "I know how it feels."

"It's okay." Brendan held her face comfortingly. His free hand caressed her rounded hip. He smiled down at her, his eyes glazed with lust. "It's okay, sweetness. Just keep coming for us. I know you love Ian so much. Let him play with your sweet cunt. It'll feel good when he fucks you."

She shuddered in Ian's arms. The pleasure kept building, and she was gripping his wrist with one hand while clinging to Brendan's shoulder with the other.

"Are you going to watch?" she whispered.

Ian grunted softly, a grunt of pure need. Fingers thrust deep into her core, one last time, right as he bit her neck. Through her cry, she heard Brendan's deep voice, and the arousal underneath: "Do you want me to, Di?"

Oh God, this was crazy, and everything meant so much more now. Before she could answer, Ian kissed her hard. Her eyes closed as she fell into the kiss. Her hand reached back to meet a large palm — Brendan's. Two bodies slid over hers, the constant contact of hot skin and cool water driving her need to a fever pitch.

As waves churned around them, she was barely aware of Ian breaking the kiss, his hand leaving her pussy. Sure hands turned her around, pinning her soft curves between the twins.

In a daze, she blinked at a dimpled smile and a cleft in a chin. Brendan was in front of her, Ian behind her. Everything was slow and syrupy and relaxed now. She clasped Brendan's water-beaded shoulder. Her other hand reached back to twine in Ian's hair.

Ian was openly fondling her breasts, his hard body up against hers. Practically offering the voluptuous swells to his brother. His erection pressed into her ass. With each movement she made, his cock jerked between her soft cheeks. Thumbs rubbed her nipples into tight buds. Her moans rippled across the water.

Brendan watched through heavy-lidded eyes. His palms anchored her waist in the lapping pool. Every time she made a noise, he stroked her hips reassuringly.

This was right, this was wrong, she didn't know what this was. When Ian pinched down on both her nipples, she let out a shuddering sigh. Brendan's *Mmmmm* sent hot desire straight to her pussy.

"You bad girl," Ian rasped in her ear. "Jumping naked into our pool. Do you know what we do with naughty little girls like you?"

"I can guess," she whispered.

She arched toward Brendan, pushed back against Ian.

Effortlessly, Brendan closed the space between them. His hands moved to her hips, lifting her in the water. A hard bulge, bursting through his swim trunks, nestled against her naked pussy.

Oh dear God, she was so soaked and swollen and needy from the orgasms Ian had given her. On instinct, her legs wrapped around Brendan's waist. Her arm circled his neck, pulling him closer. Brendan was unmistakably grinding against her tender cunt, increasing the pressure.

She moaned softly, aroused beyond belief. As Ian massaged her exposed globes, his breathing heavy, her face tilted up towards Brendan's inch by inch. Her hand went into his hair. Brendan came closer in slow motion. Her lips parted, ready to take in his tongue.

There was a tug on her wrist. Ian, moving her hand down to the waistband of his swim trunks.

"Take these off, Diana." His voice was soaked with lust. "Strip me down. You're about to get royally fucked."

Oh God, she needed it all, she wanted it all, she'd told Brendan she was overwhelmed but her body was saying *who cares?*

But if the three of them ever...if anything ever happened again between them…

Not like this.

The certainty slammed her body. She hated it for being true, but it was. It couldn't be like this. Not with Ian drunk, Brendan close behind, *I'm just glad there's a seven-foot fence* echoing in her head and probably the twins' too.

Not after a night with Ian that had stripped them both to their core, a night when they'd growled *mine* over and over.

"You guys…" she panted. She pushed against Brendan's shoulder, right as his lips brushed hers. "Wait."

Ian's hands stilled on her breasts. Brendan blinked a few times, like he was waking up. Then his heavy-lidded eyes flicked all the way open.

Diana shook her head. "I can't," she whispered to Brendan.

"You can, Di." He smiled at her. "We know you can."

She tensed between the twins, trying to get control of her body. Her mind. She was sandwiched between two muscled bodies, two aroused cocks nudging her pussy and ass, with only a layer of wet swim trunks between the twins and her bare skin.

"I'm with Ian now."

Behind her, Ian let out a long breath.

The fog in Brendan's eyes cleared. He let go of her, moving back in the water. Regret flashed across his face. She knew he was choosing to let her see it.

"I'm sorry," she began, but he shook his head.

"Don't be. Things change, right? Nothing stays the same. It's the one thing you can count on."

"I guess," she murmured. She wanted to hear Ian speak, see his expression, but she only caught the mirror of it in Brendan's face as his gaze flicked up to meet his brother's.

"Happy Independence Day, Di." Brendan kissed her cheek.

She pecked him back, blushing furiously, her skin burning where

Ian held her. A whimper left her lips, and Brendan flashed her a dimpled smile. The cleft in his chin was close enough to lick.

Splashes ruffled the water. Ian's arms tightened around her as Brendan swam to the side of the pool, heaved himself out, and strolled across the patio, sporting a very obvious bulge in his swim trunks.

In no apparent rush, he picked up a towel, wrapped it around his neck, and let himself into the house. The screen door opened and closed softly behind him.

"Diana." Ian's voice was quiet behind her, less slurred. "I know that was pretty fucking crazy. Are you okay? 'Cause—"

"Out. Now." She broke free of his embrace, need swirling through her body, and climbed out of the pool, reaching for Ian to follow. "I need you now. We can talk after."

She didn't know what she would say, or what the hell had just happened. All she knew, as they raced across the grass to the treehouse, her fingers linked with Ian's, was that she wanted him everywhere right now.

"Are you still drunk?" she panted. She was worried, but Ian stayed steady as he clambered up the slats on the trunk and held out a strong hand to help her into the treehouse.

"Sober enough to fuck you, baby."

"You better be," Diana breathed.

He pushed her backwards onto the soft pile of blankets that still covered the treehouse floor. His wet hands all over her yielding curves, squeezing her breasts, massaging her sensitive folds, were driving her insane. She stroked his damp chest, the touch her only guide at first in the near-darkness.

"You could have had both of us." Ian's voice was urgent in her ear. "You wanted it."

"Yes. I wanted it." She cupped his face in her hands. "But I love you."

"Diana..." he groaned softly. "Sweetheart."

"I just want to feel you everywhere," she whispered. "I want you to come all over me."

"You're going to." A powerful arm surrounded her, pulling her tight against Ian's hard body as he stretched out full length next to her. She buried her face in his warm shoulder, tasting skin wet from the pool, as his hand worked between her legs.

"Did you mean what you said?" he whispered. "About it being scary to want someone so bad?"

"Yes." Her legs opened to him, allowing him access to every nook and crevice, and God, her thighs were trembling. She stroked his wrist. "It's scary to love you so much."

He swore. "Yeah. It so fucking is."

"Ian—" she gasped when pressure met her clit, rubbing the exposed bud in firm circles. "I don't know anything. I have no idea what I'm doing."

"You like it that way, don't you?" His possessive touch on her silky pussy was driving her insane. "You like not knowing everything the way you do in the rest of your life. You like being on the edge of what you can handle, dirty girl. You like pushing yourself there, or me doing it for you. Am I right?"

"You're — you're not wrong." She kissed his neck.

"Didn't think so." A finger suddenly slipped inside her. He was just using one, but his probing touch was so intimate that her whole body cried out for more.

Her hands roamed over Ian's sculpted back and shoulders. God, his neck tasted delicious, salty and warm, and she just needed to wrap her mouth around it... His pained grunt of arousal told her to suck harder.

"You like the edge too," she managed when she pulled back

"You always knew that." White teeth flashed at her in the dark. "Why'd you hang out with us? I got you excited, and Brendan made you feel juuust safe enough to keep coming over."

"Are we talking about when we were kids?" she panted. "Or more recently?"

"Do I have to choose?" His hands left her body, and she moaned in protest. Ian's low chuckle met her ears. She felt him climbing over her, and silky flesh brushed her lips.

"Suck me, love," he ordered.

Jesus, there was a time when taking orders from Ian O'Brian would have seemed like the worst fate imaginable. Now, the simple command sent a wave of need over her.

Eagerly, she took him in, licking his velvet cock. The outline of his chest loomed above her face. Ian was fucking her mouth, cursing softly as she sucked. She was just getting into it, wrapping her hand around his shaft, caressing his heavy balls, urging him on with her tongue, when he pulled free of her lips with a soft pop and moved down her body.

Thickness nudged her opening, then plunged in.

"Diana. So fucking perfect." He held her tightly, unmoving, his cock fully buried in her clasping cunt.

"No, you are." She squeezed him as hard as she could, with her arms and legs and pussy muscles. Ian grunted, hugging her even closer.

"Do you need me to go easy on you, baby? After last night?"

"Another time. I want all of you."

He groaned, but held still.

"Really? Your sweet pussy isn't too sore?"

"A little," she admitted, and gasped when his cock throbbed inside her. But all he did was brush her bangs off her forehead.

"What you said today," he whispered, still unmoving. "In the hall."

"I meant it." She pulled back to stare into his eyes. "I meant every word." To get the message across, she buried her fingers in his hair and tugged. Ian's eyes opened wide, and his heavy body seized on top of

197

hers, his cock jerking again in her tight embrace. "You're good, Ian. You're so good. You're all good."

His animal growl sent a rush of heat down her whole body. "And you're bad, Diana." He gave her a wicked smile. "You're so bad."

Flexing his hips, he slammed his cock into her wetness. Diana cried out, digging her fingers into his back.

"Harder, Ian," she pleaded.

Fingers curled in her dark hair, pulling. When her head fell to the side, a hot mouth closed on her neck, sucking the soft skin. The treehouse tipped under her. She was so open to Ian, so full of his cock, shuddering from his hard, hard thrusts and his teeth on her neck.

"Dirty girl," he growled. One firm hand gripped her ass, angling her so he went deeper. Diana gasped when his cock bumped her cervix. "You insatiable little bitch. I love you."

Oh God, his crude words sent ripples of painful arousal over her body, and she was so close to coming, and right on the edge of her orgasm, Ian pulled out.

His hand blurred on his cock, the glossy rod emerging from his fist. Desire contorted his face, and his whispers were all around her.

"Fuck yes, baby, take my cum. All over your sexy body. Spread your legs, bad girl."

She obeyed, shaking with excitement. A spurt of warm liquid streamed over her breasts. When the next jet of cum hit her clit, she cried out. More cum ran down her lips. She was beyond wet, and when large fingers met her folds, she lifted her hips, the need building.

"Don't stop..."

"Come for me, you hot slut," he rasped. He was using steady pressure, rubbing their juices firmly into her cunt. Caresses on her clit made her back arch. "Soaked in my cum like I've always wanted you to be."

"Yesssss."

She felt unbelievably open to Ian, trusting him to handle her most tender places. Floating in air, sinking into darkness, there was only his hot skin on hers, until she peaked. Sensations swirled, rushing over her body, spiraling from Ian's fingers inside her.

When he withdrew, she felt like jelly, puddled on the blankets. But she managed to turn on her side and let Ian spoon her. His head rested against her shoulder, his body heavy and relaxed behind hers. Diana sighed and snuggled closer. A brief twinge of soreness made her wince.

"Oooh…" She shifted, squeezing her thighs together.

Ian stroked her hip. "Okay?"

"Mm-hm. Better than okay."

"Good." He wrapped his arms more firmly around her.

Crickets chirped rhythmically in the warm night air. Ian smelled like pool water. His damp hair tickled Diana's cheek, and his breathing, slow and even, felt warm on her neck. Her nipples tingled, wet with his cum.

The treehouse was dark and quiet. Safe. Just big enough for them to lie down together.

"Do I need to be worried?" she murmured.

"No." Ian sounded half-asleep.

"Do you even know what I'm talking about?"

"No."

"All those empty beer bottles on the patio."

Ian lifted his head. Diana turned to see him. There was just enough light from the lanterns, coming through the treehouse door, to show his white grin.

"Oh, you mean Brendan's drinking problem?"

"Ian…"

"Don't worry, baby. My brother holds his liquor better than anyone I know."

"I'm talking about you. Not Brendan."

"Diana, listen." Ian rolled into his back. Stars peeked through the slats in the treehouse roof. "This was nothing, believe me. And it's the most I've had since we got together."

She stroked one fingertip over his arm. "My parents are wrong," she said softly. "They just don't know it yet."

Ian whispered into her neck, pulling her into his arms again. "No parents in the treehouse, Diana."

"No girls either. Right? I remember the sign you put up when we were kids. Brendan tried to get you to take it down."

"Yeah, well, I make an exception if they're naked." Ian's wicked smile tempted her to laugh with him. Instead, Diana flopped onto her back and blew out a breath of frustration.

"I am never going to catch up with you guys."

"Why would you want to?" Ian stared at her.

"You've done so much—"

"And I don't even remember it all. You don't want that."

"How many girls have you brought up here?" Diana gazed around the treehouse as she lay in Ian's arms. "You can tell me. I want to know."

"One. You."

"No, really."

"Really." Ian turned to face her, his hazel eyes serious. "Diana, don't try to be like me. Don't try to be like Brendan either. We're us. You're you."

She thought it over. "I just want to be myself. Don't you?"

Silence. "With you, yeah." Something about Ian's face…the way he was looking at her…made her breath catch.

"Look, about tonight," she began.

"Tonight. Okay. Me and Brendan were pretty drunk. You were naked and burning up the pool. There were fireworks." He gave her a crooked grin. "What's your excuse?"

"Do I need one?"

"Nah. You're just crazy." When he tried to pull her in for a kiss, she stopped him with a finger on his lips.

"Seriously, what happened tonight? Did you want things to go further? Did you want to have sex with me in front of Brendan? You were practically showing me off to him."

He rubbed his damp hair, visibly uncomfortable. "I wasn't thinking about it like that," he said finally. "I guess it felt natural. It was happening, and it was hot, but I was glad when you stopped it."

"That's fair," she murmured. Someday, maybe, she'd tell Ian about her dream, where he was fire and Brendan was air. Or not. The dream was smoke, and she shouldn't try to chase it. "I had a weird conversation with Brendan in his room this afternoon."

"You mean, when you found my brother's cheap-ass handcuffs?"

Diana exploded with laughter. Ian's body shook against hers. "I— yeah. He told you?"

Ian caught his breath. "I come into his bedroom. You're bright red and Brendan gives me an 'everything's fine' look. Yeah, he told me." He stroked her back, settling on her rounded ass. Diana shivered when he smacked it lightly. "Did they turn you on?"

"They're silly," Diana said quickly. "Over the top. Too crazy for me."

"Hmmm." One large finger traced her breast. She squeezed his waist. "Didn't know there was such a thing."

"You?"

"It's hot once in a while. Brendan's really into it. He loves being in control. Big surprise there." Ian nuzzled her neck.

"Is he going to be okay?"

Ian laughed softly. "Sweetheart, Brendan's always okay."

"Always? Because I don't think that's true. As much as he wants people to think so."

The treehouse was quiet. Her fingers tangled in his hair. "Yeah. You're right. But Diana, I promise he was okay tonight. He understood. So you gave him a case of blue balls —"

"Oh, that's my fault?" Diana interrupted.

Ian chuckled. "But I guarantee he called someone else to take care of it. Girls like Brendan a lot."

"I've noticed."

Her mind flashed to a beautiful girl kneeling in front of Brendan, eagerly sucking his cock while he stroked her hair. Brendan turning her over, caressing her from behind until he coaxed her to a shaking orgasm. Handcuffs, locking her wrists to the bed while he murmured words of encouragement, then fucked her into a frenzy.

A girl with a face that could be anyone's.

She nestled closer to Ian, opening her thighs to take his leg between hers. Hot as the fantasy was, she had to wonder: *what about someone to love him?*

Ian brushed her wet bangs off her forehead. "Brendan doesn't work like you or me. There's not a lot that bothers him. You didn't hurt his feelings, baby."

"Maybe not. I suppose he doesn't allow much to hurt him." She laced her fingers through Ian's. "Except you."

Silence. "Guess so," he said finally. "That's why we've made agreements."

Chapter Thirteen

"Fuck me. Is that an O'Brian twin standing in the doorway?" Janelle craned her neck, followed by the rest of the group standing by the stage. "What's he doing here alone?"

Diana glanced at the tall male figure just inside the door. Ian surveyed the crowded club, his hands in his pockets, but his eyes didn't catch on hers — yet. She was surrounded by her friends. Everyone from her year who'd been on the literary magazine staff was here, along with half the people from her AP classes. Onstage, Shaun and his band were doing a sound check, fiddling with microphones and amps.

It was her turn for a surprise date, and this was probably an evil move on her part. But she'd been caught so off-guard meeting the twins' friends on the Fourth of July, even if it had been Brendan's fault, that she couldn't resist inviting Ian to see Shaun's band play tonight. After all, her friends had asked her to.

They still didn't know. The barbecue had pushed her relationship into the open with her parents, the O'Brians, and the twins' friends, but she'd kept the news from her own friends, even Marissa. She'd wanted to hang on to that last piece of privacy.

But it was the beginning of August now. She'd leave for Yale in three weeks, and there was only so much she could control — with Ian, with the rest of her life.

"What's he doing here, period?" Marissa repositioned herself to get a better view of Ian, leaning on their friend Lin.

"Damn, he's fine. They just improve with age. I can't tell which one it is." Janelle was practically jumping up and down.

"Whoa there." David put a hand on her shoulder.

Everyone who was a friend of a friend was here, which meant that Alex Noriega stood a few feet away from her. Diana hadn't run into him over the summer. She'd said hello and returned his hug, aware that most of her friends were watching her and expecting some kind of reaction.

"Does it matter which one it is?" Lin asked.

"Sure it matters. If it's Ian, we're three minutes away from the club going up in an explosion, and Shaun's band hasn't played yet."

"Diana, can you tell? What's your hot neighbor doing here?"

She shrugged. "Maybe he wanted to hear some good music. Obviously Shaun's show is the place to be."

"I think it's Brendan." Marissa hopped up on the stage and assessed the figure in the doorway. "He looks too happy to be Ian."

Brendan. As far as Brendan was concerned, it was like the Fourth of July had never happened. Except that their good-morning hug ritual went from affectionately sensual to one hundred per cent unsexy bear hugs, and when he ruffled her hair, it left her wanting to check a mirror afterwards.

As Brendan had suggested, she and Ian had gone on the world's most awkward double date with him and his work friend. Katherine was out of college, pretty and polished, and looked unimpressed as Diana and Ian bickered over appetizers and got in a napkin fight.

Brendan had joked about being at the kids' table, and Diana had to resist the urge to pull off his tie, lash him to his chair, and show him there weren't any kids here. That made her think of the handcuffs in his bedroom, so she switched the daydream to an innocent ice fight that involved her drink going down Brendan's pants...no, still not innocent.

Ian had just looked amused by the whole thing, and when she

grumbled afterwards about Brendan's girlfriend being boring, he assured her it wouldn't last long.

She smoothed her postcard-printed dress and occupied herself with a swipe of lip gloss, not ready to wave to Ian just yet.

"It's Ian," she announced. "Their walks are different, and Brendan would never wear that muscle tee to a club."

"It's hot in here. Right?" Lin nudged Janelle. "I think that shirt needs to come off."

Ian was squinting through the crowd, looking for her. She had under a minute and a half to do what she needed to do.

She beckoned Marissa down from the stage and put an arm around her. "That's the boy," she whispered.

"What? Which boy?" Marissa was still standing on tiptoe, openly checking Ian out.

"Ian. He's the boy."

"WHAT?" Marissa kept her voice to a whisper, but it felt like a shout. "Ian O'Brian? You're shitting me."

"I'm not."

"You are."

"I promise you, I'm not."

"What— How— Jesus, Diana, why didn't you tell me?"

"I'm telling you now. I invited him tonight."

"Oh. My. God. Oh my fucking God. You and Ian O'Brian." Marissa's eyes took up half her face. Diana turned quickly toward the doorway. Ian must have spotted her, because he was making his way through the crowd. She'd been right: Marissa was losing her shit. "I can't even process this! You should have told Janelle. She's going to asphyxiate, and it'll be your fault, and I'm making you call 911 when she does."

"She'll be fine." Diana squeezed Marissa's hand. "Everything's going to be fine. I promise. It's just Ian."

"*Just* Ian?"

"Oh my God." Janelle gulped audibly on her other side.

Diana felt a hand on her back. Not Marissa's. Not Janelle's. Ian was standing over her.

"Hi." He nodded around at her friends. Everyone was gaping at him. "Hey, babe." Leaning down, he kissed Diana on the lips.

"What the fuck," someone breathed.

"Guys, this is my boyfriend Ian." Diana wrapped her arm around his waist. Stunned silence greeted her announcement. Shock showed on every face.

Yes, she was evil, springing the news on her friends like this. And God knows the twins were used to being stared at, but she felt a little bad putting Ian through such intense scrutiny. She had to say, though: she was enjoying this moment.

"Nuh-uh," Shaun said finally from the stage above them, guitar dangling from his hand. "No, he's not. It's a prank. 'Cause you're neighbors and all. Good one, Diana. Except not, because it's completely unbelievable."

The twins' friends had had the same reaction. At least their friends had one thing in common.

"No prank here." Ian flashed a dimpled smile, all charm, and gave Diana's shoulders a squeeze. "You're Marissa, right?" Marissa waved, her eyes still wide. "And Janelle."

"You know my name?" Janelle squeaked. Diana gave her a pinch. "Hey!"

"You're taking this too far," Diana whispered. "Don't feed his ego."

"*I'm* taking this too far?" Janelle didn't bother to lower her voice. "I'm going to die, and it's all your fault. But first I have to kill you. Why didn't you tell me?"

"Alex. Good to see you again." Ian nodded to Alex. Alex didn't look too happy, but he nodded back. Automatically, Diana made the rest of the introductions. It wasn't easy, with Janelle practically panting on one side of her, Marissa making comments under her breath on the other, and Ian's hand on her back. When she finished, everyone still looked stunned.

"Excuse me," Janelle said loudly. "I think I speak for everyone when I ask: how the hell did this happen?"

Diana blinked. There were so many eyes on her.

"It just happened," she began.

"I still don't believe it's real," Shaun muttered. Marissa gave him a look.

"You know," Diana went on, ignoring him. "We're neighbors. When Ian and Brendan came home from college in May, we started hanging out. Things just..." She waved her hand vaguely. "...went from there."

Alex was peering at her, a little more closely than she would have liked. "I thought you said Ian was like your annoying older brother."

"Well, he's annoying." Diana reached for the plastic cup in Ian's hand and took a drink. She'd expected beer, but she tasted ginger ale. "And he's older."

Janelle crossed her arms. "So next you're going to tell us you're dating Brendan too."

Diana gulped Ian's soda. "Ian's enough for me. More than enough. I have my hands full."

Good thing it was dark in the club, because her cheeks were hot. A chord rang out from the stage. Shaun's band was starting. Her friends cheered, and the attention left her and Ian. Diana breathed easier, but when she turned to the right, Marissa was still looking at her.

"What?" Diana asked. Ian's hand tightened on her waist, and she sucked in her breath.

Marissa leaned in. "Anal lube," she whispered in Diana's ear.

Diana spluttered through a mouthful of ginger ale. Ian took the cup out of her hand.

"Get over it," she whispered back.

"You expect me to get over it when Ian O'Brian's fucked you up the ass? At least now it all makes sense. If anyone would wanna do that, and could talk a girl into it, it would be him."

"*Shush,*" Diana hissed. Thank God Shaun's band was loud. "He didn't talk me into it. I asked him to."

And his twin had a lot to do with it too. She clenched her thighs together, remembering Brendan teasing her, keeping her on the edge, holding her wrists with one hand to keep her from touching herself. *You're worse than Ian,* she'd moaned. *Maybe,* he'd replied.

"Is he good?" Marissa squeezed her arm.

"Yes," Diana whispered. Ian was eyeing the two of them, an eyebrow raised. "That's all I'm going to say about it."

When Marissa let go of her arm, Ian leaned close. His breath tickled her other ear. "So you didn't tell your friends."

"I liked the secret," she confessed. "Shaun was excited to play this show tonight, and back at the beginning of the summer, right before I surprised you at the gym, everyone was saying, 'Invite your hot neighbors, Diana. We know they're like your brothers, but we like the view.' I guess I wanted some drama."

"You got it."

"Are you mad?" she asked softly. "Everyone staring at you — I know you're probably used to it, but still."

Ian shrugged a bulky arm against hers. He rested his hand on the back of her neck. "I guess I'm used to it. Brendan's the one who likes the attention. He eats it up for breakfast, lunch, and dinner, even though he'd swear up and down that he doesn't." When his hand closed over the back of her neck, she sighed and leaned against him. "I'm not mad. Girls before now—" He broke off.

"What?"

"They told their friends. Everything, if you know what I'm saying."

"What does it feel like to be talked about all the time? I mean, I know what it's like to be teased." The words left her mouth now without any pain. The year away had faded. "But what about everyone acting like they know you and want a piece of you?"

"It messes with your head." Ian ran a hand over his hair, and she stretched up to kiss him. "I really like being with you, babe. Let's leave it at that."

*

Her parents rounded out the summer by insisting that Ian come over for dinner. Of course she'd be meeting so many new people at Yale, they pointed out, but she'd spent a lot of time with Ian this summer, and it was only polite to have him over. Dinner together would give them all the opportunity for a nice chat.

Everything about this idea made Diana nervous. But over the past few weeks, she'd been pleasantly surprised: after the fireworks on the Fourth of July, her parents had been almost laid-back. At least, for her parents.

They did want to know when she was out with Ian, and her mother kept dropping unsubtle hints about Brendan's manly charms. But when they saw she was staying on track — with her job at the lab, with submitting her poetry for publication in online magazines — they didn't clamp down.

She still slept in her backyard most nights, and Ian still climbed the fence, or took her out in the Jeep. He'd snuck her into the treehouse again; his room, too, and his bed felt like a luxury.

As she crossed off each day on the calendar, college seemed more real. More exciting. She'd looked up the bus schedules between Yale and UConn. Staying with Ian in the twins' apartment for an entire weekend would be pretty good compensation for spending the week apart.

But dinner with her parents and Ian involved a new level of

pressure. She came straight home from the lab to prepare, because she'd had the brilliant idea to make the dinner herself, and when her parents got home from work and saw every pot and pan in use, they did flip out.

Ian showed up in a shirt and tie obviously borrowed from Brendan, which would have made her fall over laughing if he weren't so damn quiet and collected and eerily polite. A pitcher of iced tea stood on the counter, and she wanted to swipe it with her elbow just to have something go wrong.

The first fifteen minutes were exquisitely awkward. Ian didn't even blink when she nudged his foot under the table, and everyone was grasping for conversation.

Diana had informed her parents beforehand that they weren't allowed to tell embarrassing stories about Ian as a kid or discuss her glowing future and accomplishments. This left her mom and dad at a loss, until they figured out that they could tell embarrassing stories about Diana as a kid and discuss Ian's future and accomplishments.

Somehow, they made it through the evening. Her parents didn't exactly embrace Ian with open arms, but at least everyone was smiling by the time they said goodbye, and her mom only mentioned Brendan a few times.

Late that night, as she lay in Ian's arms in the backyard and they traded soft conversation, the calendar kept rolling through her mind. Three days. Three days until she left for Yale, where everything would change again.

Chapter Fourteen

Diana sagged into her dorm room desk chair. It was Saturday afternoon. She'd arrived at Yale yesterday morning, ready for a full day of orientation. After she'd settled in and waved goodbye to her mom and dad, she'd thrown herself into meeting people. She'd gone to every activity, stayed out late Friday night, and chugged coffee this morning so she'd be ready for more.

And it was great. It was fantastic. It was everything she'd hoped for, and she just really needed a nap now.

The bed across from hers was empty. No sheets, no pillows, no blankets. Whoever her roommate was, she hadn't shown up. Privately, Diana was keeping her fingers crossed that she'd have the place to herself.

Not that she was alone right now. Two guys were making themselves comfortable in her new room, their height causing the space to seem smaller.

When she'd told Ian that freshmen were supposed to stay on campus through Labor Day, for the first week and a half of the semester, he'd insisted on driving down to see her this weekend. And Brendan had come along for the ride. Apparently he had a friend here, a girl he'd met at some leadership camp in high school, who of course had kept in touch and would be thrilled to meet up later tonight.

But until then — for the first time since she and Ian had gotten together — the three of them were hanging out the way she'd hoped for. Relaxed. Uncomplicated. Friends.

It had taken close to three months, but it was happening. And she hadn't even tried to bring it about. She and Brendan had never discussed what went down on the Fourth of July, and she didn't know if the twins had either. But maybe they didn't need to. It was in the past.

Ian was stretched out on her bed. Brendan lounged against the wall, eating french fries from a bag. Both of them looked way more at home than she felt. She'd been too buzzed last night to sleep much, and her dorm room bed was an adjustment after spending the nights outside all summer.

She leaned back in the wooden desk chair, fidgeting with her short-sleeved blouse and embroidered skirt. The blouse buttoned up the back, a little tighter than she wanted right now, and the delicate white fabric stuck to her skin, but she wasn't going to order Brendan out of the room so she could change into a T-shirt. She wanted to make the most of this time, not remind the twins of any awkwardness.

"Aren't you guys training or something?" She pointed to the bags of fast food the twins had brought. "Does this fit your diet?"

"We've got a couple months 'til the season starts," Brendan said easily. "You're coming to our games, right?"

"All the ones I can make it to. Ian's going to explain everything to me."

"Yep. There'll be a quiz. Oral only."

"Ian," she groaned after a minute. Brendan grinned at her and popped another french fry in his mouth.

Ian gave her a withering look. "It took you forever to get that. Wake up. It's too quiet in here." He rolled off the bed, put a record on her record player, cranked up the volume, and pulled her door wide open.

"Ugh, no." Diana covered her ears as cymbals crashed. Ian knew all her records now, and he'd picked the most raucous one. "I don't want to be that room."

"Sure you do. Everyone will come see where the party is."

"It's not here."

Brendan leaned over and turned the music down. Not that she needed to blare her records to get attention. Everyone, female and male, had stared as she walked through the dorm between the twins. Right now, Kate and Eleanor, the girls across the hall, were lingering in their doorway.

"Hey, Diana!" Kate called. "You made it home okay last night? This girl can *dance*," she added to the twins.

"What, without me?" Ian looked injured.

Grudgingly, Diana introduced Ian and Brendan. Her hallmates were nice, but she was completely peopled out right now, and Kate and Eleanor looked like they were settling in for a long conversation about their histories, hobbies, and life goals while Brendan encouraged them.

Diana glanced at Ian for help. He gave his brother a tap on the shoulder.

"We need to clean Diana's room now. It's a health hazard. Come visit later, 'kay?" He gave the girls a winning smile and closed the door.

"Health hazard?" Diana repeated.

He grinned. "There are some words that just make people want to go away."

Brendan shook his head and came over to her chair. "Di, you need to be out there meeting people."

"I have been." She smacked Brendan's hard stomach. He didn't blink. It felt so satisfying that she kept doing it. "I've been meeting everyone who's here to meet. You can take all the credit if you want it."

Brendan smiled tolerantly as she kept batting his abs. "Ouch," he said mildly. "Ouch. Ouch. Ouch."

"Liar. That doesn't hurt."

Ian was flipping through her records, examining them and putting them back. "It's okay, Diana. You can't be good at everything."

"How hard would I have to hit you for it to actually hurt?" she demanded.

Brendan shrugged. "You can't."

She made a face. "I thought you said I could do anything I wanted once I graduated. Remember?"

Across the room, Ian snorted.

"You're going to mess up my records," she called.

"You can do a lot, Di," Brendan said encouragingly. "You can do all kinds of things."

"Do you believe in me?" she teased.

"'Course I do. But you can't hit me hard enough for it to hurt."

"Really?"

"Maybe she can." Ian stopped rifling through the records and folded his arms. "She's been going to the gym all summer."

"Try." Brendan pulled up his shirt with a grin.

Diana blinked at his defined abs, the soft trail of hair pointing down to his fly, the belly button that went in where Ian's went out.

God, the two crazy weeks of the threesome had been all tangles and tumbles and excitement and rolling around, mostly in the dark or by candlelight. Now that she knew Ian's body so well, she saw at a glance all the faint distinctions in Brendan's bare torso. Her stomach flip-flopped.

"Just you wait." She drew back her arm and landed her best punch. Her fist bounced off Brendan's abs.

"Ouch," he said unconvincingly, while she was moaning "ow" with a lot more feeling and shaking her hand. Ian doubled over with laughter.

"Poor baby." Ian loped over and rubbed her hand. "You better get your ass back to the gym. I expect you to keep it up when school starts."

"Really, Di, you did great." Brendan was trying not to laugh.

"Oh, shut up. Could Ian hit you hard enough for it to hurt?"

"Don't make me do it," Ian drawled. "Brendan would be on the floor, bawling like a baby."

Brendan raised his eyebrows. "You want to see us fight?"

"Not fight," she said quickly. "Just, uh, roll around. With your shirts off."

Ian tugged her hair. "Only if you have your shirt off too."

"I'm eating," she protested. Ian was just kidding around, so why was she blushing? She rustled through the paper bags on her desk. "You guys brought way too much food."

"Give Brendan the rest." Ian tossed his brother a bag. Brendan caught it. "He needs the energy for later. If you know what I mean."

"Oh, right. He has to go see his leadership friend. What happened to Katherine from your internship?" she asked Brendan.

He laughed. "That was a summer thing. We're just good friends now."

"Like you are with this girl?"

"I have a lot of friends. She's a nice girl. You'd like her, Di."

"I'm sure." She busied herself poking around in a bag for more french fries.

"No, I mean, you'd *really* like her. And she'd love you. You're right up her alley."

"Brendan!" She crumpled the bag and threw it at him.

He grinned. "Wanna meet her?"

"It's okay. I don't need to meet your fuck buddy." It was easier to say things like that now, but she still felt a few degrees hotter. Ian snickered.

"Di." Brendan sounded shocked. "She's just a friend. She can be your friend too. You want to make friends, right?"

"Ian, Brendan's booooothering me."

Countless times, she'd said the opposite when they were kids, until she'd learned it was better to fight Ian back. Brendan's broad grin

215

made it clear he remembered.

Ian rolled his eyes. "Back off," he told his brother.

He crossed the dorm room — it only took him a couple of long strides — and began poking through her dresser drawers, messing up the careful rolling and arranging she'd done.

"Jeez, Ian," she groaned. "Are you marking your territory on all my stuff?"

"I'm just making sure you put everything away nice and neat. You better hide these." He rooted around in her underwear drawer and brandished two toys — a purple dildo in one hand, a pink butt plug in the other. "Otherwise you'll come in and find your roommate using them."

"Put those down before you hurt yourself," she ordered, flushing and glancing at Brendan. He gave her a wink. Thank God the door was closed. "I'm still hoping for no roommate."

"Di, everything's going to be fine." Brendan's voice was so reassuring that in an instant, she just wanted to go back to being a kid again. Back to when he'd taught her how to dribble a basketball and kept telling her she was doing a great job, she was a natural, keep going, don't quit, while Ian ran circles around them and she tried to copy his lay-ups. "You're doing everything right. Next time we see you, you'll be friends with everybody on campus."

"I don't want to be friends with everybody," she muttered. She pushed her chair back from the desk, stood, and flopped on the bed. Her bed, now. She already missed her bedroom at home, along with the open lawn of her backyard. The one time she'd moved before this, it hadn't exactly gone smoothly. "I want to stay in here until it feels like my room. And no sharing."

She pulled her pillow over her head for good measure.

The mattress sank. A warm hand closed over her shoulder.

"Are you okay?"

With the pillow over her head, she wasn't sure which twin was

216

sitting close to her. When the hand worked its way firmly down her back, she recognized Ian's touch.

"Terrified. I'm freaking out. This is way too many new people."

"You don't have to meet them all this weekend."

She groaned. "I thought I was done feeling this way. When I got here yesterday, I told myself that my rule for college is 'try everything once.'"

"Everything?" Ian repeated. He sounded wary.

"Well...most things."

"People smell fear, Diana." The mattress shifted. Arms and legs nudged her body. Ian was climbing over her, stretching out on her other side, in the space between her and the wall. One leg wrapped around hers. The bed creaked again: Brendan, sitting down beside her. "They smell it coming off you and they go for the kill or run away."

"You didn't smell it," she mumbled from under the pillow. She'd happily stay here all day. "You thought I was a stuck-up ice princess."

"Yeah, well." Ian was quiet for a minute. "You're a good bullshitter. The point is, don't be scared."

"Could Brendan tell?"

She heard muffled laughter from the twins.

"What, Di?" Brendan bent close. He rubbed her shoulder. "Were you saying something?"

She lifted the corner of the pillow. "Could you tell I was scared?"

He lay down next to her. She was enclosed by both twins on the narrow bed. An arm draped around her — Brendan's. Ian was rubbing her back, lying half on top of her, and his bulky weight was pure comfort right now.

"Yeah." Brendan's tone was soft. "I could tell. I was hoping you'd talk to us about it."

"Why didn't you say something to Ian?"

"Because he shut me down every time I brought you up."

"Every single time?"

"I did not," Ian grumbled.

"Keep doing that," Diana murmured, as he kneaded between her shoulders.

"He sure as hell did," Brendan said agreeably. "I'd start in with, 'Hey man, Diana seemed really nervous when we took her to school on the first day.' And he'd come back with, 'Yeah, nervous that she'd pull an A-minus in her advanced honors bullshit class, and nervous that it's too hot for an ice princess to be walking around, and nervous that her panties are bunched so far up her ass, she won't be able to get them out.'"

"And you wonder why I didn't want to talk to you." Diana felt around above her, skimming over Ian's firm side, until she found his ass. She gave it a pinch.

"You should have talked to both of us." Brendan's voice was more intent.

"I was scared," she whispered. "Especially of Ian. You have no idea."

"Uh-huh," Ian grunted, rubbing her back. "I'm pretty fucking frightening."

"I told you we'd help you with anything you needed." The insistence in Brendan's tone surprised her. He was pushing the conversation, pushing like he had in her dream over the summer. "We would have, Di. You should have taken us up on that."

"And what would have happened then?" she wanted to know.

A hand rested on her shoulder. "We would have been together again."

Silence hung, weighted with meaning.

"I don't know if 'again' counts for anything," Diana whispered into the heavy air. The space between her pillow and her bed felt hotter. "Things can never be the same as they were before. Right?"

"Sorry." Ian's teasing voice came under the side of the pillow. "I can't hear you. You have a pillow on your head."

She pulled off the pillow and blinked up at two sets of dimples.

"Hey, there you are." Ian bent to kiss her.

On instinct, she took his lower lip between her teeth. He ruffled her hair — no. That was Brendan, on her other side. Ian didn't ruffle her hair in a way that sneaked over the line of big-brotherly and bordered on sensuous.

Her whole body reacted. She arched toward both twins, sliding her hands up their arms. As Ian's tongue flicked hers, she craned her neck to get more of Brendan's fingers running through her hair.

For a second, no one moved. Ian's lips were soft and warm against hers. Brendan's hand twined in her hair.

Then — "Just relax, okay?" Ian murmured.

"Okay." Her eyes slid closed, and she rolled onto her stomach again. Two hands moved over her back. She heard Ian's low voice:

"She likes it when you rub right here."

"Oh really?" Brendan pressed in firmly at the small of her back, massaging in circles.

Diana sucked in her breath. "You guys—" she began, with no idea what was coming next.

"Is this helping, baby?" Ian's voice was husky.

Lust. That was definite lust coming through. The whole thing felt like a dream, in this strange room that didn't belong to her yet. It had to be a dream. She wasn't ready to wake up.

"Yes," she sighed. "You're both helping."

"Good, Di," Brendan said. "We try."

Ian's hand worked down her back to cup her ass, massaging in circles.

"Oh—" she moaned. She couldn't help it.

"Ssshhhh, it's okay." The soothing murmur came from Brendan. His fingers slipped under her blouse to rub her bare back.

"Promise?" she whispered.

"Mm-hm," came from her other side.

Ian squeezed her thigh. Brendan's hand was partly inside her shirt, so close to where she wanted his sure touch, but the tight fabric was getting in the way, and his free hand was toying with the buttons going down her back.

"You can unbutton those," she whispered.

There was a pause. A long one, almost long enough that she opened her eyes. Then the bottom button slipped out of its buttonhole. And the next.

The twins were lying so close that when she put her hands out on both sides, she immediately came into contact with two male chests.

A palm dropped to her calf. Ian was stroking up the back of her knee, exploring under the hem of her embroidered skirt. He was taking his time, pushing into her soft flesh. But in seconds or minutes, thick fingers would brush her panties, pull them aside, touch her, and he'd find out how excited she was. She was moaning into her pillow, waiting for Ian's hand to open her thighs and discover her wetness while Brendan unbuttoned her blouse.

Was she letting this happen, or making this happen? She needed to open her eyes and look at the twins. She needed to know what they were thinking, what she was thinking.

Instead, she just gave a shuddery sigh of pleasure and parted her thighs to let Ian move wherever he wanted, closer and closer to her pulsing pussy. Brendan's fingers slid under her bra clasp, and she arched her back in invitation.

As she stroked their chests, Brendan guided her hand under his shirt to brush rippling abs and the soft patch of hair she'd eyed earlier. He pushed up the puffy sleeve of her blouse. Lips trailed kisses over her shoulder.

She felt his tongue. On her skin. As he began to nibble, Ian's hand grazed her very wet panties. She bit a mouthful of pillow as his finger slipped under the elastic.

She should be opening her eyes, she should be dealing with this one way or the other, but her eyes stayed shut, and instead of talking, she could only pant "Oh God, Oh God, Oh God..."

"Look at us," Ian whispered.

Outside the door, there was a resounding thunk. Then the noisy thrust of a key in the lock.

Diana sat up, her heart beating wildly, trying to adjust her clothes. Brendan was already on his feet, swiftly doing up the back of her blouse. Ian followed, pulling her off the bed. Both twins looked flushed, and her own face was probably scarlet. Ian's hair was sticking up, and she frantically smoothed it down just as the door opened.

A petite girl with a surly expression and one enormous suitcase stood in the doorway. She looked from Diana to the twins.

"You've got to be fucking kidding me," she muttered.

"Uh, hi." Diana held out her hand. "I'm Diana."

"Sonia." The girl ignored her hand. She grabbed her suitcase, hauling it into the room.

"I can help you." Brendan started forward, but Sonia had already heaved the suitcase onto her bed with a thud. Diana eyed it nervously, then her roommate. Sonia was wiry. The girl looked like she was five feet of solid muscle.

"This is my boyfriend Ian." Diana gestured to Ian, who looked dazed. "And his brother, Brendan."

"Obviously I was interrupting something." Sonia flipped open her suitcase. "I don't want to know."

Diana bit her lip. If she'd been scarlet a minute ago, she was five shades of crimson now. Brendan patted her shoulder, and Ian's dazed expression gave way to a mischievous grin. Yes — he was actually giving her ass a squeeze behind Sonia's back, making her redder and about to splutter with helpless laughter. Later, she'd kill him.

"We grew up together," Diana went on, because she had to keep talking. Of all the roommate scenarios she'd imagined — the ways they'd meet, the first conversation they'd have — this hadn't been one of them. "Ian and Brendan live next door to me, back home."

"I really don't want to know." Sonia pulled a short, loose black dress out of her suitcase, more or less identical to the dress she was wearing. With one fluid movement, she pulled her dress over her head. No underwear. No bra. Her back was facing them, but with everything she'd seen and done, Diana's jaw still dropped. Even Ian looked taken aback, and Brendan raised his eyebrows.

"They're not going to be hanging around, are they?" Sonia asked without turning around. The new dress dropped over her head, and she shook out the fabric. "Don't tell me they go here. Who'd they bribe?"

"Nobody." Embarrassment still churned Diana's stomach, but annoyance was taking over. "They go to UConn."

"Good. I didn't sign up for a roommate with a fucking entourage."

"I'll be around," Ian said breezily. "Now and then." He seemed hugely entertained. Diana wanted to smack him. "Don't worry, Diana's a decent sleeper. She kicks, but that won't be a problem for you. If it is, let me know."

Sonia blinked, but she didn't crack a smile. "'K. Whatever." She headed for the door.

Brendan put a hand on her arm. His smile was placating, his dimples two alerts for the avalanche of charm about to pour out. Before he could say a word, Sonia stared at Brendan's hand on her arm like it was an intruding snake.

"Ex-*cuse* me?" she snapped.

Brendan raised his hands, stepping back. "Sorry." He looked too abashed to say the right thing and set everyone at ease.

Sonia just grunted and stalked out. The door slammed behind her.

"Oh my God," Diana moaned, staring at the closed door in horror. "I have to live with *that*?"

Ian draped an arm around her shoulders. "You guys are gonna get along great, Diana," he said cheerfully. "She makes the same bitchface you do."

"I do not look that mean." Diana swatted his arm.

"Not anymore."

"Not ever."

"Listen, ice princess, you were the scariest girl in school. You okay, bro?"

Brendan was eyeing the door distractedly. He shook his head and smiled. "Yep. I should get going."

He kissed Diana's cheek and wrapped her in a warm hug. Nothing except brother to see here. Ian, next to her, was being straight-up jaunty. It was too much for her to take. She broke the hug, stepping back.

"So," she began, taking a deep breath. "About before."

Ian exhaled and leaned against her desk, hands in his pockets. Brendan stood by the door, his arms folded across his chest. Both twins wore the same unreadable expression, and the truth hit her: *they don't know what to do.*

In their threesome, she'd always trusted the twins to take the lead. They were older, more confident, a hell of a lot more experienced, and they obviously knew how to share a girl in bed — at least when it came to pleasing her.

She swept her bangs off her face. A stubborn part of her still wanted to believe that the twins knew everything and had all the answers. Pushing on that want was the memory that the first woman the twins shared had been Ian's girlfriend. She'd never asked how that ended.

A buzz broke the silence. Brendan took his phone out of his pocket and looked at the screen.

"My leadership friend wants to know if I'm still alive." He tossed the phone up and caught it.

"You better deal with that," Ian said carelessly. "Don't want her sending out a search party."

Brendan nodded, but Diana felt the intensity of two pairs of hazel eyes. Waiting for her to say yes or no. What the hell could she say right now? What was there to say?

"Have fun." She smiled at Brendan. "Don't do anything I wouldn't do."

"We'll see about that." He closed the door softly behind him.

"Hey." Diana touched Ian's face as he came close to her. "I know my new roommate completely changed the mood—" She shrieked as Ian scooped her up and tossed her on the bed. "Ian! She could be back any second."

"So?" Ian crouched above her. "She got naked in front of all three of us, she can handle walking in on you and me."

All three of us. She'd let that go for now. In a perfect world, she and the twins would calmly discuss what had happened. But this wasn't a perfect world, and she had no idea what to say.

Instead, she grabbed Ian's arm. "I want to, but I really can't handle her walking in."

"Don't tell me she scares you, baby."

"She does," Diana muttered.

"I'm telling you. Best friends by the end of the semester. I'll teach you how to beat her up first if you want."

"I might take you up on that. Self-defense."

"Whatever you say. Watch this." Ian rolled off the bed. At the desk, he held up her red leather journal — the one he'd bought her at the bookstore, now half-filled with poems. "Can I rip out a page, or no?"

"Go ahead."

He tore out a blank piece of paper, grabbed a pen, and scrawled: *Busy. Please knock loud.*

"See?" He grinned at her. "I used the magic word."

Diana laughed and got some tape. "I'll put it up. It's my room."

"Look how hard you're blushing," Ian sing-songed as she opened the door. She taped the sign below the dry-erase board she'd put up and shut the door quickly.

"I hope it works." She curled up on the bed with Ian. The four walls of the dorm room surrounded them: posters and twinkle lights on her side, blank space on Sonia's. Between the room that didn't feel like hers yet, the unfinished encounter with Brendan, and her new roommate storming in and terrifying the shit out of her, she wasn't ready for sex. "This is just so weird."

"Yeah." He rubbed her back. "It's different."

"How'd it feel your first year at college?"

Ian shrugged. "Me and Brendan shared a room. We hadn't for awhile, but it wasn't like dealing with a new person. Housing tried to make us live apart, but we weren't gonna have that."

"When'd you stop sharing at home?"

"When we started high school. We got rid of the bunk beds and I moved into my own room. It took a while to get used to. I mean, for sneaking in girls, it worked."

"Already? Freshman year?"

"We just talked." He grinned at her.

"Liar."

Ian laughed. "But me and Brendan — we missed each other. Sometimes one of us would get a sleeping bag and go in the other one's bedroom. Usually Brendan would come to my room and talk at me 'til I passed out. Then he'd keep talking. I'd wake up, and he'd be talking in his sleep."

Diana snickered, rolling her face against Ian's bare arm. He gave her a squeeze. "I have no idea what that's like."

"But you will, 'cause you and that pissed-off girl are gonna be BFFs."

"More like mortal enemies. Maybe we can work out a deal where we're each in the room half the time, and we never see each other except when we're sleeping."

"Just wait." Ian slipped an arm around her to rub her stomach.

"You're all sweaty. Let's check out the dorm showers."

"Ugh." She reached for her water bottle. "I'm going to take a drink. Do not dump this on me." She sipped while Ian watched her innocently. When his eyes followed her hand wiping her mouth, she felt warmer. "What did Brendan talk about when he came to your room?"

"Jesus, what didn't he talk about? Everybody and their sisters and what they were up to. Listing off sports stats and how all the basketball teams were doing in our league and how we'd use our strengths to win. Stunts to pull and shit to get into. How to get girls." He squeezed her stomach gently. "Every so often, he'd slip you in, trying to be all subtle on my ass. *I saw Diana in the hall today. She's gotten fucking gorgeous, right? Remember the old days? Let's tell her about the party this weekend. It's not her crowd, but she'll have fun if we take her together.*"

"Wow. Subtle."

Ian gave her a wry smile. "What he said was right. I shot him down every time. But usually, he just talked to talk. Brendan doesn't like being alone."

"Is that the only thing that scares him? 'Cause there doesn't seem to be much."

"Hmmm." Ian sighed, his long body slouching against the wall. His free hand pushed her hair off her forehead, tugging lightly, sending tingles from her scalp to her toes. It did something intense to her when Ian pulled her hair, and she wasn't going to wonder why. "You're letting your hair grow longer. It's sexy."

She leaned against him, stroking the inside of his wrist. "That doesn't answer my question."

Ian sighed again, a longer sigh. "It's not that it scares him, so much. He just doesn't like it."

Diana nodded. "That's how I feel right now, except for the not being scared part."

Lips met hers in a slow kiss. Her stomach turned over. "What if we have sex in your bed?" Fingers wove through her hair, pulling harder. "Will it feel more like home?"

When she pulled Ian in by the back of his head, his hands closed over her breasts, fondling the full curves. He kissed her again with more tongue and bit her lower lip.

"It's worth a try…" She glanced at the closed door. As Ian pinched her nipples through her blouse, she stretched up, still jittery but eager for more touch. His mouth and hands were sending sparks through her body.

When her fingers brushed the heavy bulge between his thighs, he cursed under his breath.

"Do it."

"I will," she whispered. As she opened his fly, the scrape of the zipper jolted her with excitement.

Ian swiftly unbuttoned her blouse, sliding it down her arms. Her bra was off in an instant. Her embroidered skirt slipped over her hips to fall on the floor, and her panties followed.

He bent to suck on her nipple. "You taste so fucking good."

"Ian…" she moaned. He ran his tongue over the puckered bud as she worked her hand into his boxers.

"Everything's going to be okay, Diana." He bit her nipple lightly, then sucked hard. She cried out. "See? Better already." His mouth closed over her other nipple.

"Yes… But you won't always be here."

"I want to be. But you're in the big world now. Let yourself out."

Ian nuzzled her breast, his palms all over the full curves. Her nipple was a pebble in his mouth. His cock felt perfect in her hand, hidden inside his boxers, so warm, the skin smooth. A trickle of liquid oozed out as she stroked the engorged head.

Being naked for Ian while he knelt over her in his T-shirt and boxers, glancing at the door without knowing if or when it would open, smelling the clean masculine scent of Brendan still on her sheets with two pairs of hands roaming her body and too many questions in the air—

Her head was going to explode. Her body was going to explode. She moaned, tense and excited.

"That's it," Ian hissed, as her fingers tightened on his cock. He bit her nipple, soothing it with his tongue when she shrieked. "Wonder if I can make you come this way, you horny little girl?" Teeth grazed her nipple again, and she grabbed his hair. "What's gonna happen if I just keep playing with your perfect tits?"

She pulled her hand out of his boxers and scratched his shoulders. "Are you teasing me?"

"Hell yes. It's so fun." He flicked his tongue over one rosy bud.

His fingers and mouth were driving her crazy. Her body cried out for more — more weight, more force. More Ian. More gravity, when everything was new and she didn't know where she'd land.

An impulse made her ask, "Can you hold me down?"

Ian's eyes widened. He pulled off his boxers and tossed them aside. Before she could reach for his T-shirt, or stroke the thick cock pointing at her, he pushed her arms above her head, capturing both wrists in one large hand.

"Like that?"

"Ye-e-es."

A thrill shot through her. She yanked, but her wrists didn't budge. A firm palm roamed over her body, leaving heat in its wake.

"Damn, Diana. Listen to you." He was right. She was panting already. Large fingers dipped between her lips, and she gasped when they found the juices welling. "This is what you need right now, isn't it?" She lifted her hips to invite him in, biting her lip at the sensation of Ian fingering her. "So horny. So ready. Such a bad girl. You need some discipline."

"More," she pleaded.

Her pussy spasmed around thickness. Ian was stroking her from the inside, more fingers slipping into her creamy cunt.

"Fuck, you're wet and tight. You're loving this, aren't you?"

"God, yes."

"Maybe," his whisper was hot against his ear, "I should ask Brendan to drop off his handcuffs." She gasped and bucked against him. "That way, I'll have both hands free."

Fingers left her pussy. Hard flesh pressed between her legs. She was so aroused, and her body was eager, welcoming Ian in. But God, nervousness flashed through her, stoking her excitement, tightening her body.

"I'm not ready for that." Then she froze, her legs locked around Ian's waist. "Wait, he brought them?"

"Probably." Ian grinned at her. He dove down to suck her neck. The pressure ignited a path of heat down her body, and if she just pulled free, she could kiss him...but his body was heavy on top of hers, his grip on her wrists firm.

"About before." She was so excited she could barely breathe, but she had to ask. "With the three of us. What would have happened if no one walked in?"

He held still, his cock half-buried inside her, his forehead pressed to hers. His T-shirt was damp with sweat, his eyes narrow with lust.

"What did you want to happen?"

She knew what she'd wanted in that moment, but would she still have wanted it afterwards? She hadn't even been willing to open her eyes while she gave in to the twins' touch.

"God— Ian—" He was starting to move. "I liked being close to both of you. I couldn't think past that. What were you thinking?"

"I was thinking—" he pulled back, then sank deeper, smoothly — "that I wanted my girlfriend to relax. And you were really relaxing with me and Brendan rubbing your back together. And weren't we surprised when you started getting turned on?"

"That's not fair. You were taking it there."

Ian lengthened his strokes. He kissed her neck, and she shivered, tightening around him.

"Me?" he whispered. "Maybe. Guess I wasn't thinking either."

"Ian—" As his thrusts deepened, thinking went away. All she knew was the hard male body on top of hers, the friction of his cotton shirt on her tender nipples, the rigid cock moving inside her, the smooth skin of his neck under her teeth. Her hips rising to meet him, the tug of her wrists in his unyielding grip. Ian was grinding against her mound, taking her to the brink. Low grunts told her he was close to coming.

When he changed his angle, she whimpered at the overload of pleasure. "Are you going to let my arms go?"

"Do you want me to?" Ian rasped. "Or do you want me to cum in your sweet little pussy while I hold you down? 'Cause I can tell this is getting to you."

"Yes, cum…" she panted.

Ian growled and drove into her. "You really are a bad girl, Diana. Begging me to pin you down, taking me deep like the slut you are. Your roommate might walk in and see you like this. I bet you'd get off on that, wouldn't you?"

"Ian!" she gasped. Jesus, it was crazy, but as worked up as she was, his words only aroused her more. "Only if she holds the door so everyone can watch," she whispered.

His eyes opened wide. As she thrust back, matching him, he gave a muffled roar into her neck and sank deep. She moaned with him as he came, his release almost triggering hers.

"Please—"

"Fuck, yes." He gave one more thrust and withdrew, his body sweaty on top of hers. "Ask for it, baby. Tell me how bad you want it."

She didn't give a damn who walked in now. Her entire dorm floor, her professors, the chancellor, her parents. Brendan with his handcuffs.

She was in a fog of lust, Ian's face above her, his hand still grasping her wrists.

"I need you, Ian." One sentence, that was all. And it made her shiver to whisper it.

His free hand slid over her warm valley. She moaned as he massaged her pussy, her thighs spread, hot and open.

"Like that, Diana?" He found her clit and stroked the hard nub. "You want me to touch your little clit like that?"

"Oh God. Yes..." She bucked against his hand, craving the intensity that would push her to climax.

"Feel it, baby. Relax. I got you. All you need to do is come."

Ian's hand on her wrists made her heart race. His face was set with concentration, his arm straining to hold her in place. She let out a shuddering breath and relaxed into the bed. The familiar rumpled sheets from home cradled her back and ass.

"That's it, Diana." Ian's voice was husky. Fingers dipped into her opening, spreading her juices, and rubbed her clit again and again. "Come in your new room for me. Right here, right now."

He was looking at her so intently as he held her down that she felt a flash of self-consciousness. But she looked right back at him. As he fondled her melting cunt, the nerves spiked her need.

Her hands wrenched at Ian's restraining fingers. Pleasure washed over her, fed by the thrill of his firm grip. Her back arched as she came in bursts of heat.

When she went limp, he let her go and kissed her between her breasts.

"Okay?" he whispered, rubbing her wrists.

"My arms fell asleep." She rolled onto her side and smiled at him lazily. "But it was so worth it."

"Good." He shook out his hand. She pulled it to her lips to kiss his palm.

"I love you," she murmured. Strong arms wrapped around her.

"Love you too, sweetheart."

Maybe I should ask Brendan to drop off his handcuffs. Then I'll have both hands free.

It wasn't so different from what they'd done. But being cuffed to a bed, without Ian holding her — bound to her in his own way — felt more out of control, more risky, more exposed. Not to mention that Brendan's dimpled smile would be attached to those handcuffs in her mind.

The mattress creaked as Ian climbed off the narrow bed. He stepped into his boxers and shorts and gave her a devilish grin.

"Too bad your roommate didn't walk in. You were so hot and bothered, it would have set you off."

Diana groaned. "I'm so glad she didn't. It probably would've served her right, but still."

She cleaned up with a handful of tissues, found a new thong in her drawer, and stepped into a fresh dress. Hopefully she'd get used to seeing her clothes in the dorm room closet.

Just as Ian reached for his shirt, the door banged open. Sonia charged in. She gave one disgusted look at Ian's carved chest, then sat down at her desk and opened her laptop.

"Um." Diana cleared her throat. "The sign said to knock."

"Oh," was all Sonia said. She tapped her keyboard. Apparently, that was the end of the conversation.

Ian whistled as he pulled his shirt on. Diana eyed the door, prepared to make a break for it as soon as Ian got his ass dressed.

"Well, uh, we're going to dinner."

She picked up her purse. God, when was she going to stop stammering? Each time she thought she was over the shyness for good, it cropped up again.

"Yep." Ian paused by Sonia's chair, a friendly smile on his face. "Wanna come?"

No, Diana mouthed frantically at him, but Sonia glanced up. Then she closed her laptop and heaved a sigh.

"Fine. Why not." Her tone implied she was doing Ian a colossal favor.

Diana was too irritated to say anything as the three of them walked down the dorm hallway. Sonia kept her scowl pointed straight ahead. Ian's walk was carefree, but he didn't single-handedly manage the conversation the way Brendan would have. Instead, he whistled all the way down to the dining hall, where Sonia put a finger in front of his lips.

"Stop," she ordered.

If any other girl had done that to Ian, Diana would have itched to push her hand away, but there was nothing flirty about Sonia's gesture. It was too direct to be threatening.

"Oh, you have a problem with it?" Ian asked innocently.

"I have a problem with you."

"That's fine." He grinned at Sonia. "Everyone does. I'm used to it."

Diana bumped him with her hip, a little too aggressively. "I don't have a problem with you."

"Sure you do. I'm your biggest problem. You're mad at me 'cause I invited your roommate to our romantic dining hall dinner. Don't worry, I brought the candles anyway."

"Ian," she hissed.

"Sorry to crash." Sonia didn't sound sorry as they made their way through the lines in the dining hall. Maybe she enjoyed the awkwardness, Diana thought. This was going to be a long year.

"By the way," Sonia said abruptly, after they'd sat down at the end of a long table with their food. "About the 'please knock' thing. I knew you guys were done screwing. Half the hall heard you. I waited until the noise went away."

Diana winced. "Half the hall?" She dropped her fork with a clatter when she saw Ian rocking with laughter. "Shut up." She pointed the fork at him. "You don't go to school here."

"Come on, Diana. You're starting the year with a bang."

She was ready to argue, but something was happening with Sonia's mouth that was almost a smile. Just one corner lifting, but it was better than nothing.

Sonia shrugged. "It wasn't half the hall. I exaggerate. Four other people."

"And you all bonded, right?" Ian grinned at her.

"Hell, no." Sonia took a long swig of her juice. "I'd be happy if I never saw them again."

"You didn't want food?" Diana eyed the glasses and mugs in front of her roommate, with no plate to keep them company. Juice, tea, water. She'd loaded up her own tray, wanting to try everything, and Ian was eating enough for all three of them.

"I prefer drinking to eating," Sonia announced. "And no, there's nothing wrong. It's just a preference."

Diana took her glasses off and rubbed her eyes. She'd never felt so normal. Maybe there was a silver lining to living with someone who was quirkier than she was.

"I like drinking too." Ian flashed his dimples.

"That's because you're a dumb jock."

Diana stiffened, but Ian just laughed.

"Hey now, don't be judgmental."

"Oh, he used a three-syllable word," Sonia commented to Diana.

Diana smiled grudgingly. "He knows a few."

"Did you teach them to him?"

"Absolutely. I taught him everything he knows." It was so untrue that she began to laugh.

"Did you housebreak him, too?"

"Nope. That was his brother's job." She shot a glance at Ian, who just nodded agreeably.

"Oh," Sonia said, her hint of a smile gone. "I forgot about your brother," she informed Ian. "I like you better as an only child."

A tall male figure appeared behind Sonia. Diana cleared her throat. Ian looked up just as Brendan clapped him on the shoulder.

"You need to keep your phone on, bro. I've been trying to call."

Ian slapped his pocket, then shrugged. "Guess it's in Diana's room. And Sonia's room."

"Right." Brendan winked at Diana, like the incident an hour ago had never happened. He turned his dimples on Sonia, moving cautiously, like she was a feral beast he was trying to tame. She ignored him.

"Probably fell out while you were fucking," Sonia remarked. Her expression was so deadpan that Diana snorted with laughter. She grabbed her napkin and coughed.

Brendan shook his head. "Do you need the car tonight?" he asked his brother.

"Nah. I thought we were driving back to school."

"We can go back tomorrow." Brendan messed up his brother's hair. "No rush. You want the time with Diana, right?"

Diana pushed her plate away. Obviously things were going well with Brendan's leadership friend, which was great. Fantastic. And here he was, trying to arrange Ian's life again.

"Where's Ian going to sleep?" she asked. "In case you didn't notice, I have a roommate."

Sonia shrugged. "I don't care."

"Really?" Diana stared at her.

"I go to bed really late, and I like to be out. As long as you guys aren't at it when I come back, it's fine. Since I have to share a room, I don't give a shit if there are two people or three people in there." Her sour glance at Brendan added, *Just not four.*

"Oh. Wow." Diana almost pinched herself to make sure she was awake. "I kind of love you now." Sonia's bluntness was rubbing off on her.

"Ugh, don't." Sonia got up without ceremony and went to get

more juice.

"See?" Ian leaned over to whisper. "Best friends."

"Not exactly. But I think we'll be okay."

Brendan was looking after Sonia, an odd expression on his face. Then he leaned down. "Di, I think you need to be careful with your roommate. She doesn't seem like the most stable person."

"There's nothing wrong with her." Ian buttered half a roll and tossed it in his mouth. "She just doesn't think you're the nicest guy in the world, which puts her in the minority."

"She pulled her clothes off in front of total strangers." Brendan's whisper was urgent. He actually looked worried. Diana hadn't seen worry crease Brendan's brow before. "That's not normal behavior."

"You thought it was okay when I did it, right?" she whispered back. Ian chuckled softly. And Brendan — he fucking blushed. His eyelids flickered.

"That was different."

"Uh-huh. Because you were telling me to do it with those girls from the club, and I was drunk and high. Sonia surprised you, and she was sober."

"It was a different situation," Brendan insisted. "Don't tell me it wasn't weird, Di."

Diana shrugged. A little part of her enjoyed messing with Brendan. "Hey, she had a nice body." Ian chuckled again, and Brendan held up a hand in a *please stop* gesture. "Okay, yeah, it was weird, but I don't think she's going to do any harm."

Brendan heaved a sigh. "Just be careful."

"Thanks." She squeezed his hand. The brief touch left her off-balance. Dammit, why? This needed to stop. She was with Ian, she wanted to be with Ian, and that was the whole story. *Brendan equals brother.*

As soon as Sonia reappeared, Brendan said goodbye. He gave Sonia a nod — clearly Brendan couldn't be rude back, though she just gave him a bored look in return — and hurried out. One female head after another whipped toward him as he left the dining hall.

"Do you only hang out with people who look alike?" Sonia asked.

"Yep." Shaking off thoughts of Brendan, Diana laughed. Sonia's abruptness was beginning to feel less jarring. "If you don't have a twin, I can't spend time with you."

"Good." Sonia stood up with her tray. "I'll leave you guys alone. I'll be back around 3, 4 am. Just keep your shit out of my side of the room, okay?"

"Uh-uh. Sorry," Diana giggled. The dining hall was noisy enough that she didn't worry about being overheard. "We're going to do it in your bed. I'm going to be the roommate from hell."

"That's what I was afraid of."

"Really?" Diana stopped laughing. "You thought I was going to be the crazy one?"

"You *are* the crazy one." Sonia squinted at her like the truth was obvious. When Diana appealed to Ian, he just nodded emphatically.

She shook her head. "I'll try not to be too obnoxious."

"Yeah, you can try." Sonia left without saying goodbye.

Diana watched her go, then turned to Ian. He leaned back in his chair, a satisfied smile on his face.

"Told you so."

"I saw what you did," Diana whispered. "You completely won her over. I wouldn't have. Even Brendan couldn't."

Ian shrugged. "Ninety-nine per cent of the time, Brendan's better at that. But I know when someone has a chip on their shoulder and they're trying to compensate."

"Oh, really?" She tickled his side through his shirt. He kissed the top of her head.

"Know it better now that we're together."

Chapter Fifteen

As August turned into September, and October gave way to November, Diana did her best to balance trying everything at Yale and seeing Ian on weekends. Her world was wide open now, big and exciting. But tugs came in all directions from her social life, her boyfriend, and working to be the best in a school packed with bests.

She texted with Marissa and Janelle, which kept her feet on the ground. Her parents were glad she called them each week.

But with every conversation, the question hung in the air: *Are you still dating Ian O'Brian?*

Yes. She was very much dating Ian. Until Thanksgiving break, when he had to travel for basketball, they didn't miss a weekend together. Diana had expected a two-and-a-half-hour bus ride to UConn every time she wanted to see her boyfriend, but Sonia stayed true to her word and said she didn't mind when Ian came to visit.

Ian had been right. While "best friends" was a stretch, Sonia was an excellent roommate. She had her own habits — staying out till all hours doing who knows what, sleeping late — but she slept like a rock. She still changed clothes with zero modesty, and she was blunt and abrupt, but Diana always knew where she stood with her. It was refreshing.

Even more surprising, Sonia and Ian hit it off. The second weekend he visited, Sonia let out a surly grumble that might have passed for 'hello.' In response, Ian burped loudly in her direction. And instead of the volcano Diana expected, Sonia cackled with laughter. Ian was okay in her book after that.

It was nicer to visit the twins' apartment, though. A double bed to share with Ian, a room to themselves all night long, flannel sheets that smelled like him. A kitchen where she baked cookies and teased him with the frilly apron she'd bought.

The twins' roommates, Jeff and Steve, mocked Ian about being totally whipped, and whenever Diana went out with him on campus, there was a stir of whispers. Comments, too, about how Ian was drinking less and showing up more to class. He took her to her first frat party, where a drunken group wanted to know how Ian O'Brian had bagged a freshman girl at Yale and she was too tipsy to do more than giggle.

But her wild times with Ian didn't happen in public. They happened in private: in his room, inside the Jeep when he picked her up from the bus station, in her dorm bed with one flickering candle and her record player turned low.

She'd brought her red dress to Yale, the one she'd worn to the club night with the twins. The dress that had amped her curves up and soaked in the scent of smoke and beer, only to end up on the floor of a strange girl's bedroom. But it hung in her closet, unworn.

Brendan was friendly when he saw her, which wasn't often. Mostly, he was out of the apartment when she and Ian were in it. When they did cross paths, he was rarely alone. He was with a pack of guys, or a girl, or a group of both.

One Saturday night before Thanksgiving, he did come home while she and Ian were curled up on the couch in front of a movie. He teased them about being an old married couple, down to the fleecy blanket they were snuggled under, but he sat next to Diana to watch the rest of the movie with them.

It was late. She'd had a long week. As the screen flickered, her head drooped between the twins, and her eyelids drifted closed.

The squeak of the front door woke her. One of the twins'

roommates was walking into the apartment — Jeff, jangling his car keys.

The twins were fast asleep, lounging on either side of her. Her head rested against Brendan's solid shoulder, her legs were draped across Ian's lap. The blanket had fallen to the floor, and her skirt was rumpled around her thighs. When Jeff met her eyes, he gave her a funny look.

Right. It would make more sense for Brendan to be sitting on the other side of Ian. She shrugged sleepily and smiled at Jeff. He shook his head, giving her one more glance between the twins, and went to his room.

There was absolutely nothing there with Brendan. Since Sonia had walked in on the three of them in August, neither twin had made any move to talk about what had happened in her bed. She didn't bring it up, either.

Sometimes, though, she had to repeat "Brendan equals brother" to herself , ignoring the tingles in her body, when he pulled her in for a hug and kissed her on the cheek. And she definitely noticed all the cute guys at Yale. They were there. She saw them.

But Ian was the one whose eyes she wanted to look into, Ian was the one she wanted to fall asleep next to, Ian was the one she wanted to have soft conversations with in the middle of the night with the phone pressed against her ear.

The one she wrote love poems for — ripped from her new journal, folded into paper airplanes, and mailed to UConn.

After Sonia walked in on a private Skype session, she announced that if Diana wanted to have long-distance sexy times with Ian, she should just reserve the room and tell her in advance. Diana turned red, but she took her up on it. And honestly, putting on a show for Ian, slowly toying with her sexiest underwear while he growled dirty advice, was shockingly hot.

But afterwards, she always wanted Ian's arms around her. You didn't get that from a screen.

Chapter Sixteen

"I'm going to kill him." Diana pitched her phone onto her bed and leaned back in her desk chair. Outside, early December night was falling over campus. Her literature homework was spread over the desk.

"Not Ian." Sonia stretched lazily next to the closet. Weeks into the semester, it had become clear that Sonia was one of those people who never seemed to study but aced all their classes. Used to pushing herself, Diana couldn't relate. It was unusual for Sonia to even be in their room right now.

"Yes, Ian. Do you have an objection? Because he deserves it. I was supposed to go see him this weekend—"

"And he canceled?"

"No," Diana said grudgingly. "I canceled. I have too much work. I'm falling behind."

Last weekend had been Thanksgiving. She hadn't seen Ian then either, because he had to travel for basketball. Which meant a total of three weeks apart until they were together again. The ache of missing him filled her body, but papers and problem sets were piling up. Spending every weekend in his arms had been a beautiful distraction.

"Don't sweat it."

"I don't know how to not sweat it. I don't fall behind with schoolwork. That's not who I am. I can let go to a certain point, but I have to do my best."

"You need to dominate. I get it."

"Stop," Diana groaned. She closed her laptop and flopped across her desk.

"You want a blue ribbon?"

"I just want to make the most of being here. And I'm going to kill Ian, because when I told him I couldn't come this weekend, he said he was sending me a package. So I go to the mailroom to pick it up today, I rip the box because I'm so excited, and the biggest, I mean fucking huge, vibrator falls out in front of everyone else getting their mail." Her cheeks went hot, remembering. Sonia let out a peal of laughter. "Oh, and a note fell out too. It said, *Now you can come this weekend. Tell me about it when you do.* And when I informed him of my utter humiliation, he just texted back to ask if I'd used it yet."

Sonia propped an ankle behind her head. "Kill his twin. Let Ian live."

"What's your problem with Brendan?" Diana flipped her pen between her fingers and reached for the giant mug of coffee on her desk. "You've only met him once."

"Once was too much. Your boyfriend's one of the few decent guys I know, but his brother's the devil incarnate."

Diana choked on her coffee. "Brendan's not the devil," she coughed between giggles. "He's no angel either, but he's a good person."

"I don't like people who everyone else likes. Or who want everyone to like them. Is it just me, or is he used to running his brother's life?"

"It's not just you." Cautiously, Diana set her mug down, far away from her laptop. Her roommate's powers of observation were uncanny. Neither she nor Ian had ever discussed his relationship with Brendan in front of Sonia. "They used to be attached at the hip. But not anymore."

Sonia rattled the hangers in her closet. "Thank Jesus. I can't imagine being so tied up with someone else. Now Ian's free."

Diana stacked her papers, re-ordering them. "I don't think it works that way. No one's ever totally free."

Her wrists tingled, feeling the grip of Ian's fingers. She'd asked him to hold her down again. Twice, since the first time in her dorm room.

The raw force of Ian pinning her to the bed got her so excited it took her breath away. The pounding of her heart filled her ears, her blood rushed, and desire saturated his handsome face. The reality of letting go so intimately with him, looking into his eyes, stripped down and helpless beneath him — God, it was huge.

But the third and last time, the sensations of spinning, falling, and hurtling through air had been so strong that they scared her.

She hadn't welcomed the fall, the way she had in her bedroom after the boxing match, in her bed here when she first arrived at Yale, in her dream about overtaking the twins on her bike and them taking her over as smoke. No, she'd clenched up tight, everywhere.

Ian had taken one look at her face and let her wrists go. He'd been so nice about it, gentle as they finished making love. It was up to her to ask for it again if she wanted it. And she hadn't asked for it.

But now, her body remembered the first time. A strong hand restrained her, then hard plastic. Her mind wrapped her boyfriend's brother's handcuffs around her wrists. Her curves arched up, inviting Ian to take her somewhere neither of them knew.

"Eh." Sonia shrugged, breaking in on her thoughts. "I try to be free."

Brendan's amused voice brushed Diana's ear. *It's nice to be with a special someone. But your options just aren't the same.*

"And Ian's my baby," Sonia went on. "I just want to put him in my pocket. No one fucks with his life."

Diana snorted. Some girls might be put out if their roommate had an oddball friendship with their boyfriend. But she could trust Sonia to be completely transparent, and Ian to be completely uninterested.

"He's older than you are."

"Doesn't matter."

"Brendan has good intentions," Diana protested. "He genuinely wants everyone to be happy. I trust him more than almost anyone else I know."

Sonia gave her a funny look. "How well do you know your boyfriend's brother?"

"Oh...we all grew up together." Diana turned to her laptop, her cheeks pink. "We know each other pretty well."

Over the summer, she'd wondered if anyone would suspect the threesome. But her friends were too dazzled by the light of the O'Brians to really believe she was with Ian, let alone guess she'd slept with Brendan too.

Sonia was another story.

"Want to go out tonight?" Diana asked abruptly.

"Where?"

"To party. It's Friday. I'm not going to mope around over missing Ian or sit with my lit paper tonight. I'll bang it out tomorrow."

Sonia gave her a disgusted look. "I don't party."

"You're out 'til all hours."

"Yeah, but I'm not drinking or shoving my tits into other drunks." Sonia stalked around the room, rustling the hangers in the closets. "You're the wild one."

"I'm really not," Diana began, but a flash of red from her closet caught her eye.

Yes. She was the wild one. She would be.

*

At eleven pm that night, Diana walked across campus, arm in arm with Kate and Eleanor from across the hall. The red dress clung to her frame. Her high heels clicked on the paved path. Underneath her knee-

245

length coat, the wind blew up her skirt and stung her bare legs.

She'd knocked back a shot of tequila in Kate and Eleanor's room, then chased it with a second one to keep it company. The alcohol flushed her body, warming her to take the chill off the whipping breeze.

"Where's your boy?" Eleanor asked her.

"At school. I'll see him next weekend." She flipped her hair back.

Her curves were covered by her purple wool coat, but it nipped in at the waist and outlined her hourglass figure. As she looked up and out, stares caught on her face, the thrust of her breasts, the jut of her hips, the expanse of pale leg that was showing. Male stares, female stares.

Each pair of eyes were embers, coals that clung to her body and sparked flames to lick her skin. She was so used to going out with Ian, gazing at his face only, wrapping herself up in him. And that was how she wanted it, of course it was, but — she'd missed this. Strutting down the pavement in heels, attention rippling toward her, power rippling out from her. She'd tasted it so briefly after high school graduation. The gazes were like a drug, spiraling through her body and sharpening her senses.

"Let's hit the frats," she announced.

"Sig Nu is having a party. They're this way." Kate tugged at her arm.

As they walked up the stone steps, a guy waved them past the line. Diana stepped inside and the noise surrounded her.

Holy shit, there were guys everywhere. Someone was taking her purple coat and putting it behind a couch. Heads whipped toward her as the red dress was revealed. The bright fabric made a shocking contrast to her pale skin and dark hair, clinging to every exaggerated curve.

She pretended not to notice the lust that thickened the air as she laughed with her friends, but attention pulled in to her like iron filings to a magnet.

Drinks appeared, offered from all directions. She waved them away, pulled Kate and Eleanor to the bar, and ladled out three cups of punch. They clinked glasses and sipped. Bodies pressed in on every side.

The punch was as sweet and fruity as the drinks the twins had bought her when they took her out after graduation. This time, she tasted the alcohol.

A guy was trying to talk to her. No, two — make that three guys. Music pounded through the room, lights were flashing, and she barely heard a word they were yelling.

One of them held out a hand. Why not? It was just dancing. Her friends were getting more drinks, striking up conversations. She grabbed the male hand stretching toward her — there was a name attached to the hand's owner, but she hadn't caught it in the noise — and let him lead her onto the dance floor.

Bass thumped through her body, the singer's voice pulsed over her in waves, and the room rolled beneath her feet. The masculine body behind her, the hands on her hips, were all part of the atmosphere that fed her energy. The headiness of moving with a packed room of people, letting every worry and responsibility go — each sway of her hips intoxicated her.

The guy behind her was getting more aggressive, his hands roaming over her stomach. She wriggled free, shouted something over her shoulder, and threaded her way to the bar.

Punch, jello shots, mixed drinks — they all looked good, but she didn't have time to waste sipping a drink. She needed to dance.

She remembered the twins tipping their heads back at the club, knocking back two shots each of clear brown liquid. She could guess what it was now. She knew how to have fun, and she wasn't scared.

"Two shots of bourbon," she commanded.

The blond guy who was tending bar looked her over. Then he

grinned, upended a bottle, and handed her two tiny plastic cups. She downed the first one, gasped at the burn in her throat, and chased it with the second.

"More?" he offered.

"Later." She raked her bangs back from her forehead. She was starting to sweat. Perspiration gathered on her skin and in the valley of her cleavage. Her legs longed to be back on the dance floor.

"Come back soon. I'll take care of you as long as you want. This —" he banged the bottle of bourbon down on the bar — "has your name on it."

"Aren't you sweet." She blew him a kiss.

"You know…" He leaned forward. "I've been having kind of an off day. But you're really turning me on."

She laughed and swiveled away. Her hips rolled as she walked off. She didn't have to look back to know his eyes were glued to her lush ass.

What are you doing? a little voice asked in her head.

Nothing. None of this counts.

Back on the dance floor, she went straight for the platform in the middle, brushing against innumerable bodies. People helped her up. Her high heels clicked on the wood. One helpful guy took both her hands, pulling her into the center of the platform.

Tall, dark-haired, handsome — she almost saw Ian in front of her. She squeezed both his hands, laughing and matching his movements. He was a good dancer. Ian had rolled his hips like that at the club, when the twins had taken her out for her graduation present, inviting her to shed every last inhibition and follow him anywhere.

But he'd had help. Brendan, behind her, had stoked her desire as much as Ian in front of her. Coaxing where Ian challenged. Persuading her to cross every line, act out every last fantasy. If she'd been alone with Ian that night — it was hard to imagine — she wouldn't have ended up in someone else's bed.

248

When she spun out from the guy in front of her, still holding his hands, her back brushed a hard male chest. Instead of pulling away or apologizing, she deliberately bumped him again. And when he moved in closer, she thrust back.

Hands closed over her hips, pulling her up against whoever was behind her. The guy in front of her raised his eyebrows. Then he smiled and moved in so she was sandwiched between two firm bodies.

This — yes. This was what she'd been missing, this was what she needed. Just for a little while. Just for now. She closed her eyes and lost herself to the waves of the music, the roll and thrust of her body between two men, the jiggle of her curves and the hands that were getting bolder.

Ian was going to bend down and kiss her, any minute, and her neck tingled, waiting for Brendan's tongue. Everything was fine. The three of them were unbreakable, dancing together was what they needed to do, and tomorrow morning she'd be all Ian's again. They all understood.

There were no secrets between any of them, no words left unsaid.

She couldn't wait, she needed to kiss Ian and show him how happy she was. She reached up, her eyes flickering open.

But that wasn't Ian in front of her, grinning broadly and gyrating his hips into hers. It was someone else, someone she recognized: Raj, from her writing seminar. And it wasn't Brendan behind her, squeezing her waist, grinding against her ass with a very noticeable erection. It was — oh Jesus, some drunken stranger.

She'd been loving the attention, the stares heated her skin, the two bodies against hers were very male, but in an eye-blink, it all felt less safe, and…Ian. She wanted Ian. Right now.

"Excuse me," she giggled to Raj. As she stepped to the side, the room tilted, hazy.

"I got you." He caught her arm. "You want to go somewhere?"

"I need to go outside. Get some air."

"I'll go with you."

She straightened and pulled her arm from his. The stranger had a hand on her back. He and Raj were making eye contact, clearly wondering where this was going and whether they should cooperate.

"I just really have to go. By myself. It's urgent." She smiled, waved, and lurched forward. Fortunately, someone helped her down from the platform.

Where was her coat? She fought her way to the pile behind a couch, fishing through endless black parkas until her fingers closed around a purple wool sleeve. Shouts and whistles followed her. Were they meant for her? When she straightened up, someone started giving her a back rub. She looked over her shoulder. Cute guy. Unfamiliar guy.

"Do I know you?" she giggled.

"Not yet."

"I have to go." She pushed past him and edged out the door.

Getting her coat on was awfully challenging, and it was taking longer than usual. She stumbled down the stairs and found a quiet spot on the lawn by a low stone wall.

Perfect. It was so warm out here — at least, she was so warm — and she missed lying on the grass. She'd done that practically every night, all summer. How had she not lain on the grass even once at Yale? Time to fix that. She dropped to her knees on the lawn, tried to button her coat, gave up, and curled up on the grass.

So peaceful. The night was clear. Even with the lights of campus, stars sparked overhead.

This. This was good. This was right. But Ian wasn't here. She needed him to make this complete.

Fumbling in her pocket, she searched for her phone. No, not there… Maybe her other pocket… Not there either. She lay on her back, watching the stars. Maybe her phone was gone forever. But wait — there was another pocket. She felt inside her coat until her fingers brushed the hard shape of her phone, tucked inside the inner pocket by her chest.

Yes. She'd call Ian, and he'd be here, and everything would be all right.

It only took a few tries to pull up his number and tap it. But when the call went through, Ian's phone rang and rang. After an eternity, his voicemail picked up.

Hey. You've reached Ian. Leave me a message and maybe I'll call you back.

"Hi Ian," she cooed. "I have a message for you. Call me back."

After a minute, she hung up. She waited patiently, following the shape of Orion in the sky and counting the stars in its belt. But Ian wasn't calling back. She tried again and again. Nothing.

The December air was sweet. Crisp with a hint of smoke. She should be cold, shouldn't she? How long had she been lying on the grass? Her head was beginning to throb, and when she sat up, it took enough effort that standing seemed like a bad idea.

"Maybe I need some help," she giggled. People were coming and going, up and down the steps of the house, but she was out of sight, sitting by the corner of the wall. "I can let nice people help me."

She eyed everyone milling around the house's entrance. Then she looked down at her phone, tapping through her address book, searching under *S*.

Unlike Ian, Sonia picked up.

"What?" she demanded. There were no hellos with Sonia.

"Can you help me?"

There was a pause. "Where are you?"

"I'm outside Sig Nu. On the grass."

"You're an idiot. Are you alone?"

"Yes."

"Can you walk?"

"Um…kind of?" Diana stood up experimentally. Bad idea. Very

bad idea. She swayed, grabbing the stone wall for support. "I just really wanna lie down right now."

"Where are those bitches you came with?"

"Don't start, Sonia. They're good people, okay?"

"I mean it. They shouldn't have left you alone."

"I left *them* alone. They're probably inside."

"Fuck 'em. They're probably as drunk as you. I'm coming. I'm halfway across campus now."

"Thanks. You're so great. You're really fierce, you know? You're like a really fierce mama bear."

"Uh-huh. Keep talking."

By the time Sonia showed up, Diana was sitting down again, leaning her head against the wall. The stars turned overhead in slow circles.

Texts were coming through to her phone, from Kate and Eleanor. *Where are you?* She'd ignored them while she was waiting for Ian to call.

Right here, she texted back, fumbling with the phone. *Where else? Sonia's taking me home.*

Home. Where was home? Her bedroom. Her backyard. The twins' treehouse. Their Jeep. Ian's room with posters plastered all over the walls. If there were a lot of places that felt like home, did you feel more at home in the world? Even if you weren't in any of them?

"Seriously, Diana?" A disgusted voice cut through her reverie. "Look at you squatting in front of America's favorite frat. I thought you were smart. Like, actually smart."

Sonia was standing over her, bundled in a scarf, beanie, and mittens. Maybe it really was cold out.

"I'm on vacation," Diana said confidingly. "From being smart."

Someone knelt down next to her, but it wasn't Sonia. It was a guy.

"Need some help?" he asked in a friendly tone.

"She's fine," Sonia said firmly.

Diana squinted at his messy blond hair. "Hey, you're the bartender! Aren't you supposed to be tending bar?"

"My shift's over." He grinned at her. "I saved you the bourbon. If you can walk inside with me, it's yours."

Sonia gave him an icy glare. "Go. Away."

He batted a hand at her. "Come on, I'm just making sure your friend can walk okay. Are you a freshman?" he asked Diana. "I have a special for freshman girls. Two drinks for the price of one."

She pointed at him, giggling. "You can't fool me. They're all free."

Sonia pushed up her sleeves, her stance reminding Diana of the boxing match Ian had taken her to.

"What part of 'Fuck off' do you not understand?" she spat. "Do *you* need some help? Get out of here."

Bar Boy stepped back. "Okay, okay. Sheesh. You're her guardian angel, aren't you?"

Sonia didn't reply. Diana tried to look fierce from her spot on the grass. When Bar Boy lurched up the steps to the house, Sonia sprang into action.

Holding out a hand, she hauled Diana to her feet. A supporting arm looped around Diana's back. Funny, the way her legs wobbled underneath her. Very funny. Sonia was surprisingly sturdy, her arm like steel.

"You're really strong," Diana giggled, as Sonia steered her off the lawn. "You're all petite and stuff, but I bet you could just go, like, pow through a wall."

"Oh my God." Sonia shook her head. "Just walk."

"Is this really America's favorite frat?"

"Who cares?"

They started across campus. Diana was grateful for Sonia's firm grip, because her ankles weren't always cooperating. But that was okay. They were just ankles. She began to hum.

"Are you singing? Really?"

"Yes, really." She hugged Sonia with both arms.

"Stop."

"No."

"You're such a happy drunk," Sonia remarked disdainfully.

"'Course I am. Everything's great. I'm gonna sing again, okay?"

"No. What were you doing out there?"

"Lying on the grass. Oh, first I was dancing with some guys. But then it was time to go. Without them."

"They didn't follow us, did they?"

"Shit, I didn't even think of that." And she'd been so goddamn careful about guys for so many years. Diana lurched, trying to look over her shoulder. Sonia looked too.

"No one's back there," she confirmed. "You know Raj? He was one of them."

"Harmless. He won't bother you."

"I didn't know the other guy. The one who was behind me."

"You were between two guys?" Sonia rolled her eyes.

"It just...happened," Diana explained. "The one behind me was saying something before I left. Really loud, in my ear. It seemed important. I think he was saying, 'My penis is so happy right now.' Ew," she added belatedly.

They passed one building after another, closed and locked for the night.

"You want me to go back and fix that for him?"

"God, no. Don't let go of me."

"Fine. But what the hell, Diana? You have Ian."

"No-o-o. Not right now I don't. And I need him. He's not answering his phone, and I don't know where he is, and I want him now —"

"All right. Okay. It's okay, Diana. He'll call you back."

"But I neeeeeed him. I need him so bad." Her breath made white clouds in the cold night air.

"Maybe he's staggering around like you. Too bad you can't be idiots together."

"Him and Brendan are idiots together," Diana hiccuped. "They're stupid boys."

"I wonder," was all Sonia said. "Step up."

She wrestled Diana up the dorm stairs. Somehow, they made it to their room, and oh yes, her nice soft bed, which Sonia got her into so helpfully and gave her a cup of water, all while delivering a long, obnoxious lecture about how alcohol was concentrated poison.

"Okay. I get it," Diana groaned. "I know what it does to my brain cells. And my liver. And my everything else. And my bed is better than a lawn somewhere." Her body felt more solid. The furniture looked more solid. Her head, she wasn't sure about. "I'm in your debt forever."

"Yep, you are. Just buy me a smoothie tomorrow. You're not going to puke, are you?"

Diana thought about it. "No."

"I'll leave you alone now. Go to sleep."

"K. Thanks, Sonia."

"Whatever." A smile sneaked onto Sonia's face. "I won't say 'any time.' But you're welcome."

"Leave the lamp on?"

Sonia nodded and quietly closed the door behind her.

The desk lamp cast a warm glow over the room. Diana flung an arm above her head and stared up at the ceiling. Sonia had helped her out of the red dress and hung it up in the closet. Her lacy black bra lay over her desk chair. Her high heels stood by the bed. Her panties were the only piece of clothing she still had on.

She should be nodding off to sleep right about now, but her eyes refused to close. Her body felt heavy, still warm.

Heaving herself up, she reached for her phone to try Ian once more. This time, the phone picked up on the second ring.

"Hey, Di," a familiar deep voice said.

She sighed with sweet relief and snuggled under the covers. "Hey, baby."

He laughed softly. "It's Brendan."

What? Of course. Brendan called her 'Di;' Ian never did. Unless he was impersonating his brother.

"Is this really Brendan?" she asked, toying with the covers.

"Yep, it's me." There was a smile in his voice. "Who else?"

"Ian, for starters. You're answering his phone."

"I saw you called a bunch of times, cutie. I figured you'd want an answer."

"Where's Ian?" Panic seized her gut. Brendan sounded relaxed, but that was how Brendan always sounded. Almost always. "Is he okay?"

"He's fine, Di. My better half's passed out right now. I got him to his bed."

"What?" She sat up.

"He had a lot to drink tonight. He's sleeping it off. Once in a while, Ian needs to rage really hard, and he hasn't in a long time. He'll be fine in the morning."

"Ohhhhh." The air and tension rushed out of her. "I just got put to bed too. Because I also kind of drank a lot. But Ian—"

"He's totally fine," Brendan repeated, his voice assured. "Are you okay?"

"I think so," she giggled, lying back down. "Your 'better half.' I've never heard you say that before. Who thinks Ian's your better half?"

"Just me, Di. And you."

And Sonia, she thought. "No, you're good too, Brendan. You're a good boy. I know you are."

"Thanks." He laughed softly.

"Were you drinking also?"

"Mm-hmmm."

She'd always figured Brendan wasn't capable of getting totally wasted. That, or he just didn't drink enough to lose control. But there was a definite slur in his voice. She could see him lying back, his solid body relaxed, his eyes half-closed and a dreamy smile on his face.

Her thoughts were drifting, swirling. "How come you have all those old pictures of us on your wall at home?"

"Guess I'm just sentimental that way."

"You probably don't even think about us or remember the old times."

"I remember all of it, sweetness."

Sweetness. The nickname sent warm ripples through her body. Brendan hadn't called her that since the Fourth of July.

"Mmmmm," she sighed. "I like it when you call me that. Was it real with you and me and Ian? Or was it a dream?"

There was a pause. "Both, Di."

"It was really nice."

"Mm-hm. You're nice."

"No, you are," she argued. "Even if you're secretly bad and naughty, you're the nicest boy I know. I always thought so when we were kids."

Brendan's laugh was nice too, but even through her soft haze, she heard a note of regret. "Makes me wonder what boys you know, cutie."

"I know enough. And you always have the best intentions."

"Except when I fake it," he said softly. "Or protect Ian too late. I know that's what you think, Di."

"I have thought that," she murmured. "But I don't blame you anymore. You both made your choices. We all do."

"Thanks." Brendan's voice in her ear made it seem like he was next to her. "I mean it."

She wished she were face to face with Brendan. Cuddled in bed together, his warm body close to hers, his long-lashed hazel eyes steady. Preferably Ian's bed, with Ian stretched out on her other side, sleeping peacefully and obviously okay so she wouldn't worry. He'd stir and slowly come awake as she and Brendan talked, joining in the conversation with a drowsy joke, soothing her naked curves with his hands…

"You and Ian don't make your plans anymore. You don't have your agreements. That's good, right? It's good."

"We have other agreements, sweetness. And we kept some old ones."

"Okay," she said sleepily. "Do you like the girl you brought home a few weekends ago? 'Cause she was really loud. In bed, I mean. You know, through the wall."

"You're loud too, Di."

"Oops. Sorry."

"'Sokay." A chuckle broke through his dreamy voice.

Diana pulled the covers over her head like a tent and curled up with her phone. "Did you use your handcuffs on her?"

"Is that any of your business?"

"No. Uh-uh. But pleeeease, Brendan? I wanna know."

Man, she really was drunk. That was the same pleading little-sister voice she'd used when they were kids and wanted Brendan to teach her how to pop a wheelie, or how to climb the gnarled tree that stretched over the creek in the park.

He chuckled again. "Not telling. But I got nicer ones. They're soft and comfy on the inside and hard as steel on the outside."

She was so blissfully muzzy that she only snuggled her head into her pillow and said, "Mmmmm."

"Anyway." Brendan's voice was soothing. "I'm glad you and Ian are having fun."

"Me too." She was starting to giggle again. She felt so heavy and relaxed. "And I see what you did there, Brendan. I see right through you. You didn't answer my question. You didn't tell me if you liked the girl."

"I like everybody, sweetness."

"Yeah. That. Sonia doesn't like you because of that. Or no, wait, she doesn't like you because everybody else likes you. I think it's both. And she's kind of like your handcuffs, 'cause she's soft on the inside and hard on the outside. She's bossy like you, too."

"Your roommate?" Brendan sounded a little less dreamy. "Why are we talking about her? You want to kill my buzz, Di?"

"Nooo. Never. I just want you to be happy all the time, the way you want everyone to be happy."

"That's sweet." His voice relaxed. "You're a really sweet girl. The sweetest."

"I mean it." She stretched in bed. Her head rolled against the pillow, everything moving slow in such a pleasant way. "I like you like that. You make me happy. Sooooo happy." It seemed very important that Brendan know that. "The way you let your voice pour over me like warm honey...mmmmm...and you can pet me everywhere and make me feel good...and be here in my nice warm bed with me, because Brendan makes everything better... Miss you, Brendan..."

Oh. Oh God? A tiny, wakeful part of her told her to stop talking.

There was a long silence. Very long. A few seconds, or maybe a few years.

"Di, take it easy tonight, okay?" Brendan said finally, sounding a lot more sober. "Drink some water. Get some rest. Let your roommate take care of you. I'll tell Ian you called. Sleep tight."

Another pause. Then he hung up.

Shit, shit, shit. Diana stared at the phone in her hand. Then she turned it off and shoved it under her pillow, rubbing her throbbing forehead into the plump down.

She wanted Sonia to come back. She wanted to tell someone about those head-spinning two weeks with the twins, even if that someone would declare her certifiably insane. She wanted Ian's firm body crowding her in bed, taking up the mattress, his leg wedged between her thighs while he quenched her desire with hot kisses and a slow grind against her clit.

And oh God, she wanted Brendan there, naked against her back, his hands roaming all over her, and she'd be the one whispering reassurances now. Whispering that everything would be fine between the twins, nothing could separate them, definitely not her and she didn't want to.

Maybe that was how it had to be and there was no other way, but did it have to hurt?

Her hand drifted down her collarbone to cup one full breast. Sprawling on the sheets, she let her eyes close. She felt Ian's hands and mouth, squeezing her lush curves hungrily, taking her everywhere, as she cuddled against Brendan and he kissed her cheek.

All too soon, those kisses trailed down her neck. She arched her back, exposing her throat, and God, she had one hand in Ian's hair, pulling him closer, and the other hand exploring Brendan's muscled arm as he began to caress her breast, and the three of them were whispering. Laughing together. Ian was teasing her about how much she was moaning, and Brendan was rolling her nipple between assured fingers to make her moan louder.

As two hands eased her thighs apart, spreading her open to two very different kinds of touch, the twins shared a look above her head. It lasted only a second, but it said more than a night of talking.

"Please..." she whispered. She sat up, reached for the top drawer in her dresser, and felt around the piles of panties and bras for the vibrator Ian had sent. Curling up in bed again, she eased it in, just barely.

Oooh...it really was enormous. Did Ian think she'd actually try to use it? Or was it just a joke? Right now, it didn't matter. She needed to be filled so badly.

"Everything's okay, right?" she whispered into the still air.

Oh Jesus, Brendan was taking the vibrator from her and penetrating her slowly with the huge toy, one warm hand holding her thigh against the bed. Whispering calming words, telling her he knew she could take this dildo in her sweet cunt, because she'd come so far already.

As she opened to him, trusting his steady voice, fingers flicked her clit, sending twinges of sharp sweetness through her full pussy — Ian, his eyes narrow with lust.

"Promise me everything's okay," she insisted.

I promise, Di. Brendan smiled down at her, dimples flashing. He looked delightedly at her soaked folds, clutching the smooth rod that he slowly pumped into her, and his brother's fingers pinching her clit.

Promise, baby. Ian held open her other thigh, crouched over her bare curves, naked and gorgeous, his face dark with lust. The dorm room blurred as her pussy convulsed again and again on the cylinder half-buried inside her. She groaned into her pillow, pleasure and longing rippling through her body until they diffused into a hazy glow. *Everything's gonna be okay. Better than okay. Everything's fucking perfect.*

Chapter Seventeen

The next morning, Diana went to breakfast alone, grateful she didn't have to chat with anyone. Sonia was fast asleep, a silent lump under the covers in their room.

Had she really danced between two guys? And then Brendan on the phone... She stuffed French toast into her mouth, cradling her aching head. She needed to tell Ian everything.

But when she dialed, the call went straight to voicemail, every time.

Heaving her bag over her shoulder, she went straight from breakfast to the library. On the way, she passed Kate and Eleanor.

"Hey lady!" Eleanor called. "You were the life of the party until you disappeared last night."

"You looked ready for a happy ending," Kate added. "Did you get lucky? Are you still dating the basketball player?"

"I hope so," Diana muttered, hefting her bag.

"What?"

"Yes," she said firmly. "Yes, we're still dating. Nothing happened last night."

"There's two of her boyfriend." Kate elbowed Eleanor. "Remember the beginning of the year?"

"I try to never forget it."

"No," Diana broke in. "There's one of him. And there's one of his brother."

"Same difference. Woman, you were hilariously thrashed. I didn't know you had it in you."

Diana pushed her glasses up her nose. "I guess we all need to cut loose sometimes."

Worry tugged at her, connected to the silent phone in her purse. Maybe she should have spent last night in the fucking library, catching up on all the work she needed to do this weekend. But that would be hiding, wouldn't it? Wasn't she done hiding? What was she hiding from right now?

"Anyway, it's fine," she went on. "Sonia helped me get home."

"Oh, shit. Hope you didn't freeze where she touched you."

"No. No, she was really great. And I'm fine. Eleanor, on the other hand… I saw you and those jello shots."

Eleanor grinned weakly. "My head. It's still here. That's all that matters." She and Kate blew kisses as they left.

*

The library was familiar, safe, and quiet. Right now, she desperately needed all three of those things. Diana settled into a third-story carrel, opened her book, and dove into studying. Finals were starting on Monday this week, and she saw more than one all-nighter in her future. She needed to crack down. She'd been so busy experiencing college life during the week, so wrapped up in Ian on the weekends, she'd almost forgotten how it felt to lose herself in books.

As her pen scratched paper, she waited to be totally absorbed in the subject. In high school, studying had structured her life, but it had also been her happy place. She could get lost in words, numbers, facts, and ideas. Safe in her own world.

But in the carrel, her body and heart kept distracting her mind. Generations of Yalies had decorated the carrel with scrawls and pictures. Words crowded the wooden walls, shouting at her. And sex was everywhere.

My nipples ache to be touched, said the scribble directly in front of her, with a helpful illustration. Standing her book on end, she shoved it against the carrel to cover it.

An hour later, her notes were done. Sketchy, but done. She flipped open her laptop to start her paper. Her fingers tapped her keyboard in rhythm, sentences were building on her screen, and she was finding the groove.

That was when a buzz came from her purse.

"Hello?" she whispered, cradling her phone between her shoulder and ear. She wasn't in the silent part of the library. As long as she kept her voice down and the conversation short, she'd be okay.

"Hey, sweetheart." Ian's voice was hoarse, cracked almost to nothing. It was sexy. It made her feel warm. It also made her worried.

"What happened? Your voice is gone."

"Baby, it's the sign of a really good, crazy night," he whispered. "It'll be back tomorrow. There's nothing to worry about."

"Yeah. About the whole crazy night thing."

"By crazy, I mean enough alcohol to float a raft. But nothing else."

"Okay." She stood up and glanced across the row of carrels and the tables in the middle of the room. "I had a crazy night too."

"Oh, really." What was left of Ian's voice changed its tone. "What juicy details do I get?"

"I went to a frat party with Kate and Eleanor. I was having fun, I got pretty drunk… And there I was." She took a deep breath. "Dancing between two guys."

Silence. "And?" Ian said finally.

"Nothing happened. I didn't want anything to happen. In my mind, it was you in front of me." And Brendan behind her, which she wasn't going to say. "I was remembering that night at the club, after graduation…" She trailed off. Ian didn't fill in the pause. "When I figured out that it wasn't you, I left. No big deal."

"Christ. How much did you have to drink?"

"A few shots, more than usual. I just liked the thought of getting wild."

"Why?"

"What do you mean, why?" she snapped. Her head throbbed. "I thought you liked that about me. You encouraged it from the start."

"Yeah, when I'm with you."

"Isn't that what you did last night? Go wild, without me."

"Diana…" Ian's rasp made her want to wrap her arms around him and rewind the last twenty-four hours. "Going wild's overrated. Way overrated."

"Says the expert."

"I am the expert." Ian's voice sharpened, louder now. "And I'm telling you so you don't wake up somewhere you don't want to be, with no idea how you got there."

She dropped onto her chair and closed her laptop.

"Look," she said quietly. "I missed you. I left. Nothing happened. I didn't want anything to happen. I went outside and lay down on the grass to take a nap, but then I called Sonia and she walked me back to the dorm and got me in bed."

"Oh yeah? I'm buying Sonia flowers."

"You never buy me flowers."

"I bought you a vibe. Flowers die. Rechargeable vibes don't."

Diana laughed. The hint of a grin in Ian's voice encouraged her to go on. "And, uh, I called you and got Brendan, who said you were passed out and snoring, and we got to talking."

"Uh-huh." Ian exhaled on the other end of the line. Now she heard the tease. "He told me all about that." Ian's voice went high. "'Brendan makes everything better. Help me, Daddy Brendan!'"

"I did *not* call Brendan daddy," Diana hissed.

Heads turned in the library. She whipped around to face the wall, fanning her burning cheeks with her free hand.

"Oh really?" Ian's tone was all innocent surprise. "He told me you did."

"Forget it," Diana grumbled.

Ian obviously didn't think anything of her drunken Saturday night ramblings, and neither did Brendan. In the light of day, sober and facing a week of finals ahead, she was determined to forget it too.

Chapter Eighteen

Lines of water drizzled down the bus window. Diana leaned her forehead against the glass, letting her eyes slide closed as the rain-washed landscape streaked by.

On the seat next to her, in her tote bag, was a box of M & M cookies she'd baked in the dorm kitchen. The scents of butter, sugar, and melted chocolate filled the air, and it took all her self-control not to sneak one.

Nestled in the bag by the box of cookies was her entire collection of sex toys, wrapped up in a silky chemise she'd bought over Thanksgiving break while she was missing Ian. A book lay open on her lap.

It was Friday night, a week since she'd worn the red dress and called Sonia for a rescue. Since then, she'd survived her first finals at Yale. She'd pulled two all-nighters, gotten sick mid-week, staggered around campus in a pair of sweats she'd borrowed from Kate — for three days straight — that she never would have been caught dead in otherwise, and popped caffeine pills when she couldn't face another cup of coffee.

Grades weren't out yet for most classes. She had no idea if she'd scraped by or pulled As. And in this moment, she was too exhausted to give a shit. She was done with fall semester.

All the ingredients were coming together for a celebratory weekend: toys, lingerie, cookies, and Ian. But she was too worn out to feel like celebrating, and she didn't know where she and Ian stood.

They'd talked between finals. It was exam week for him too, and he actually seemed to be studying. Diana had no idea how he was doing in any of his classes, and he wouldn't tell her. She tried not to push for information. He was on the basketball team; that meant he'd gotten his grades up. Still, she worried.

And she'd been terrible on the phone. Thinking back on their conversations, she'd acted every inch the humorless ice princess. The stuck-up goody-two-shoes who never broke a rule. And this time, unlike high school, she'd known she was doing it.

She'd brushed Ian off when he said sweet things, ignored his jokes and silly comments, and refused to take the bait when he made suggestive cracks. She'd been aloof, even cold, while wondering underneath if she and Ian were okay. The times she did sleep, guilt woke her up.

When she tried to bring up their drunken nights apart, he laughed it off. She didn't ask about Brendan.

Now she was done with finals, but the last thing she felt like doing was letting loose.

The bus pulled into the station. Ian was waiting, the hood up on his sweatshirt, when she disembarked.

She went straight into his arms. The hug felt good, and she let the rain fall on them, hoping it would wash her clean.

Ian let go and tipped her chin up for a kiss. His lips were warm, but when his tongue slipped into her mouth, she pulled back, self-conscious in front of all the people at the bus stop.

"Are you getting shy on me?" he teased.

"Maybe." She straightened her glasses. He pulled the tote bag off her other shoulder to carry it. "Or just wet."

"That's more like it." He grinned, pulling her to the Jeep.

"Ian," she groaned. "Do you have to think about sex all the time?"

He stopped in front of the passenger door. When she saw his face, she wished she hadn't said it. He quickly covered with a laugh.

"I've been asked that before. But never by you, bad girl."

"I'm sorry."

"Are you thinking about it enough for both of us? If you want to give me a break, I'll take it." He opened the door for her.

"I guess I'm the one on a break right now." She settled into the passenger seat and gave him a remorseful look. "This has been the least sexy week of my life. You should look inside my bag when you get in the car."

Ian paused, one hand on the Jeep. Then he shrugged and closed the door. Swinging himself into the driver's seat, he unzipped her tote bag.

"What's this?" He tore into the box of cookies. "Are these for me?"

"Of course. Will you share?"

"Always."

He offered one to her for a bite, then popped the rest in his mouth. The M & Ms were little puddles of chocolate. The heat was running in the Jeep, and Ian's fingers were warm against her lips.

Dammit, she would relax if it killed her. Everything would be fine.

Ian handed her another cookie, took a second one for himself, and pulled out of the parking lot.

*

"Can we go to your room?" she murmured, as Ian twisted the key in the front door of the twins' apartment. "I just want to be close to you —" She broke off as they walked into the living room. "Hey, Brendan."

"Hey, cutie." He smiled at her from where he was stretched out on the couch. The TV was turned on low. "'Sup," he added to his brother. Ian nodded.

"You're not going out tonight?" Diana asked.

"Nah. I'm taking it easy after finals. Jeff and Steve already left for winter break. You guys have fun."

Even with the dimples, it was an obvious dismissal. Brendan turned back to the TV, sipping his beer. Diana sighed, letting Ian pull her into his bedroom.

She dropped onto his bed. The flannel sheets were soothing. She wanted to wrap herself up in them and nap for a hundred hours.

Ian sat down next to her, pulling his shirt off, then his jeans. She sagged against him as he undressed her.

"Foxes shouldn't wear other foxes," he whispered, as he peeled off her fox-printed sweater.

"Funny," she murmured. She just wanted to sleep.

Ian unbuttoned her corduroy skirt and worked it over her hips, unzipped her riding boots and took them off, pulled her tights away from her body. She let him unhook her bra and slide her panties down her legs as she dropped her glasses on his desk.

"So pretty." He nuzzled her neck. "Come on in bed."

She curled up close to him under the covers. The thick bulge in his boxers brushed her crotch. Ian was kissing her, rolling her nipple between his fingers, caressing the curve of her breast in a way that would normally drive her insane.

When Ian was gentle with her, it did something beyond words. God, when Ian was rough with her, it went beyond words too. Her body always responded.

But right now, nothing, except the friction of his hand on her breast.

"Ian—"

"Just take it easy, baby. You've had a long week. You work too hard." His hand slid between her legs and into the crevice of her thighs.

"Wait," she whispered, but Ian was already parting her folds. He blinked in surprise when his fingers met her pussy. She wasn't wet at all.

Diana moved his hand away.

"Okay," he said. "That's different."

"I'm sorry. I'm just not—" she broke off. She hated to say it.

"…in the mood?" Ian finished. His dimples showed.

"Yeah. It's been a rough week. It's not about you." She buried her face in his pillow and breathed in the clean scent. What the hell was wrong with her?

"It's okay, Diana. It happens."

"No, it's not okay," she mumbled. "I miss you so much when we're apart. I haven't seen you in three weeks. Every minute should count."

"Don't force it." Ian rubbed her back. "We've got the whole weekend."

"You're obviously not having this problem." She looked down at Ian's boxers. The erection pushing out the plaid cotton didn't seem as hard. Dammit, this was not turning out the way she'd hoped. "I can just give you a blow job."

"Just?" he repeated. "You're obviously not feeling this right now. I don't want it either unless you're into it." He folded his arms under his head. "If you need a nap, go to sleep."

"No, I feel bad."

"Why?"

"Because of last weekend. I missed you. I went a little wild, and I thought I had everything under control, but it's all just… And you were mad, but you got even more wasted than I did, and Brendan on the phone…" She bunched up the pillow in her hands.

"Diana, I'm just gonna come out and say it," Ian interrupted. He propped himself up on his elbows. "You think you know everything now because of me and Brendan. Guess what? You don't. You said so yourself. You're insanely smart, but you still have a lot to learn."

"Brendan said the same thing this summer," she snapped. "Did you coordinate?"

Ian heaved a sigh and sat up, leaning his head against the wall. "You don't know your own limits yet. You push yourself too hard.

271

With school, with…fun. For now, just take it easy on the alcohol when I'm not around, okay?"

Her eyes opened wide. She sat up straight and pulled the covers over her breasts. "That's controlling."

"I'm not trying to control you, Diana."

"That's exactly what you're doing. Sorry, no."

Ian rubbed a hand over his hair. He hadn't had a haircut in awhile, and he looked so messily gorgeous that she wanted to eat him up — or would, if she weren't royally pissed.

"I'm worried about you. You were on the edge of losing it when I talked to you this week. And the party last weekend…that 'try everything once' thing... You don't have to try everything once, babe. Really. There's a lot of shit out there you can stand to skip."

Diana glared at him. "What's happened to you? You used to be all about the bad girl hidden inside little Diana who lived next door. You were all about bringing out the real me. Remember when you and me and Brendan were in your Jeep going to that club after graduation—" yes, dammit, she was going there, even as Ian's eyes widened — "and you said everyone in the car knew the truth about me? You guys are the only ones who know the truth. And now you don't even want that to be true."

"Jesus, Diana. All I said is that I'm worried. It's different now, okay? You're my girlfriend. I worry."

"Then stop. Stop worrying." She was winding up, going too far, but dammit, she wanted Ian to push back. "Stop being my dad. Brendan does that just fine."

Ian's eyebrows shot up. "Then you stop being a bitch."

"Fine," she growled. "I will, when you stop being a controlling jerkface."

"Jerkface?" Ian looked like he wasn't sure whether to laugh. "You really have been studying too hard. It's drained your brain. You can do better than that."

272

"Well, maybe I'm too busy worrying about you too. You won't tell me anything about your grades or let me look at your papers, which I get, because *I* don't want to mess with *your* business, but I don't even know if you're staying on top of everything and I can't stand to see you kicked out of school and..."

"Diana, can you please just trust me?" Ian's face was suddenly so naked.

"Yes," she said quietly. "Can you trust me?"

Ian blinked at the "yes." "To do what? To take care of yourself? To not go overboard on everything? I want to, but I don't know if I can. 'Cause I think you want to go overboard. No, I don't think, I fucking know."

"Well, why don't you just spank me?" she snapped.

Silence spread outward as they stared at each other. A surprised gleam lit Ian's eyes.

"For real? Or are you just saying that?"

"I —" she swallowed. "Yes," she heard herself say.

The anger in his expression was fading. He threw back the covers and sat on the edge of the bed.

"On my lap, little girl."

Oh no. Oh yes. She'd fantasized about this moment before, but she'd never known how, exactly, to ask Ian to spank her. Not just a flirty slap or a smack on the ass as he drove into her, but an honest-to-God, full-on spanking.

Naked, goosebumps pricking her skin, she climbed onto Ian's lap and lay across his legs.

In an instant, a strong arm pressed into the small of her back. A pinch on her ass made her twitch. Heat flushed her body, and she was wide awake now. Ian rubbed all over her bare cheeks, making her shiver, his erection pressing against her hip.

"I'm not mad at you anymore," she whispered. "Are you still mad at me?"

"Mad? Hmmm..." He squeezed one cheek firmly. "Not exactly." She couldn't see his face, as she stared at her glasses and clothes lying on his desk, lit by the haloed lamp. She could only hear the broad grin in his voice. "But you have a lot to be spanked for, Diana."

"Yes, I do..." she moaned, squirming against the bulge in his boxers. Then a large hand descended on her ass.

"Ian!" She jumped.

"Naughty girl." He spanked both her round cheeks. "Not getting enough sleep, not taking care of yourself, being mean to your boyfriend..." He punctuated each statement with a satisfying smack.

Oh God. She never could have handled this at the beginning, or even over the summer. She felt so vulnerable lying across Ian's lap, totally at his mercy, that she started to giggle. Her pussy was waking up, warm and tingling. Her ass, too. Ian wasn't spanking her hard, but there was a definite sting in his slaps. When she gasped, he switched to massaging her ass, soothing the warm cheeks.

"I'm sorry, Ian." She made her voice extra remorseful. "I'll be good. I promise."

He groaned softly above her.

"You can try, Diana. Like you said, though. We both know the truth. You can't be a good girl. Not for long."

Squeezing her curvy flesh, his hand slipped down to her warm valley. Fingers explored her pussy, sliding through the juicy folds.

"What's this?" Ian's voice dripped with mock astonishment. "Is this hot slut getting turned on by her punishment? Very, very bad."

"Ian! Ooohh..." But she was tilting her ass towards him, inviting his hand. "More."

He sucked in his breath. When he spoke again, his voice was rough.

"Here I was thinking that you needed a cuddle..." He spanked her again while he massaged her clit, making her cry out. "Some tender loving care..." Another smack, with a pinch on her clit. "A couple kisses while I listen to you..." Her pussy hugged Ian's fingers as he worked them inside her. "And instead it turns out you want to be spanked like the bad girl you are."

She groaned, squirming against Ian's hand as he peppered her full cheeks with smacks.

"I like that other stuff too," she panted.

"Sure you do. But it's not what you need right now, is it? You've told me everything, baby. I know it all. All your naughty fantasies and your dirty little dreams." He fingered her more firmly, flexing and twisting in her tight pussy. Jolts of pleasure ran through her body as he kept spanking her. "I've read every poem you've ever written. I know all your secrets. I know how scared you used to be, and how horny. You never thought about your perfect date in high school the way your friends did. Nooo, you fantasized about screwing every boy in class. Then you'd hand in your perfect homework like a goody two shoes and run straight home to rub your hot little pussy. And you'd come so fucking hard, you little slut."

"Yes, oh God, yes," she gasped, lifting her ass, urging him on. Her head felt light. She was going to come soon, quivering around Ian's fingers, her ass warmer and warmer under his hand.

"Unbelievable." He squeezed her full cheeks, and she groaned. "You just want more and more. Maybe I should call my brother in here to witness you getting every last" *smack!* "fucking" *smack!* "punishment you deserve."

"Yesssss," she hissed, thrusting desperately toward him as hot juice dripped from her pussy. "Get Brendan."

Ian's hand froze on her ass. Shit.

"I was kidding, Diana."

She twisted around to look at him. His handsome face was incredulous. "Uh, so was I."

"Don't lie to me, little girl." Ian gave her a firm pinch, and she let out a shriek.

Oh God, Brendan had to have heard that over the TV. Not like he didn't know — firsthand — but this was so awkward, and she had no idea what to do.

"I love *you*," she whispered. "I want *you*. And you're the one who brought it up."

Ian let out a breath. "I know, Diana." Then a wicked grin split his face. "And you're still pure slut."

"Then why don't you teach me a lesson?" The words left her mouth before she could think.

"You know I will."

Ian stretched a long arm to his desk, snagging his phone. He texted rapidly, then held the glowing screen in front of her flushed face. His thumb hovered over 'send.'

Diana's getting spanked. She's been bad. Want to watch? Delete this

And Brendan's name at the top.

"Ian…?" Dear God. Her nipples were two hard buds, rubbing against Ian's comforter. Her pussy ached with need as his hand left her folds. A smack on her cheek sent ripples through her flesh.

"Yes or no, bad girl?"

This was insane. Brendan wouldn't want to. They'd all moved on. The three of them were in the past, long in the past. Why bother him? It would be so rude, to intrude on his quiet evening of TV watching and beer drinking. He'd say no, without a doubt.

And…on the tiny off-chance he said yes…he'd just be watching. He'd just be witnessing his brother punishing her, driving her crazy with need, making her his while she writhed on his lap… Maybe Brendan would give her a dimpled smile, murmuring that he knew she could take it, encouraging her to be a good girl for Ian…

"Yes." It came out a breathy whisper.

Ian hit 'send.'

Chapter Nineteen

The TV in the living room went silent. Moments passed. Neither she nor Ian moved. Her heart thudded in her chest, and Ian's hand was frozen on her ass.

In front of her face, Ian's phone buzzed.

You sure? the screen said.

Ian didn't respond. He was waiting for her, Diana realized. She nodded.

We're sure, Ian texted back.

At the light knock on Ian's door, Diana's head jerked up. Ian gave her ass a squeeze, but he didn't speak.

"Come in," she called.

The door opened with a soft creak. Brendan stepped into the room. Diana took in his well-worn T-shirt, his gray sweats, and the hesitation in the way he moved — a hesitation that was new for Brendan.

His face opened into a broad smile as his eyes traveled over her bare body, draped across Ian's lap. Her breasts were pressed into the covers, and Ian's hand rested on her ass, but Brendan saw enough, she knew.

He closed the door behind him.

"Did you do something wrong, Di?"

She flushed. Ian gave her a firm smack.

"I guess…"

"You guess? Ian wouldn't be spanking you if you didn't, would he?"

Oh God. Words failed her. Brendan swiftly crossed the room to stand in front of her, the bulge in his sweatpants beyond obvious. Crouching by the bed so their eyes were level, he took her chin in his hand.

"What did you do, sweetness?" His voice was so understanding. "Tell me."

"I—" she began. Her head swam. "I went kind of wild last weekend. I wanted to do my own thing, but I also missed Ian, and I missed the three of us—"

She broke off at Ian's intake of breath. It felt so crazy and completely right to confess to Brendan while she lay naked over Ian's lap, but how far would she go?

"And I didn't get enough sleep... And I went overboard studying... And I was mean to Ian... And I came on to you on the phone when I was drunk," she whispered. "I wanted the three of us together."

"Brendan told me," Ian said in a low voice. "He told me all about your phone call."

Diana stiffened on Ian's lap.

"And," Ian went on, giving her ass a lingering pinch, "he told me you were sad that him and me had secrets from each other now. You missed us being close."

"I do," she murmured. "I didn't know how to tell you that."

"Diana, after my brother and I took you together, and after all we've been through, you could do me the favor of telling me the truth. The whole fucking truth. No secrets."

"I wanted to be totally honest with you," she panted. "But I thought maybe it's better to forget it."

"Things like that don't stay forgot." Ian's eyes were half-closed, locked on her when she twisted to look up at him. "I'd rather know. And I'd rather hear it from you."

"Okay." She let out a breath.

Her eyes met Brendan's, and he raised his eyebrows. She wanted to look at Ian too, see them both at the same time. But that would mean sitting up, which would mean showing Brendan her breasts, and she wasn't at all sure where this was going. She stayed in place across Ian's lap.

"The whole fucking truth is…" She was sweating. "I want Ian to be my boyfriend. I don't like Brendan that way. But I miss the three of us together. I miss you guys together, I don't want to drive you apart, I want you to be close but better than before, without the good twin-bad twin bullshit. And, and when I got off the phone with Brendan — I touched myself afterward."

She gasped when Ian spanked her again, making her flesh ripple. "Naughty girl," he hissed.

"You did, Di?" Brendan looked startled, then delighted. He ran a thumb over her lower lip. "You played with your pussy? Did you make yourself come?"

Shock ran through her body, and it didn't help when large fingers slid through her folds, right as Brendan murmured the word "pussy." She was wet now. Very wet.

"Ye-e-esss," she moaned. She needed to tell them everything. "I used that insanely huge toy Ian sent —" "*Jesus,*" Ian muttered above her. "And I thought about the three of us in bed together laughing — and everything was okay — and I didn't know if it ever would be —"

"Poor baby." Brendan smoothed back her bangs. "We're right here. And Ian's helping you, isn't he? I bet you're really wet now."

"Yes," she breathed. Ian was slowly, firmly rubbing her clit, sending sparks of pleasure through her pussy. His cock was rock-hard against her hip.

"What do you want, Diana?" Ian's voice was low and rough. "Do you want Brendan to watch while I give you what you deserve? While I teach you how to be good? Or do you want to be the bad girl we all know you are? Do you want my brother to do more than watch?"

Oh God, oh shit, of course she did, but she was with Ian now, and what would this do to all of them?

"I'm yours," she whispered. Ian's cock pulsed against her at her words. "We all know that."

Brendan had a slight smile on his face. His hand still cupped her chin, and his thumb rubbed her cheek in circles. He was holding back, she realized. Not trying to run the show.

"Answer me, Diana." Ian flicked her clit, and she cried out. "Yes or no?"

"What do *you* want?" she parried.

"I want you to tell me the truth, baby. I always want you to tell me the truth." Jesus, he was massaging her pussy now, making her quake. She didn't have a chance.

"Yesssss," she moaned. "I want Brendan—" she gasped when Ian pinched her clit — "to do more than watch."

Ian let out a low groan, pushing his cock against her hip. Brendan's eyes lit up, but he didn't move.

"How much more, sweetness?" He tipped up her chin.

For a minute, she could only pant as Ian stroked her wet core. That had to be enough of an answer — but no, they were still waiting.

"Everything," she whispered. "I want to give in to you and Ian and let you decide. I want you to make agreements. I want you to work together."

Brendan's eyes flicked to his brother's. Ian slapped her ass one last time.

"Get in bed, Diana. Me and Brendan are going out to talk. You can touch yourself, but if you come, you'll be in trouble."

Diana gaped at him. Out of the corner of her eye, she saw an approving look on Brendan's face. "What kind of trouble?"

"You don't want to know. Now do it."

Holy shit. Ian had taken charge that wild night before the Fourth of July, but he'd dominated her with his body. The sex had been all raw physicality and strength. Now he was giving her orders? And expecting her to obey?

She reached for Brendan. Fine, she'd do what Ian said. After all, that's what she'd asked for. But she'd do it her way.

Strong hands grasped hers, helping her off Ian's lap. As she straightened up, she did a slow turn so both twins could see her bare curves from all directions. Nerves and desire heated her skin.

Brendan's eyes lit up, roaming over the heavy swells of her breasts and the puckered nipples that were deep red with excitement. Ian let out a low growl. Her stomach fluttered, and an insistent pulse beat between her thighs. She put a little strut in her walk.

Keeping her gaze on the twins, she climbed into Ian's bed and pulled the covers up to her chin.

"Bye," she breathed. Her heart was hammering. "Have fun. See you soon."

Ian led Brendan out of the room, closing the door behind them. Out in the hall, deep voices rose and fell. Bursts of laughter came through the door, snatches of "Remember when...?" and "How about we..."

She closed her eyes and let her hand drift over her body, but she was too nervous to do much.

Her eyes flew open at the creak of the door.

The longer she'd dated Ian, the less the twins had looked alike to her. Now, as they walked into Ian's bedroom together, she had to squint for the cleft in Brendan's chin, the freckle under Ian's left eye, because she could barely tell them apart. Gorgeous, muscular, wearing boxers and huge, identical grins.

Sweet Jesus, what had she gotten herself into?

Brendan was holding something behind his back. As the twins approached the bed, she craned her neck to see what it was, but large hands cupped her jaw — Ian, pulling her into a kiss that clouded her vision. When his mouth left hers, Brendan's hands were empty.

Drawing the moment out, she pulled down the covers until the tops of her breasts were exposed to two hungry pairs of hazel eyes.

The mattress sank when Ian leapt on the bed and straddled her, then again when Brendan sat. The covers brushed her skin as they slipped further down, baring her to the waist. Ian's hands closed over her breasts.

Diana shivered, feeling the force of Brendan's gaze along with Ian's touch. As crazy as it had been the first time around with the twins, it felt even more naughty now, more forbidden, more secret to be with both brothers, now that Ian was her boyfriend.

"So…" Ian squeezed both her breasts, the generous flesh spilling between his fingers. "You said you want us to make agreements."

"Yes."

"You want to give in to me and Brendan."

"Yes," she whimpered.

"You're letting us decide." Leaning down, Brendan licked her ear.

"That's what I said." A little shyly, she reached up to stroke his hair.

"Okay, baby. The agreement…" Ian pinched her nipples to rosy peaks, then released them, rubbing them with his thumbs as the blood rushed back, "is that Brendan stays here until the sun comes up. And you're ours until then, Diana."

"Meaning…?" As her eyes locked on Ian's, hooded and dangerous with desire, her nerves sharpened.

"You'll find out."

She opened her mouth to respond, and Brendan's lips closed on hers. She gasped at the suddenness of his soft mouth, his warm tongue. Brendan's tongue, playing with hers. As she fell into the kiss, Ian tossed the covers off the bed. The mattress was moving. He was opening her legs. Firm hands parted her thighs, making her gasp again.

"Ian," she moaned into Brendan's mouth. "Oh Jesus—" Strong fingers met her soaked cunt, rubbing and stroking. "Brendan—"

"Is Ian playing with you, sweetness?" Brendan broke the kiss to smile down at her. "Is he touching your little pussy?"

"Oh…" Diana moaned. A finger dipped inside her, just as Brendan pinched her nipples. "Brendan!" she yelped.

Fiery pleasure radiated out from the tight buds. He kissed her again, his lips as juicy as she remembered. As she relaxed into the kiss, his hands slid over her breasts and along her shoulders. Gently but firmly, he eased her arms upward until her wrists crossed above her head.

"Stay like that," Brendan ordered. He reached over to the desk.

Diana obeyed, looking confusedly down at Ian. He just grunted. His tongue traced impossibly hot lines over her eager clit, her silken lips, and her tight opening. Moaning from all the stimulation, she reached for him on instinct.

Brendan's voice stopped her. "I said stay like that, Di."

What? Ian's head was right there, his hair tousled, inviting her to yank and tug. And who'd put Brendan back in charge?

"Ian?" she gasped.

He lifted his head, his lips glistening with her juices. "You heard Brendan, baby. Do what we tell you. Both of us."

A pleased smile broke over Brendan's face at that "we," that "us." Ian's words sent waves of heat rolling over her body.

She groaned in frustration, wrapping her fingers around the slats of the headboard to keep her hands in place. Ian was licking her soft folds, parting them with heavy slurps of his tongue, nudging her opening over and over and totally ignoring the swollen bud of her clit.

Brendan dropped a warm hand on her knee, urging it open to give Ian even more access to her pussy.

"I'm proud of you, Di," he murmured. "You're already doing amazing."

Diana focused on Brendan's smile, on his muscled body in the glow of the lamp. There was something in his other hand.

The light gleamed on a pair of handcuffs.

These cuffs were metal, lined with fur. Not the plastic loops she'd seen on the Fourth of July.

A curl of excitement and sheer nerves unwound in her stomach. When a thick tongue pushed against her tight core, she shivered.

"Congrats. New handcuffs," she managed to say. "Now that I see them, I believe you. I thought you were going to keep the glow-in-the-dark ones forever."

At the snort of laughter from between her legs, her hands dove toward Ian, tugging his thick hair. She was giggling too. Strong hands grabbed her wrists and pinned them swiftly above her head. She squirmed against Brendan's unyielding grip, laughing harder.

"Are you going to model them for me? Or is Ian going to?"

"Come on, sweetness." Brendan lifted her chin with two fingers, his other hand firm on her wrists. The light touch sent a shockwave through her body, straight to Ian's tongue on her cunt. "You know who these are for tonight."

Her fingers tightened on the headboard, and a shudder of arousal ran over her full curves. She knew. Of course she knew, but this was a whole new level of trust. She couldn't— she wanted— oh Jesus. She was so scared suddenly, and so curious.

Ian raised his head again, his lips glossy with her juices. The little smile on his face was an open challenge.

"Can you handle it, baby? Being tied up for me and Brendan?"

He'd picked the right words. Indignation sparked her body.

"I can handle whatever you give me." The words came out husky.

A hot tongue stroked her ear. "Do you trust us, Di?"

Of course she did. She'd told them both, every time Brendan had asked her...

No. Brendan hadn't asked. He'd ordered. *Say you trust us,* that first time in the treehouse. *You can trust us, sweetness,* in the Jeep on the way to the club. He hadn't asked, until now.

Her lashes fluttered. "Completely. More than anyone."

Then her eyes flew wide. A single teasing suck on her clit made her hips thrust toward Ian again, just as he pulled back to give her an infuriating smirk.

In one fluid motion, Brendan stood, dropped his boxers, and straddled her. He was totally naked, perfect, his muscles outlined in the lamplight, leaning over her just like she'd imagined when she found the handcuffs. Pointing toward her face was his hard cock, as gorgeous as she'd remembered. A pearl of liquid hung from the tip.

Smoothly, he clasped a handcuff around one of her wrists, looped the chain through Ian's headboard, and closed the second cuff around her other wrist.

Click. Click.

Moving off of her, he surveyed the pale expanse of her skin and his brother's head between her legs with frank appreciation.

"Delicious," he murmured. "I've wanted this for a long time, Di."

She shuddered, hugging Ian's face between her thighs, but he pushed her legs open and held them down.

"Me too," she whispered. "For so long."

Ian raised his head from her eager cunt, drinking in the sight of her arched back and her arms above her head. The position pushed out the generous swells of her breasts and made every curve available. The sheer lust on his face made her shudder with need.

"Fuck," he muttered.

Heat was moving over Diana in waves, starting with her bound wrists and ending at her toes.

"I thought you said this was Brendan's thing," she murmured.

"Doesn't mean I don't think it's hot." Large hands spread her thighs wider, squeezing the creamy softness.

Diana bit back a moan. The hunger in Ian's eyes was almost too much to take, and with her hands restrained, she couldn't do a thing about it. When patient fingers stroked her breast, exploring the

285

sensitive underside, she began making noise. All kinds of noise.

"That's it, sexy," Brendan murmured, rolling her rosy nipple between his fingers. "Let go for us."

He bent down, and his lips covered hers. Too excited for words, she opened her mouth, and his tongue slipped in. Dear Lord, Ian's mouth was so hot and soft and demanding on her pussy, and she was openly making out with Brendan now, kissing him eagerly, sucking his lower lip as she adjusted to being bound and exposed.

Every movement felt more intense, and as her excitement built, it was harder to breathe.

"You guys—" she panted, pulling at the handcuffs.

Ian lifted his head and gripped her thighs. "Sweetheart. Relax."

"Just like you wanted, beautiful." Brendan pulled back to kiss her forehead, his hand comforting on her breast. The twins' steady touches calmed her. "Give in to me and Ian, and we'll give you what you need. How long have you wanted it like this?" He nodded at the cuffs.

"Months," she breathed.

"Since the summer?" Ian was still looking up at her from between her spread legs.

"Yes. But I didn't think it could happen."

"It's happening, baby." He buried his face in her pussy. She squeezed his head with her thighs, thrashing.

"Easy, Di." The reassuring look on Brendan's face was all big brother, but the pinches on her nipples, teasing them to tight buds, were as far away from brotherly as you could get. "We know you can do this, but if you need us to slow down or stop, say so. Okay?"

"Okay."

Her eyes fluttered shut when Brendan's mouth closed over hers again. His lips were warm. His hands were knowing on her breasts, rolling her nipples between his fingers just as lips captured her clit. With a gasp, Diana thrust against Ian's tongue as he licked and licked the little bud. She was so close to climax, so close to dissolving under two hungry mouths…

But he pulled back from her slickness. Brendan sat up and gave her a wink. Her wrists strained at the cuffs as she tried to beckon them both to her.

"Not yet, beautiful." Ian's laugh was heavy with lust. "Not for a long time."

"What?" she screeched.

"Hang in there, sweetness." Brendan's broad grin infuriated her. "Don't worry. We're going to give you everything a bad girl needs. Once you earn it."

Before she could retort, Ian was on his knees between her legs, pulling them wide. His cock, warm and thick, sank into her in one long plunge.

"Oh God. Ian…"

He grunted, holding himself still. She stared up at him. Desire contorted his handsome face.

"I'm gonna fuck you, baby," he whispered.

She writhed on the soft flannel sheets. Ian was relentless, holding one of her knees up while he braced himself on the bed with his other hand, and she was so wet and slippery that he was able to go fast almost right away. She was shaking again, beyond grateful for Brendan's hand in her hair, his warm palm stroking her throat and the swell of her breast.

"Brendan," she moaned, seeking reassurance. "Help me."

He gave her breast a squeeze. His thumb pressed gently at the base of her throat, and she gasped. Ian was watching it all, his thrusts bouncing her on the bed, and the look on his face made her blood rush.

"What do you need help with, sweetness?" Teeth closed on her lower lip, biting like he had all the time in the world. She moaned again, giving herself up to Brendan's kiss as Ian drove into her. "Aren't we taking good care of you? I know you love being fucked so deep."

"I need to come." Her wrists tugged the cuffs. Ian growled,

pulsing in her tight embrace.

"Only good girls get to come, Di." Brendan lay down close to her, looking entirely too comfortable. His flushed erection, his hot skin against hers, and his smoky eyes were the only clues to how aroused he was. He flicked her rosy nipple. Sparks shot through her body, making her spasm around Ian's cock. "Have you been a good girl?"

"Maybe not…"

"Ian doesn't think so. Why else was he spanking your sexy, naughty ass?"

She heaved a ragged breath as he sucked her nipple into his mouth.

"Diana's not a good girl, Brendan," Ian grunted. He leaned on both hands, slowing his strokes, pacing himself. Her body was sweaty where it joined with his. His eyes glittered with lust, moving between her pleading face and his brother's mouth on her breast. "She's got a long way to go. All night long."

"Easy for you to say," she panted. "Are you going to wait to come too?"

White teeth flashed at her. An especially deep thrust made her cry out, bucking her hips fruitlessly against Ian.

"Some other time, we can play that way. Not tonight. Goddamn, you feel incredible."

His eyes flicked to Brendan's, and the twins exchanged nods. Before she knew it, Brendan was straddling her. He leaned forward, cupping her face. The smooth skin of his cock brushed her lips.

Shaking with excitement, she flicked out her tongue to taste him. He was warm, velvety, musky. His shaft was thick and veined, his balls full and soft. He looked like Ian, of course, but she'd never compare them. This was Brendan's cock. She remembered it so well. And she remembered how he turned into a babbling mess when she sucked him.

"Uh," Brendan groaned. "Oh yeah, Di. Take me in, sweetness." He massaged her head, burying his fingers in her hair as she opened her lips.

This was happening. Her fantasy was real. She was handcuffed, closed in by hard male bodies, licking Brendan's cock as Ian fucked her deep. She felt so vulnerable, so out of control, but somehow secure.

This was exactly where she wanted to be. Her heart raced, her head felt light, and she was giddy with lust.

As Brendan groaned with pleasure at each swipe of her tongue, hands squeezed her ass. The possessive touch calmed her, and she hugged Ian's waist with her legs, rocking against him.

"That's it," he rasped. "Now you're opening up to me. Let us both in, baby."

Hard flesh bumped a sensitive spot inside her. Diana moaned around Brendan's cock, her wrists straining at the cuffs. He caressed her hair and murmured soothingly to her, easing back to let her swirl her tongue over his head. His eyes were glazed, and she knew he was close to crumbling.

"So beautiful," he murmured. "You suck me so good, Di. I missed your sweet mouth. You've been doing this for Ian a lot, haven't you?"

"Mmmmm-hmmmm," she moaned, taking him in again.

Her jaw ached a little, but no way was she stopping. Brendan's handsome face contorted in lust. "Oh yeahhhh...mmmmm...oh fuck, Di, don't stop…"

He let out groan after groan of pure pleasure as he spurted into her mouth. Oh God, Brendan's cum, warm and creamy. The first she'd ever tasted. More jetted out as she caressed his cock with her tongue, and she felt a thrill of satisfaction at driving him wild with need.

"So good, baby." He pulled free of her lips, kissed her forehead, and lay down next to her. She swallowed and caught her breath. As her heart pounded, insistent hands pushed her knees to her chest. Ian leaned over her, his face dark with need.

"Ian," she gasped. Her cunt was so hot and sensitive and she was so fucking close...

"Christ, Diana." Ian's voice was rough. "You really are pure slut. I thought a spanking would teach you a lesson, but you need so much more than that."

"Please," she gasped.

"Take me, you bad girl." He thrust deep inside her, gripping her legs. "Uh...so fucking hot... Take my cum, baby."

Oh, his words pushed her so close...she wanted to go over the edge with him...but Ian was already coming, his eyes wide. When she thrust back, squeezing him, trying to grind against him, he held her hips down on the bed, keeping her still.

Brendan rubbed her jawline, smiling down at her. "Not going to happen, Di. Not 'til we say so."

A hot tear of frustration trickled down her cheek. Brendan wiped it gently away with his thumb. His half-hard cock throbbed against her hip.

"Jerk," she muttered. "Don't tell me that turned you on."

"Sshhh, baby, everything's going to be okay. You're doing so well." Brendan turned her face to his, capturing her lips in a soothing kiss.

Ian finally eased out. He lay down on her other side and gave her stomach a squeeze. Every touch was delicious agony, every inch of her skin aware of the twins. She pressed her legs together, trying to find relief. When they fell open again, Brendan stroked her creamy thighs, making her shiver.

"Ian's right, sweetness." He dimpled down at her. "He's been right all along, You're a bad girl. Do you want my fingers on your pussy?"

"Yes..."

"Touch her." Ian pinched her aching nipples, making her squirm. "Drive her out of her fucking mind."

Diana's eyes fluttered closed at the command. The first time around with their threesome, Brendan had been the bossy one. Hearing Ian tell his brother what to do with her almost made her come on the spot.

A large hand cupped her mound. Fingers slipped into her warm valley. She moaned at the first contact. Brendan's touch was so...Brendan. Sure and sensual. When she looked over at Ian, his eyes were narrowed to slits, fixed on his brother's hand between her legs. She arched against Brendan, straining at her bonds.

"So soft, baby." Brendan caressed her juicy cunt. "So perfect."

"Brendan, I need you," she pleaded. "I need Ian."

"Of course you do." He stroked her swollen lips with infuriating slowness. "I've never seen you this wet for us." His thumb pressed gently on her clit. "And I've seen you really, really fucking wet."

She lifted her hips, circling against Brendan's hand. A heavy arm pressed across her hips and pushed her to the bed. Ian was holding her down, his eyes challenging her. He sucked her throbbing nipple into his mouth.

She tried to protest the tease. She was desperate to come, desperate for either twin to get her off. But this was what she'd wanted, right? Asked for. Insisted on. Giving in to the twins, letting them take her over.

She still wanted it.

But as Brendan tickled her wet cunt, she bucked furiously.

"I hate you, Brendan." She yanked at her bonds. Brendan chuckled, caressing her pussy with a feather-light touch.

"What was that you said to Brendan about him being the nicest boy you know?" Ian smirked at her. "He told me you did."

"Fuck you," she growled. "Fuck you both."

"Careful, Di." Brendan's dimples creased his cheeks, but his hazel eyes held a warning that made her gush onto his teasing fingers. "You don't want to make us mad when you're right on the edge."

When Ian kissed his way up to her neck and sucked hard, her head swam.

"You guys." She twisted from side to side. "I need— I can't—"

"You can do this." Brendan's voice was low, firm, and encouraging. He stroked her more purposefully, spreading her juices. A warm hand rested on her thigh. "You can do this for us."

And at the same time Ian rasped, "You can't what, baby? You can't handle this? You want us to untie you?"

Did she?

Brendan was right. She'd been longing for this moment. And Ian was right; she loved the edge.

She couldn't stand another second of sweet torment, and she wanted it to last forever.

Identical faces watched her, waiting. Behind the glazed hazel eyes, there was clear concern on Ian's face, endless patience on Brendan's. She panted for breath.

"Diana." Ian's voice was gentler now. He was trying to get himself under control. "Too much? I know we're coming on really fucking strong..."

"I want this." Her voice was the softest whisper. "But I'm scared."

"I'm here." Ian stroked her face. "We're here."

"Open, Di." Brendan's tone was so persuasive that her thighs fell open. She groaned as he massaged her dripping pussy. "Take me in."

A large finger slipped inside her, then another. She squeezed down on thickness. The twinges in her pussy rippled into pure pleasure.

"More?" Brendan asked. Ian was nuzzling her neck, playing with her breasts, whispering the sweetest, dirtiest things.

"More," Diana breathed.

"Mmmmm. I'm giving it all to you, baby."

Excited, she clutched his fingers, feeling as full as she had with Ian's toy a week ago. But better, because it was Brendan inside her, real and alive. Because Ian was next to her, sucking on her breast. Because her wrists caught in the fur-lined cuffs were exquisite torture, and because none of this was a fantasy.

One whimper after another slipped from her lips.

"Brendan…"

"That's right, Di." He beamed down at her. "Four fingers in your pussy. This is what bad girls need."

"But I'm good," she moaned, quivering around him. Her cunt was soaked with cream. Brendan's fingers felt huge. She craved every touch.

"No," he said simply. "You're not, Di." Slowly, firmly, all those fingers fucked her pussy. "You're bad."

Ian kissed her on the lips, soft, then hot. "I love you so much," he whispered. "You're my good girl."

Brendan saying she was bad, Ian saying she was good — she didn't stand a chance.

"I love you too…"

Ian's hand snaked down to her mound. "Let Brendan in, sweetheart. We're going to give you what you need. We understand you, Diana."

She sobbed with pleasure, and her tightness relaxed around Brendan's probing touch.

"Fuck. That's it." Sudden lust contorted Brendan's face, in a way she'd never seen before. "So sweet. So open. So ours."

He began fingering her more roughly, and she gasped as his thrusts became harder, firmer, deeper. A cry flew from her lips, just as Ian's fingers surrounded her swollen clit, soothing it with gentle circles.

"Stay with us, Di," Brendan ordered.

"Give in to us, Diana," Ian coaxed. "Let go, beautiful."

The room was spinning. Intense lust on Brendan's face, reassurance on Ian's face —Looking pleadingly at both twins, she came.

And came, and came. Her cries filled the dimly lit room as her pussy clutched Brendan's rough fingers. Her clit responded to Ian's caresses with a cascade of sweet spasms that spread through her body.

As the waves of sharp pleasure ebbed, she dropped to the bed.

Brendan eased his fingers out of her. Ian unlocked the handcuffs and helped her free her wrists.

Soft kisses covered her face. Hands rubbed her tingling arms back into wakefulness. Murmurs played over her head, and she couldn't tell if the twins were talking to her or to each other.

Right now, she didn't care. She snuggled contentedly between two sweaty muscled bodies and let the room go dim.

When she woke, her cheek was resting on a chest that rose and fell with even breaths. A hand cupped her head. Someone was stroking her back with a possessive touch.

She was cuddled against Brendan, with Ian's hand on her back. Her sigh turned into a purr.

Then the bed moved. She felt shaking against her back.

"Ian?" she demanded, rolling her head toward him. "Are you laughing at me?"

He nipped her shoulder. "I've been wondering for a long time, Diana."

"Wondering what, exactly?"

"What it would take to wear you out."

"You haven't found out yet—" she began. "Oooh, Brendan." He was rolling her nipple between his fingers. "Enough."

He released her and gave her a wink. "We're on the right track. Right?"

"Yes. Absolutely. But let's save it for later." She raised her head to glance at Ian again. "If there's going to be a later."

Hooded eyes met hers. "There's going to be a later. If you can take it. I'm pretty damn sure we did wear you out."

"Not even close," she insisted, flopping onto her back. "This is just...really nice." Her hands crept to each side. The twins' fingers linked with hers. "It's nice to lie here with both of you."

Ian squeezed her hand. She traced a fingertip over the veins in

Brendan's wrist and up the inside of his arm.

"Mmmmm." He smiled at her. "Feels good."

Does this feel as wild for you guys as it does for me? she murmured. I know you've done this with other people.

"This is special, Di." Brendan nuzzled her hair, while Ian was saying, "No one I was in love with. And we didn't lie around and talk afterwards."

"Have you been in love before?" Diana asked. This was one conversation they'd never had.

"Not like this. You?"

She laughed. "I thought so. But it wasn't love. It was stories in my head that I made up about guys I barely talked to. I wasn't laying myself open and they weren't either. We weren't giving anything to each other. I was just obsessing and masturbating my brains out and being ridiculous."

Ian's arms tightened around her. Brendan chuckled softly.

"Brendan?" She rolled to face him. "Have you ever been in love?"

"I don't fall hard the way Ian does, sweetness. Maybe someday. But this... It shouldn't have taken so long."

She raised her head from the pillow. "You mean, it shouldn't have taken so long for us to all jump into bed after Ian and I started dating?"

"No. I didn't expect that. I wanted it, but I didn't expect it. I just mean, it shouldn't have taken so long for the three of us to be together again. In any way. You were lonely, Di. It kills me. And we both missed you."

She stared at Brendan's serious face. This was Brendan, stripping himself bare. More naked than she'd seen him before. Even the time he'd come to her room after the wild club night last June, all the sunny charm gone.

"You can't fix everything, Brendan. I learned a lot, being lonely." Ian was lying quietly next to her, rubbing her hand between both of his. "Even if you think I don't know anything."

"I never said that." He sighed. "You should never have to be alone."

"I think everyone needs to be alone once in awhile, just to know what it's like. Ian and I — we've talked about it."

"We should have been there for you."

"You tried. More than once. Unless you were just trying to get in my pants."

"You don't wear pants, baby." Ian ran a lazy finger over her stomach.

"Then up my skirt."

"What?" Brendan looked at her innocently. "Us? Never."

"What if I'd said yes in high school? What if I'd said, Brendan, I do need some help? From both of you? With everything?"

Brendan cleared his throat. He looked awkward, and Diana had to admit — she was kind of enjoying it.

"It wouldn't have gone as far, obviously. Maybe. We would have done whatever you wanted to do, Di. But yeah, you were beautiful. You've just gotten more gorgeous."

"Eh, she's okay," Ian mumbled from her other side. Diana whacked his arm. "That's all you got?"

"Don't try me, Ian."

Brendan's serious expression shifted to a smirk that could have come off his brother's face. "You're right, Di. It's good that nothing happened. Ian couldn't have handled it. He would've exploded from touching you. He would have lasted under a minute. Two minutes, if you were lucky."

"Fuck you," Ian said amiably. He stretched like a cat.

"I probably would have exploded too," Diana giggled. "Then Brendan would have cleaned everything up."

"I'm good at that."

"Very good. But you don't have to do it."

She played with Brendan's fingers. He smiled at her.

"Have you guys—" She hesitated. "Have you tied anyone up together?"

Laughter. "Uh-uh," Ian said. "Told you it was Brendan's thing."

"Why do you like it?" she wanted to know.

Brendan kissed her forehead. "It's fun and sexy. It works for me. I get to be bossy." He tickled the underside of her breast, and she wriggled in Ian's arms.

"Like you're ever not."

A hand moved between her legs. Unlike the beginning of the night — it seemed like hours and hours ago — she was ready for Ian this time. Big fingers explored her juicy core, getting her wetter.

"Do you want more, baby?" Ian's tongue traced her ear. "Because we can give you more."

"Yes," she breathed. "But no handcuffs this time. I want to touch you both."

Brendan gave her breast a gentle squeeze. He was kissing her neck. The trail of his lips over her collarbone was driving her mad.

"Turn over, sweetness."

The soft command seized her body. Desire was beginning to fog her mind.

She rolled onto her stomach. Ian moved to the head of the bed and propped the pillows behind his back. He gestured to his cock, rising from the thatch of dark hair. The silent movement spiked her arousal.

As she crawled toward him, Brendan was behind her, between her spread legs, massaging her back. His hands moved downward, kneading slowly, surely.

It felt so right to open her lips and suck Ian's cock into her mouth. She caressed him with long slurps of her tongue, cupping his balls with one hand while stroking his thigh with other. Low groans bathed her ears. Strong fingers tangled in her hair.

Brendan gripped her soft ass, spreading her open.

"Beautiful," he whispered. "So ready."

Ian grunted, thrusting into her mouth. As she sucked faster to keep up with him, Brendan's fingers slipped into her folds. God, she was absolutely dripping on his hand, and his coaxing whispers just invited more hot juices to flow over his fingers.

"So sexy, Di. You're doing so well. You're a good little cocksucker for Ian, and you're creaming all over my hand like a slut in heat."

She moaned in shocked arousal. Ian had called her a slut more times than she could count. But Brendan? Never, not once.

"Yes, baby." Brendan's voice was soothing. One finger sank into her pussy. "That's what you are for us. Who else would give it up so completely to her boyfriend and his brother? And we love it."

"We?" she pulled off of Ian's cock to pant. He tugged her hair, growling.

"I," Brendan murmured. As her lips closed around Ian's head again, his free hand gave her ass a firm pinch. "I love it. I love you like this. So sexed-up and dripping wet and hot for me and Ian."

Hard flesh pressed against her pussy, working in with steady pressure.

Oh. God. Her boyfriend's twin was fucking her. Her whole body tightened in excitement. She pushed back, and he groaned with pleasure.

"You feel amazing, sweetness." His whisper floated around her. "Just like I remembered." At his words, Ian's cock twitched between her lips.

She'd never thought this would happen again. She'd never expected to feel Brendan's sure, deep strokes in her tight sheath as he handled her hips to pull her back on his length. Each time he was fully buried inside her, he held her to him for an extra second murmuring to her as she squirmed, before releasing her and easing back.

Oh fuck. Oh yes. Her sucks on Ian's warm cock became more frantic as she quivered around Brendan's shaft. So close...

"Please," she gasped, pulling back from Ian's cock. "Touch my clit."

A firm smack on her ass cut her thrusts short. She bucked, her body tightening.

"No, Di," Brendan's deep voice chided. "We decide when you come."

Ian's fingers twisted in her hair. "Don't stop, baby," he ordered. "Not till I say so."

She felt dizzy as Brendan plunged into her, but the hazel eyes above her told her not to push. Obediently, she lapped up the pearl of liquid oozing from Ian's head, slathering his cock with her tongue and fondling the softness of his balls. God, Brendan kept slapping her ass with a large hand as he fucked her, whispering what a naughty girl she was. A girl who needed all the discipline he and his brother could hand out. She couldn't take much more of this.

Ian was pulling his erection from her mouth. Brendan's cock eased out, leaving her empty. As she moaned with need, two pairs of hands guided her to her knees, stroking her everywhere. Brendan stretched out next to her, the lamplight glowing on his body, his cock glistening with her juices, pulling her on top of him. Ian gripped her hips, growling at her to straddle his brother.

This time, she knew where this would lead. She knew she could handle it, she knew she could take both the twins inside her. But nerves flared through her body, laced with unbearable excitement.

She braced her knees on either side of Brendan, shaking with anticipation.

Ian bent over the desk, looking through the drawers, his body flushed. He met her eyes, and the want there would have burned her to ash if it weren't for Brendan's steady touch.

"It's okay, sweetness." Brendan rubbed his cock over her crotch, fondling her breast with his free hand. She clutched his arms to support herself as thick flesh nudged her opening. "It's just me and Ian."

"Just you? It's all you. It's only you."

Tears from the intensity were already trickling down her cheeks as she sank onto Brendan's cock. She gripped his shoulders, and he pulled her down for a slow kiss.

As her ass lifted, hands spread it open. Cool lube dripped down her cleft. A finger stroked her rosebud. When she moaned, Ian's finger slipped into her ass. His probing touch, as Brendan fucked her with little thrusts, almost sent her over the edge. She fluttered around him as he withdrew, desperate to be filled.

Firm roundness lodged against the pucker of her ass. As a low male noise came from behind her, she drew a ragged breath, opening to Ian. Thank God he was going slow. He was stretching her, but she was ready. Welcoming his heavy erection, slippery and hot, hugging him in her narrow channel. Her juices bathed Brendan's shaft as the twins eased in and out.

"I love you, Ian," she breathed.

"Fuck, Diana." He shuddered behind her, his cock jerking between her cheeks. "I love you too, baby."

Brendan's fingers played in her hair. When he pulled, she shuddered, her pussy and ass contracting on two rigid cocks. "Tell him," he murmured. "Tell him how good he is."

Heat bloomed down her body. This was so personal. As up-close and personal as it got.

"You're amazing. You're so pure and good in every way." She dug her fingers into Brendan's muscled shoulders as Ian worked into her tightness with controlled movements. God, it was true. When Ian's lips met her neck, she bent to kiss his twin. "And I love you, Brendan. I love you a lot."

Ian groaned softly in her ear. Brendan's face lit up in a surprised smile. He pulled her down for another kiss, a deeper one.

"I love you too, Di." His thrusts were longer, grinding against her sensually. "You know that."

Ian's cock throbbed in her ass. He felt huge as he eased out, then sank further, alternating with his brother's deep strokes. His thighs were hot against hers. Cupping her chin from behind, his thumb brushed her mouth, and she sucked it in feverishly. She was filled beyond full, barely able to contain both twins.

There were no more words. Only breaths, hard and soft. The push and pull of the twins as she rolled between them. The slide of slick skin. The more she tipped toward Brendan, tilted toward Ian, the more the boundaries dissolved. They weren't three. They were one.

Whispers dropped through the air above her, from Ian's mouth to her ear.

"Come." An insistent finger stroked her clit, caressing the swollen bud. "Come, Diana. Come. Come. Come."

"Let go," Brendan murmured beneath her.

"Take us with you."

"Do it."

"Ours."

"Yours."

"Mine."

"Ours."

Everything flooded her body at once. Flames, wind, waves. She burst, clasping the twins inside her.

The air was thick, but she was soaring. Then she fell and slammed back into her body. The twins were solid, not smoke. Heavy and real and hot and moving. Ian's growls above her, Brendan's groans below her, the hand in her hair, the wide-open hazel eyes that stared right into hers — this was real. The hard cocks spurting inside her, the sounds of pleasure, were no dream. Her orgasm seemed like it would never end.

Their breath slowed. Ian eased out of her first, and Brendan followed. She collapsed between them, her crotch sticky with cum. Her heart was still beating fast, but she couldn't move. She was sinking into Ian's flannel sheets, cushioned by the weight of the boys next door.

They lay still. She traced a path on Ian's arm with her finger. Brendan brushed her damp hair aside to kiss her neck.

"Shower?" Ian's hand covered hers.

"I thought it was impossible for me to get clean," she teased.

There were quiet chuckles — the same laugh from both twins.

"We can try."

Powerful arms scooped her up. She gazed up at the freckle high on Ian's cheek as he carried her the bathroom. Brendan adjusted the water, turning it hot enough that steam rose from the tub and filled the room.

No one spoke. Sleepily, Diana lathered a firm chest on one side, a broad back on the other. She sighed at the feeling of four soapy hands sliding over her skin. A few bubbles floated through the warm fogged air. She popped one with her finger and watched the others float away.

Back in Ian's bedroom, she laughed out loud when Brendan began to strip the sheets off the bed. Ian gave his brother a look and finished the job.

*

Hours later, Diana blinked awake in the soft darkness, woken by low voices. It was the middle of the night. She was naked in Ian's bed, lying on fresh sheets, her face resting on someone's chest. A muscled leg was between hers on one side, a solid arm flung over her on the other.

"I mean, Diana— she's amazing." That was Ian, his chest rumbling against her cheek, his arm around her waist. "Sometimes it messes with my head, I love her so fucking much."

"You always have," Brendan replied from behind her.

Diana lay still, half-awake. She didn't want to eavesdrop, but she was curious. She squeezed her thighs around Brendan's leg and reached back until her hand brushed his. She felt his sleepy surprise, then the slide of his warm fingers through hers.

"Guess so." Ian lifted his arm, then wrapped it around her again. "But being with her, it's a different world than thinking I'd never touch her. Being with a real girl instead of dreaming about her — really being with her, together, like there's never been anyone else...I don't know how to say it any better than that. But I know I can't do it any other way now."

"Well, when you figure out how to say it, let me know," Brendan murmured. He was drawing circles on her palm. She sighed into Ian's chest.

"You want that?"

"Not yet. But eventually. What you guys have... Look, I like people, but sometimes I think no one can really love anyone else unselfishly and everyone's just out for themselves. You and Di give me hope."

Quiet descended in the room. Diana wondered if the talk was over when Ian spoke.

"Thanks, bro."

"Yeah. I mean it."

*

She woke again when someone shifted behind her. Brendan was climbing out of bed. The first slivers of morning light peeked between the blinds.

"Love you, Ian." Brendan reached over her to clasp his brother's shoulder. Ian mumbled a sleepy response. "Love you, Di."

Lips brushed her cheek. She reached up to Brendan, burying her face in his firm chest. Then she tipped her head up to graze his lips with hers. Brendan cupped the back of her head, stroking her hair as he held her in a kiss.

"I love you too, Brendan," she whispered.

"Be good for my brother."

"I will. When he deserves it."

Brendan chuckled. "Ian always deserves it." He bent to kiss her again. Then he pulled on his boxers and closed the door quietly behind him.

Behind her, Ian stirred, his voice a low rumble. Strong arms wrapped around her, pulling her close.

"You awake?" she asked.

"Mmm. Were you okay with everything?"

"Yes." It came out on a sigh. "Completely. Were you?"

"Yeah. It was pretty fucking amazing." His arms tightened around her. "And now I want you all to myself again."

"I'm yours." It was all she could say. "I love you so much."

"Always."

Epilogue

Three and a half years later

Diana filed out of commencement with the other graduates in a row of black caps and gowns. The May sunshine lit the grass. She shielded her eyes and saw her parents waiting for her, the O'Brians at their side.

Her parents hugged her proudly.

"Smile big." Ian held up his phone to take pictures of them, and Diana hugged her parents again.

"Now us." She handed her phone to her dad and went to Ian. He took her face in his hands and kissed her on the lips, and she kissed him enthusiastically back. She had no shame in kissing him in front of her parents now.

Every time Diana had come home during college, her parents had more or less asked if she was done with Ian yet.

Now that they'd been together for four years — through her junior semester abroad in London and his travel for basketball, the ups and down of college, his job in the real world at a gym and her preparations for grad school — her parents had stopped asking. Her mom was even beaming at Ian right now, asking about his promotion to assistant manager like he'd been on the approved boyfriend list all along.

She wasn't done with Ian. She wouldn't ever be done with him.

"Congratulations, dear." Mrs. O'Brian kissed her on the cheek. "I can't believe how much you've grown up."

Diana had hoped Ian would make it to her graduation. Bringing his family with him was an unexpected bonus.

Brendan bent to kiss her too. There was no reason for anyone to think his lips against her cheek meant something beside brotherly affection. Or the hug he gave her, or her tight embrace around his neck.

"You smell good," she whispered.

"Congratulations, sweetness," he whispered back. "I know how hard you worked for this."

She stepped back, flushed, when he let go. Someone tapped her shoulder, and she turned to see Sonia standing behind her.

Diana stretched out her arms. Sonia grinned and put up with a quick hug. She rolled her eyes when Ian hugged her too, but looked pleased. Brendan gave her a professional smile, and Sonia shrugged in response.

"Diana was lucky to be paired with a roommate she wanted to live with for all four years of college," her dad commented.

"Not that I expected it," Diana said under her breath.

"Hey, Brendan," Ian said innocently. "Did you know Sonia's moving to Washington too? You'll be neighbors. You can say hi."

"That's great." Brendan's professional smile was back. "Absolutely."

Sonia gave Brendan a pointed look and muttered something unprintable. She waved to Diana and Ian as she walked off with her family.

Two years ago, for the twins' graduation, Diana had taken the bus to UConn for the last time. Her parents couldn't make it. She'd promised to send pictures.

Graduation was on a Sunday morning. The twins' roommates had cleared out right afterward, and Mr. and Mrs. O'Brian had driven home.

Back at the twins' apartment, Diana had looked around at the familiar couch, Ian's flannel sheets, everything that had been her home away from home for the first two years of college, and asked mournfully,

"Can we hang out for a little while before we pack everything up?"

She'd sat between them on the couch to watch a movie. Halfway through, the sitting turned to snuggling. Under her favorite blanket of Ian's, the tangle of arms and legs had felt so cozy. Innocent — at first.

Then the snuggling turned to kissing. Slow and hot, paths of lips over skin. And those paths led to clothes coming off.

Ian was unzipping her dress. Brendan massaged her thighs, soothing her as he worked his way upward. She wrestled with their shirts, trying to pull them both off at once.

Being the girl in between the twins — it hadn't happened since that December night her freshman year. The three of them had been easier with each other since then, the twins closer without being locked into good and bad. The question of whether the threesome would ever be repeated teased her fantasies, but it hadn't driven her crazy.

"Is this just for now?" she whispered.

The twins glanced at each other. A volume passed between them in the space of a second.

"How about 'til tomorrow?" Ian licked her ear. Her body tightened, and the ache between her legs beat in a pulse. She reached out to both sides, stroking the bursting bulges in the twins' pants. Their groans only raised her pleasure.

"Well, you did just graduate," she giggled.

Ian had let her tie him up. Wrists cuffed to the bed, muscled body gleaming with sweat, arms straining, growling as she sucked his hard flesh. Brendan stood behind her, massaging her ass, stroking her soaked folds with sure fingers until she whimpered and backed up against him, needing his thick cock to enter her and his soft dirty whispers to fill her ears.

God, she'd done everything possible with the twins over those two days, and some things she'd didn't know were possible. In between, the moments of talking and joking, the ease among the three of them, felt so right. When the end came, it was right to kiss Ian as her boyfriend, and Brendan as something else. A lover, going back to being a brother.

She didn't know if the threesome would happen again. She knew the twins didn't either, and that was okay. She liked it that way.

The noise of commencement brought her attention back. Her parents and the O'Brians were snapping pictures of her and Ian like they were celebrities.

"They look so attractive together," Mrs. O'Brian sighed.

"Brendan, get over here." Diana beckoned to him.

Brendan's dimples flashed. A solid arm draped over her shoulders. Ian wedged her against his brother so she was caught between them. As flashes went off, his hand dropped to give her a firm pinch on the ass. Hiding a burst of laughter behind her smile, she pinched him back.

She didn't dare do the same for Brendan. Not here, in public, with happy graduates and families everywhere. But it crossed her mind.

"It's so nice that Ian and Diana will be in the same city now," Mrs. O'Brian exclaimed. "And moving in together! We couldn't be happier."

Diana's parents made agreeable noises. She knew they were still recovering from last night's conversation. After rehearsing five times in front of a mirror, she'd calmly told them she was going to share an apartment with Ian. There were fireworks, just like the Fourth of July that first summer, but everyone had come out okay. There was no question that she knew the real Ian.

"Brendan's so far away in Washington, though," Mrs. O'Brian continued. "I hope you'll all be able to see each other often."

"Brendan, maybe it's time for you to settle down." Mr. O'Brian clapped his son on the back. "We get the feeling you're burning the candle at both ends. You should follow your brother's example."

Diana and Ian burst out laughing, and Brendan grinned. "I don't know if I can be as good as Ian. But I'll try." His father rolled his eyes.

They all went out to dinner together. Over the meal, stories flew about Diana and the twins growing up. When they got to the year the Coopers had moved away, Mrs. Cooper shook her head.

"Maybe it wasn't the best idea. Diana became so much quieter that year. And when we came back, she refused to see the twins! Thank goodness that's all in the past."

Under the table, Ian squeezed her hand. A foot nudged her ankle on the other side. She looked up, startled, at Brendan's sympathetic gaze. She let her leg rest against his.

"It wasn't a good year, Mom." Diana sucked down her iced tea. Both the twins were watching her. "It really wasn't. But it's over, and the past isn't everything, and it's never going to happen again."

After dinner, she said goodnight to her parents and the O'Brians. Everyone seemed to expect that she'd hang out with both twins that evening. They got drinks and ended up in the twins' hotel room, sitting on the balcony, talking lazily about college and the real world. More stories were told, the kind they hadn't shared with parents around.

As the conversation slowed, Diana leaned back, her eyes half-closed. The twins were watching her like they had at the restaurant, but with something very different in their gazes.

"Congratulations, Diana. You've come so far. What do you want for graduation?" Ian's voice was husky.

Her eyes opened all the way. Slowly, she took off her glasses and set them on the table.

Everything started slow. Kisses on her jaw from Brendan, licks down her ear from Ian. Each time she tried to kiss one of them back, a hand would grip her hair to hold her in place, or close on the back of her neck.

A swift palm slipped under her dress to fondle her breast. Ian was touching her out in the open, with the city spread out below them.

"You guys — oh God — anyone could see."

She tugged Ian's hair, pulling him down for a kiss that didn't end. The zipper down the back of her dress parted, inviting male hands to slide it over her shoulders and follow with the satin straps of her bra. Her hand went under Brendan's dress shirt, exploring hard abs and soft hair and the warmest skin. As his fingers wandered down her arm, they toyed with the crevice of her elbow in a way that just escaped tickling and connected straight to the desperate ache between her legs.

"Anyone could see," she whispered.

She came out there. They made her come, outside. Under the stars and above the skyline, with her dress bunched around her waist, her bra lying on the table, and her lacy thong pushed aside by insistent male fingers.

Brendan swallowed her moans in long sensuous kisses, one hand rolling her puckered nipple and the other massaging her clit. Ian's fingers filled her again and again, while he whispered words so filthy that her gasps of laughter threatened to pull her apart.

When her palms traveled down two sleek chests covered with too much fabric, bumping over belt buckles to cup two heavy bulges, her laughter deepened to uncontrollable moans.

As her cunt hugged Ian's fingers in a long burst of need, his other arm circled her shoulders, holding her close as his brother teased her clit to peaks of desire and release.

She'd been through more than she'd ever imagined with both the twins. With Ian. But out on the balcony in the open air, about to graduate and take another step into the world, coming between Ian and Brendan, she'd never felt so vulnerable yet so safe.

Strong arms carried her inside. Clothes came off and scattered the hotel room. Everything after that was a sensual blur.

Brendan, bending her over for a spanking because Ian had assured him she needed one, and the things he'd done to her while she was in that position... Ian pinning her wrists down while she squirmed under

Brendan's hands, until he fed her his thick rod because she'd begged to taste it… The hazy glow of both their cocks inside her, her body locked between theirs, climaxing uncontrollably as the twins fucked her.

The bliss of puddling in their arms afterwards.

Diana woke at the first light of dawn. She was naked, wrapped in crisp sheets and muscled arms and legs. The unfamiliar hotel room confused her, but the deep breathing close to her ear — close to both her ears — brought everything back.

She'd graduated Yale. She was between one part of her life and another, with no idea what to expect next. The twins lay on either side of her, and she was the girl in between them.

She lay still, savoring the moment. Then she shook Ian awake. His hair was messy, his body warm, his leg thrown over hers. The pillow had left adorable creases on his cheek. Brendan was fast asleep, a peaceful smile on his face.

She and Ian stumbled sleepily into the bathroom to shower, where they blinked at the bright light. Afterward, she woke Brendan up, which wasn't easy, for one last kiss and a few whispered words. His smile made everything seem right in the world.

Ian's arm around her as they walked to the Jeep, their fingers intertwined as they drove to her apartment, made everything right in their world.

Streaks of orange broke through the sky, lighting the purple-gray streets and buildings. Diana's bag rested by her feet. Inside was the red journal Ian had bought for her when they started dating.

She'd filled it up with poems the past four years at Yale. Some were sexy, some were raw, some were aching. Some were better than the poems she'd written in high school, and some weren't. But there was one big difference: they were less lonely.

There was a single blank page left, the last page, and she knew what she'd be writing on it tonight.

She squeezed Ian's hand and broke the sweet silence. "You're okay with it all?"

"Fuck yes. I wouldn't have started this if I wasn't."

She leaned back in the passenger seat. The Jeep came to a stop at a light.

"That was really amazing," she murmured. "Thank you."

"Don't thank me." He smirked at her. "You were hot as hell. We just wanted to give you a little something for graduation, but you gave as good as you got."

"I love you," she said abruptly. Ian's hazel eyes pierced hers. She took a breath, because it still took courage to put her feelings out there. "We've been through a lot together, and it's always been you. You still make me flutter, but I'm so sure about you."

He held her gaze. "Then how about spending the rest of our lives together?"

She stared at him, squeezing his hand, speechless.

"This isn't a joke," he added.

"Yes." She found her voice. "Yes, yes, yes." Laughter bubbled up. "Oh my God, you just asked me that."

"Yep." Ian wore the same foolish grin he had when they'd said *I love you* for the first time. The day she'd told him she only wanted to be with him. He leaned in to kiss her, brushing her bangs off her forehead. "I didn't plan this, so I don't have anything to give you yet…"

A horn honked behind him. The light was green. He stepped on the gas, turning his attention reluctantly to the road.

"It's okay. All I want is you." She stroked his leg, giddy. "Can we tell Brendan first?"

"Well, yeah." Ian laughed. "Who else? He won't be surprised. He already talks like we're old and married."

"No secrets from each other?" she asked softly.

"We don't tell each other everything. But we tell each other enough."

"You don't think it's crazy to be deciding this right after what the three of us did last night?"

"Of course it's crazy." Ian's thumb stroked her palm. "That's who we are. Are you all right with it?"

"Yeah." She leaned back in her seat and watched the sun rise. "We're just crazy like that."

"I love you, Diana Cooper." Ian pulled into a spot by her apartment, parked, and took both her hands. "I always have."

"I love you, Ian O'Brian." She let her forehead rest against his. "Even when I didn't know it."

In front of them, her apartment building rose, outlined by the early morning sun. She'd moved every year in college. In a few hours, this wouldn't be her house anymore. She'd be starting a new adventure with Ian, in a new city.

Nothing stayed the same. Life changed, and anything could happen.

She kissed Ian.

"Everywhere with you is home."

ACKNOWLEDGEMENTS

Thank you for taking this journey with Diana, Ian, and Brendan! *The Girl in Between* began as a vignette — a peek at Di and Ian during a visit after a rough finals week at Yale. When Brendan joined them, it grew into a short story, then a novella, and finally a full-blown novel.

Many thanks to everyone who's supported this novel as it's come into being:

My wonderful beta readers — Ava T. Argent, Finn Mitchell, F. Evans, Stacy, and Bruce — for giving indispensable story feedback and sharing their reactions.

V.K. Torston, for offering valuable insights on the early chapters, along with literary cheerleading.

The romance community on Twitter and Facebook, for its encouragement.

The readers who picked up *The Boys Next Door,* thought it should have a sequel, and asked for more.

My husband, for his unwavering support through all the ups and downs of writing.

ABOUT THE AUTHOR

Miranda Silver writes sexy stories with a twist. She's happy to be putting her English degree to use, along with her love of drama, secrets, steam, and words. Miranda lives on the West Coast with her family, where she spends time outdoors whenever possible. Her other books include *The Boys Next Door*, *Priceless*, and *Crave*.

mirandasilver.com
Facebook.com/MirandaSilverBooks
Instagram: @mirandasilverbooks
Twitter: @silvermusings

Made in United States
North Haven, CT
18 June 2022

20370044R00189